DAW Titles by C.J. CHERRYH

THE
DEEP BEYOND

CUCKOO'S EGG
SERPENT'S REACH

C.J. CHERRYH

DAW BOOKS, INC.
DONALD A. WOLLHEIM, FOUNDER
375 Hudson Street, New York, NY 10014

ELIZABETH R. WOLLHEIM
SHEILA E. GILBERT
PUBLISHERS
http://www.dawbooks.com

DAW Book Collectors No. 1337.
DAW Books are distributed by Penguin Group (USA) Inc.

First Paperback Printing, August 2005
1 2 3 4 5 6 7 8 9

DAW TRADEMARK REGISTERED
U.S. PAT. OFF. AND FOREIGN COUNTRIES
—MARCA REGISTRADA
HECHO EN U.S.A.

PRINTED IN THE U.S.A.

CUCKOO'S EGG

I

He sat in a room, the sand of which was synthetic and shining with opal tints, fine and light beneath his bare feet. The windows held no cityview, but a continuously rotating panorama of the Khogghut plain: a lie. Traffic noise came through.

His name was Duun. It was Dana Duun Shtoni no Lughn. But Duun was enough for day-to-day. They called him other things. Sey: general. Mingi: lord. Or something very like. Hatani: that was another thing. But Duun was enough now. There was only one. Shonunin the world over knew that, and knew him; and when the door chimed and they came to bring the alien to him, whose who carried it would not look him in the eyes, not alone for the scars that a shonun could see, the pale smooth marks traced through the fur of half his face like the limbs of a lightning-blasted tree, the marks that twisted his right ear and left his mouth quirked in permanent irony and one eye staring out of ruin.

He was Duun, of *Shanoen*. He reached out hands one of which was marred, like his face, and took the closed carrier that they gave him, marking how their ears slanted back and how they turned their heads from his for horror—not of what they saw: they were meds, and had seen deformity. It was the force in him: like a great wind, like a great heat in their faces.

But his hands were gentle when he took the carrier from them.

They went away, appalled and forgetting courtesies.

He waved the door shut and set the carrier on the

table-rise, opened it and gathered the small bundled thing from it.

Shonunin were naked when they were born, but downed in silver that quickly went to dapples and last of all to gray body coat and black on limbs and ears and crest. Duun held the creature on its discarded wrapping, on his knees; and its downless skin was naked and pink as something lately skinned, except for a thatch of nondescript hair atop its skull. It waved soft limbs in helpless twitches. Its eyes were shut, in a face flat and not unlike a shonun; between its legs an outsized organ of curious form and various (they said) function. Its mouth worked restlessly, distorting the small face. And Duun touched it with the sensitive pads of his fingers, with the four fingers of his left hand and the two of his maimed right, exploring the hot, smooth feel of the bandage-patched belly, the chest, the limbs. With the merest tip of a claw he drew down its soft lip to inspect its mouth—nothing but toothless gums, for it was mammalian. With the claw he lifted the lid of a sleeping eye; he saw it white and milky, centered with blue, restless in natural shiftings. He touched the convolutions of the stiff, small ears; explored the visible organ and discovered reaction: so it was sensitive. That was of interest. He examined the fat, clawless feet, all one pad as far as the toes. Unfurled a five-fingered hand with the careful touch of a single clawed finger, and the tiny fist clenched again, stubbornly. It waved its limbs. Fluid shot from the organ and fouled Duun's clothes.

Any shonun would have flinched seeing that. But Duun gathered up the wrap about the infant and mopped at himself patiently, with infinite patience. So. Likewise shonun infants performed such obscenities, if more discreetly. It let out cries, soft and weak and meaningless as all infant cries. It struggled with less strength than his own infants had shown.

He knew what it would be, grown. He knew its face. He knew every aspect of its body. He gathered it against his breast in the stinking blanket and rose, went to the package they had brought him that morning and left on the riser by the bed. He held the softly crying creature in the crook of his left arm for he was still more able with the right hand, two-fingered as it was. He managed to open the case and to warm the milk—not milk of shonunin; by synthesis the meds provided, of their own ingenuity.

There was data, which had come days ago; he had memorized it. The creature wailed; so shonunin wailed, exercising infant lungs. And it breathed the air shonunin breathed: and perhaps its gut would take the meat shonunin ate one day. The meds thought that this was the case. The teeth that would grow would, some of them, be pointed like the major teeth of a shonun. "Hush, hush," he told it, joggling it against his chest. He drew the warmed bottle from the case and thrust the nipple into the soft mouth that quested among the blankets. It suckled noisily and quieted, and he crossed the sand to the riser he had left, sat down cross-legged, rocking it, whispering to it.

"Be still, be still."

Its eyes closed in contentment; it slept again, fed and held. It could not, like a shonun, be taken for granted. He was delicate with it. He laid it finally in the bowl of his own bed and sat beside it, watching its small movements, the regular heaving of its tiny round belly; and when the view in the windows changed and became the nightbound sea, he still watched.

He would not soon tire of watching. He did not bathe. He was fastidious, but he inhaled the smell of it and the soiled blanket, the smells of its food and its person, and did not flinch, having schooled himself against disgust.

They were dismayed when they came, the meds—to deal with him, to examine the infant and to take it back to the facility down the hall to weigh it and monitor its condition. He stalked after them as they carried it in its closed case; he offended their nostrils with his stink.

And never once in all this dealing would they meet his eyes, preferring even the face of the alien to the chance of looking up into the stark cold stare he gave to them and all their business.

They weighed the infant, they listened to its breathing and its heart, they asked quietly (never glancing quite at him) whether there had been difficulty.

"Duun-hatani, you might rest," the chief of medicine said the second day that they came for the infant. "This is all routine. There's no need. You might take the chance to—"

"No," Duun said.

"There—"

"No."

There was uncomfortable silence. For days Duun had looked at them without answer; now the chief cast a searching, worried glance full into his eyes, and immediately afterward found something else to occupy herself.

Duun smiled for the first time in those days, and it was a smile to match the stare.

"You dismay them, Duun," the division chief said.

Duun walked away from the desk on which Ellud sat, gazed at the false windows, which showed snowfall. Ice formed on the branches of a tree above a hot spring. The sun danced in jeweled branches and the steam rose and curled. Duun looked back again, the thumb of his maimed hand hooked behind him to that of the whole one, and discovered another man who preferred to study something just a little behind his shoulder. The false sunlight, it might be. Anything would have served. "It's in very good health," Duun said.

"Duun, the staff—"

"The staff does its job." Never once had the eyes focused on him, quite. Duun drew a deep breath. "I want Sheon."

"Dunn—"

"Sheon belongs to Duun, doesn't it? I tell you that it does."

"Security at Sheon—"

"I stink. I smell. Notice it, Ellud?"

Long pause. "The estate—"

"You offered me anything. Wasn't that what you said? Any cooperation? Would any shonun in the world prevent me anything—if I want a woman; if I want a man; if I want money or your next of kin, Ellud—if I want the president turned out naked and the treasury to walk in—"

"You're hatani. You wouldn't."

Duun looked again at the false spring bubbling up in its wintry vapors. "Gods! but you do trust me."

"You're hatani."

He looked back with the first clear-eyed stare he had used in years. But not even that could hold Ellud's gaze to his. "I'm begging you, Ellud. Do I have to beg? Give me Sheon."

"Settlers have moved there. Their title's valid by now."

"Move them out. I want the house. The hills. Privacy. Come on, Ellud . . . you want me to camp in your office?"

Ellud did not. They had been friends. Once. Now Duun saw the guarded lowering of the ears. Like shame. Like a man taking a chance he wanted. Badly. At any cost.

"You'll get it," Ellud said. Never looking at him. Ellud's claws extended slightly, raked papers aside as he looked distractedly at the desk about him. "I'll do something. I'll see to it."

"Thanks."

That got the eyes up. A wounded look. Appalled like the rest. The agony of friendship.

Of wounded loyalties.

"Give it up," Ellud asked, against self-interest; against all interests. The loyalty jolted, belated as it was.

"No." For a moment then, eye to eye, no flinching from either side. He remembered Ellud under fire. A calm, cool man. But the gaze finally shifted and something broke.

The last thing.

Duun walked out, freer, because there was nothing left. Not even Ellud. Just pain. And he wrapped that solitude about him, finding it appropriate.

*   *   *

He came to Sheon's hills in the morning, in a true morning with the sun coming up rose and gold over the ridge; and the wind that blew at him on this grassy flat was the wind of his childhood, whipping at his cloak, at the gray cloak of the hatani, which he wrapped about him and the infant. Ellud's aide showed distress, there on the dusty road that led toward the hills, in the momentary stillness of the craft which had brought them there, over in the meadow. The aide's ears lay flat in the wind, which blew his neatly trimmed crest and disarranged the careful folds of his kilt. The wind was cold for a citydweller, for a softhands like him. "It's all right," Duun said. "I told you. There's no way up but this. You don't have to wait here."

The aide turned his face slightly toward the countryfolk who gathered out of the range of hearing, who gathered in knots, families together, uncaring of the cold. The aide looked back again, walked toward the gathered crowd waving his arms. "Go away, go away, the mingi has no need of you. Fools," he said then, turning back, for they gave only a little ground. He stooped and gathered up from the roadside the little baggage there was, slung the sack from his shoulder. His ears still lay back in distress. "Hatani, I will walk up with you myself."

It was a wonder. The aide met his eyes with staunch frankness. Ellud chose such young folk, still knowing the best, the most honest. Duun felt for a moment as if the sun had shone on him full; or perhaps it was the smell of true wind, with the grass-scent and the cleanness. He felt a motion of his heart toward this young man and it ached.

But he grinned, old soldier that he was, and glanced at the uphill road, for this time he was the one to flinch, from the youth's innocence and worship. "Give me the sack," he said, and stripped the carry-strap from the young man's shoulder and took it to his own, his right. The infant occupied his left arm, warm and moving there, nuzzling wormlike among its swaddlings beneath his cloak.

"But, hatani—"

"You're not going. I don't need you."

He walked away.

"Hatani—"

He did not look back. Did not look at the mountainfolk who lined the road near the copter. Some of them were the displaced, he was sure. Some of them had held Sheon, having gotten it since he was renunciate. Now they were abruptly dispossessed. He felt their eyes, heard their whispers, nothing definite.

"Hatani," he heard. And: *"Alien."* Whisper they need not. He felt their eyes trying to penetrate his cloak. They came to wonder what he was as much as they wondered about what he brought. "Hatani." There was respect in that. "What happened to his face?" a child asked.

"Hush," an adult said. And there was a sudden, embarrassed hush. It was a child. It had not learned what scars were. It was only honesty.

Duun did not look at them. Did not care. He was hatani, renunciate. His weapons were at his side beneath the cloak. He asked one thing of the world. These hills. This place.

A little peace.

That a hatani dispossessed them— The countryfolk living at Sheon had surely thought their title secure. The land was fallow; the house vacant; ten years renunciate and it was theirs by law.

But it was what he had told Ellud: there was nothing he could not ask and obtain, nothing in all the world.

He felt their eyes. Perhaps they expected him to speak. Perhaps they expected him to care, to offer words to reassure them.

But he only walked past them up the road, the dusty road to the heights and the house made of native stone, deep within the hills.

He heard the copter lift. It beat away with small thumps like heartbeats echoing off the mountainside. It had come and gone often here yestereve and three days before, with other craft, seeing to provisions, to special equipment, to all such things as satisfied Ellud and Ellud's ilk.

Nuisance, all of it.

*   *   *

He prepared himself. He knew that Sheon would have changed. He gathered up his resolve in this as in other things. He needed virtue. He sought it in abnegation. He sought it in lack of caring, when he came, in full noon, to the mountain heights, and discovered the things country-folk had done to Sheon, which he expected: a sprawl of new rubble-stone building, which destroyed the beauty Sheon had once been, a creation of smooth artistry indistinguishable from the living rock of the mountain wall that flanked the house. The house sprawled now, artless and utilitarian, the yard about it cleared and dusty. He was not dismayed.

Only when he came inside and discovered what Ellud and his crews had done—that, that afflicted him. Instead of the country untidiness he had expected (different from the time of his childhood, of stones carefully polished, of spacious halls and a sand-garden where the wind made patterns), the government had worked sterility, lacquered the stone walls, sanded the floors in white, not red, installed a new kitchen, new furnishings, all at great expense; and the smell of it was new and pungent with fixatives and paint and new-baked sand.

He stood there, in this clean, sterile, unremembered place, with its abundant stores, its furniture new from the city—

For the infant. Of course, for the infant. The meds feared for its health. They wanted sanitation.

And destroyed—destroyed—

He stood there a long, long time, in pain. The infant squirmed and began to cry. And he was very careful with it in his anger, as careful as he had ever been. He searched the cabinets for new cloths; fround the cradle prepared—

The infant soiled itself. He knew the cry, smelled the stink, which had surrounded him, stronger than the lacquer and dry-dust smell of sand.

He laid it down on the sand; he put off his cloak and laid his weapons down on a riser near the fireplace. He listened to it scream. It had grown. The voice was louder, hoarser, the face screwed up in rage.

He took cloths and wet them and knelt and cleaned

its filth in starkest patience; he heated the formula and fed it till it slept. He walked aimless in the halls afterward, smelling the stink it had left on him, and the stink of new plaster, new lacquer, new furniture.

He had run barefoot in these halls, laughed, played pranks with a dozen sibs and cousins, rolled on the floorsand, till exasperated elders flung them out into a yard well shaded with old trees.

The trees were gone. The new wing stood where the oldest tree had been. So much for homecomings.

He made a fire. There was that one thing left untouched, the old stones of the hearth he had sat by as a child, and there were scraps of demolished outbuildings and fences, in a towering pile near the rocks. He made a fire of them, burning others' memories of home.

He took the infant outside with him, well wrapped against the cold; he took it about the house with him, in the kitchen, at last before the fire itself; he sat on the clean deep sand before the hearthstones and held the infant in his lap.

He had grown accustomed to it. The flat, round face no longer disturbed him. The smell was his smell, compounded of its sweat and his. Demon eyes looked up at him. The face made grimaces meaningless to both of them in the wavering firelight, the leaping flames.

He took its skull between his hands, the whole and the maimed one, and he was careful as if the skull had been eggshell instead of bone. He smiled, drawing back his lips from his teeth, and gazed into eyes which perhaps saw him, perhaps not.

"Wei-na-ya," he sang to it, "wei-na-mei,"—in a hoarse male voice unapt for lullabies; *little bird, little fish*—the house had heard that song before. "Hei sa si-lan-nei. . . ." *Do not go. The wind is cold, the water dark, but here is warm.* "Wei-na-ya, wei-na-mei."

And "Sha-khe'a," he sang, but softly, like the lullaby, which was a hatani song.

It was the deathsong. He sang it like the lullaby. He smiled, grinned into its face.

"Thou art *Haras*," he said to the awful, demon face, to the slittted eyes with their centers like stormcloud. It was the sadoth he spoke, the language of his hill-dwelling ancestors. "Thou art *Haras*. *Thorn* is your name."

It gazed solemnly up at him.

Unafraid.

It waved its hands. *He,* Duun reminded himself. He. Haras. Thorn. The wind howled about the house, skirled in the chimney and set the flames to flickering in the hearth.

He grinned and rocked the child and did a thing which would have chilled the blood of any of the countryfolk who doubtless huddled together in their dispossession; or the meds; or Ellud in his fine city apartment.

He held it as if it were a shonun child and washed its eyes with his tongue (they tasted salt and musty). There was nothing he spared himself, no last repugnance he did not overcome. Such was his patience.

II

They came from the capital. Copters landed, and meds made the long trek uphill carrying their instruments; and downhill going away. They were not pleased. Perhaps the countryfolk frightened them, gathering in their sullen watchfulness at the foot of the road, where the aircraft landed.

They came and went away again.

Duun held the infant, talked to it as he watched them go, mindless talk, as one did with children.

It. Haras. Thorn.

"Duun," Thorn said, infant babble. "Duun, Duun, Duun."

Thorn made busy chaos on the sand before the hearth. His cries were loud, ear-splitting; shonunin were more reserved. He still soiled himself. When this would cease Duun did not know. How to teach him otherwise he did not know. Thorn's appetite had changed; his sleep was longer, to Duun's relief.

"Duun, Duun, Duun," the infant sang, on his back before the fire. And grinned and laughed when Duun poked him in the belly, squealed, when Duun used a clawtip. Laughed again. Enjoyed his belly rubbed, fat round belly which began to hollow now, the limbs to lengthen. "Duun." Duun leaned forward, nipped at Thorn's neck. Thorn grabbed his ears, and Duun sat back, escaping the infant grip, disheveled. He had let his crest grow; it sheeted raggedly down his back and strayed now in front of his ears.

He went for the throat again on hands and knees and

Thorn squealed and kicked. Clawed with small fat hands,
with nails which were all the defense he had.

Duun laughed aloud, well-pleased.

Thorn ran, ran, ran on tottering legs, out of doors, on
the dusty earth where outbuildings had been; naked in
the warmth of spring.

Duun knelt. No one nowadays saw Duun's body, the
lightning-blasted scars of his right arm, the scars that
skeined across his side and leg. But here he wore no
more than the small-kilt, in the warmth, with the hiyi
flowering by the back door and drifting blossoms down
pink as Thorn's smooth skin. Infant hair had gone, come
in gold, darkened again in winter metamorphosis. Perhaps it was seasonal; perhaps a phase of Thorn's life.
Duun held out his arms to Thorn and Thorn laughed as
he plunged into Duun's arms, all dusty-smelling.

"Again," Duun said, and set him upright, crouching
again a little distance off to make Thorn run. Infant legs
tried and failed, exhausted. Duun caught him, hugged him,
licked his mouth and eyes, which Thorn did to him when
Thorn had stopped laughing and gasping, clenching small
five-fingered fists into Duun's trailing crest and the shorter
hair of his forelock, and digging his face for a sly nip into
the hollow of Duun's neck when he got the chance, but
Duun ducked his head aside and got in a nip first. Small
unclawed feet drove at his lap, the small body strained
and Thorn ducked down to bite him ungently in the chest.

"Ah!" Duun cried, seizing him in both hands, kneeling,
lifting him kicking and squealing aloft at arm's length.
"Ah! Devious!"

He hugged him again and Thorn bit again. He had
gained teeth, and strength, but they were not teeth like
Dunn's. Duun bit at fingers and Thorn caught Duun's
mouth and pushed back his lip to try his fingers on Duun's
larger, sharper teeth. Duun nipped and Thorn rescued
his hand and squealed.

There were more visits. "Bye, bye, bye," Thorn bade
the meds sullenly from the porch. He squatted down

naked as he was and grimaced then. He had bit the chief med, and the med had come within a little of flicking an impudent youngster hard on the nose.

But the med had stopped himself. Duun was standing there, hatani-cloaked in gray, arms folded.

The meds went away. Thorn made a rude sound and urinated on the step.

Duun went and snapped him soundly on the ear with thumb and forefinger. Thorn wailed.

"Bad," said Duun. The wail went on. Duun went into the house, into the kitchen and got his hand wet in the sink. Thorn followed, naked, holding hands out, wailing all the way and dancing in his distress.

"Shut up," Duun said. And flicked cold water in Thorn's face. Thorn blinked and howled and clawed frantically at Duun's legs, not in rage. Pick me up, that meant.

Duun picked him up, armful that he had become, rocked him with a swinging of his body in that way he had learned the infant liked. A small face nuzzled its way to his neck; this did not always mean biting. This time it did not. Thorn clung to him and snuffled, soiling his cloak with running eyes and nose.

"You were bad," Duun said. To such simplicities the philosophy of hatani bent nowadays. He swung from side to side and the sobs stopped. The thumb went in Thorn's mouth, irrepressible, though Thorn ate meat now, which Duun chewed for him and spat into his mouth. ("Not advisable," the meds said, obsessed with disease. But he did it, which was an old way, a hill way, and easier than urging a spoon past Thorn's dodging mouth, or cleaning up when Thorn fed himself and smeared it everywhere. Duun's mother and father had done this for him. He took perverse pleasure in performing this dutiful service. It shocked the meds. That gave him perverse pleasure too. He smiled at the meds. It was strange. They had become familiar with him. They looked him in the eyes, at least more than once in the visit. "Ellud-mingi sends regards," they said. "I send mine," he said in return. And perversely added: "So does my son." *That* sent them on their way in haste. Doubtless to take notes.)

He rocked Thorn and sang to him, absently: "Wei-na-mei, wei-na-mei." And Thorn grew quiet in his arms. "You're getting too big to hold," Duun said. "Too big to make puddles on the step."

That night, when they sat before the fire (the spring nights were cold) Thorn crawled into his lap and sat there a while; and got up on his feet in the triangle between Duun's crossed legs and touched Duun's face, the scarred side. Duun caught the hand with his maimed one. And let it go.

"It's a scar," Duun said.

He did not prevent the exploration. He made himself patient. He shut his eyes and let Thorn do what he liked, until Thorn pulled savagely on both his ears, which was challenge. Duun's eyes flashed open.

"Ah!" Duun cried, drawing back his lips in a grimace. Thorn recoiled and stumbled on Duun's legs; Duun caught him in mid-fall and rolled with him, rolled holding him in his arms, never coming on him with his weight. Thorn screamed, and gasped, and when Duun bit, bit back, and screamed and squealed till Duun clamped a hand over his mouth and held it there.

Thorn grew still. The eyes stayed wide with shock. So. So. Fright, not fight.

Duun gathered him to his breast and licked his eyes till Thorn had begun to pant, recovering his lost breath. For a moment Duun was worried. Small hands clutched at him.

He gripped Thorn by both arms and held him up. Grinned. Thorn refused to be appeased.

That night Thorn waked howling at Duun's side, short sharp yelps, gasps for breath. "Thorn!" Duun cried, and turned on lights and snatched him up, thinking he had rolled on the infant and hurt him in some way; but it was the nightmare.

Thorn held to him. It was Duun Thorn feared. That was the nightmare.

"Ah," Duun cried, falling back, dragging Thorn atop him. "Ah! you hurt me! You hurt me—" To give him the upper hand. He had no pride in this.

"Duun," Thorn cried and snuggled close.

Sometimes genes were truer than teaching. Alien. Thorn clung to what had frightened him.

"Duun, Duun, Duun—"

Duun held him. It was all Thorn understood.

There was a day, in the morning bath, that Thorn noticed his own naked skin. Thorn scrubbed at Duun's belly and at his own with a rough-textured sponge. Dropped the sponge and put both hands on his own belly, rubbed it thoughtfully. When he looked up thoughts passed in his milk-and-storm eyes, with a little knitting of his brow. "Slick," he said of himself. His speech did not go as fast as a shonun child. But there was a difference of mouths and tongues. "Slick."

Perhaps Thorn wanted to ask, if his young mind had thought of it, when his own pelt would begin to grow. The hair on his head was abundant, tousled curls, which had finally settled on a faded, earthy brown. The eyes had never changed. It was a dangerous time.

Duun took Thorn from the bath and held him in his left arm, hugged him close in front of the mirror. Thorn had seen mirrors. He had one for a toy. He had seen this one many times.

Today there was distress in young Thorn's eyes, and thoughts were going on. Thorn had never seen a shonun child. He had never seen other shonunin, except the meds. Perhaps some terrible thing was dawning on his mind, put together of little wordless pieces, images in mirrors, smooth bellies, a facility for making water in a long, long arc, which was for a time his nuisancefully chiefest talent. He spread his five-fingered hand at Thorn-in-the-mirror, in a way that should bring claws and did not; he grimaced at this Thorn as if to frighten him to flight. (Go away, ugly Thorn.) He flexed the fingers yet again. Made faces.

Duun turned them both away. Bounced him to distract him.

After that Thorn did not mention the difference of their skins. Only from time to time there were small moments which Duun caught: a moment of rest when Thorn, lying beside Duun, reached and stroked his arm, turning the fur this way and that. Another when Thorn, finding Duun's hand conveniently palm up, dragged it closer to him across Duun's lap and played with it, fingering the dissimilar geometries of the palm, working doggedly at the fingers to make the claws come out. Duun cooperated. It was his right hand. It was not the deformity Thorn explored, but an ability which surely Thorn envied; and Duun was suddenly aware of a silence within the child, a secrecy which had grown all unawares, that small walled-off place which was an independent mind. Thorn had arrived at selfhood, a self which came out to explore the world and retreated with scraps of things which had to be examined with care, compared (sign of a complex mind) against other truths: Thorn had arrived at self-defense, disappointed in his body, it seemed. Aware of his own deformity. And not, truly, aware of Duun's. Duun was Duun. Duun had always had scars; they were part of Duun as the sun was part of the world. There was no past. Thorn had not been in it: therefore Thorn could not imagine it.

But Thorn's hands were not like Duun's. His skin was not. And Thorn had begun to take alarm, suspecting imbalance in the world.

Duun gathered him close, as he had done when Thorn was smaller, rolled him into his lap and poked him in the belly, which Thorn resisted for a moment, and writhed, and finally gave way to, in squeals and laughter and abortive attempts to retaliate in kind. Duun let him have that victory, sprawled backward on the sand before the fire, belly heaving under Thorn's slight weight, in laughter which was not reflexive, like Thorn's. To be touched on throat or belly went against instinct. There was a sense of peril in that abandonment.

But a child had to win. Sometimes. And lose sometimes. There was strength in both.

*   *   *

"Follow, follow," he urged the child, looking downhill. The rocky incline was a great trial for small legs, and Duun's stride was long. Thorn stood with legs apart, arms hanging, and staggered a few more knock-kneed steps. "Keep climbing," Duun said. "You can."

A few more steps. Thorn fell and cried, a weak, breathless sobbing. "I can't."

"You have breath left to cry, you have breath to get up. Come on. *Up!* Shall I be ashamed?"

"I hurt my knee!" Thorn sat up, clutching it and rocking.

"I hurt my hand once. Get up and come on. Someone is chasing us."

Thorn caught his breath and looked downtrail, still hiccuping.

"Perhaps it will eat us," Duun said. "Get up. Come on."

Thorn let go his reddened knee. Limbs struggled. Thorn got to his feet, wobbled, and came on desperately.

"I lied," said Duun. "But so did you. You could get up. Come on."

Sobs and snuffles. Wails of rage. Thorn kept walking. Duun walked with shorter strides, as if the way had gotten steeper for him as well.

"Again." Duun gave Thorn another small stone. Thorn threw. It hit a rock not so high up the cliffs as before. "Not so good. Again."

"*You* do it."

Duun threw. It sailed up and up and struck near the top of the sheer face. The child's mouth stayed open in dismay.

"That is what I *can* do," Duun said. "Match that."

"I can't."

"My ears are bad. Something said can't."

Thorn took the rock. Tears welled up in his eyes. He threw. The stone fell ignominiously awry and lost itself among the rocks at the bottom of the cliff.

"Ah. I have frightened you. Thorn is scared. I hear *can't* again."

"I hate you!"

"Throw at *me,* then. I'm closer. Perhaps you can hit *me.*" Duun gave Thorn another stone.

Thorn's face was red. His eyes watered and his lips trembled. He whirled and threw it at the cliff instead.

So.

"That was your highest yet," Duun said.

III

The meds came back. Ellud was with them. "Ellud," Duun said.

"You look well," Ellud said, with one long searching look. With a furtive sliding of the eyes toward Thorn, who stood his ground in the main hall of the house, where the hated meds prepared their discomforts. Thorn scowled. The sun had turned his naked skin a golden brown. His hair, which Duun cut to a length that did not catch twigs or blind him when he worked, was a clean and shining earth color. His eyes were as much white as blue. His nose had gotten more prominent, his teeth were strong, if blunt. He stood still. His poor ears could not move. Only the regular flaring of his nostrils betrayed his dislike.

"Thorn," Duun said. "Come here. This is Ellud. Be polite, Thorn."

"Is he a med?" Thorn asked suspiciously.

Ellud's ears sank. A rock might have spoken to him in plain accents and shocked him no less. He looked at Duun. Said nothing.

"No." said Duun. "A friend. Many years ago."

Thorn looked up and blinked. A med came and got him and prepared to take his pulse.

"Come back to town," Ellud said. "Duun, come back."

"Is that a request or an order?"

"Duun—"

"I'd remind you that you promised me anything. Not yet, Ellud."

That evening Thorn was silent, gloomy, thoughtful. He did not ask about Ellud. Did not discuss the meds.

Thorn slept apart now. There were changes in his body which made this advisable. He went to his room of the many rooms in the house and curled up into his privacy. Duun came to check on him.

"Are my ears going to grow?" Thorn asked, looking at him from the pillow as he stood in the doorway.

Ears. Maybe that was the easiest, least painful thing to ask. Duun stood silent. He had planned how he would answer about claws and hair and the shape of their faces and the difference of their loins. He had planned everything but ears.

"I don't think so," Duun said. "I don't care, do you?"

Silence, from the small shadow in the bedbowl.

"You're unusual," Duun said.

A snuffle.

"I like you that way," Duun said.

"I like you," came the small, disembodied voice. Another snuffle. "I like you, Duun." *Love* was, Duun recalled, not a word he had ever used in Thorn's hearing. Like you. As one liked a warm fire. The sun on one's back.

"I like you too, Thorn."

"I don't want any more meds."

"I'll talk to them about that. Do you want to go hunting tomorrow? I'll give you a knife of your own. I'll show you how to keep the blade."

"Hunting what?" Snuffle. Shadow-child wiped his eyes with a swipe of an arm; nose with another. There was interest in the voice.

"I'm hatani, Thorn. That's something hard to be. That's why I push you hard."

"What's hatani?"

"I'll show you. Tomorrow. I'll teach you. You'll learn to do what I can do. It's going to be hard, Thorn."

Another wipe of the eyes.

"Tomorrow, Thorn?"

"Yes."

"Get to sleep, then."

Duun went back to the fire. Wind howled outside, in cold. The fire leapt. The last of the old countryfolk lumber was gone. They began to use an old log from down-slope. He cut it with the power saw he had ordered with supplies and brought it up, bit by bit. None of the countryfolk from the valley would bother the pile he had made on the roadside below. They kept out of his sight and left no sign near the house. But he knew that they were there.

They would know hatani patience. Countryfolk had patience of their own. Perhaps things would change. Perhaps the hatani would die. Perhaps the alien would meet with accident. Perhaps their title would become valid again.

Perhaps they had bad dreams, down in the valley, on the other side of the mountain, out of his sight and mind. Perhaps they dreamed nightmares, imagining that their woods were no longer their own.

Or that the woods might not be theirs again, forever.

He had asked for the house and lands of Sheon. He had not used the lands, till now.

He took his weapons from the top shelf of the locked cabinet where they had remained out of the way of curious young fingers. He had taken them out many times to care for them, and never let Thorn touch them, to Thorn's great frustration. A child should have unfulfilled ambitions; should know some things forbidden. Doubtless Thorn had tried. Children were not always virtuous. That was to be expected. And dealt with.

"Have you ever tried these?" Duun asked, when Thorn sat opposite him, across the blanket from the small array of knives, cord, wire, the two guns, one projectile-firing and one not. "Have you ever handled them?"

"No," Thorn said.

"Will you ever, if I tell you no?"

Alien eyes lifted to him, in startlement that at once dilated and contracted the irises: swift, furtive decision to agree, the easy course, swiftly to be violated—perhaps. If a child wished. There would be a quick flick of a reproving finger against an ear. Perhaps a cuff to make the eyes water. Thorn could endure that. There was no permanency. Nothing was forever. As he lacked a past, he lacked a true future, and believed nothing could thwart him forever.

There was no *can't* for Thorn. Duun had taught him so.

"I am not asking you," Duun said, holding up the solitary finger of his right hand. "I am telling you a thing. I want you to believe this. Will you ever pick these up if I tell you no?"

From childish excitement, from game to perplexity. Thorn's brow contracted in a spasm of anxiety. Perhaps Duun would break his promise? Perhaps he was being teased?

Duun took off the cloak and dropped it behind him. He picked up the *wer,* a middling blade. He stretched out his bare left arm, fist clenched, and set the knife against his forearm.

"No!" Thorn cried suddenly. A game? A threat? Something he had done wrong? Duun was teasing him?

Duun slowly brought the blade down and down, deeply. Blood sprang out and rained in steady, heavy drops on the weapons and the blanket. He kept his fist clenched and held the arm steady, resting the knife butt on his knee. Thorn's eyes were wide, his mouth open with nothing coming out.

"That's what weapons are for," Duun said. The blood poured, soaked the blanket. "Each time you take them up, remember what they're for."

"Stop it," Thorn cried. "Duun, stop it bleeding!"

Duun held out the knife, the wounded arm still spurting. He turned it in his maimed hand and offered it hilt first to Thorn. "Can you do it?"

Thorn took the bloodied knife. His eyes still were wide. His lips set themselves, drawn in. He held out his own clenched fist and set the knife to his skin. He drew the blade down the same way, and his face was red and his eyes poured tears; his nostrils and his lips went pale. He drew the knife down. Blood began to drip. The small hand drew away, the knife wobbling in tremors that convulsed the knife-arm and began to involve the other. As

Duun had done, he set the knife hand on his knee, and his face was all white and beaded with moisture, while the blood ran down and made another darkening of the blanket.

So. So. Duun had expected last-moment flinching. His own head grew light. His cut was deeper and bled abundantly. He held out his hand and took the knife back. He saw the terror in the child. (What more, Duun? What else? What worse? I'm *scared,* Duun!)

"It is not a game," Duun said. He put down the knife and pressed his right hand to his wound. "You can hold it. Hold it tight." He got up from his cross-legged posture without using either hand. He went and opened the med kit and pressed a sealing film on the wound. He came back to Thorn with another square of the gel, and pressed the film to Thorn's arm and held it, warming it with his hand until it took and stayed, soft and blood-reddened, over a wound that would scar. Duun held the arm. Alien eyes looked up at him, white all round. He was tender in his grip. "You won't forget," Duun said. "You won't forget what weapons are. You will never pick them up when I tell you not."

"No." A small weak voice.

"You will use them when I say. And you'll set them down when I say."

"Yes."

"Good." He slid a bloodstained hand past Thorn's head and rubbed Thorn's nape in the vise of his maimed hand till the tension left and Thorn's body gave to and fro with that motion, his eyes still fixed on Duun. "Believe me, Thorn. Believe me in this. You hurt now. But you did what I asked. That was brave."

Muscles in Thorn's face shook, as in some dire chill. His limbs convulsed. Stopped. Duun kept on his massage until the shiver passed. Thorn's eyes lost their wild look. They were wide and moiled with forethought and calculations. (What else does he want? What did I win? What did I do? What next?)

Duun let go. Motioned at the bloodstained weapons. "Clean them. I'll show you how."

Thorn stirred, edged closer to the array of weapons on the blanket. "You said—" he began.

"I said?"

"We'd go hunting. You said—we'd go hunting today."

"That we will. We won't eat tonight if we don't take something."

Thorn's eyes flicked up a second time; Thorn could do that, without turning his head. The look hoped for a joke and Duun made his face implacable.

There was no question, of course. The place was full of unwary game. No one hunted it much. Yet. And a hatani could, in the most desolate place, find some sustenance.

But Thorn would discover this when he was hungry. When he had tried for himself and understood that he was too loud and too awkward.

When he had seen what was in the land, and what the wild things knew.

"I promised you a knife."

A glance upward, wary interest. A stare of white wide eyes.

"The *wer*-knife. The one you used. That would be a good one for you. You can have it if you like. It's a very good blade. You have to keep it spotless. Even fingers stain it. I'll show you how to keep it."

Thorn picked it up again, by the hilt. Held it.

The gangling boy came up the trail, thinking he was alert: Duun knew. Thorn looked this way and that: his callused feet made very little noise on the dusty track among the rocks.

"*Up,*" Duun hissed. "Look *up*."

Thorn's head came up. Duun had already moved, lost in the brush.

The boy was still looking up when Duun hit him in the back with a thrown stone. Thorn spun about and threw. Thorn's stone rattled away down among brush and rock. Duun had evaded it with a fluid shift of his hip, and stood untouched.

"Too late," Duun said. "You're dead. I'm not."

Thorn's shoulders slumped. He bent his head in shame. Whirled and sped another rock underhand.

Duun evaded that one too without more than shifting stance. Thorn did not look surprised, only exhausted. Beaten at last.

Duun grinned. "Better. That *did* surprise me." The grin faded. "But your choosing this track up didn't. *That* was your first mistake. How did I know? Can you figure that?"

Thorn gasped for breath. Hunkered down on the path, arms on scabbed knees. "Because I was tired. The climb's easier."

"Better still. You're right. Think ahead next time. And think in *all* directions. You know this path. You should have seen these rocks in your head before you came to them."

No answer. Thorn knew. Duun knew that he knew. Thorn wiped his forearm across his face and smeared dust across the sweat. Even at this range he stank of heat.

"Also," Duun reminded him with delicacy, "when you came round the mountain the wind was coming at your shoulder, at an angle to the rocks. Do you see why that should have warned you?"

Thorn blinked sweat and wiped again. He had grown rangier, longer of limb. The belly had gone hollow beneath the ribs, ridged with muscle above the wrap about his loins. Brush-scars showed white on his skin. "Scent," he said. He gasped for breath. There was chagrin in his half-drowned face. "Sorry. I'm sorry, Duun."

"Sorry won't save you. Scent-deaf doesn't mean the world is. You're dead, Thorn."

"Yes, Duun." A faint, hoarse voice. Shoulders slumped again. "You won't catch me again."

"Won't I?"

"Duun—*I'm hungry, Duun!*"

Duun spun around the other side of the tree, leaned there looking at him and scowling. "Hunt, then. Fool. Don't tell me what your needs are. I'll know where to find you. Don't trust me, Thorn."

"I'm not playing, Duun!"

"Then neither will I be." Duun spun round again. Headed downslope. "I'll hurt you this time, Thorn!"

"Duun!"

Fire crackled, there in the clearing. They made peace. Thorn nursed bruises. It was Duun's catch Duun divided with him, meat which Thorn took gingerly, dancing it from one hand to the next while it cooled down.

"You do well," Duun said.

"For someone who can't smell," Thorn said hoarsely. "Who falls into traps."

Duun flicked his ears. "Good, you worry about your lacks. You'll think of them. You won't forget again."

"Duun, what's wrong with me?"

The question stopped him. The meat burned Duun's fingers and he shifted it in haste, back and forth again, and laid it on a rock. "Wrong. Who said wrong?"

Silence from the other side of the fire. Grievous silence.

"You're different," Duun said. "Or maybe *I* am. Does that occur to you?"

It had not. Thorn blinked in shock. Then disbelief crept in. There were the meds. There was Ellud. Thorn was not diverted. Duun was pleased with that, too.

"You're smart," Duun said. "You're quick, you're clever. Brave. All those things. You're Thorn. What if you were the only one? What if? What if I were the only Duun? Would that make a difference? You're all you can be. You don't need anything else. I don't."

"Make sense, Duun!"

"The world's wide, boy. Wide. There's nine seas. There're cities. There're roads and highways. People in a hurry. Cities are full of noise. Sheon's best. That's this place, Sheon. The gods made this whole world and they made Sheon first. You talk to the winds, Thorn. You hear the gods talk back? Do you?"

"I don't know."

"You can't hear that in a city. Cityfolk are scent-deaf. Too many smells. Gives you a headache." Duun tore off a bit of meat and swallowed. "The gods made the world

and they made shonunin last, out of the leftovers; and
they were missing some. And they were sorry, so one of
them gave up a bit and another gave another bit and
they filled up the gaps till there were parts enough.
That's what we are, all scraps and a bit of the gods' own
selves. All patchwork. With good parts and bad. So you
can't smell. I've got just six fingers. And you've got five
on just one hand."

"How did you—?"

Ah. The fish bit. Duun had thought that bait would
lead him astray. Duun shrugged. "I made a mistake. See?
Even I make mistakes. And I'm good, Thorn, I'm very
good. You don't know how good."

Thorn choked down a bite. He had to chew more than
Duun did. Sometimes in his haste he forgot this. He
struggled. Stayed silent after. "What happened?" Thorn
asked finally. "Duun—what did happen to your—?"

"Ah. Well. I hunted something that bit back, you
see?" He held up the maimed hand. "You put your hand
into things, young Thorn, you may not get back what
you want."

"What was it?"

Duun took another bite. Swallowed. "Eat. It's getting cold."

"Duun."

"Maybe I'll tell you. When you can beat me, fair or
foul."

"I never will!"

"Ah. Maybe you won't. But you're several fingers
ahead of me. You're younger than I am. My knee aches
when it rains."

"Couldn't the meds—?"

"Maybe I didn't want them to."

Thorn's mouth was open. He closed it and stopped
asking. His eyes were muddled with unasked questions
and too many answers. He had become too wary a
hunter to go down a trail that likely to have snares.
Thorn took another bite and ate in silence.

"I'll teach you to shoot," Duun said. "You almost hit
me with that stone."

Thorn looked up. Distracted again, lured on and promised. (O young fool. Fool who loves me. Thorn.)

"Another sequence," Duun said. "Base ten this time. The numbers are sixteen, forty-nine, fifty-two, ninety-seven, eight and two."

Thorn sat on the back porch of the house. The hiyi flowers bloomed. The insects hummed and made pink petals fall in delirium. Thorn shut his eyes. His brow knit. "Two hundred twenty four."

"Divide by the third in sequence."

Thorn put his hands against his eyes. Pressed hard. "Four point three." He looked up. "Can't we go hunting, Duun? I'm tired of—"

"More decimals."

Another shutting of the eyes. Hands pressed to shut out the light. "Point three zero eight."

"Add nine. Subtract four, eighty-two. Six."

The hands came down. Eyes blinked. "I'm sorry, Duun, I lost it, I forgot—"

"No. You didn't remember. Think. Name me the numbers."

"*I—*"

"Am I about to hear *can't?*"

"Didn't"

"Didn't. Didn't. There was a nest of maganin; here and here and here! How many were they? Which groups? Where? *They've eaten you, fool!*"

"Maganin don't come in fifties!"

"I am ashamed." Duun thrust his hands into the waist of his kilt and walked away.

"Duun—"

Duun turned, ears pricked. "You've remembered."

"No! No, I haven't remembered! I can't remember! I don't remember!"

"Then I'm still ashamed." Duun laid his ears back, turned and walked on.

"Duun—"

Duun did not look back. There were tears back there. Rage. It was Thorn's nature.

So was it Thorn's nature to come trailing back into
the house, finally, when it was dark, when Duun had
made a fire and sat on the sand before the hearth. Duun
had cooked food. He had eaten. He had brought Thorn's
supper outside and set it wordlessly on the step. Thorn
was not to be seen. But it was in Thorn's nature to admit
defeat when night came.

Thorn came and stood on the sand beside him. "Two
hundred twenty-four," Thorn said.

Duun's ears pricked. "Plus nine. Minus four. Eighty-
two. Six."

"One forty-one."

"Ah. You can."

Thorn knelt. Leaned on his hands. "What in the world
comes in two hundred twenty-fours?"

"Stars. Trees. Kinds of grass. The ways of a river. The
stubbornness of a child. The world is wide, young Thorn.
I can reckon the speed of the wind, name the stars, the
cities of the world. I can read a man's intent in the pupils
of his eyes."

Duun swung around and struck, open palmed. Thorn's
open palm was there to meet it, stopped it, held and
trembled.

"Ah. You are hatani, are you? Back away, little fish.
You're not ready to take me. Drop the hand."

It was a trap. Thorn refused it. Thorn held still, eyes
wide and white-rimmed, palm trembling against his palm,
and Duun lowered his ears.

"Now what will you do?" Duun asked.

"Let me go." The tremor grew. "Let me go, Duun."

Duun reached out his maimed right hand and encircled
Thorn's wrist gently with the span of his two fingers.
Pulled. The hand refused to leave contact with his palm.
The arm shook. Thorn's eyes were dilated, watched his
feverishly.

"What are you going to do now, little fish? You have
a problem now, don't you? You've let me get two hands
into it."

Thorn lifted his other hand. It froze in that lifting,
trembling.

"Not wise. Not wise at all," Duun said. "You're over-matched. You'd better stop. Don't you think?"

"Let go."

"Relax. Relax and trust me."

"No!"

"There was a time I told you, do you remember?—when you took up the knife, I said that you would take it up when I told you; and when I told you, you would lay it down. This is the time, Thorn. Now I tell you to let go. Do you hear me? I tell you to lay it down, Thorn."

The tremor grew. The palm slowly left his palm. Duun clenched his hand on Thorn's wrist and jerked him against his chest. Thorn, utterly off his balance, collapsed against him. Duun grinned, grasped him by both arms, claws out, shook him back in that grip and stared into eyes face to face. "I would have torn your throat out just then. Do you believe it?"

"No."

"Why would I not?"

"I don't know, Duun!"

Duun let him go. Thorn collapsed onto his rump and sat up and rubbed his arms. There would be bruises and clawmarks. Duun knew.

"Are you a fool, then?" Duun asked. "Why did you do that?"

"You would have hit me," Thorn said, perfect logic.

"Yes," Duun said.

Another change. Thorn sat with his jaw loose, stunned silence in his watering eyes. The boy discovered chaos in the world, sums that had no right answer. "The world's full of two-way bad choices," Duun said. "Numbers always work out. You can trust them. That's why we learn numbers. To set some order in the world. There's no other part of life where things work out. Do you see that?"

"Yes." Thorn's teeth chattered. "I see."

"You are hatani. Wei-na-hatani, little fish. A small one. A hatani is not the weapons. Is not the knife, the gun. A hatani is not these things. I told you that the time would come to lay these things down. Now you have no

need of them. You can pick up the knife and lay it down
again. A hatani is not the knife. Do you understand? Not
the skin or the claws or the eyes. Do you understand? I
teach you. You become hatani. Inside."

Thorn blinked rapidly. Gasped for breath. "Duun, where
did you get me?"

"Where do you think?"

"I don't know."

"But you trust me. Don't go to every morsel, little
fish. Some are traps. Don't I teach you? Use your wits.
Add only what can be added. Remember all the figures,
even so. Never lose one. That one will surely come from
behind and kill you. There are no second tries in the
world. Nothing is twice."

"How can you know anything?"

"Remember all the numbers. Even the long-ago ones.
Never drop any. You don't know when they'll be needed.
Reject nothing. You don't know what you might need. I
give you these things."

"Where did you get me?"

"I pulled you from the river, little fish. You were
drowning and I saved you."

"Is that truth, Duun?"

"I lied." Duun reached out the finger of his hand and
brushed Thorn's cheek, where a light down had grown.
Hair began to grow and darken elsewhere on Thorn's
body. Thorn's hope and his despair. (It's worse than
nothing, Thorn cried, before the mirror in the bath. I'm
all in patches, Duun!) Other signs were on him. "I tell
you, I think you should cut this, little fish; you're right:
it's here and there—I'd make it even."

"Stop it. *Don't distract me!* I want an answer, Duun."

"Ah. You uncover my tricks, do you?"

"I want an answer, Duun."

"The minnow has hatani tricks."

"I want an answer, Duun."

Duun pursed his lips. Laid his ears back. "Put that
answer with my hand. Beat me and I'll answer you."

Thorn's shoulders slumped. His head bowed. True defeat. Then he glanced up with a piercing, anxious look.

"Duun—Duun, tell me the truth. One truth. Be fair to me. Do you know?"

"Yes," Duun said, and gazed at him steadily until Thorn turned his face away.

IV

Faith am I when all you trust has died;
Truth am I when all you know has lied.

Choice I bring when the choice you had is sped;
Promise am I when all other faith has fled.

Vengeance am I but I come to you at cost;
One gain am I when all else you want is lost.

Thorn sang. It was a hatani song. Duun listened, as to the other lessons, listened half-dreaming as he played. There was a sweetness in Thorn's voice, all unsuspected, a skill in his hands which ran upon the strings. Perhaps it was a native fierceness that made the boy love this song; perhaps it was the innocence of that downlands child who questioned a hatani's scars, happy in ignorance. Perhaps Thorn only loved the tune. He sang it well.

Duun took over the dkin and strummed out a new rhythm with his two-fingered right hand. Rapped the beat on the sounding-board, and Thorn with native skill took the beat on the small drum.

The young head bent to the music, young eyes looked up slyly from beneath a fall of dark hair, lately shaven lips widened in a grin. Thorn had given up on the hair of his face. That on his body he still cultivated. Besides, the razor burned. (You look better, Duun had told him, when Thorn had done the deed and crept out for approval. And Thorn looked profoundly relieved.)

Vulnerable. Oh, vulnerable, young Thorn.

Green beneath the summer sun,
White beneath the snow,
All fair my land,
And fair the one I know
Whose paths run down
To mine in evenglow.

Love and women and things of the world.

"A hatani has no kin," Duun said while his hands played on. "When you are hatani to the heart you will not have me."

The drum stopped. But there was no question. Thorn had betrayed himself and Duun had gone no further; Thorn kept his own counsel, grown wary in his years. And having done that much, Duun kept the melody going, gentle harmony. "When I lost the most of my hand, I thought I would never play. I recovered that. Other things I lost. You gain no virtue from loss you never know. There will never be love, Thorn. Never. Do you know that word? —Take up the beat."

Thorn picked it up, bowed his head till his eyes were hid.

"I tell you," Duun said in the low beat of the strings, the counterpoint of the drum. "There's always something left to lose. When you think there's nothing more you're a fool, Thorn; there's something till you're dead. And after that—gods know. Do you know how old you are?"

Thorn looked up. The beat skewed, recovered itself.

"They know in the city. I know. The meds don't come. Half a year and they don't come. You know why, Thorn?"

A move of the head. No. There was dread in Thorn's eyes.

"Well," Duun said, "they don't. Maybe they know what you are."

The beat kept up, regular as heartbeat and as painful.

"What am I?"

Duun looked at him sidelong. "Hatani. Like me. Self-sufficient."

Thorn only stared at him, knowing his tricks. (Foul, Duun-hatani. Wicked and foul.)

"You have a wound, little fish. You bleed into the water. Don't you know this?"

Thorn's jaw set. His eyes were alive with thoughts. "I didn't feel the wind, Duun-hatani. You caught me."

"—again."

"Meds."

Duun looked up.

"You talked about meds, Duun, and cities. What about them?"

"Oho. The minnow takes to deeper water."

"You mean to say something, Duun-hatani. You never say anything you don't want to say."

"Deeper still."

"You called them. Did you?"

"No." The music grew under Duun's fingers, shifted and changed.

"They called you."

"Ellud called."

"Why?"

"To ask how you are. I told them. Improving, I said. Growing. They were satisfied."

"What's Ellud? Why does he want to know? Why do the meds care? Why do they look at me and never at you?"

"Ssss. There's time. There's a little time, isn't there?"

"Time for what?"

"Tksss. Fool. Walk and breathe at once, can you?"

The beat picked up again, changed, became another thing, strong and temperful.

"Defy me, do you?" Duun launched into a thing more complex.

The beat followed. "Time for what?" Thorn asked. Duun shrugged.

"For Sheon."

"The city? The meds?" Thorn's eyes grew wild, dilate. "Gods—go there?"

"Did I teach you profanity? No. I taught you respect.

You're still a child. What a leap of reason. Did I say go to the city?"

"What do you mean—time?"

"That." And Duun launched out on another tune. "Time was, I thought you might beat me, little fish. I thought you might come at me in my sleep. Fair or foul, I said. You ever think of that?"

"I thought of it."

"Why didn't you?"

A long hesitation. "I like my own sleep, Duun-hatani."

"Ah."

Thorn gave him a wary look. Duun grinned at him in no merry way. So Thorn got the joke as well. Jaw set. Eyes flickered in alarm.

(Guard your sleep, little fish. The rules just changed.)

Thorn smiled suddenly, darkly, without humor, and complicated the drum-pulse, making irreverent changes in hatani songs.

(What is a hatani? Duun. Duun is Duun. Like the sun. You become Duun, little fish, and never ask what Duun might be. Duun is the trees and the mountain, environment. Duun is faith kept. You sing the song. Hear the words, Thorn, wei-na-mei, minnow in my brook.)

Thorn poured the tea, sitting cross-legged on the riser in the room before the fire. His hand trembled and there was a shadow about his eyes, a bruising where no one had struck. "Eat," Duun said, on its other side. "You'll climb the mountain today."

Shadowed eyes lifted to him. Shoulders were already slumped. Perhaps Thorn thought of protest. If so he gave it up. Thorn knew the game.

"The black thread," Duun said, sipping at the tea. "Across the door last night. It's a very old trick. Did you know that?"

"No."

Duun grinned and swallowed down a mouthful. "Eat. Eat. You'll break your neck on the rocks."

Thorn filled his mouth and choked it down. He had shaved. He had washed himself. He had waked last night with a knife being laid at his pillow. "You're dead," Duun had whispered, ever so softly, the fifth night, the fifth night of Thorn's sleeplessness.

Thorn had started up, grasped Duun's wrist and lost that battle too, in the pitch black, in the haze of sleep caught for night upon night in fitful snatches.

"You'll try to sleep today," Duun said quietly, over tea. "It might be wise."

Thorn looked at him in bleak dismay.

Duun grinned. "On the other hand, it might not be. Want to sleep, minnow? You might take me now, face to face."

"No. There's a pebble in the pot, Duun-hatani."

Duun stopped in mid-sip. Looked at the haggard face.

"I've drunk no tea," Thorn said.

Duun set the cup down on the riser, in front of his crossed ankles.

"I won't ask my question," Thorn said hoarsely. "That was foul. I'll take you fair. With warning."

Duun drew in a long breath. Thorn had braced himself. Centered himself against the chance of a blow. And Thorn trembled.

For a long moment Duun did not move. Then he held up his left hand in a slight gesture that meant no attack forthcoming, and reached to his belt with the two fingers of this right.

He laid the pebble on the smooth surface.

Thorn glanced at it. There was only that. His eyes lifted, strangely clear.

"I would have given it to you before you left," Duun said. "I would have given it to you when you told me. But, minnow, you offered me quarter. To offer that to *me*—"

"I'm sorry, Duun."

"The thread was clever. To change the rules was cleverer. Then pride blinded you. Minnow, you've changed the rules. Do you understand?"

A hoarse whisper. "Yes, Duun-hatani."

"Be wary of everything, minnow. And never grant quarter to a hatani. *Fair* is a teaching-game. *Fair* is a box

I drew. Should I have used all I had and discouraged you? Now the walls are down, minnow. What will you do?"

"I'd be a fool to tell you, Duun-hatani."

Duun nodded slowly. Thorn picked up his bowl to eat. Set it back then, with a soft click of the spoon against the bowl and looked up at him.

"Yes," Duun said. "It would be good to wonder what's in the food. Wouldn't it? Eat, minnow. I give you that grace. It's quite safe."

Thorn edged back on the riser, set his leg over the edge. "You said no quarter. I believe you."

"And not my telling you it's safe?"

"No." Thorn got to his feet and walked across the sand, gathered up his weapons from the shelf, his cloak from beside the door. He stopped there and looked back.

Turned and left then. Running, feet thumping down porch steps.

Duun sipped at his tea and set it down at his knee. Thorn expected a little start. Such things he took for granted.

Duun got up, gathered up his own weapons, and his cloak.

No quarter then.

Thorn ran, ran, knowing that there was no time. There was no time to rue the attack, no time for any regret, only the running and the land—

("Wind and land, wei-na-ya: wind and land.")

("Scent-blind: but my knee aches when it rains—")

Turn and turn and turn: a fool's need rules his wit; a wise man's wit governs need.

("A hatani dictates what another's need will be.")

Fool, to do what a hatani said to do!

Thorn caught his breath and sprang for the rocks, bare feet doing what claws might do, shaping themselves to stone as Duun's could not, clinging with their softness: bare hands clinging where Duun's hands might not— swinging on a branch that gave a shortcut round the cliffside, dropping to a slant where Duun's feet would skid, where Duun's leg might fail—

The wind, O fool, the wind is at your face; Duun had checked the wind this morning. There was no corner Duun-hatani did not see around before his quarry even saw the turn—

The pebble in the tea—

Upland or downland? Do what Duun said and surprise him with obedience? Or do the opposite?

Run and run: he was quicker than Duun, that was all he was. He had grown up in these hills; and so had Duun. Thorn was more agile. He could take the high slope on his bare feet at greater speed than Duun—

—but Duun knew that.

Wild choice, then. Logic-less. He darted downslope.

Wind in his face, wind carrying his scent; and he had to get around that bend first, around the mountain shoulder.

Duun was at his back. It was not the pain Thorn dreaded, though pain there would be. It was Duun. Duun himself.

The wind carried scent and Duun breathed it—*fool,* Duun thought, at the edge of the rocks; *but twice a fool is a hunter too secure.* There was the easy temptation— to win at once, to take the rash chance, the wide chance.

But it was hatani he hunted. No more minnow, but fish in dark water.

He smelled the wind and knew Thorn's direction and his distance; he knew the branch of the trail that gave access to the cliff and knew the way Thorn could take that he could not—he knew every track in the hills.

Thorn knew he knew. That was the conundrum: how well he had taught the fish.

And what kind it was, how native-adept, what skill was bred into its bone and blood . . . what intelligence, what instincts.

Five-fingered hands; a surer grip; a talent at climbing: these it had. It had youth: strong legs, that felt no pain.

It knew—if it used its wits—how a once-maimed sho-nun had to compensate for these things.

And it would, being hatani, try to predict; try then to seize events and turn them.

It smelled of fear and sweat, even when the wind had cleaned the scent. It stank of something else, a bitter, acrid taint.

Run and run: it was speed Thorn had first for advantage. It was agility—Duun's was greatest, hand to hand. But Thorn's was more in distance, in the rocks, in the quick scaling of a tilted tree across a crack—

(Fool! he'll know—)

(But it will cost him time.)

And Thorn had gotten the mountain between him and Duun, gotten stone between them, to confuse the scent.

But Duun could smell where a hand had been, if he got his nose down to it. So Duun claimed.

(Run, minnow. I'm coming, little fish. . . .)

Downland. The opposite of what Duun had said he ought to do: should he confound the choice? What was there to do that he had never done?

(Gods, his gut, his bowels ached. Fear? The chase? The jolts from rock to rock?)

(Something in the food?)

Duun tripped the support. The log rolled down the gravel slope. Hastily done. Rife with scent. He spotted the second trap too, the limb drawn back, and drew back his hand in time.

Double-snared.

(Good, fish. Well done, that. But not good enough.)

Thorn knelt on hands and knees. He had reached the road and crossed it, leaving tracks; he paused to set a rock up on a twig, on a slope where haste might set a foot, then hurled himself downslope, leaving further tracks, leaving a bit of skin on the stones below.

He miscalculated further, sprawled. His face stung with shame. He gathered himself up again, doubled over a little farther on sweating and resisting the easy support of a tree.

(Touch nothing, leave no trace—)

Duun would hurt him. That was nothing. It was the look in Duun's gray eyes. The stare. The scorn.

Thorn bent and caught his breath; and wits began to work. He looked up at the slope he had left.

(Take me now, face to face.)

(The walls are down, minnow. What will you do?)

(Did Duun sleep? Could Duun sleep more than he did these last nights in the house?)

Was Duun-hatani lying awake each night—thinking a minnow might try him? Expecting it?

Was Duun as tired as he?

(Fix the breakfast, minnow. Hear?)

Hatani tricks. A hatani decides what his enemy will do. A pebble in the tea. (Fix the breakfast, minnow.)

And what his enemy believes.

Anger came into him. He purged it.

(Wield anger; it has no place, else.)

(Is there a use for fear?)

Duun stopped, not yet in the open. There was the land below. There were the treetops black and green downslope. There was, beyond the trees, the great flat plain, the river-plain, the valley of the Oun, which watered it, narrow in its folds.

And a sudden bleak thought came to him.

Predictive. His heart doubled its beats. He had chosen the hunter's part. It was that part habitual with him; Thorn seldom turned, only tried to disarm his attacks, to defend—to set snares. It was wise in Thorn.

(Face to face with me—Thorn challenged, and: no, said Thorn, when I offered him a fight.)

It was constantly the running tactic. The evasion.

(Find me, Duun-hatani. Find me if you can. Find me where I choose.)

In a different place, a change of grounds.

Duun dared not run. That was always the pursuer's hazard. Thorn's traps were halfhearted, token; but there was no tokenness in a downslope fall. Thorn supposed in him a certain degree of care.

And Thorn was quicker. Younger. Sound of wind.

Duun set out quickly. Anger rose in him and died a quick death.

(Well-done, minnow, if this was your plan. I am not ashamed. Not of you.)

Duun saw his hazard. And being hatani-trained, perhaps the young fool knew what he did.

Perhaps.

Thorn ached still. The first cramps had bent him double. (O gods, gods, gods, his guts.) He heaved himself down at a streamside he had never hunted yet, bathed his face. Livhl-root. He knew the herb. He knew others and chewed the leaves, a foul taste, but it stopped the spasms in his bowels. He had left sign. He had made mistakes when the pain drove him. He chewed the sour leaves he found and swallowed, splashed his face with icy water from the spring. His hands were white with the chills that racked him.

Fool, to challenge Duun. To have offered quarter. To have changed the game. Nothing was safe. He flung himself up again and ran down the stream—

—Old trick. Ancient trick, Duun would say. Do something original.

He had no strength left. His knees ached with the struggle with the water and the rocks, his bones ached with the chill: his joints grew loose and ached and strained with the sudden turn of river stones. The cold got into his bones and set him shivering.

(Can one die of livhl? *Was* it livhl?)

His ankle turned; he saved himself from a plunge in icy water, waded to the shore, his arms and the legs under him jerking with shivers like drugged spasms. (O Duun, unfair.)

No quarter. None.

Downhill again.

The sun went past zenith. The drug had worked. Duun caught the livhl-stink, though Thorn had been wary, and fouled the brook to kill it. It was in his sweat, on the things his hands had touched. He had taken to the stream and followed that—no craft at all to conceal his exit-point. A snare was possible, if Thorn's wits were not addled. Duun went around the place, picked the trail up without difficulty, though water had killed the scent somewhat. (Well-thought, minnow; the brush is thick, the chance for ambush all too great. Am I to follow you into a thrown rock, a deadfall?)

(Where's the breaking-point, Thorn? The killing-point? The point you turn?)

(Or do you fall first? How long, Thorn?)

Duun hastened. His limp betrayed him. There was a pain within his side. (Old man, old man—they put you back together; you should have let them replace the knee, regrow the hand—now you rue it, late.)

He found another way—he guessed which way Thorn must head and guessed amiss.

(So. He learned that lesson all too well. Does he read me? Does he know? Or is it random choice he tries? Knowledge or fool's choice?)

(How old is he in his own terms? Not man yet. Not grown. But near.)

(Thorn-that-I-carried. *Haras,* Thorn, that wounds the hand that holds it, the foot that treads it, that tangles paths and bears bitter blooms and poisoned fruit.)

The shadows multiplied in the sinking sun. Thorn gasped for air, withheld his hands from their instinctive reach after support on trunk and log and stone as he descended the valley. He sighted on a stone and went to it, for his legs wandered. He sighted on the next and followed that. Such little goals led him now.

(Get beyond the pale, get to paths strange to both of us. Duun knows the mountain too well—far too well.)

(Go where Duun would not have me go—make him angry—anger in my enemy is my friend, my friend—)

He smelled smoke. It was far away in the valley, but he went toward it.

(Let Duun worry now. Let him come here to find me.

Here among the countryfolk. Here among others. Other people.)

(Run and run. Stop for wind. Let us play this game in and out of strange places, in among stranger-folk who know nothing of the game.)

—There must be food, food for taking with hatani tricks. ("They're herders," Duun had said. "Herder-folk. No, little fish, not hatani, nothing like. They respect us too much to come here. That's all. They lived here once.")

(Where houses are is food, is shelter: he'll have to search, he won't know if they'd lie, these countryfolk, or hide me—perhaps they would.)

There was a trail. There was a stink of habit here even his nose could tell, musty, old dung, the frequent passage of animals.

Thorn jogged up it. Stink to hide his stink. To confound Duun's nose. Tracks to hide his tracks. Let Duun guess. Thorn gathered speed and coursed along the trail. There was the taste of blood in his mouth.

("—They never bother anything," Duun said of farmer-folk. "They don't ask to be bothered and we don't go there.")

("Couldn't we see them, Duun-hatani? Couldn't we go and see?") Thorn wondered if they were like the meds and Ellud; if there were—

(—O gods, if there were some like me.)

In all the wide world Duun spoke of, there must be more like him.

It was what Duun had thought. Fool! he cursed himself. Fool! To maneuver the enemy and not to see it— that was the greatest fool in the world. Scent-blind, sick with livhl, Thorn was seeking a hiding-place, seeking some place rife with scents, with smoke, with tracks and confusion. Cover himself in shonun-scent.

Thorn was going to the one place forbidden him. Change the rules. Upset the game.

Find outsiders and raise it another level still.

(Duun, what's *wrong* with me?)

(*Slick,* the infant said, rubbing at his stomach.)

Faces in the mirror.

(Duun, will my ears grow?)

Duun laid his own ears back and put on speed, risking everything now, risking shame, that a minnow might trap him.

But Thorn already had.

There was a house in the twilight—not a large house like theirs up on the mountain, but a ramshackle thing part metal and part wood. There were fences, put together the same way, of bits and pieces. *Fences*—Thorn guessed that word: *fences,* Duun said, kept countryfolk cattle from the woods: and *cattle* Thorn had seen, from high on the mountaintop, white and brown dots moving across the flat in summer-haze. ("City-meat comes from those," Duun told him. And Thorn: "Can't we hunt them?" "There's no hunting them," Duun had said. "They're tame. They're stupid. They stand there to be killed. Staring at you. They trust shonunin.")

("And they *kill* them, Duun?")

White animals huddled in their pens. Lights burned near the house on a tall pole in the twilight. Thorn saw the power lines, that led from there two ways, the house, and off across the land— (The power unit's far away then. Can there be other houses near?) He skirted brush, came up nearer, where he had a closer view of the house, the dusty yard beyond its fence. Hiyi grew there, along the row, all in leaf in this season, flowerless. He heard high voices, the closing of some door. "I'll get you," someone shrilled, but there was laughter in the voice. "I'll get you, Mon!"

More shrieks. Thorn came closer, taking to the road. Beneath the lights, in front of the porch, two small figures ran and raced and played chase.

"Come in here!" a voice called from the open door. "Come in, it's time to eat."

They were children. They ran and shrieked and yelled— Duun's kind. Thorn's heart stopped. He stood there in the road and looked beyond the fence and likewise the children stopped their game and stared, they on their side, he on his.

They were like Duun. Like him, in grayer, paler coats. With Duun-like ears, eyes, faces—with all that made up Duun.

"Aiiii!" one screamed. The other yelled. They hugged each other and yelled—to frighten him, he thought; he stood his ground, trembling at the sight. More of Duun's kind came out.

But children were like Duun. Children were not born hairless; he was not a child gone wrong, failed in growing—

—He was—

(Duun!)

He drew back. A man had run out onto the step. "Get in! Get inside!" Thorn thought it meant him, and delayed. "Ili! *Ili!* Get the gun!"

(O gods! Guns! Duun!)

He spun on his heel and ran. He heard doors slam, more than once. Heard running come toward the fence, heard voices at his back. "Gods, it's *him!*" one yelled, and others took it up. "It's that thing—*that thing!*"

It was a trap. Duun had made it. Duun had snared all his paths, all the world: there was no way, nothing, anywhere, that Duun had not seen and set up to trap him—

(Got you, minnow, got you again—)

Thorn snatched breath and left the road, darted into the undergrowth, hearing the howl of animals at his back, hearing shouts raised—*"The thing on the mountain!*—It's him, it's come!"

(O *gods,* Duun—gods—) Breath split his side. Branches tore at him. He ran and something in him had broken, ached, swelled in his throat—

They hunted him. They all did. There was no help.

No quarter.

Leaves burst into flames near him. Beamer. He heard the whine of projectiles.

Splinters burst into his face. He flung his hands up, hit a tree or some such thing: impact numbed his arm and spun him. The ground came up. He felt twigs stab his hand, earth and leaves abrade the heel of it. He scrambled to turn over and get his knees, his legs under him, eyes pouring tears; the numbed arm flopped at his side. He heard more shots whine.

"There he is!"

He dived and dodged and stumbled to his knees again, aware of shock. Once he had fallen from the rocks and been like this, numb from head to foot, and scared and breathless—had risen and walked and run again and known only later where he was, to find Duun gazing down at him from the high rocks.

To find Duun coming down to him, game abandoned, to take his face in his maimed hand, jaw pinched between thumb and forefinger, and look into his eyes—

"You hear me, little fish? You hear me?"

Duun!

Thorn slipped to one knee and got up again, turned, his shoulder to rough bark. There were lights, the howl of beasts, there were shapes behind the lights, people shining lights wildly this way and that into the brush, over him.

"Get it! There it goes!"

He put the tree between them and him and ran again, left arm swinging like a dead thing at his side. (I was hit. It was a shot that knocked me down. They shot me. Am I allowed to use my knife?) He ran and ran, sliding on the slopes, tearing himself on brambles. (Is this real? Is it game? Duun—Did you set this up? Am I supposed to kill? Duun, I'm *scared!*)

He came down the slope, skidded at the bottom, spun on one foot and ran left along the streamcourse.

A shadow rose up in his path. He flung himself aside to escape it, but it was *there,* shonun-smelling, blocking the strike of his right arm, and a voice said: "Thorn!" before a two-fingered grip came up at his throat and spun him off-balance and crushed him in a choking hold. Thorn bent, caught one-handed at the arm and tried a throw. Sickness jolted through him to the roots of his teeth. He was pulled back and back stumbling in the leaves, and a grip twisted his wounded arm. "Get out of here!" Duun hissed into his ear. "Thorn, Thorn—it's me! Run for it! Get home!"

Duun's hand let go and shoved hard in the middle of his back. Thorn ran. He ran and slipped on leaves and ran again; his side ached. Fire shot through it. His arm ached and the pain jolted through each step.

(Get home!)

(Do I believe you, Duun—do I do what you say? Is it a trap, Duun?)

A gun cracked. Several. He heard the echo off the hills. There were shouts—there were voices, the howl of beasts.

(But Duun's back there.) Thorn stumbled to a stop, hit a tree in his blindness and leaned his back on it. His sight hazed. The pain was one vast throbbing now, beyond pain, or it had gotten to his heart. He blinked the night as clear as it would come. There were lights. There were more voices raised—shouts and cries and howls; again the discharge of a gun.

(Duun!)

Thorn began to run downslope, holding the loose arm still as he could. Branches jabbed into his face and he ducked his head aside, ran blindly, trusting the slope of the land to tell him downhill from up—fended brush finally with the right hand and let the left drag on the brambles in cold, vast shocks. He heard his breathing, felt the tearing of his chest—there was no more night, no more world: it had shrunk to body-size, all sound diminished to the sound of his breath and his heart.

(They'll kill him like the cattle! Duun!)

A branch thrust into his way, wrapped living round him, locked and held. "Thorn! Dammit—fool!"

Thorn hung there, on Duun's arm. Duun's strong grip spun him, seized him by both arms and shook him, snapping his head back.

"Fool! Where were you going?"

He could not answer. The pain came on in waves. Duun shook at him again. It was Duun. It smelled of Duun. (Scent-blind. Scent-blind fool.)

"I had to hurt someone," Duun said. It was anger. Duun shook at him. "You hear me, fool! I had to hurt someone for your sake."

"I think—I think—" Shock came on him. His jaws passed his control, locked and chattered. And Duun took him to the ground. ("How many times did they get you? Gods. Gods. I see it. . . .") He stretched him out there on the forest slope and probed the arm, while here and elsewhere came and went for him.

"Why?" he asked Duun. "Why did they do it?" While his jaws spasmed and chattered and the pain came and went. "Duun, were they supposed to do that?"

"Shut up," Duun said. And hurt him, whether by intent or accident. Thorn went out a moment, came back with Duun slapping gently at his face. "Can you move the fingers? I've got a gel on it. Move the fingers. Hear?"

Thorn tried. He thought they moved. He clenched his jaws, because Duun hauled him up against his shoulder and pulled him to his feet. The world went upside down as Duun's shoulder came into his groin and heaved. Pain. The arm swung. Jolting pain as Duun moved. The world went black and red, phosphenes darting in his eyes, in the dark. Branches raked his back. There was instability as Duun climbed, so that he dared not move. But the pain, the pain. . . .

There was a darkness. Duun swung him down and let him to his knees on the slope, holding onto him. Duun's breath was in his face.

"You've got to walk," Duun said. "Hear me? Hear me, Thorn? You've got to walk now." Duun got an arm about him and pulled up on him. "Walk. Hear me?"

Thorn heard. He tried. He heard Duun's gasping breaths, leaned on him, struggling for purchase on stone and earth and mold. "Climb," Duun said. "Dammit, climb!"

Howls rose behind them in the woods. They lent Thorn strength. Duun's curses did. Duun carried him a time, and flung him down in the leaves with a jolt that knocked the breath from him. And slapped him after. "Breathe, dammit, breathe."

He tried. He gasped. And Duun lay down on him and

panted. Their hearts jolted one against the other and the pain kept time with it.

Another climb. Duun had gotten him on his feet again. Thorn had no memory how. "The road's not far," Duun said. "They won't come above it. Come on."

And sitting then, sitting on a flat roadside stone where Duun set him, Duun holding him with one hand about his arms and the other against his chest. There was color in the world. It was dawn.

"Breathe. You've got to walk again."

"Yes," he said. He questioned nothing. Duun was Duun, source and force. Like the sun, the wind. He sat a moment and got up again, his heart hammering, his body swaying in the height of the world, with the treetops like black water whispering below them.

They walked. He and Duun. Duun's hand in his belt; Duun dragged his sound arm about his ribs and held it by the wrist. Going was easier on the road. Thorn's feet discovered pain, lacerations that small stones wore at. His mouth was dry as the silken dust. The wind was cold on his bare skin and Duun was warm.

Another rest. "Sit down," Duun said. "Sit down." And drew him against him and held him in his arms.

"Why did they shoot?" Thorn asked, because that answer eluded him. "Duun, why?"

"You scared them," Duun said. "They thought you'd harm them."

Scared them. Scared them. Thorn recalled the children. He shivered. Duun's arms clenched him hard.

"Fool," Duun said. He deserved it. He was ashamed.

He slept. He opened his eyes on the ceiling of the big room in the house with no memory how he had gotten there from the road. He heard Duun coming and going. (Guard your sleep, minnow. Dared he sleep?)

"Drink," Duun ordered him, lifting his head, setting a cup to his lips. He turned his head away, not wanting to be twice victim. (Fool. Won't you learn?) "*Drink,* damn you, Thorn."

He blinked, all hazy. "Livhl—"

"Dammit, no. I'm telling you drink, this time."

He drank. It was sweetened tea. It hit his stomach and lay there inert and he was glad to have his head down at level again before it should come up. "I lost," he said. "You beat me, Duun."

"Be still." Duun's maimed hand brushed at his hair. (Duun holding him, Duun playing games, Duun touching him that way long, long ago.) "Meds are on their way. I called them. Hear?"

"Don't want meds." (Ellud standing in the room. An old friend, Duun said. Be polite.) "Duun, tell them don't."

"Hush. Be still." The touch came at his hair again. At his face. "Rest. Sleep. It's all right. Hear?"

(Duun in the bedroom door at night. Go to sleep, little fish. There were no black threads in the doorway. No games. Go to sleep now, minnow.)

V

"They'll pay for it," Ellud said. Ellud had come with the meds. The house stank of disinfectants, of bandage and gel and blood. And Thorn's distress. Duun folded his arms and gazed at the hearthstones. At dead ash. "They have to," Ellud said. "Don't they?"

There was criticism implied. Duun looked around at Ellud and stared. Ellud flinched as Ellud had done sixteen years ago. But it took longer. There was wrath in Ellud now. There was offended justice. "Anything," Duun reminded him hoarsely. "But no. Don't charge them."

"You've left me with no choice. They fired on you."

"Did they? I don't remember that."

"They called the magistrate. They confessed. They know what they did."

"So." Duun walked away toward the closed door. The medicinal smells offended his nostrils. His ears lay down. He limped. Every muscle he owned was strained. Ellud wore his city clothes, immaculate. Duun wore nothing but a small-kilt. And let the scars show. He might have worn the hatani cloak. He had left it hanging. "I'll talk to them, Ellud. No charges."

"They can't do a thing like that and get away with it—"

"Because I'm sacrosanct?" Duun turned back to him, ears flat. "You promised me anything, Ellud. I'm asking you. No charges. Deed Sheon back to them."

"They tried to kill you!"

"They damn near did. Good for them. They're not

bad, for farmers. Do I have to take this on my shoulders too?"

Ellud was silent a moment. His mouth drew down.

"So you get what ought to make you happy," Duun said. "I'm coming in. I trust you'll find a place."

More long silence. "It's about time. It's about time, Duun. I'll have a copter up here. Lift you out."

"He'll walk down," Duun said. "Day after tomorrow. He'll be fit."

"Past *them?* Gods, hasn't there been enough trouble?"

"He's hatani, Ellud." Duun met the darkness in Ellud's stare and matched it. "Understand that. He'll walk out on his own."

Thorn gained his feet after the meds left. Duun thought he would. "Sit down," Duun said, sitting himself, on one of the risers that rimmed the room. The floor sand was trampled, dotted with darkness. Thorn had bled on it, amply. Thorn hung now in the doorway with his arm slung in a cord about his neck; his skin had an ugly waxen color, excepting the arm, where blood-reddened gels plastered an incision. There would be a scar. A long one. It had missed a major nerve; so the meds said. The bone was chipped but not broken. "You've got a lot of plasm in you for blood, boy. Left most you owned down in that valley. Come sit down."

Thorn came. Duun was polishing his weapons. Thorn sank down on the riser on his knees and sat down carefully, one leg off. There was sweat on his hairless brow. His hair clung to it.

"We're going," Duun said, "to the city. We'll live there now."

"Leave here—"

Duun looked up at him. Sheon was lost. Twice now. There was darkness in his stare; and Thorn stared back at him with alien, clouded eyes, with thoughts going on, and dread. (Why did they shoot, Duun? Is this revenge? Is this against me? Was I wrong, Duun? What did I do, down there?)

"I don't want to go, Duun."

"They'll come later and gather up the things we'll want. These—" Duun polished the blade. "These we take."

"I don't want to go."

"I know that." Duun looked at him. Tears shimmered in Thorn's eyes. "The countryfolk get the land. It'll belong to them now. It'll pay, maybe, for what I had to do. Do you understand me, Thorn? Haras? Do you hear?"

"Yes, Duun-hatani."

"We'll fly out of here. We'll go to a place where the wind stinks and you won't understand a thing you see. You'll ask me your questions in private. There'll be people around us. Always. No more hunting. No more woods. Just steel. Just thousands and thousands of people. A lot of shonun like that life. You'll learn to."

Thorn bowed his head onto his arm, against his knee. Duun was aware of him. Duun looked only at the blade, gently polished the razor steel in small strokes of an oiled cloth. Oil-smell and steel. Steel and oil. His half-hand held the cloth, the whole left hand held the blade.

"Give it away, Thorn. You're hatani. Hatani own nothing. Only the weapons, the cloak on your back. This time it's only a place you lose. When you're what you will be, you'll own nothing at all. I only used this place. You and I. It was a stage. It's gone now."

Thorn's face lifted. He had smeared his face with wiping it. His lashes were wet. "I'm sorry, Duun."

Duun's hands stopped in a long silence. Then he took up the motion again. "You lost a year, perhaps. A year here. Maybe two. Then we'd have gone, all the same. It's not much, two years. Your eyes are running. Do that tomorrow and I'll beat you. Do you hear?"

"Yes," Thorn said.

They started in the dawn: they walked slowly on the winding track and there was no anger evident in Duun. "Joiit," Duun said once, naming a birdsong. Thorn thought then that in the people-teeming place Duun described to him there could be no birds; and the sound from the woods made his heart ache. The very wind in the leaves did that. The silken feel of the dust under his sore feet. His arm ached as he walked. His head was light. They had closed up the house and walked out of the yard. And once Duun had looked back and Thorn did, just when the house was going out of view. It looked no different than it ever had when they left it in their hunting. The light was the same on the brown stone walls, with the hiyi growing here and there in lavender-edged green; all of it was from this distance, in the morning, stained and tinted like the earth. It was like every morning. The house appeared to wait for them. Would go on waiting, through the days. Someone would come, Duun said, to strip the rooms. The countryfolk would come and take it back. The children would explore the rooms, play tag in the yard—

—hunt in the woods. They would know the old tree that was good to lie on in the sun; the hollow rock that overlooked the little pond back in the hills; they would know the tracks and trails where Duun had led him—

Thorn shed no tears. When his heart hurt that much he looked away at the sky, the road, he said something, no matter what, he clenched the fingers of his wounded arm, which made it ache and took his mind away.

He did that when the bird sang. And when the wind blew in the leaves that way; and when he realized he could smell things even scent-blind as he was, like dust, and grass, and the rough-raw scent of lugh-flowers, which was strong when one bruised them, when Thorn-the-child pulled off their heads and found his hands all sticky with sap, all one flavor with the sunlight and the giddy golden blooms—

Everything came flooding in. Sights afflicted him with farewells, all along the road. And Duun was silent for the most part. (Duun was young here too. He knew the old tree, the stone—the paths—he showed them to me. I took them from him. Duun!)

The trees spread away from the road in a purpling-green flood of treetops. Beyond them the valley fell away where countryfolk lived, a pale haze of land beyond that,

flat as flat: and vast sky, delirious blued violet, and
streamers of cloud like pond-ice, high, high above the
plain, going off into milky white.

Terror afflicted Thorn. The sky was all too large beyond the mountain. To fly, Duun said. There were machines; Duun had mentioned them. Now and again when
the meds came he had seen one far away, before it went
out of sight behind the mountain. Sometimes there were
white trails in the sky: planes, Duun said. People fly in
them.

(Where, Duun? Where do they go? Why do they go?
Can they see us? Thorn-the-child had waved at such
planes, standing dizzily atop the tallest rock he could
climb: "Here I am, here, here!")

(Notice me. Give me a sign you see. Here I am, are
you like me? Do you see other children where you go?
Have they skins like mine? And eyes like mine? And
have they five fingers too?)

(Thousands and thousands of shonun in the city. Will
there be some like me?)

The road wound down and down, among the trees and
out of them. Far away was a sound the wind never made,
that grew: machine-sound, thumping in ominous accents
that always spoke of meds.

"They're coming in," Duun said. "They'll be early.
Waiting for us."

The strangers came up the road to meet them. Not the
meds, but others, dressed from neck to foot in blue and
gray. Wearing weapons. Thorn hesitated when he saw
them, but Duun kept walking, so he knew they were
acceptable. "You didn't need to," Duun told them when
they met. "We have orders," one of them said; that was
all. Thorn stood still in the encounter at a turning of the
road. They looked at him, these strangers, and they
looked away, as if he had no importance, being only an
appendage, Duun's. And the blue-clad folk led off, walking down again, with one of them behind them, another
by Duun's side.

The mountain stopped being theirs then. Strangers
owned it. Strangers came to get in the way of their last

moments with it, his and Duun's. He knew why Duun
wanted them away. But Duun would not tell them no,
and walked without looking at things like trees and
stones, as Duun had looked about him before they came.
Without talking to him. Duun was bitter. Duun hurt.
Thorn knew it. (My fault. My doing. All of it. They
should take me and go away and Duun would still have
his mountain.) But no one offered Thorn that choice.
Perhaps it did not exist.

Down and down, the last little distance to the flat,
around the last turning of the road.

A machine sat in the meadow; it had huge blades. It
had flattened a circle all around itself in the milky green
grass. There were broad dusty roads that met there, and
people stood there at that crossing, far removed.

"We've kept them off," said a man who had not spoken before. Only not a man like Duun, like Ellud, like
the meds. This one was broader-hipped, walked differently, had a quiet, smaller voice. *Woman,* Thorn thought,
hearing that, and his heart picked up its beats.

("Women are," Duun had told him, when he was
small, "us and different.")

("How different?" Thorn asked.)

("Inside. Outside, in some things. They have a place
inside they make babies. Men put them there; women
make them.")

("How?" child-Thorn asked. "*That* does it," Duun
said, and showed him what this was. "I haven't got that,"
Thorn had said, looking at himself. "Duun, I haven't got
that. Mine's all outside.")

("You're different," Duun had said.)

("Am I a woman?")

("No," Duun said. "You're a child. You're going to
be a man.")

("How do women make babies?")

Duun had not answered then. Or he had forgotten.
Thorn knew the answer later. ("See this," Duun had
said. Showed him the young inside a deiggen Thorn had
killed. "They're babies. You ought not to kill the does.
See the eartips. Don't hunt that kind.")

Thorn remembered that. But he had gotten a deiggen-baby out of its womb and laid it out on a flat rock to see it. It was not the death he remembered strongest, or the blood. It was that it had had no hair, was naked-skinned like him.

(I was born and grew wrong. They got me out too soon.)

He watched the foenin mate. (*That's* how? He was appalled and interested at once in the black bodies one on the other's back, the curious spasms they made as if one of them were sick.)

("Shonun do it face to face, usually," Duun said. Thorn was twice appalled. It was odd enough to do from the rear. Having someone watching back right in one's face—)

This—woman—had a gun on her hip. She swayed when she walked. She had a bright white crest but she had shaved it far back as did all the cityfolk, not like Duun's, which was black and long and swung freely when he walked.

Thorn thought of the foenin. Clenched his hand to drive that thought away. He had made enough difficulty for Duun. It was not spring. It was not appropriate. There was something about smell, but Duun refused to discuss this with him.

They walked out onto the flat toward the machine and foenin blurred in the waft of oil and warm metal. The copter. They would go up in the air in that. It looked too heavy. Thorn forgot about women. His heart began to beat in terror. (Fool, he told himself. Duun had warned him. The thing had gotten here, it would get away again with them inside. He would not be afraid in front of strangers. He would not stink of fear where others not scent-blind could smell it. He would not shame Duun. *I will beat you,* Duun had said, to get his attention; now Thorn remembered that and knew why Duun had threatened him. Not to be shamed by him. He would not flinch when they led him in.)

It was the countryfolk Duun watched, the spectators the guards had kept far off on the other road. He kept his ears aslant, shutting out what words the wind might

bring him. He smelled the scent of them even at this
range. His mind painted him hate; and fear. He was a
fool to shut down his hearing; one of them might have
brought a gun.

But they had called the magistrate and turned themselves in. In fear, he thought bitterly, of more general
retribution. In responsibility, late-arrived. Sixteen years
they had waited, in the hope of Sheon's land.

(So it's yours. Enjoy it. And be damned.)

He was ashamed of the thought. He had come here
for virtue and took away—

—took away this shadow at his side. And the cold
stares of those who had seen a hatani bend his vows.
Who had lived for sixteen years in fear of what happened
on the mountain they coveted.

Well, well. It was not a mistake, perhaps. Duun looked
toward the copter, exchanged perfunctory courtesy with
the guard-captain, snagged Thorn with a gentle clawtip
on his inner arm. "Come on," Duun said looking at the
captain. (Be done with it. Don't draw it out. Get us out
of here.)

Thorn walked by him, lifted his head to wonder at the
blades—Duun hit him in the back. "Fool, keep your head
low beneath these things!" Thorn ducked and went; but
the rotor was only lazily turning now. Not even enough
for wind.

Up the steps then, to a metal world, to plastic seats,
the smell of oil and fuel. Duun settled Thorn—"There,
that's the buckle. Push, that's right. That lets it loose.
That tightens it. Keep it on." He looked Thorn in the
eyes, which no one else would meet, and saw stark terror
there. Duun frowned and worked his way past Thorn to
his own seat to buckle in.

The crew took places. The guards climbed aboard aft,
making the craft rock on its runners. The pilot brought
the engines up—whup, whup, whup! Thorn looked toward
the side window, looked ahead, looked his way. Duun
reached over the shared armrest and gripped his arm,
once, sharply, with the claws all the way out. (Behave!)

Thorn settled then. And the whup-whup-whup grew

louder, the aircraft tilting as it lifted, tilted and swung its
tail about as the countryfolk ran in the dust the blades
kicked up.

Wh-wh-wh—! Sky in one view, ground in the other.
He gave a look at Thorn, saw the cords in Thorn's neck
stand out as he braced himself. Another grip of claws.
Thorn visibly relaxed. Turned his face to Duun's with
studied serenity.

So. Duun slipped his finger down Thorn's arm, to the
place on Thorn's wrist where veins lay next the surface.
The pulse throbbed beneath his finger-pad as if the heart
that drove it was going to burst.

"Keep your eyes on the horizon," Duun said into
Thorn's ear. "Helps your stomach."

"I'm not scared," Thorn shouted back. But the copter
turned off for the west then, sharply, and Thorn's fingers
clenched on his armrest.

The great flat, more hills, an hour and more of trees
and roads and herds that raced beneath them in a brown
tide. Suddenly the great sheet of a bay spread itself beyond a brown rim of trees, water shining silver in the
sun and going on forever to the south. Thorn forgot his
terror and pointed—"What's that?"

"Djohin Bay," Duun shouted back. "That's the sea
out there, minnow! That's the great wide sea!"

Land came up eastward beyond that shining surface:
outthrusts of the city, a stain against the sky. "What's
there?" Thorn yelled into the rotor noise.

"That's Pekenan," Duun said. "That's the port town.
The city's coming up. There—that's the shuttle-port, see
that gray ribbon there."

"What's a shuttle-port?" Thorn asked. "What's a port
town?" His skin was white in the sunlight that streamed
through the copter's side windows. He sweated. It was
too soon to have traveled. Sights and strangeness
multiplied. (Don't faint on me, minnow, not here, not
now. There's more.) "Here." Duun fished out an inhaler
from the kit at his feet. He had brought it with their
gear. "Put that in your mouth— Breathe in hard." He
pushed the spray and Thorn choked, coughed. Fell back

against the seat with a shocked offended look. But he lost the waxen taint. His pupils dilated. "There. Want more?"

"No, Duun," Thorn said earnestly. He turned and looked out the window.

Duun had little desire to look. He knew what he would see. The capital. Dsonan. The tall buildings where shonunin lived one on top of the other.

"Look at those!" Thorn cried suddenly, pointing at the city-center.

"I've seen them, minnow." Tall buildings failed to interest him. "We're going to land on one. We're going to live there. Inside." To explain more than that took too much shouting. The rotor noise depressed him. He remembered the perspective of the concrete canyons, the buildings passing under them. He took Thorn by the wrist and held his finger on the pulse. Thorn looked at him, knowing what he was doing, looking as if he were vastly ashamed of a heart he could not control. "Look down," Duun said as they began to fly over the city. "Get used to it."

Thorn did not flinch. The pulse sped as the perspectives shifted beneath them. ("What's that?" Thorn asked, when a train whisked below them.) What's that? Duun had not wanted questions yet. There would have been time. The pulse fluttered beneath his fingertip with unbearable rapidity. "Are we coming down?"

"They never miss," Duun said. "Watch the roof, minnow. See the circle there. That's where we land."

VI

The window gave them a brook, a woodland. Duun cared nothing for it. The wind from the air-conditioning brought wood-scent. It was, like the opal sand on the floor, synthetic and expensive. Thorn marveled at it, touched the window—"Are we turning?"—because the scene moved. "No," Duun said with acerbity. "Have you forgotten? There's city behind that wall. Behave yourself. You don't own this. I don't. It's all *here*, that's all. Don't be impressed with it.

("Whose is it?")

Duun regretted then bringing up the matter. And perhaps Thorn suspected then that he had been in the company of more than one illusion maintained for him. Thorn's ebullience ebbed away and left a look of pain, the fine-drawn look of someone scant of resources. The lack of sleep for days, the purgative, the hunt, the wounds; a heart which had worked harder than the engines had in the copter flight—which had had, perhaps, all a heart ought to bear for a while. Duun went into his room, delved into his kit and took out a sedative, went into the kitchen and mixed it in milk.

The apartment was larger than the house had been. There were four bedrooms, the kitchen, a sitting room, dining hall, office, bath, gymnasium, sunroom (a lie); there was a library; a viewing-room; a sauna; a robing-room; a pantry; a laundry; a servant's quarters, but that was vacant. A security post. That was not. But Thorn knew nothing about guards and monitors and the hall outside. There were several rooms that feigned sunlight well enough to have growing plants, if one bothered. The bath and master bedroom had a wraparound tridee screen that doubled as windows—gods knew, it was not all nature scenes the builders meant with that. And a man grew tempted. There were recourses in the city. There were places a man or woman could go, amusements to be had. A hatani would be discreet. But even a hatani might—with a woman of discretion—find some out-of-season comforts. Duun laid his ears back. Hours in this place and it was as if sixteen years had not happened. Except for the presence which turned up at his shoulder.

He turned and handed Thorn the cup. "This is yours. Drink it. Go lie down."

Thorn took it. Perhaps Thorn was not quite that scent-blind. His eyes acquired wariness. And weary puzzlement.

"Sedative," Duun said. "Drink it. Go lie down. You'll sleep."

"Duun." Thorn set the milk on the counter. His face was white again. He leaned against the wall, not so strong as he pretended; he had been limping when he came in. "Have you been here before?"

"I lived here." Duun picked up the milk and picked up Thorn's hand and joined one firmly to the other. "Drink that. Shall I convince you, Thorn?"

Thorn drank it. All. He set the cup down again.

"So you've found out what you don't know," Duun said. "Does the world scare you, Thorn? You have to pick out the illusions here, that's all. You have to know what's real and what's not."

"You'll be with me."

"Haras-hatani. Thorn. What do I hear? Is that need? Is that something I have and you don't? What is that thing?"

"Courage." Thorn's voice was hoarse and hollow.

"Do I hear can't?"

"No, Duun-hatani."

"The meds want you. They want to take you and take

that arm apart again; they want to put their machines on you and get pieces of your hide and measure you up and down. I told them to wait a day or so."

Silence. Thorn's eyes were dilated. It was not all the sedative. "Thank you, Duun-hatani."

"Get to bed."

Thorn went. Limping.

So. So. There was no rebellion. Thorn might have. Duun stared out the vacant kitchen door. The place smelled of remodeling, beneath the wood-scent. Beneath the false wind and the false images. And the sand under his stone-callused feet felt too light, like powder.

He walked into the bedroom and found Thorn in bed. It was night. Duun's senses knew that, though the wall-images were out of synch and showed mid-afternoon. Thorn slept, the pale blue sheets clutched in a brown, smooth hand. The face had taken on a hollowed look, the jaw lengthened, the cheekbones more prominent.

Final changes. Almost-manhood.

Duun selected for night-image. The lights went out and a dust of stars shone on the walls, about the sleeper. The air-conditioning breathed a noncommittal scent, something synthetic and vaguely like the sea.

"Well, Duun?"

Duun tucked up his feet cross-legged on the riser (city manners came hard after sixteen years), rested his arms on his thighs and let his hands fall limp into his lap. (Well?) He looked up at Ellud, who sat on his desk, surrounded by the appurtenances of office, monitor, communications. Worm-in-web. Lines went everywhere from here, all over the world. "He's well," Duun said. "I don't think there was damage. A scar or two—what's that?"

Ellud looked at him; Duun looked back with a forever-twisted smile. It was humor and Ellud seemed finally to decide it was and not to like it. "The deed's been settled. The countryfolk are abjectly grateful. The matter is closed."

"Good."

"I'm fending queries off your neck, Duun. You know that."

"I know. They'll keep their hands off him. Tell them all that. He'd never seen a copter. He can run all the household things, well, the dishwasher he'd not seen. He's what I am. I told you that. The meds will respect him. Or I'll deal with them. No. *He* will. I'll give him leave."

"I wouldn't advise that."

"He's hatani, Ellud."

"A handful of farmers damn near killed him. For the gods' sweet sake, man, they'd have killed him! What were you doing about it?"

"Running. They almost killed me, you know. A half dozen men with guns aren't to disregard. I didn't teach a fool. And they surprised him. Not with the guns. With their reaction. They're lucky he ran. They're very lucky. Even with the guns. You can tell your staff that."

"They won't provoke him."

"They're not to talk to him. That rule still holds. Please, thank you, and sit down. Breathe in, breathe out. No comments. Nothing. And respect. They'll respect him. I do mean that."

Ellud drew a long, long breath and let it go. "How mature is he?"

"Very—in some ways. Not at all in others. I'm telling you: no one talks to him."

"For how long?"

"As long as it takes."

"They want to use the tapes."

Duun frowned. "Give me a little time with that. I'll say when."

"You've had sixteen years!"

"So has he. Who knows what he needs? I want your meds away from me, Ellud. Or I find another place. Somewhere the other side of the world if I have to."

"As long as it takes, is it?"

"That's the way."

"All right. I'll keep them off your neck. I'll talk to staff. Maybe you should get some rest. Have the meds check you too."

"That's not what I need."

"What is?"

"Is Dogossen still around?"

A silence. "She moved to Rogot, a husband. Second, now."

The years caught up to him, all in one dull ache. "Well. Hounai? Same?"

"You want a woman, Duun? I'll ask around on the staff. Maybe—"

"No hatani." He looked down, studied the patterns of his hands, whole and half. "I don't want a hatani. Nothing like. It's been a long time."

"I hope to the gods it has."

Duun looked up. It had been half a joke. Ellud's ears drew back and lay down tighter to his skull under Duun's stare. "Believe me," Duun said. "*Hire* someone. I don't want conversation. By the gods I don't want another wife. Let's keep it business. Not a staffer either. Someone at the port. Let security worry itself."

"I'm not your—"

"Call it friendship." Duun's voice was rough and hoarse. His hands clenched and unclenched when he knew it. And Ellud's ears lay back. Ellud went on looking at him as if Ellud wished to look away.

"Duun-hatani—" Carefully. With fear and offended sensibilities and prudent questions boiling in him Ellud would never ask. Like harm. And solitude. And sanity. The silence stayed there a long, long time.

"I'll want staffers too," Duun said. (So what have you done, Ellud no Hsoin? What do you dread? Violence? Old friend—what do you expect?) "Good ones. Young ones who know how to take orders."

"That's a contradiction in terms." Ellud's laughter was hasty as if he much wanted to laugh, to turn matters elsewhere. To be light with him. But the laughter died. "How many?"

"Four, five. Male and female. I'll let you do the picking. He's got to learn people. They can be older. Say— twenty, twenty-five. They'd better to the gods be stable. You understand."

A long silence. "I want those tapes started."

"You've forgotten," Duun said softly. "This is your office. But you don't control things. I do. Old friend. I'm not your backwoods employee come to the big city. I'm not one of your staffers."

"They're putting pressure on me, Duun."

"They."

"The council."

Duun drew a deep breath. Shut his eyes and thought again of the woods.

"Duun."

His eyes opened. Ellud sat there as if frozen. "They don't run this either," Duun said. "Sixteen years. Memories are short."

Two members have died. Rothon and—"

I know. I read all the news out there. What do you think I was doing? I know who's in and I know what they can do; and that's too bad: they dealt with a hatani. They can't undo that."

"Duun—they might try to kill you. Even that."

Duun laughed.

"Politics," Ellud said. "They'd be fools to try, but politics has made fools before. Don't take it lightly, Duun. That's my guard at your door. You'd better thank the gods it is. And the woman will be from my staff. I'd feel better. Be polite, Duun-hatani. Some of these young fools worship you."

He laid his ears down. "Dammit, Ellud."

"You want to work off something else than that, Duun-hatani?"

"Rescue me from fools."

"I'm trying to. From one I used to love, Duun."

Duun stayed still a long, long time. Grinned finally, and felt the scar pull at his mouth. Laughed once shortly; Ellud looked alarmed. "Gods," Duun said, "I'm drowning, and someone has a rope."

Ellud looked the more disturbed. His eyes showed whites.

"I own the world," Duun said. "Women don't see my scars, my charge adores me, and my last friend calls me a fool." He laughed again, flung his feet down to the sand and stood up. "I cherish that," he said. And left.

*   *   *

Young muscles strained, knotting and stretching under a hairless, sweat-drenched back: the arm held, and Thorn hauled himself upward on the exercise bar, up and down, up and down. Duun walked up on this in the gymnasium, walked up quietly on the well-trampled, sweat-pocked sand and stood there with arms folded a while. Finally Thorn's efforts flagged, became an upward struggle. In perverse humor Duun landed a swat on a vulnerable backside, claws out, and Thorn flinched and made the lift, then dropped, turning in the movement. Gasping then for breath, but bright-eyed with the morning and his health. Duun pursed his mouth. "Not sore, is it?"

"No." And a little wariness crept in. Duun studied him. Thinking. Thorn had gotten easy; and now Duun was thinking, and looking at him that way, and that was cause enough for wariness. There was a great deal in this place where things went on behind the walls, where Thorn waked to find himself adrift in the night sky, and stifled a scream which would have brought Duun's swift disgust. So Thorn turned on the stars each night himself, and walked dizzily to his bed, and flung himself down and made himself look up, about, lying wide-limbed as he had lain on a summer hillside, undefended against the sky that slowly turned. He remembered how it felt to fly. Remembered the land turning giddily under his sight, and the shifts of weight, the falling-feeling amplified by height enough to turn cattle into insects and valleys into folds of cloth. And the dark and the stars took him and whirled him until that flying sensation was back, and he lay there deliberately, overcoming his fear, and going to sleep with it. Some fears Duun set into him for a reason; at this one Duun would laugh, Thorn felt that this was so—and Duun's scorn was worse that the heights, worse than any falling. He hoped now for Duun's approval . . . the quickly hooded glance, the tightening of the mouth— for such small things he worked, but they had meaning. The slap that stung—that was a joke; Duun joked with him, and dared him, and that meant—meant perhaps an end to Duun's restraint with him—Duun's pity. Duun's—

(he felt)—disgust with this place and what had brought him to it. (Forgive me, Duun-hatani. Forgive me for all of it. For us being here. For me being helpless and disappointing, and, gods—don't be angry, Duun.)

Duun poked him in the belly. Hard. Thorn withstood that. He centered himself, expecting—some sudden move. A blow that could take his head off. Because Duun knew he could turn it. Thorn thought of that. Suddenly he was not thinking of the blow; timing-sense deserted him and he shivered, flinched, knowing it. And Duun saw that too.

"Where's the mind, Haras?"

Thorn centered himself again. Duun walked around behind him. Thorn's ears strained. He listened to the soft sound of Duun's tread on sand. His own rapid breathing dimmed his hearing and endangered him. He did not move until he heard Duun on his left, then turned his head, pursuing the movement which teased the tail of his eye.

Slowly Duun extended his right hand toward Thorn's face—(Attack?) Thorn's heart jumped and in a critical moment the hand had passed his reaction-point and he let it, let Duun touch his jaw. A two-fingered grip settled gently on either side, where no one's hand belonged but his teacher's, but the slow-moving hand too quick for him if he should move. He was vulnerable to that. He knew it. He cherished it. When Duun discovered weaknesses in him he attacked them, but this was the allowable one, this one was his safety that kept the games all games. Duun never took that away. Duun's dark eyes were on a level with his own, poured force into him, like the dark of night, like the dark and all the stars in which he whirled and perished.

"What is your *need,* Haras-hatani?"

(O gods, Duun—don't.)

"What is your *need,* Haras-Thorn? Why did I get through your guard? To what are you vulnerable? Name me that thing."

"You, Duun-hatani. I need *you.*"

The grip hurt. Bruised. "What am I to you, minnow?"

Words failed him. The grip grew harder. Gentler then. The eyes shifted, let him go and he could blink. Duun drew his hand back and Thorn was shaking.

"You understand what I did to you, minnow? You understand how easy it was? Do you think I could do it again?"

(Duun holding him by the fire, Duun touching him, all the warmth there was. Not to be touched again. Not ever to allow that to Duun or anyone—) Tears stung Thorn's eyes. (Your eyes are running. Do that tomorrow and I'll beat you.) "Yes," Thorn said. His chest ached. "Yes, Duun-hatani. Right now you could."

Duun's eyes on his. Dark and deep and cold as the artificial night. A second time Duun's hand lifted. (I'll hurt you this time, Thorn.) Thorn lifted his hand ever so slowly and opposed it. Duun seemed satisfied. Walked around him again and the skin of Thorn's back crawled. His buttocks tensed. Once more to the side and in front of him.

Like a lizard-strike this time. Thorn flung up his hand and palm hit palm with a slap that echoed. No force then. No pushing, from either side. Duun signed with his other hand. Thorn accepted it, maintained wariness while Duun disengaged his hand and put it behind him.

Inviting a strike. (Try me, fledgling.)

"I'm not a fool, Duun-hatani."

"You're less one than you were," Meaning the matter of the farmers, Thorn thought. It was all in these days Duun had ever hinted on the matter.

"I'm not ready, Duun-hatani."

"The world doesn't always ask if you're ready, Haras. It's not likely to." Duun set his hands in his belt. "You're going to have other teachers. Oh, I'll be here. For now. But there'll be others. Other young people. They're not hatani. They know you are."

(People like me, Duun? Are any like me?) But the question hung in his throat. ("What do you *need*, Haras-hatani?") It was deadly. It opened him up in ways he knew better than to confess. "When?" he asked. (Duun, I don't *want* other teachers.)

(*Want,* minnow? Do I hear *want?*)

"Tomorrow. Mind, don't show off. You'll be better in some ways, worse in others. You're good in math; you'll learn to work new ways—not in your head, this time. On machines. They're not hatani. If you hit one of them you'd kill him. Do you understand that? Your reactions are too quick. And they don't know how to stop you. So your reactions have to be quicker. To keep from reacting at all— Do you understand that? Lay down the knife. Lay it down when you're with these people. Let yourself be open. So. Stand still." A third time Duun reached toward his face. Thorn's hand lifted—stopped in indecision. (Trick? Or what he means?) He let Duun touch his jaw, let the touch trail down and beneath it. "That's good," Duun said. And drew the hand back again. "Remember that. They're like that. None of them could stop you. None of them would have a chance. None of them know how to stand, how to move. They won't touch you. That's the one thing they'll understand. Even if they forget that—don't react. Understand, Thorn?"

VII

They were five: Elanhen, a youth whose back had black tipping on the gray, broad of shoulder, with a wary eye turned to the world and a diffident and ready grin; he was first and easiest in his manner (wisest, Thorn thought: the manner is all he gives the world, he keeps all the rest reserved.) There was Cloen, a smallish fellow whose belly-fur had dapples—("Don't remark on it," Duun warned Thorn in advance when Duun described Cloen that way. "His baby-mark's still with him.") And Cloen was least outgoing, and quickest to frown. (He has a wound, Thorn thought; it bleeds into the water. Cloen would be an easy mark. If I were after him.)

And Sphitti, lank, unkempt Sphitti. They called him that, which was a kind of weed (like Thorn). Sphitti would sit and think and think and he hardly talked.

Lastly there was Betan—who was female; who moved with a wide-hipped stride, whose grin was sudden and whose wit was quicker than the rest. Betan *smelled* different. Betan wrinkled her nose at him and grinned in a way no one had ever looked at him, which frightened him. (Confidence. She *knows* things. She knows things I don't and knows she knows and she knows she can take me.) If Duun had looked that way at him and laughed inside like that Thorn would have gone cold to the soles of his feet. He would have eaten nothing and drunk nothing Duun could have dreamed of touching and not dared sleep in his bed. That a stranger looked at him this way was devastating. He stood staring back the first time that they met and put on his most frozen, expressionless face.

(They don't have the moves, Duun had insisted. But Duun had lied before.)

They met, all five of them, in a room Duun took him to, on a floor above the floor where they lived. "Go inside," Duun said, and under the eyes of a watcher at the door, made to leave him, which prospect alone filled Thorn with panic. "Mind your manners." Duun did not say, mind what I told you. It was what Duun did not say that always weighed heaviest. Thorn was expected to remember those things without being told. "Yes, Duun," Thorn had said, and committed himself on his own, as the watcher opened the door to let him in. The touch of Duun's hand in the middle of his back was a dismissal, not a shove.

Four strangers got up off their seats when he passed the foyer, four strangers whose commingled scent was artifice and flowers, in a white-sanded room as large as the gymnasium: it had five desks; and the windows in this white sterility showed a thicket like Sheon's woods, a tangle for eye and mind. He would smell of fear to them. He stopped still. "Hello," said the one he discovered as Elanhen. "Hello," Thorn said, and put the best face on he could, a face he had seen in Duun when he met the meds. "I'm Haras." Haras he was to outsiders, his hatani-name. They told theirs. That was how it started. "We're a study-group," Elanhen said. "They say you're good."

He might have been furred as they were, four-fingered, with ears and eyes like theirs. (I'm *different*. They shot at me at Sheon. Aren't you shocked, the least bit?) But no one affected to notice.

(Duun, Thorn thought, Duun knows them. Duun set this up. Duun arranged it all.) He felt the walls of a trap about him. He let them invite him to the desk that was to be his and show him the computer. "You have to catch up with us," Elanhen said. "Sit down, Haras-hatani."

He did. He took the keyboard onto his lap and tried. He had trouble with the keys, but not with the math. He fouled the machine once and he was ashamed, looked up at Sphitti, thinking to meet scorn.

"Try again," Sphitti said. "From the beginning." Without rancor.

The others watched him. Thorn centered his mind, recalled Sphitti's instructions and got it right this time.

"That's good," Betan said, and Thorn looked guardedly her way. *Good* was not that easy a word to win. He suspected humor at his expense. (What are they up to, when will it come? What game are they playing?)

He tried not to make mistakes. He listened to things and remembered them.

Duun did not mention the matter of the school that day or the next. (When will he move?) Thorn slept lightly, feared his food and ate with attention to taste. (He won't warn me the next time. He won't. He'll move. How? And when?) A panic had settled on him, a sense of things slipping away from him, the chance that Duun himself might go, now that there were so many others to take care of him.

(What is your need, Haras-hatani?)

He might wake one morning and find Duun gone, only because Duun knew how desperately he needed him, and needing him was wrong.

Perhaps Duun was waiting for something. (For me to attack *him,* for me to start it this time. . . .) But Thorn would lose. Events had proved that. And he nursed a more dreadful suspicion: that if he did not he would lose all the same—for Duun would not abide defeat. Duun would go. He would be alone finally, utterly alone, among all the meds and the strangers they foisted off on him. So he wished only to hold his own. Forever. And not to displease Duun, which seemed mutually impossible.

He played the dkin for Duun. He sat on the riser. ("We're in the city now," Duun said, "and cityfolk don't use the floor except to walk on." It seemed unreasonable to Thorn. He liked the warmth of the sand and the ability to shape himself a place in it. But Duun said; and he did as he was told.) He played the songs he knew. Duun played him others. This had not changed, and it soothed him and made Duun smile.

> *I one day wandered down a road*
> *that I had never known;*
> *I one day came upon a path*
> *that I was never shown.*
> *It wended up and down the hills*
> *And wandered through the dell,*
> *And there I met a clever man*
> *Whose like no song can tell.*
> *I never met a man his like:*
> *I never hope to say*
> *How he was like and unlike me,*
> *This man I met that day.*
> *He had my look, he had my eyes,*
> *He had my ways, for true.*
> *Why, fool, he said, and sang the song*
> *That I've just sung to you.*

Thorn laughed when Duun had sung it. Duun smiled and adjusted a string. "Let me have it," Thorn said.

"Ah, there's no revenge. My repertoire is endless." The scarred lip twisted. It did that in such a smile. "Damn." The string had snapped. Thorn winced. "It's old," Duun said. "Quite old. I'll get another tomorrow." Duun gave the dkin to him to put away, and Thorn took the instrument and put it carefully in its case. "Get some sleep," Duun said.

"Yes," he said. And turned, again, on his knees on the riser, for Duun had gotten up and come up behind him, and Thorn was wary of that. He looked up. Duun stared at him a long moment and turned and walked away. The silence left Thorn cold. He snapped the case shut.

(He was thinking something. He was planning something. He meant me to know. Gods, what?)

Duun stopped in the doorway that led back to the other rooms. Looked back again. Walked on.

(Waiting for me to do—what?)

(Does Duun ever do anything without a reason? Does he ever make the least move without a reason?)

(I'm scared of those people. Does he know?)

A confusion of white light and white sand—the gymnasium spun and the sand met Thorn's back: he rolled and came up on his feet with lights exploding in his eyes.

"Again," Duun said.

Thorn's left knee buckled and went out from under him. He landed on his knees in shock, feeling the abrasions. The skid had cost his shoulders too. Sweat stung there. He knelt there and lifted a hand to signal a wait till the daze should pass.

Duun walked over and took his face between his hands, pulled his eyelids back to face the light, felt over his skull.

"Again," Thorn said. Duun shoved his head free with a force that rocked him, cuffed his ear and backed off.

Thorn got to his feet and stood there wide-legged and wobbling.

"So you haven't learned it all, minnow. Slow, this time. Step by step again."

Thorn came, reached out his hand in the slow dance Duun wanted, turned and turned and ended up again in the way of Duun's slow-moving arm.

"That's how. Do it, minnow."

There was a counter for it. It arrived against Thorn's ribs in slow-motion and he evaded the feigned force of it. Sweat flew from him and spattered the sand, flung from his hair as he snaked his body back. Duun faced him, hands on knees. Duun did not sweat. His tongue lolled at times, his mouth open and showing his sharp teeth. But it flicked and licked the saliva clear. Duun bent now and invited attack. "Keep it slow, Thorn. I've still got tricks."

Thorn had thought he knew them. The light that danced in Duun's eyes alarmed him. He had never seen Duun extend himself against him. Not truly. He understood that now.

Duun's hand flicked out and touched him on the cheek when he came in. "You're dead. Dead, Haras-hatani."

Thorn wiped his face. His centering was gone. He recovered it. (Don't be bluffed. Turn off the fear. Turn it *off,* minnow.)

Duun got a grip on him. Bent him back, holding him from falling. Duun let him go; but Thorn rescued himself from that shame with a tumble up again, sand coating his sweating skin.

Duun turned his back on him and walked off.

"Duun. Duun-hatani." His face burned.

Duun turned. "You don't have to say can't. You are that thing. The world doesn't wait for your moods, minnow."

"Try me!"

Duun came back and laid him straightway breathless on the sand, then stood looking at him. "Well, it wasn't *can't* that threw you that time. Did I promise you a miracle?"

Thorn rolled over and tried to cut Duun's ankles from under him.

Thorn ended on his belly this time, spitting the sand that glued itself to his face and hands and body; Duun's knee was in his back, his arm twisted painfully. Duun let him up and sat down on the sand.

(Invitation?) But Duun held up his hand. "No." Duun said, "not wise." Thorn knew where that attack would have taken him—into Duun's grip when he refused to go sailing over Duun and halfway to the wall. And Duun's teeth at his throat. Never grapple, Duun had hammered home to him. Nature shorted you, not me. And Duun had grinned at him that day to make the point.

Thorn tucked his knees up and locked his arms about them, panting. Sweat ran into his eyes and he wiped a gritty hand across his brow, flexed the fingers and held them out.

"You're pulling your claws, Duun-hatani." Pain welled up and hurt his chest and it was not all the pain of several meetings with the floor. "You'd have me in tat-

ters. You'd tear my throat out. Anybody normal—
would."

"Eyes," Duun reminded him, with a touch at his own
brow-shadowed eye. "That's worst. You let me at your
face. Never."

"I'm sorry, Duun."

"You wouldn't be sorry. You'd be blind. Damn right
I pull it. You do that again I'll scar you. Hear?"

Thorn rocked his body in something like a bow. He
hurt. His bones ached as if they had all been reseated.

"Yes, Duun."

"But as for the claws—they might take you if they
could touch you. If you were a fool. I'm very good,
Thorn. Doesn't that tell you something?"

Thorn paused a long time. The ache got into his throat
and stuck there, embarrassing him. "That I might be."

"Did you touch me?"

"No, Duun-hatani."

"Do I hear *can't* now?"

"No, Duun-hatani."

"The outsiders have gotten into your head. Their
moves have infected you. Do you let them touch you?"

"They touch each other. Not me."

"They touch you—here." Duun touched his brow.
"You lose your focus. Youth, Thorn. Give that up too."

Thorn drew another painful breath. (They're yours.
Aren't they? A hatani dictates the moves others make. . . .
Duun-hatani.) "What can they teach me you can't?"

"What is ordinary. What the world is."

(The world is wide, minnow.)

"Duun—they act like I was nothing unusual."

Duun shrugged.

"They're lying, aren't they?"

"What does your judgment tell you?"

"They're lying. They're pretending. You sent them.
You're in control of all of it."

"Tkkssss. You have a suspicious mind, Haras-hatani."

"You've always been. Is that close enough to beating
you? *No one's* like me. There aren't any. I'm different.

And they're so busy not noticing it they shout it. *Why,* Duun?"

"You build bridges in the sky."

"On *rock*. On what I see and don't see." Thorn's muscles began to shake; he clenched his arms about his knees the harder and tried not to show the shivering, but Duun would see. Duun missed nothing. "What's wrong with me? How did I turn out this way?"

"Doubtless the gods did it."

The blasphemy shocked him, from Duun. He piled one atop it. "The gods have a sense of humor?"

Duun's ears went back. "We'll talk about it later."

"You'll never give me my answer. Will you?"

A long silence. Yes and no trembled on a knife's edge. For the first time Thorn felt Duun was close to answering him and a breath might tip the balance. He held that breath till his sides ached.

"No," Duun said then. "Not yet."

"He's intelligent," Ellud admitted. Duun clasped his crossed ankles and returned a stolid stare. "Did I say not?" Duun asked. "What else do your young agents say?"

Ellud laid back his ears. "I handed them over to you."

"Come, Ellud. How many sides do you face at once?"

Ellud shifted uncomfortably on his desk. "I'm fending rocks, Duun; you know that."

"I know that. I want to know who you're talking to."

"The council. The council wants to talk to *him.*"

"No."

"You say no. They get no from you and come to my back door. I'm getting supply shortages; I'm getting delivery delays; I'm getting records lost."

"Not coincidence."

"Not at this rate," Ellud said. Duun drew a deep breath and straightened his back; Ellud held up a hand. "I'll take care of it, Duun. I'd have come to you if I couldn't."

"How does Tshon report me?"

Ellud's mouth dropped. "Duun—"

"I'm not offended. How does she report me?"

"I—told Council you're quite stable. Her report was an advantage. To both of us."

Duun smiled. With all the horror that expression had for the beholder; and he was always, with Ellud, aware of it. "I sent Council a letter. If they want a hatani sanction individually and singly—let them forget their contract. The government made it. They've got it to my dying day."

"Or his."

"Are you telling me something, Ellud?"

"I don't remember telling you anything. I'd have to swear I didn't."

Few things disturbed Duun's centering. This was one. Ellud grew very still, hands loose in his lap, for a long while staring at that stare.

"If there were to be an accident," Duun said.

"I don't know how it would come. He's hatani, you said. He wouldn't be easy. Duun—you have to understand. It's not just Council; it's public pressure: the matter at Sheon—got out."

Duun said nothing and Ellud lifted a modifying hand, sketched diffident explanation. "They called the magistrates, the magistrates called the province head—back when they thought they'd run afoul of the Guild, when they thought they'd hatani troubles up to their armpits— well, the matter got blown up larger: a few offices got onto it, and a few wealthy landholders at some dinner party— Well, a note went out to political interest here. And Rothen's successor—"

"Shbit."

"Shbit. Exactly. Wants to play politics. On the issue the whole thing's gone sour." Ellud made a helpless motion. "Duun, hard as it is to think anyone could be short-sighted enough—"

"I don't find it hard at all. "I have a very fine appreciation of venality. And stupidity. Tomorrow doesn't come and a stone cast up doesn't come down. For a renunciate, I'm a very practical man, Ellud. You should remember that."

"I remember." In a small, hoarse voice. "Duun, for the gods' own sake—they're trying to get between you and the Guilds. You know that's how they'll work. They're trying to slow my office down with their paper-delays. They want documentation of malfeasance. I'm making duplicates of everything. I've got them in a packet in hands that will get them to the Guild—if—anything should happen."

"Wise."

"People are frightened, Duun."

"Go on guarding the back door. I'll take care of the front. *I* will."

"For the gods' sakes—"

Duun gave him a cold stare. "Calling on Shbit would solve it."

"You couldn't get to him."

"Couldn't?" Duun pursed his mouth. He drew in air that stank of politics and his blood ran faster. "Watch me."

"Gods. Don't. Don't. Ammunition's all I want. Listen—Duun. Just let me take it awhile. Let me handle it. What happens to me when the pieces start hitting the ground? You've got the Guild. I've got no cover. You think I can't manage it? I managed it while you were rusting in the hills for sixteen years. For the gods' sake, leave politics to me and get me what I need. You've got enough in your lap. Trust me for this."

Duun scowled. "Meaning?"

"Just—let me pile up data. Awhile."

"The Guild's another answer. He might make it."

"Gods. You don't mean that."

"We're very catholic."

Ellud's ears sank in dismay.

"I'm working on it," Duun said. "I tell you that. But he's not ready yet."

"You know what that would cause?"

"And prevent."

There was a long silence. Then: "The tapes, Duun. For the gods' sakes, *start* them. Can you do that?"

Duun stared and thought about it. "Yes."

* * *

They sat together, Elanhen and Betan and Sphitti and Cloen: "This is the way it is," Elanhen said. "We get scored together. All of us. You're the one they threw into the group. If you don't learn, we fail together."

"We get thrown out of our jobs," Betan said.

"What's your *job?*" Thorn asked, because everything they said puzzled him.

Their faces went closed to him then, on secrets they would not share.

"You've got a problem," Betan said, leaning over his shoulder while he plied the keyboard in his lap and watched the window across the room become a glowing display. Lines blinked and intersected. "That's the trajectory. With that acceleration where will you intercept?"

Sometimes the problems made vague sense. And sometimes they did not.

(What in the world comes in two hundred twenty-fours?)

(Stars. Trees. Kinds of grass. The ways of a river. The stubbornness of a child.)

(I can reckon the speed of the wind, name the stars, the cities of the world—)

". . . in order, the particles—"

Betan brushed his arm as she bent above him. She smelled of something different. She had no reticence with him. She took no care how she leaned past him. The column of her throat was undefended, her body sleek coated and ripe with musk—

"You got it right," Sphitti said as they clustered about his desk sitting on its edges. "Here's an application now. If you were drifting in midair—no friction and no gravity—"

(They're trying to trip me.) "You can't."

"Say that you could."

Betan flicked an ear at him. Perhaps it was a joke at his expense.

"Write it down," said Cloen.

"I don't have to."

"Let him do it his way," Sphitti said. Then he had to get it right.

"That's right," Elanhen said then, checking what he said.

"Damn hatani arrogance," Cloen said when he was not quite out of earshot, when he and Elanhen were off together at Cloen's desk.

It hurt. Thorn was not immune to that.

(Duun, what do I do when people insult me? When they hate me? How do I answer, Duun?)

But he never asked it aloud. The shame of it distressed him. And he thought that he should come up with that answer on his own.

"Just the sounds," Betan said. "It doesn't matter what it means. It's a test of your recall. Listen to the tape and memorize the sound."

"It's not words at all!"

"Pretend it is. Just try. Record it. Play it back till there's no difference."

Thorn looked at Betan, at Sphitti. At two gray pairs of eyes. He felt indignation at this, as if they had made this one up. But they had never joked with him, not on lessons.

He put the plug into his ear and listened. Tried to pronounce the babble. (They'll be laughing. It sounds like water running.) He looked around at them, but they found other things to do, with the computer and with their own studies. He turned back to his work, put his hands over his eyes to shut out the world.

(Remembering days on Sheon's porch, the hiyi blooms—)

He mouthed the noises. He slowed down the machine and ran it fast and memorized the sequences. It was harder than Sphitti's physics. The plug gave him an earache.

"I've had enough of that," he said after he had gotten the start of it down and they gathered about to hear it. He would never have said that to Duun, but they accepted such things.

"That's all you're supposed to do in the mornings," Elanhen said. "You keep at that."

Thorn sat there amid his desk. He thought that he could beat any of them (even Betan, because Duun had made him believe that he was good).

"Get to work," Cloen said.

"I'm going home," Thorn said.

"You can't. The door's locked. The guard won't let you."

"Shut up, Cloen," Betan said. "Thorn, *do* the work. Please. I'm asking."

Thorn glared at Cloen. At Betan too. (But it was pleasant that they said please to him. No one did. It occurred to him that they had to worry what they would do if he grew recalcitrant; and that they had to fear him (even Betan) the way he had to fear Duun. And that was a pleasant thought.)

He cut off the tape, found his place in it again as the others drifted back to their places; and he did what Betan had asked until his ear hurt and his head ached.

But when they were leaving he contrived that Cloen should brush against him.

He sent Cloen against the foyer wall with a move of his arm. And stood there, in a shocked tableau of fellow-students and the guard outside the open door.

"I'm hatani. Lay a hand on me again and I'll break it."

Cloen's ears were back. His jaw had dropped. He stood away from the wall and looked at Elanhen. "I never touched him!"

Thorn walked out. An escort always came to bring him home. Duun's idea, Duun's direction. Thorn swept a gesture at the man waiting for him outside and never looked back.

"Go to the gym," Duun said when he came out of his office; and this was not habit, but Thorn went, and stopped and turned. Duun shoved at him.

"I think you hit me," Duun said, with a darkness in his eyes; and sudden fear washed over Thorn like ice-water. Thorn backed up. He had not hit Duun; and one thing came to him at once: that someone had been on the phone when he came in. "What should I do about it?" Duun asked. "Well, Haras-hatani?"

"I'm sorry, Duun." Thorn sweated. (Gods, *move* on me! Come *on!*) His concentration shredded. He dared not back out now. And he had never faced Duun in temper; he had never looked to. (O gods, Duun, don't kill me!)

"The knife, minnow. Lay it down. Do you hear me? I'm telling you—lay it down."

Thorn went off-center, shifted his balance back with a lifting of his head. Stood there with his arms loose and a quaking in his knees.

"That's good." Duun patted his cheek. "That's very good."

(O gods, Duun, *don't!*)

The clawtip traced a gentle path down to his jaw. "I want to talk to you." The hand dropped to his arm and took it, hurling him staggering to the center of the floor.

"Duun-hatani, I'm sorry!"

"Sit down."

He sat down on the fresh-raked sand. Duun came and hunkered down in front of him.

"Why are you sorry?" Duun asked. "Because of Cloen or for me?"

"You, Duun-hatani. I shouldn't have done it. I'm sorry. He—"

"What did he do?"

"He hates me. He hates me, that's all, and he's subtle about it."

"More subtle than *you?* Haras-hatani, I am confounded by his capacity."

Heat rushed to Thorn's face. He looked at the sand. "He tries to be subtle. Anything I do is wasted on him."

"You're different; just like Cloen with his baby-spots. And you suspect everyone's noticing. And you want to make sure they respect you. Am I halfway right?"

"Yes, Duun-hatani."

"You have a need, Haras. Do you know it? Can you say it to me?"

"Not to be different."

"Louder."

"Not to be different, Duun-hatani."

"Was it reasonable, what you did?"

"He won't despise me!"

"Is that so important? What do you own? What does a hatani own?"

"Nothing. Nothing, Duun."

"Yet here we live in a fine place. We have enough to eat. We don't have to hunt—"

"I'd rather hunt."

"So would I. But why are we here? We're here because of what we are. You own nothing. You have no self-interest. If this Cloen should ask you to remove him from a difficulty you would do it. He would have no right to dictate how you did it; or when or where—but Cloen is your charge. The *world* is your charge, Haras-hatani. Do you know—you can walk the roads and go from house to house and no one will refuse you food or drink or a place to sleep. And when someone comes to you with a thing and says: help me—do you know what to warn him: Do you know, Haras-hatani? Do you know what a hatani will tell him?

"No, Duun-hatani."

"You will say: 'I am hatani; what you loose you cannot recall; what you ask you cannot unask; what I do is my solution.' There was a wicked man once who called a hatani. 'Kill my neighbor,' he said. 'That's not hatani business,' the hatani said and went away. The wicked man found another hatani. 'My life is wretched,' the wicked man said. 'I hate my neighbor. I want to see him die.' 'That *is* a hatani matter,' the hatani said. 'Do you give it into my hands?' 'Yes,' the wicked man said. And the hatani struck him dead. Do you understand the solution?"

Thorn looked up in horror.

"Do you understand?" Duun asked. "His problem was removed. And the world was eased. That's what you are. A solution. The helper of the world. Do you want *my* solution for your problem?"

Thorn's heart beat very fast. "What should I do, Duun-hatani?"

"Tell Cloen to hit you once. Tell him to use his judgment in the matter."

He looked at Duun a very long time. His gut ached. "Yes," he said.

"Remember the lesson. Do as you're told. Someday you'll be wise enough to solve problems. Until then, don't create them. Do you hear?" Duun reached out and closed his hand on Thorn's shoulder. "Do you hear?"

"I hear."

Duun let him go.

VIII

"It certainly didn't help matters," Ellud said, with the report aglow in his lap. He flung it aside and the optic draped itself over the stack of real paper and went on glowing with ghostly, damning letters. "I chastised my staffer. I don't know why I picked him. But, dammit, Duun—*you* passed him."

"For his faults," Duun said. "As well as his virtues. I never expected perfection. I didn't want it. That's why I stayed by your choices."

"Damn hatani tricks," Ellud said after a moment. "I understand what you're doing. But I don't like it with my staff. Cloen could have been killed."

"I didn't judge so. In that, I was right."

"It's in the record what happened. It was too well witnessed. I can't get rid of it. And with all the sniffing about the Council's doing, I wish to the gods I could."

"What did happen was my fault. Power without restraint. I counted on two more years at Sheon. Haras *was* restrained. I'll tell you something which should be evident. Hatani solutions are too wide for young minds. His morality is adequate to hold his power back. It isn't adequate to use it."

"To make him hatani—Duun, *that's* what's sent the wind up the Council's—"

"I know."

"I took it for a figure of speech. That it was all you could teach. It was what you knew how to teach."

"Come now."

"Well, that it was easier. But you mean to go all the way with this. When they get that rumor—"

"Try to be discreet."

"If the Guild could just devise something—clever, if they could find a halfway status—"

"There's no halfway. To give him what I've given him—with nothing but restraint to manage it? No."

Ellud reached and turned off the recorder. There was dismay on his face. Terror. "For the gods' sake, Duun. Have you lost your senses? What are you after? *What are you after, Duun?*"

"Shbit will have gotten my letter by now. Things should be quieter, from council quarter."

A brief silence, no more comfortable. "What did you tell him?"

"I offered him salutation. I felicitated him on his council appointment. I wished him health. I signed it. It was a simple letter. He hasn't answered. I expect your supply difficulties to clear up slowly, but I do expect them to clear up."

"You're not the man I knew." Ellud fidgeted with the hem of his kilt. "I don't know how to understand you."

"Old friend. You had courage enough to stay in office this long. I trust you'll keep on with it."

"I have to. Without this office I'm a naked target. They'd go for me. Shbit and his crew. Dammit, I've got no choice. They'd eat me alive."

"I'm here. Trust me."

Ellud stared at him.

"Did Cloen hit you?" Duun asked when Thorn got home. Duun leaned easily in the doorway of his office, ears pricked.

"No," Thorn said. There was no satisfaction in that tone. (How much do you control, Duun? Do you know already? Do you always know?) Duun gave him no clues. " 'Cloen,' I said. 'I was wrong in what I did. I'll let you hit me once.' Cloen stood there with his ears back and he raised his hand *no* then. And walked off across the room and got busy."

Duun turned and went back into his office.

"Duun?" Thorn pursued him as far as the doorway.

Duun sat down and turned on the computer. "Duun, did I do what you wanted?"

"*Did* you do what I wanted?"

Thorn was silent a moment. "I tried, Duun."

"Do I hear can't?"

"No, Duun."

The sounds grew less hard. Thorn worked, his eyes shut, his lips moving in repetition of the tape. When it played back it was the same.

"It sounds identical," Cloen said. "I can't tell a difference."

Cloen was careful, since that day. Cloen's face never betrayed anything but respect. And fear. There was that too.

"I've finished it then."

"That one." Cloen licked his lips and looked diffident. "They sent another one. It's not my doing," Cloen said quickly.

It had to be believed. Cloen did not have the look of lying. Cloen drew the cassette from his pouch and offered it.

"I like chemistry better," Thorn muttered. He felt easier with them since the day Cloen had not hit him. He could say such things and hint at everyday needs, the way they did. He put that manner on and off at the door. It occurred to him that it made them easier with him. He could laugh with them, sometimes, because he had convinced himself he was not the object of laughter. Or if he had been, it was of little consequence.

(But I hate these sound-lessons. I hate this nonsense. I think they like giving them to me. Like a joke on the hatani they can't beat any other way. I play jokes too. I can make the computer give Sphitti a readout he never expected. He'd think it funny. I wish I *could* do more physics and less of this.)

(I wish Betan would sit here with me instead of Cloen.)

(I daren't think that. Duun would break my arm.)

"Thanks," he said dryly and pushed the new cassette into the machine.

Cloen let him alone. They were growing apart. Thorn's shoulders widened. Poor Cloen's baby-spots persisted.

Betan was absent a time. ("It's spring," Elanhen said, and sent heat to Thorn's face. "She's been taking a suppressant but she wants to take a holiday. She'll be back.")

"It's spring," Duun said that evening. "I understand Betan's gone on holiday."

"Yes," Thorn said. He had the dkin on his knee, tuning it. He went all cold inside, for reasons he could not plainly define, except the matter of Betan was a place he protected from the others like some galled spot. And Duun knew unerringly how to find these things. "They said she was on suppressants but she wanted to go on holiday. I think she has some friend."

"Probably," Duun said matter-of-factly. "I'll warn you to be polite at school. Men don't have seasons. But their sisters and their mothers and half their friends do. And Elanhen and Cloen and Sphitti do have lives outside of the school, you know. Don't put any pressure on them."

(What about on *me?*)—You're hatani, Duun would say. If Thorn were fool enough to ask. Hatani don't have needs.

(Gods, I don't want to get into *that* with him, not today.)

Betan did come back. She came sailing in one day all smiles and what had been an all-male society of careful courtesies and few pranks became lively again.

(As if the heart came back into the place.) Thorn felt something expand in his chest, as if some anxiety had let go. Spring was over.

"Have you missed me?" Betan asked.

The others flicked ears and rolled their eyes in a way that they would do when they talked about forbidden things. So it had a ribald flavor.

"Yes," Thorn said simply. Dignity seemed best. (They're

joking about her being in season. I'll bet none of them got close to a woman this spring.)

(Neither did I. Neither *will* I. A hatani has nothing. Owns nothing. Betan has property in the city. She doesn't have to marry. She could have all her children to herself.) Between Duun and the ribald jokes Thorn had learned some few things. (But I'll bet someone will make her the best offer he can.)

"When Ghosan-hatani came to Elanten there were two sisters who asked her to judge between them and their husband. They had married the same man for a five-year, each in succession. They all three were potters and he was promised a potter's shop from his mother's heritage, so a marriage seemed profitable. But during the fourth year of the first sister the second sister bore a child which was only hers. The husband refused to consummate the second marriage if the woman did not disinherit this child. And both women would lose all they had invested in this shop. 'This is a small matter,' Ghosan-hatani said when the sisters came to her. 'Judge it yourselves.' Of course the husband was not there. He had no desire to have it judged. And the second sister looked at Ghosan and lost her courage. 'Come away,' she asked her sister. 'We were mad to ask this hatani.' And that sister ran away. But the first sister stayed. 'I want a judgment,' that sister said. So Ghosan-hatani went door-to-door in Elanten and asked everyone in the village what they knew. And she asked the magistrate. And everything confirmed what the sisters had said. 'Give me a pen,' Ghosan said. The magistrate gave the hatani a pen. And Ghosan wrote in the village records that the shop belonged to the child and to his descendants; and if not to them it belonged to the village of Elanten."

"They would hate the child," Thorn objected.

"Perhaps they would," Duun said. "But when the child was grown and the husband was beyond his prime, what would keep him from turning the husband out? The husband not only consummated the marriage, he wanted to marry the women for good, but they only married him one year at a time for the rest of his life, even through he was very kind to them and to the child. The industry still exists in Elanten, and exports all over the world."

"Do hatani marry?" Thorn asked. He was thinking about Betan. His heart beat fast. (Ought I to have asked that? It wasn't the point of the story.) But there was a feeling in him that came in the night, when he had a vague and disturbing dreams, when he waked ashamed of himself. But Duun said nothing about these times, Duun only looked at him with that guardedness that did nothing to reassure him. (Does Duun do these things in the night? Something is wrong with me. Why shouldn't it be? Who were my mother and father? Was I like that child?)

(Did some hatani judgment take me away from my mother? Was it Duun's?)

"There are instances," Duun said.

"Were *you* ever married?"

"Several times."

It shocked Thorn. (He's done—that—with a woman.) Thorn's face went hot. (I might.) He thought of the foenin in the woods. And shifted restlessly, and hugged his knees. (Think of something else. What else has Duun done? What made his scars? Is it all one story?)

"There was a hatani named Ehonin," Duun said. "He had a daughter with a woman not his wife. This daughter when she was grown trekked to another province where Ehonin was by then. She asked him to judge between him and her since her mother had married and disowned her. Ehonin made her hatani. She died in her schooling. This was her patrimony. Ehonin knew she was not able. She was weak. But he gave her what he had. To kill the wife wouldn't have helped."

"He could have made the daughter marry."

"That would have been another solution, but there was no other participant. He could hardly drag someone into the situation who wasn't involved. That's never right. When the hatani himself is involved in the case, the judgments are never what they ought to be: the fewer people the hatani has in the case to judge, the fewer solutions are available."

"He could have made the woman's husband adopt the girl!"

"Indeed he could, and there was a husband. If the girl had asked him to judge between herself and her mother's husband he might have done that. That was also how Ehonin suspected she would not be hatani. She asked in haste even when she'd had ample time to think. Or she didn't want anything to do with the husband. That's also possible. In any case he had nothing to work with: to have gone to the mother and asked her truth would have been pointless. There was no recourse in her. And the daughter had asked none. That left himself and the daughter for principals. He had no other answer."

"If she hadn't asked him a hatani solution he might have helped her."

"Indeed he might."

"She was a fool, Duun-hatani."

"She was also very young and angry. And she hated her father. None of those things helped her."

"Couldn't he warn her?"

"She was old enough to have walked across a province. What point to warn her? But perhaps he did. Anger makes great fools."

"This is the velocity of the system through the galactic arm."

"Is it absolute?" Thorn asked. He had learned to ask; and Elanhen looked pleased. "No," Elanhen said. "But consider it so for this problem. . . ."

They were back to physics. At least two of every five-day set.

There was history. ". . . In 645 Elhoen calculated the world was round. This was his proof. . . ."

". . . in 1439 the hatani took down the shothoen guild and set up the merchant league in its place—"

". . . in 1492 the Mathog railway joined the Bigon line and cities grew along the route—"

". . . in 1503 Aghoit made the first powered flight. By 1530 Tabisit-tanun flew across the Mathog. . . . He crashed in the attempt at a polar crossing. His son and his daughter inherited his interest in the guild and the daughter was lost in a second attempt when ice on the wings forced her landing in Gltonig Bay. That was the last radio message. The plane was found abandoned and no one knew what became of her. The son made the flight successfully in 1541."

". . . Dsonan became capital . . ."

". . . The Dsonan League took the Mathog. Bigon resisted. The hatani refused to involve themselves without an appeal from Bigon and there was bloodshed until both sides appealed for settlement. It was the first use of aircraft—"

". . . Rocket-bombs were first developed—"

A great unease stirred in him. He turned and looked for help . . . not Cloen's. About the room the others were at their desks. He held the keyboard on his lap and put in Betan's name.

"W-h-a-t?" the reply appeared white-lettered at the bottom of the screen.

Thorn hesitated. Typed. *"W-h-a-t y-e-a-r a-r-e w-e i-n?"* His face burned. He waited for an answer with his heart pounding. Nothing touched the screen. He looked up and saw Betan leave her desk and walk across the sand to him with a puzzled look on her face.

"I don't need your help," Thorn said. "It's just a question."

Betan looked at the screen and looked at him. Her ears flicked down and up and her fine mouth pursed. Standing this close, she smelled of warmth, of flowers, and he wanted Sheon back, he wanted the world as simple as it had been, and the smells of earth and dust and the answers he used to know. "It's 1759," she said. And gulfs opened up about him. Doubtless Betan thought him a fool. Of course they had all grown up in the world and he had had only Sheon. She laughed at him. "Why?"

"It never came up, that's all." He sent the screen on another scroll. It stopped at 1600. Ended. "I need a new cassette."

Betan sat down on the edge of his desk, rested her hand above his knee. The touch burned him. He looked desperately elsewhere, searching with the tail of his vison for where the others were, but they were all on their desks.

"I'm sorry," Betan said. "I shouldn't have laughed." And she smelled of difference and warmth and his heart pounded against his ribs. She pressed against his ribs. She pressed on his knee and strained his leg and he wished he could get her hand off before something else happened. "Sheon's not quite the world capital, is it? Look, if you need help with that I'd be happy to stay."

"Duun wants me to be in the gym by noon."

"Ah." She gave his leg a pat and got up. "But it's 1759. The 19th of Ptosin. It's summer out."

He was suddenly, overwhelmingly conscious of the blankness of the school's white walls. The falsity of the windows behind which (sometimes) was the noise of machinery. The world closed in on him like the clenching of a fist about his heart.

In Sheon the leaves would be green and the hiyi pods opening; the foen-cubs would come tottering out and hiss at the—

—curious countryfolk children. Mon was the name of one. They owned his house now. They lived in its rooms. Sat by the fireplace on the warm sand, all together.

Mon. Mon. Mon. He hated that person.

The city closed about him. Imprisoned him. But it was his fault. All his fault. His difference caused it.

"Haras?"

"I can't."

Betan gave up and wandered off, went back to her desk and sat down cross-legged with her back to him. Thorn picked up the keyboard again and looked at the screen.

A message came to him. *"BETAN: Well, tomorrow, then. I could answer questions, things that bother you."*

He watched it scroll by three times. His heart beat faster and faster. *"B-e-t-a-n,"* he typed, addressing the response. *"Y-e-s."*

*　　*　　*

Thorn picked himself up and dusted the sand off. He bowed. "Yes. I see."

"Again," Duun said. It was not always that Duun stripped down to the small-kilt for practice. Duun did that today, so that his scars were evident, like lightnings through the gray and black hair of his body and his maimed arm, of one fabric with the scars on his face, so that they acquired a fearsome symmetry which Thorn had sensed in those years before he knew that they were scars, or knew that every man in all the world was not marked as Duun was marked, or had not but half a right hand, or did not smile after that permanent fashion, which Thorn knew now was enough to daunt any opponent Duun ever faced. It daunted him now. (He means to put me to it today. He has something in mind.) And it came leaping into his mind in one fatal rush that it had been a very long time that Duun had left him in peace. (Not to interrupt my studies—surely that was why. Or I've gotten better and he won't try—)

That thought vanished in one missed attempt, in the far too lengthy offbalance moment he had to fall as Duun took his feet from under him.

Duun often grinned at such moments. This time he stood there with a dour face, signed no attack and watched with hands on hips as Thorn recovered himself from his drop-and-rise.

"Again."

"Duun-hatani, show me that move to the side again."

Patiently Duun showed him. Thorn bent himself to it and tried a trick in the midst of it, a joke.

Duun's hands closed on him and dumped him to the ground. (He saw it.) Duun might have laughed, but Duun's face never changed. Thorn hesitated on the safety of the floor a moment, looking up at him. (Gods. He's got something in mind. Something's wrong.) Thorn shook the dazzle and the thoughts and the day from his head and brought himself to his feet again, centered in the tightest possible focus, no thought to anything, no thought, no heartbeat but the beat of the dance, the light and the dust. It was not the city, it was Sheon's noon, and the yard about them, and Duun faced him in purest simplicity.

Pass and evade, strike and recover and pass and turn.

"Better," Duun said, and that one word ran down his nerves like fingers on the dkin. "Better. Take the offensive."

No hesitation. Thorn struck and caught and Duun spun off across the sand, up again in a move that never stopped.

Counter again and attack.

Again.

Again. Thorn floated out of a kick aimed at his hip and struck.

His hands met flesh and he spun again in distress, in time to find Duun coming up again from the sand and a kick coming at him he only scantly evaded.

Time, Thorn called, lifting his hand. Thorn's breath came in great gasps. Duun straightened not quite entirely, breathing no easier, and put his hand to his left side. (Gods, I *hit* him, I hurt him, O gods, his ribs—)

"That was good," Duun said. "You got through my guard."

(He wasn't going to stop. If I hadn't called halt—)

(—he'd have kept coming. He'd have taken me.) Thorn found himself trembling in the knees when he understood that.

(Not another pass, please, Duun, not another—)

The darkness ebbed from Duun's eyes. Reason came back. Duun straightened, pricked his ears up and gave a left-sided smile that with the permanent quirk of the right side, held a deceptive innocence. "Hot bath," Duun said. "Both of us. You're shaking, minnow."

"I didn't pull that. I thought—"

"We'll do simple figures tomorrow. I thought you were getting to that stage. We can hurt each other. No more ungoverned practice. It's gotten too dangerous."

(I didn't win, I didn't beat him, there's no beating him without killing him—)

Duun walked away from him. Duun was limping, but

not much. Thorn wiped sweat from his face and found his hand shaking.

(In everything he ever promised me—he always knew that.)

He was abysmal in his lessons. The figures floated past without meaning. He studied his history and the dates settled into his mind but the names eluded him.

"Something's bothering you," Sphitti said. "Do the sound-routines. You can do that."

It insulted him. (I'm hatani, he wished to shout at Sphitti; things don't bother me.) It was the worse because it was patently true. Cloen walked warily around him. Elanhen worked silently at his own console on something abstruse and statistical, while Betan gave Thorn looks over her shoulder and said nothing.

Can I help? the message said in the bottom of his screen.

After, he sent back, and nothing else.

(Duun had cheated him. Duun had maneuvered him all his life. But why did Duun spend his life on one student? Why did Duun have so much wealth and the countryfolk live in a tin-roofed house—but now they had Sheon; and Duun had this place, which was at the top of one of the tallest buildings in Dsonan, in the capital of the world, where power was. Why me? Why Duun? Why all this effort?)

(Why do I know so little about the things I want and so much I never wanted to know, and why do they lock the doors and guards take us where we go in this building? Guards for what? What do they guard? Us? Someone else?)

(I used to live here, Duun had said.)

(Ellud's an old friend.)

(I grew up at Sheon. So did Duun. Where did he know Ellud from?)

The numbers blurred. Thorn keyed in letter function.

Betan Betan Betan, he wrote, and again, *Betan,* and filled the screen with the repeat key.

The hours dragged. The clock came up noon and in

silence they shut down terminals and got up off their
desks. But Thorn kept his terminal alive. He had told
the guard who walked with him that he would have extra
work to do. "I have to catch up in my history," he said
when Sphitti asked. The others passed him without a
word to him, talking to each other—perhaps Betan had
changed her mind, perhaps Betan would forget, it had
only been a casual thing to her. He heard the door snick
shut and turned about on his desk and saw Betan come
back in.

Thorn stood up. Betan walked to his desk and they
both sat down knee-to-knee on the side of it. She was
grave and looked at him in a quiet way no one but Betan
used, not even Duun. She sensed something amiss. He
knew. His heart sped and his breath grew tight; but she
smelled of flowers and herself, she always did, like sun
and warmth. "Something's wrong," she said, but it was
different the way she said it. Her face was vastly concerned, open in a way no one else was with him. "What
is it?"

"I almost beat Duun yesterday." Thorn was dismayed
by the way the exaggeration leapt out so easily and then
he could not take it back.

"Was he angry?"

"I don't think so." His breath grew tighter. "Betan, I
lived at Sheon—" (but she knows that, this is a stupid
way to start) "—I don't know the city, I've never been
outside, except once, when I flew in— You do, a lot,
don't you?"

"Oh, yes. I go to the coast every spring."

(Conjuring ribald jokes and student humor and mystic
somethings every male in the world knew but him, more
marked than Duun, scent-blind and naked as something
newborn.) Betan sat close, knee touching his knee. Her
eyes were wide and dark. "I never learned," he said, and
lost track of what he was saying, (not hatani, no: she was
not; he did not need to be, for once he did not have to
be complex, only simple, with Betan, who used to frighten
him and now set her hand on his knee and slid it up.)
He put his on hers, and felt the silkenness of her fur and

felt the muscles slide, alive and taut as she leaned and stretched and came up against him with her hand on his body. "I never learned—"

He felt things happening to him all at once, felt things vastly out of his control and brought it back again. It was all very clear suddenly what he wanted and what his body was doing on its own, and he held her against him and maintained that good feeling as long as he dared, until he felt everything slipping again, and he took her belt and unfastened it quickly. She unfastened his. Her head burrowed underneath his chin and she leaned on him, all warm, and her smell had changed.

It was fear. He flinched, jerked her back by both arms and she twisted in his grip—*"Betan!"*

The door opened beyond her. A man walked out into the foyer. Betan jerked out of Thorn's hands and scrambled off the riser.

Duun.

Betan stopped, of a sudden crouched and backing away. Thorn got to his feet. "Dammit—*Duun!*"

Duun stepped marginally out of the doorway and waved Betan to it. She hesitated.

"Get out!" Thorn cried. (Gods, he'll kill her—) *"Betan! Get out!"*

She skittered out the foyer doorway and through the outer door like escaping prey. Duun glanced after her and looked back at Thorn.

Thorn shook. He stood with one foot on the sand and one knee on the desk and shook with reaction as he put his clothes together. Duun stood there as if he would wait forever.

"Leave me alone," Thorn said. "Duun, for the gods' sake leave me alone!"

"We'll talk later. Let's go home, Haras."

"I haven't got a home! A hatani doesn't have anywhere! He hasn't got anything—"

"We'll talk later, Thorn."

Thorn shivered convulsively. There was no choice. (There's never been a choice. Come home, Haras. Give up, minnow. Pretend nothing's wrong.)

(But she was scared. She panicked. Scared of *me*—)

"Come on," Duun said.

"I wish you'd been a little later!"

Duun said nothing. Held out his hand toward the door. Thorn left the desk and the room blurred. (Your eyes are running, Thorn.) He walked out and in a vast blurred haze Duun walked beside him down the hall to the elevator. The silence lasted all the way to their door and past the guard there. That watcher was noncommittal, as if he read them both.

Duun closed the door behind them. Thorn headed for his room.

"There was no choice," Duun said. "You know what you'd have *done* to her?"

"I wouldn't have hurt her!" He spun about and faced Duun squarely, at the distance of the hall. "Dammit, I wouldn't have—"

"I have to be more plain to you about anatomy."

"*I wouldn't have hurt her!* I'd have—I'd—" (I can't; couldn't; but touching her, but her touching me—)

"I can imagine you'd have tried." Coldly, cooly, from age and superiority. "Common sense was nowhere in it, Thorn. You know it."

"Tell me. Lecture me. Gods, I don't mind what you do to me, but you came in like that on her—What do you think you did to her, Duun-hatani? Is *that* your subtlety?"

"I promised you an answer. Years ago you asked a question and I promised you an answer when you could beat me. Well, you came close yesterday. Perhaps that's good enough."

Shock poured over Thorn. Then reason did. He flung up a hand. "Dammit, *dammit,* you're maneuvering me! I know your tricks, you taught them to me, *I know what you're doing, Duun!*"

"I'm offering you your answer. That's all. What you are, where you came from—"

"*O gods, I don't want to hear it!*" Thorn turned. He ran. He shut the door to his room and leaned against it shaking.

The intercom came alive. "When you want, you can

come out, Thorn. I don't think badly of you. Not in this. Even a hatani can take wounds. This is a great one. Come out when you can face me. I'll wait for you. I'll be waiting, Thorn."

He was dry-eyed when he came out. He unlocked the door and walked out into the hall, and down the hall into the main room. Duun was there, sitting on the riser that touched the wall. The windows were all stars and dark. Nightview. Perhaps it was. Duun did not look at him at once, not until he had crossed the sand and sat down on the riser in the tail of Duun's view.

Then Duun turned his face to him; and there was no sound except something mechanical behind one window and a whisper of air from the ducts.

"Have you come for your answer?" Duun asked.

"Yes," Thorn said. He sat upright, hands on his thighs, ankles crossed. He looked unflinchingly at Duun.

"You've studied genetics," Duun said. "You know what governs heredity."

(Be quick. Drive the knife in quickly, Duun. O gods, I don't want to sit through this.) "Yes I understand."

"You understand that genes make you what you are; that every trait you manifest is no matter of chance. A harmonious whole, Haras."

"Are you my father?"

"No. You had none. Nor mother. You're an experiment. A trial, if you will—"

Thorn was strangely numb. Duun's voice drifted somewhere in the half-dark, in the timelessness of the view. The night went on forever and he went on hearing it.

"I don't believe this," Thorn said finally. Not because he did not believe it was something equally terrible. But that he saw no way to accomplish it. "Duun. The truth. I'm something that went wrong—"

"Not wrong. No one said wrong. There are things right about you. But you're different. An experiment. You know how conception takes place. You know genetic manipulation's done—"

"I don't know how it's done." (Clinically. Precisely,

like a lesson. It could not be him they discussed, a thing
in a dish, a mote floating in a glass.) "I know that it is
done. I know they can put things together and come up
with something that didn't exist before."

"You know when someone wants a child and there's
a—physical impediment—there's the means to bring the
embryo to term. A host. Sometimes a volunteer. In other
cases a mechanical support system. An artificial womb.
That was so in your case."

(A machine. O gods, a machine.)

"There's nothing remarkable in that," Duun said.
"You have that in common with a thousand, two thousand ordinary people who couldn't be born any other
way. Medicine's a marvel."

"They made me up."

"Something like that."

He had struggled not to cry. The tears welled up out
of nowhere and ran down his face, endless. "When they
were putting me together in this lab—" He could not
talk for a long time and Duun waited for him. He began
it again. "When they made me did they bother to do it
twice? Is there anyone else like me?"

"Not in all the world," Duun said. "No."

"*Why?* For the gods' sake *why?*"

"Call it curiosity. There are undoubtedly reasons adequate for the meds."

"The meds—"

"They're your fathers if you like. After a manner of
speaking Ellud is. Or others in the program."

"What are you?"

"A hatani solution."

Small warnings went off. A prickle of alarm. (Self-
preservation. Why should I bother? Why should I care?)
But there was fear. "Whose?"

"I might have done many things. I chose to give you
the best chance I could give. The only chance I'm
equipped to give. Like Ehonin and his daughter."

"Who asked for it?"

Duun was silent for a long time. "The government."

"Asked a hatani solution?" The enormity of it washed over Thorn like a flood. Duun's stare never gave him up.

"You are one of my principals. I gave you all I could give. I'll go on giving that. It's all that I can do."

The stars glittered on, awash. "I wanted to love her, Duun."

"I know."

"I want to die."

"I taught you to fight. Not to die. I'm teaching you to find solutions."

"Find this one."

"I've already been asked."

Thorn shuddered. All his limbs shook.

"Come here," Duun said. Held out his hands. "Come here, minnow."

Thorn went. It was a pathetic thing Duun offered, shameful for them both. Duun took him in his arms and held tight till the shuddering stopped. After that he lay still against Duun's shoulder for a very long time, and Duun's arms cradled him as they had done before the fire, in Sheon, when he was small.

He slept. When he woke Dimn had fallen asleep over him, and his back ached, and it was all still true.

IX

"Well," Ellud said, "we're still tracing the files as far as we can. When official channels decide to fake a record they can do it with remarkably few tracks."

"No matter." Duun kept his back straight. The cracked rib and a twisted night put slowness in his movements; and he sat cross-legged on the other riser in Ellud's office with a cup of herbal tea in his hands. He savored the warmth and the quiet. "I congratulate the Council. The security service background—true or false—accounted for the way she held herself."

"Young and bright and probably indebted as hell to someone."

"Try Dallen Company. Trace it and make as much noise as you like. It ought to keep Shbit prudent awhile."

"I'm embarrassed about this."

"She cost them. A lot of years forging that identity. What worries me is how she got out of the building untracked. Dammit, how did they foul that up?"

"We're trying to find that out too."

Duun stared at Ellud a moment and poured himself another cup of tea from the vessel which sat at his left knee. He lifted the cup and looked at Ellud again, making his face expressionless, his eyes uninformative as glass. "He's growing to be a man, all fine points aside; the matter was bound to come up. Betan was a solution when I picked her. I sensed she had the nerve to deal with him. That was understatement, at least. Thorn, gods know, could take care of himself—up to a point. But at least she was bent on creating an incident. That's likeliest. And at worst case, she would do that and kill him in the process. If she could. She had nerve for it. Pity the Guild didn't get her."

"Free-hatani?"

"I've thought of that. I don't think so. Free-ghota, maybe."

"Good gods, if you thought that—"

"Hindsight. She might be the same vukun as Shbit's own bodyguards. They're capable. Maybe even one of Dallen Company's guilded hire-ons. She botched it up if killing was what she intended, but she wasn't bad. And I doubt it was all that simple." Another sip of the tea. "You won't find her, not now, I think. She likely did clear the building. Look for old friends in Security."

"I'm doing that."

"She'll probably suicide after she reports. I embarrassed her, and not in her youthful modesty. Shbit will see the body disappears. I'll be glad to see her go to him, frankly. It'll make solutions a lot neater."

"I don't *like* this kind of thing."

"I don't like it either. I may yet visit Shbit. But this discomfiture ought to slow him down a while. He can't bring his witness to light now. That's all spoiled—the charges of assault and ravishment—" Duun drew a deep breath. Ellud's distress was evident. "Well, it's over. For a while. I put him to work in the gym this morning, refused all further questions, and poured a sedative down him afterward. Right now he's sleeping and Hosi's standing over him. Tomorrow, well, we'll change that school situation. I think it's best. With thanks to your staff. I'd like to pull him out, get him out to the country—"

"Gods, no! We just had one security breach. You want another business like Sheon?"

"—but I know it's not feasible."

"Duun. Duun-hatani." Ellud reached beside him on the desk, picked up the optic sheet and waved it. "I'm getting inquiries. We've got a slow leak that's going to become a panic, for the gods' sake, Duun! We haven't got that much maneuvering room left. I want that program to go on, I want it back on schedule. I'm telling you this. It's not just Shbit now. It's coming from the provinces. We're getting inquiries. Do you understand?"

"I've always understood. There's a limit, Ellud. The mind has limits. I want him tranquil. I want him whole. He's closer now than he ever was. But give him room."

"He doesn't know about Betan, does he?"

"How could I explain that without getting into the whole Council business? That's why I couldn't stop her on the spot. What would I say? Some people want you killed? He already avoids mirrors. Let the scars heal over before he gets the rest." It was the two-fingered hand that held the cup. Duun contemplated that, rolled it in his fingers and set it down. "Put Sagot on it."

"She couldn't."

"Ask her. No, I'll explain to her. She's old, she's canny, and she's female, and that's the best combination I can think of to handle this."

The guard still stood at the door, the same as always, and Thorn turned to look at the guard who escorted him to the upper floor—not a hard look, not vengeful. (*He* put Duun onto it.) At first Thorn had thought of Cloen. But Thorn had not been devious, had not—truly—thought of covering his tracks, not thought he had to.

Going through that ordinary door this morning was all that he could do. ("Betan's gone," Duun had told him yesterday. "She's been transferred. It was her request.") ("Did you kill her?" Thorn had asked, cold and shivering a second time. It was not a rational question, perhaps; but the very air felt brittle, full of doubts, full of duplicities. And Duun looked him in the eyes when he answered: "No. No such thing—" as soberly as ever Duun had answered him, as ever Duun had told him half-truths, had kept the world from him until Betan let it in.)

(What year are we in?)

(I shouldn't have laughed. Sheon's not quite the world capital, is it?)

Thorn walked in, into the foyer with its stark white walls, its plain white sand, the severely arranged vase-

and-branch on its riser. The sand showed the raking it got at night; a solitary line of footprints led around the corner into the large main room in which all the windows were white and blank.

He followed it and stopped in the archway in front of all the vacant desk-risers. That single track led to the farther desk in the stark white room, the one that had been Elanhen's.

A stranger sat there, legs crossed, hands on thighs. The nose and mouth and eyes were rimmed in white that graduated to a dusting, except the eartips. The crest was stark white. The arms were gaunt. Thorn stared, thinking he saw disease.

"Come closer." It was a thin voice, matching the body. He walked closer and stood staring. "You're Haras. Thorn."

(Gods, doesn't he know?) Laughter welled up like blood in a wound, but he could not laugh in this great sterile quiet. (He?) Thorn suddenly suspected not, for reasons he could not quite define. "Where's Elanhen? Where's Sphitti and Cloen?"

"My name is Sagot. You're staring, boy. Does something about me bother you?"

"I'm sorry. Where are the others?"

"Gone, Sit down. Sit down, Thorn."

He did not know how to refuse a voice so gentle. Duun had not taught him how to say no to authority. He had learned it on his own; and the world was too perilous to go recklessly in it. He sought the nearest riser and sat on the edge of it, feet dangling.

"I'm Sagot. You haven't seen anyone old before, have you?"

"No, Sagot." Saying anything seemed difficult. (Age. Gods, she's so brittle—it *is* she, it has to be. Will I get like that? And she knows me . . . she's a friend of Duun's—)

"I'm going to teach you now."

"Not them?"

"No. Just you. Shall I call you Haras or Thorn? Which do you prefer?"

"Either. Either, Sagot." (What do I call her? Is she hatani? Or one of the meds? Oh, get me out of here, Duun, I want them back! Even Cloen, if not Betan, at least Sphitti! At least Elanhen, at least someone I know!)

"I've had two children. Both boys. They're grown and have children of their own and their children have grown children. It's been a long time since I taught a boy. I always liked it."

(O gods.) The gentleness found quick flesh, slid in like a knife: shocked the tears loose again so quickly there was no retreat, no covering it; Thorn put his face into his hands, disgracing himself and Duun, and his chest ached as if something had broken there. He sobbed. He shook with tears. When he had gotten control again he wiped his face and nose with wet hands and looked up because he had to.

"You're a fine young man," Sagot said. "I like you."

"You're lying, you're lying, Duun put you up to this—"

"Doubtless he did. But you're still a fine young man. I can see that in you. I can see more than you think I see, I've brought up too many boys not to have had a young man wail and pour his troubles into my lap now and again, and young women too—I confess to you, even a few who weren't so young, all wailing and shaking with the troubles that were great to them then. Lamentations like that, they're like great storms. They're good for you. They come sweeping through the woods and break a few limbs. But they herald change. They bring the turn of seasons. They make things new. There, that's good. Your eyes are bright—very handsome eyes, if different. They're blue, aren't they, when they're not running."

"Let me alone!"

"It's amazing how much young men are alike; first the wails, then the shouting. I know it hurts. I've buried two husbands. I know something about pain."

"Are you hatani?"

She smiled. "Gods, no. But I know Duun. You know a hatani can do a lot of things, but when it comes to others, well—reason can't solve everything. 'Take care of him,' he said, 'Sagot, talk to him, teach him—' 'Now why should I do that?' I said. 'I've got my work, I've got things to do, I've got fourteen great-great-grandchildren, I don't need another boy—' But then I got to thinking, it's been so very long. They're all grown. I'm a hundred fifty-nine, young lad, and I've traveled all over the world, I've trekked down rivers, I've been to the two poles, I've written books—some of the books you study, by the by; I've had nine husbands, lovers I've forgotten, a few I haven't, and I've patched young knees, set bones, birthed babies and seen enough in this world not to be shocked at anything, that's the truth."

"Maybe that's why Duun wanted you with me." Bitterly. But somewhere in the chatter the pain in his chest stopped, and Sagot made it stop, and he had no more wish to run away. He sat there with his feet dangling, his five-fingered hands in his lap and the remnant of tears drying on his naked face. (But Betan's furred skin was silk and tasted like she smelled—)

"I don't think you think enough of yourself," Sagot said. "It's very well to be hatani, but you're not *all* that thing, you know, the way you're not just that pair of eyes or that pair of hands or that sex between your legs—" (The heat flew to his face.) "Oh, well, boy, I know, I know, you've only now discovered it and for a while it's the most of you, but that passes, it gets less important, the more of you there gets to be, the more abilities, the more thoughts, everything changes and shifts until the world's so wide and the things you are get so complex there's no containing them. You're not just Thorn who was born in a lab, right down this hall; you're Thorn the hatani, Thorn my student, Thorn who'll go places and do things and be things Thorn hasn't even thought of, and I haven't, and you'll find answers to your questions and questions yet to answer, which makes life, after all. So wail and take on if you have to, and if you want to come here every day and pour it all in my lap, well, that's doing some good, if you need to. But when you're done with that and you're quite ready I've got a lot of things I want to give you—it *is* giving, you know, a kind of gift. When you've lived as many years as I have you want to leave something in the world, and my teaching's that thing; it's what I do."

Another sob overtook him, unexpected, like a sudden breath. But it hurt less. Thorn wiped his face with a swipe of his hand, quick, distasteful. He slid back on the riser and tucked his feet up. There was no choice. Sagot left him none. "I'm listening, Sagot." (O gods, what has she got to teach?) Sagot teemed with secrets, frightening as Duun. As implacable. As difficult to get around. "Are you sure you're not hatani?"

Sagot laughed and even that was gentle, a fragility about her voice. "I take that for a compliment. What do you like best, what study?"

"Physics."

"Physics, then. Show me what you know. I'll find out where to start."

"If an object were traveling at the speed of light, and a man traveled on it to the nearest star—what is that star?"

"Goth."

"And distant—?"

"Five light-years."

"5.1. Be precise for this. And this man was forty; and he left a sister on earth when he went. . . ."

"There's a kind of parasite infests the brains of cattle on the Sgoht river. I remember once seeing one—"

"You were there?"

"Child, I lived nine months on the Sgoht, and I had a village magistrate for a lover. He had a ring threaded so, right through the side of his lip, and it looked odd, I'll tell you, when he smiled. He had been married six times and he had a great notch in his nose where one of his wives took a stick to him, but she was a crazy woman and her daughter was crazier. She took it into her head to sell her mother's land, that's right, without owning it—she was going to sell her *expectation* of inheriting it to this man she was living with so she could get the money to go downriver and get a husband who owned a grocery, don't ask me why, but I think food was quite all she could think of—she must have weighed two hundred, all of it. Well, the magistrate my lover finally gave her the money to get her out of town, and that fool man she was living with went after my lover with an axe—"

"Gods, Sagot!"

"He did. And chased him round and round the office and out into the street before someone shot this crazy man. Rumor had it the cattle sickness got him, that that woman fed him from diseased animals; but my lover the magistrate said anyone who married that woman was crazy from the start."

"Watch the monitor. This is a simulation game. This is an instrument panel—there's your fuel, do you see, there's your altitude, there's your compass. . . . You remember your ride to the city, don't you?"

"Of course I remember."

"Well, this isn't a copter. It's a plane. Use the toggle and the keys—let me show you. Here's the runway—this is an old-fashioned plane. But we'll start with that."

"Can you fly?"

"Oh, well, yes, I used to. My eyesight's against me now. I stay to the commercial planes."

"Commercial."

"Dear lad, planes go back and forth all over the world all the time, how do you think one would go?"

"Rail."

"Oh, well, it's all mostly freight, nowadays. Let's try taking off again; I'm afraid we've just crashed."

At some time the pain stopped. Thorn woke up one morning and realized he was past the sharpness of it; and that it had gotten to a kind of regret in which he did not have to work so hard at self-control; and finally, at breakfast with Duun on still another day, he hurt with a different pain, that he and Duun had had little to say to each other beyond the necessities of two people living with each other, and Duun's teaching him in the gym. There were no tales in his life but Sagot's; there was no sound in the house, but sometimes in the long evenings

he and sometimes Duun played the dkin with indifferent
passion—Duun aimlessly or working out long and vexing
compositions that frayed Thorn's nerves; Thorn playing
gloomy hatani songs or the lightest, most trivial ditties
he had known from childhood, like accusations hurled at
Duun. And Duun would sit and listen, or retreat to his
office for peace and (sometimes, for Duun's side pained
him) Duun would take a sedative and close the door of
his room.

He was Sagot's ward. Duun only lived with him and
went turnabout at fixing meals, and saw to his drill and
his practice (but Duun ached when he breathed and even
that was indifferent).

(He held me all night, that night. That must have hurt.
He could hardly move when he woke up. He never
complained.)

(Is it ever going to heal?) In one part of him the sight
of Duun reduced to walking into the gym and giving
instructions and walking out again gave Thorn satisfaction.

(But he's too quiet. He doesn't talk to me. What's he
waiting for?)

(O gods, I wish he'd yell or frown at me or even look
me in the eyes. His shoulders stoop. He moves like Sagot
does. I'd never have caught him in the first place, but
his balance was on his bad side in that pass. If he was
younger, if he hadn't ever been hurt, gods, he must have
been impossible to beat. I'd hate to have met him then.)

(O Duun, *look* at me!)

(Why should I care that he took Betan, he took Elanhen, Sphitti, even Cloen, he takes everything I care for,
he sent Sagot and someday I'll walk in and he'll have
sent her away too, everything, everyone.)

(He spied on me. He's probably tied into the computers there at school, I know he could, all you have to do
is put the codes in, we're in the same building. He knew
everything, he read everything Betan and I passed back
and forth, probably the guards reported to him.)

(O Duun, I don't *like* this quiet. I don't like you looking like that, it hurts.)

But one noon he came back from Sagot and Duun was in the gym, was waiting for him when he had shed down to his small-kilt and got out on the sand. Thorn waited for instruction, but Duun walked out, swinging his left arm a bit and working it back and forth.

"Duun, be careful."

"Thorn, I don't need *you* to tell me careful. Just remember what I told you: no all-out strikes. Let's go a fall or two."

Duun took him. It took a good long while, and it was craft that worked Thorn off his center and brought Duun's foot against his back.

"I'm dead," Thorn said, and sat down on the sand. Duun sat down less quickly, breathing hard, licking at his teeth. Thorn panted for breath and leaned on his knees and stared back at him. Grinned suddenly, because getting beaten by Duun was in the nature of the world and made it feel less lonely.

Duun grinned back. No words. It was better after that. Duun played that night, one old familiar piece after the other, and the music brought them back, dkin and drum, not the sad songs but the songs with tricks, hatani humor, subtle and cruel.

Thorn slept that night, and waked about the middle of the dark with the stars giddy about his bed and the air breathing false chill winds as if they came off winter snow; everything was still, and he had some vague terror that he could put no name to.

(Duun was here. He was here a while ago.) Perhaps it was a subtle scent the air-conditioning had dispersed. But the door was closed.

Thorn's eyes searched the room, the dark, seeking outlines and knowing Duun's skill. (Is he still in the room? Is he waiting till I move?) Thorn's heart raced, the veins pounding in his throat. (This is foolish. How could he pass the door? It's noisy; I couldn't sleep that soundly.)

(Could I?)

His heart hammered wildly. (He wouldn't. He *couldn't*. Not after Betan. He knows I'm mad. I hate him. I hate him that he does this to me.)

He hurled himself out of bed. (Never trust him. Never take Duun for granted—) But there was nothing there, only the false stars in their slow dizzy movement.

Thorn sat down again on the edge of the bed. His heart still slammed against his ribs.

(What's the world like? Full of Sagot's kind? Or Duun's? What's he up to? What was I made for? Why does the government care whether I live or die—enough to call on a hatani to solve my problem? He could kill them. Kill me. He gives me a chance, he says . . . a chance against *what?*)

(A hatani dictates others' moves. A hatani judges. A hatani wanders through the world setting things to rights again. A hatani can leave a pebble in your bed—in your drink—can pass a locked door and track you in the dark. He's a hunter . . . not of game. Of anyone he wants. What else is he?)

(Everything Duun does has a cause. And Sagot's his friend. Maybe—maybe Betan was. No. Yes. O gods, maybe it's *all* set up. Could Betan take a thing like me by *preference?* Was she curious? Curious—about what she'd let do *that* with her?)

(Sphitti laughing and joking with me, Elanhen too, from the time we met. Wouldn't it be natural to flinch? But they were prepared for it. They *knew* what I'd look like. Maybe Cloen was the only honest one—the only one who ever told me the truth.)

(Fool, you knew that, you knew it from the time you walked into that room and you wanted to believe something else. You saw how Betan moved—you thought *hatani* then and put that thought away.)

(She flinched at the last, she flinched and I reacted— I smelled the fear, her nerve broke—I pushed back, it scared me, it was reflex, she was up against me and I smelled the fear—)

(Thorn, where's your mind? Did you leave it at Sheon, on that hill, when you went back for him? Can you forget how Duun works?)

(I love him. Does he love me?)

(Is even Sagot real? All her chatter—from the start—
'I like you, boy.' Thorn, you fool.)

(Did Duun tell the truth, what I am and where he
got me?)

Thorn sat there with his hands locked between his
knees; and at last he got up and turned on the lights,
checked the bed, as if there could be a pebble there.
There was none.

(I hate him. I hate him for what he's done to me.)

(It was the best thing in the world when he smiled at
me today.)

X

"Again."

They used the *wer*-knives this time, the blades cased in clear plastic. Duun bent and took the pass, snaked from Thorn's strike and Thorn evaded his, fell and flipped up on his feet a distance away. "Is that a move you invented?" Duun asked dryly, and Thorn lowered his head and looked under one brow in that way he had when he had done something foolish. "I invented it just then," Thorn said, "when I landed on my heel. I'm sorry, Duun."

It was well-done, nevertheless. Duun laid his ears back. "Again."

Three more times. The *wer*-knives met in a way they never met when they were naked steel, plastic touching plastic and giving too much resistance. Duun floated back and stripped the cover from his blade. Thorn's eyes betrayed dismay, but Thorn pulled the sheath from his and threw it aside.

Naked steel. Duun gripped the knife in his maimed right hand, held the left close to it, ready to change off on short notice. Thorn did the same, maneuvering and watching nothing but his eyes and that blade.

Duun moved, not the feint that was his habit, but straight attack, aborted at the last instant when he saw Thorn cover; evade; to a feint, double-feint, hand-shift, retreating circle, sideslip, hand-shift.

Blade hissed on blade and slid clear; continuing drive, a floating attack.

Thorn escaped it with a fall and roll, came up again with sand in his hair and a desperate parry, for Duun kept coming and the wall was coming at Thorn's back.

Thorn sensed it and moved, too quickly. Duun shifted hands and blade rang on blade as Thorn backed up in free space again.

Duun called time. "Dammit, that steel's too fine to be treated like that! Keep edge off edge!"

"Yes, Duun." Thorn sucked breath in. Sweat ran in his eyes and he wiped it.

"It's that damned handedness again. You know what you did?"

"Went to the right," Thorn said. His shoulders sank. He wiped sweat again. "I feinted left."

"But you went to the right, fool!"

"Yes, Duun. I thought you'd think I'd go left this time for sure."

"Not when you never do it! Gods, surprise me once!"

Thorn's face was all chagrin.

"Up!" Duun struck, lizard-quick. Thorn escaped, escaped, escaped, attacked and escaped with a ringing of the blades.

Duun hit him then, averted the blade and struck his arm up with his fist. Thorn flung his own arm up to lessen the force, skipped back and covered himself again.

Duun called time again and Thorn looked down at his wrist as if he expected to see blood. "At least," Duun said, "you didn't stop when I hit you."

"No." They had hammered that one out in painful lessons, beginner habits unlearned with bruises. "I'm sorry." Breathless, with another wipe at the sweat. Thorn meant the blade-touch.

"You've developed a whole new form of fence, the artful covering of your mistakes! You're best at your escapes!"

"I'm sorry, Duun-hatani."

"This isn't hand-to-hand. In this, young fool, you've got a damn sharp claw! Rearrange your thinking and use it. Again!"

Thorn came at him. He evaded it, struck, evaded, struck.

"Hold!"

Thorn flinched back. Stood there with the breath rasping through his mouth and sweat running in his eyes. He straightened. "I'm sorry, Duun." It had gotten to be a refrain. There were always mistakes. His look was contrite.

Duun reached a hand toward his face, slowly. Thorn stepped back. There was threat in that stance, wariness. Duun smiled.

Thorn straightened his shoulders back, panting. (Why do you shout at me? Why do you curse me? What's wrong today? I'm trying to listen, Duun, don't make fun of me like that.)

"Let me touch you, minnow. This once."

The knife-hand lowered. Thorn stood still. Duun came close and put his palm in the middle of Thorn's chest, on flesh gone pale without sunlight, on flesh slickly sweating so that hands slipped off it, if one grappled without claws. The heart jumped beneath his hand in steady, labored pulses. There was no flinching. No shivering. Duun moved the hand up to the side of Thorn's neck and felt the same pulse. A slight flinching. Reflex. Or teaching. He looked into alien white eyes: it was curious how little the blue centers had changed from the first time he had looked into them, an infant lying on his lap; a round-bellied child clambering on his crossed ankles and trying to pull his ears; a boy's face gazing up at him in sudden shock at finding him on the trail—

They had never seemed to change size. The bones about them did. The face became hollow-cheeked and the jaw lengthened and its skin roughened in dark hair Thorn kept shaved. . . . (They'll laugh at me, Duun; my body hair just doesn't get thick enough and I'm not going to grow it on my face like that, all patched up and thick here and not there.") Thorn shaved his body here and there too, where the patchiness was worst. Clipped and groomed and gods, *tried,* not to grow a coat any longer, but at least not to let the changes in his body overcome the Thorn they both had gotten used to. Thorn smelled different than he once had. The chest and shoulders were wider and muscled, the belly flat and hard, the loins narrow, the legs long-muscled and agile. Strong, Thorn could lift *him* nowadays, though gods knew Duun had no intention to let him try.

Strange, Thorn was not ugly. Seventeen, nearly eighteen years, and Duun looked at him eye-to-eye, even having to look up a little lately. And there was in Thorn a symmetry that made that face probable on that body and the composite of him fit together in a grace of motion that no aesthete could deny. ("When you get used to him he's beautiful," Sagot said. "Frightening, like some big animal you've gotten closer to than you wanted. But you want to watch him move. There's a fascination to such things, isn't there?)

The pupils dilated and contracted with thought. With anxiety. (Is this a game, Duun? Am I supposed to do something?)

Duun walked away, turning his back on that look. Perhaps Thorn picked up his anxiety. It was acute now.

("We've got to go with it," Ellud said. "Duun, you're put me off; first it was: Wait till he's got the first tapes down. Then it was: The Betan business has him upset. Now it's: There's a last few things I have to teach him. Duun, we're out of excuses.")

Duun picked up the cap for the *wer*-knife. Looked back across the room where Thorn was doing the same thing. Ripple of muscle, the reach of an arm. Thorn was whole this morning. Duun wished to remember this.

"These are the words: I know you can remember them. You won't need much study. *Ship. Sun. Hand. Warning.* They're equivalents to these sound patterns." Sagot played the tape in the recorder wand she held. It was all a complicated thing, and Thorn centered himself, not to diffuse his concentration on his surroundings. The guard had not brought him to the familiar room this morning, but two doors down, into a place with the slick, bare floors that shouted *meds*, a place that was large enough, but there were two large risers and a clutter of cabinets: the windows showed illusory desert, which only made the place seem starker, less comforting. Sagot was there waiting for him, sitting cross-legged on a desk with a keyboard in her lap; there was a keyboard and monitor at her knee. "Sit down," Sagot had said, and the guard went out and closed the door on them.

"I. He. Go."

Thorn had thought *simulator* when the guard brought him to a strange door. He enjoyed that, the fast interaction with the computer, the imagination of flight, and land skimming beneath illusory wings. Gods, they had a screen in one room that made it all seem real. He sat in a machine in that room that had controls very like the copter controls had looked, and the whole machine could move under him, incline and tilt with the screens so that the first time he had had to clamp his jaws to keep from screaming when he lost control and the room spun. He was better at it now.

("Meds?" he had said at once to Sagot, alarmed. "Sit down," she said, "it's patterns today.")

"Stop. Man. Radio. Stop."

"Is it some kind of language?"

"Do your patterns, boy."

(Something's wrong. Sagot's mouth is hard. Did I ask something wrong? Is she worried about this place?)

"Concentrate."

Thorn worked at it. He put meanings with the patterns. Sagot left him listening to his tapes over and over again and he hated them. He mouthed the sounds, resenting it. It was not a good day. Duun had been surly at breakfast; surly in Duun's way, which meant quiet and thoughtful and not giving him anything from inside him, only the surface, like a puddle frozen over. Sagot gave him stark orders and went off and left him in this room, disappearing through the inner door and coming and going in perfunctory checks on him.

(They've been talking to each other. Duun's mad at me and he's told Sagot. I haven't done anything to make Sagot mad.)

(I was stupid about my moves yesterday, I can't stop going to the right all the time, I'm worse when Duun yells at me, I wish he'd hit me, even, I don't mind his hitting me, I deserve to get hit when I leave my side open like that. It's like I've reached a point I can't improve anymore, and Duun knows it, and I'm not good enough to be hatani, not quite. He's worked so long to teach me, and I go off to the right like a fool and he ought to shout at me, he should have cut me and maybe I'd remember after that.)

There was a scar across his forearm and one on Duun's. (I always remembered that.)

"Boy."

The machine went off, Sagot's intervention. He blinked at Sagot, who had brought him a pill and a small cup of water. (Gods, it *is* meds. What's wrong? Do they just want to look at me?) "Sagot, I don't want to swallow that. I'm not sick."

She went on holding it out. There was no choice, then. He picked the pill off her black, wrinkled palm and put it in his mouth. He had no need of the water to swallow it, but it made his stomach feel better; it threatened upset. (Is that what has Sagot acting strange? Is there something really the matter with me? Does Duun think so?)

"I want you to go next door with me," Sagot said. "Yes, it's meds. You're going to lie down a while and I want you to be good about this."

(You smell afraid, Sagot. So do I, I think. Gods, what's this about?)

He got up. He towered over Sagot, but Sagot reached and took his hand. (I'm hatani, Sagot, you're not supposed to—) But he never told Sagot no. She led him by the hand to the door in the side of that room, and led him through it into a small room that left no illusions about meds in this room. It was a cramped small place, all machinery and a table. Sagot's hand held his. She was evidently not going to argue the matter. (She's afraid. What should *I* be?) But he stood there while meds came out and told him to take off his kilt and lie down.

"I'll be all right," he told Sagot; he did not want to undress with her there, not because he would shock her—(I have fourteen great-great-grandchildren, boy)—but precisely because it would not, she would look on

him as a child, and child-Thorn was already too naked.
But Sagot stayed, and Thorn turned his back and unfastened his kilt and got up on the table when the meds told
him to. His head swam; his limbs felt distant from his
brain; he drifted in a vast calm which itself alarmed him.

(It was a drug Sagot gave me. Does Duun know? Does
he know where I am, what they're doing, did he order
this?)

They pasted electrodes about his body. He felt this far
distant from him. They spoke in whispers or his hearing
had gone wrong. They adjusted a screen above his head.
Something soft and rough settled over his naked body
and he realized vaguely that someone had put a sheet
over him; he was dimly grateful. (It's cold in here; they
never realize how cold I get sometimes, they've got a
coat and I don't and I'm sweating now—) Something
tight went over his legs, once again over his chest. "*Talk*
to him, for the gods' sake, he's not a piece of meat
you're handling."

"Sagot-mingi, we have to ask you to be still, with respect, mingi Sagot."

Something weighed on his shoulder. Shook at him.
"Keep your eyes open. Look up."

Thorn obeyed that voice. He heard the sound of his
tapes over and over again.

"Blink. That's right. You can blink when you have to."

"He's following that, isn't he?"

The voice drifted out again. He heard another voice
babbling at him; there were images, he was in the simulator; more voices, more images, there were people like
him moving in the dark, there were faces that babbled
at him, there were machines and more machines—

He tried to leave this.

Eyes stared at him, mirrorlike. More machines that
spun in dark and arms that moved—

He fought. He evaded and escaped and fought.

"This is your heritage," a voice told him out of the
dark. "Accept it, Haras-hatani. This is your heritage. Accept what you hear and see. Stop resisting. Accept this.
This is your heritage."

Chaos of images.

"Listen to the sounds. Learn this, Haras-hatani. Remember these things."

"Wake up."

He was lying on the table. The sheet was over him. He was drenched in sweat. He wanted only to lie there and his eyes stung as if sweat were in them; it might be. Someone wiped his face and the cloth was neutral-feeling, wet and rough but neither cold nor hot. Someone lifted a weight off his chest and legs. "Are you sure you ought to? He's not awake yet." He was, but he preferred to keep that secret to himself, and stare at the stark steel of the machinery, ignoring the faces and the touches, the sudden nakedness of his body as they peeled electrodes away in small twitches he ought to have felt keenly and did not.

"His color isn't good."

(I'm cold, fool.)

Something stung his arm. It was not a great pain. In a moment he began to feel his heart thumping the way it did in nightmares.

(Go away. Let me alone. Don't touch me.)

"Hold him, don't let him move."

He blinked. Meds held his limbs in a hurtful grip. He lifted his head. "Let go. I'm awake. I want to sit up."

They looked foolish, with a dropping of their ears. After they had mulled it over they let him go and one at his side got a hand beneath his back and one and another helped him sit up, holding him.

"Are you through?" Thorn said.

"We're through," one said. They rarely spoke to him at all. "We'll put you to bed awhile."

"I'm going home." Thorn gave a sudden heave and landed with his feet on the floor. His feet were numb, but his knees held. The med reached and he stopped that reach with a backhand lift of his arm, slow-motion, gentle warning. The med took the warning when his stare followed the turn he made, and backed off.

"Sagot," someone said, "Sagot, get in here fast."

Thorn waited then, if Sagot was coming. He remembered he was naked. "I want my clothes." A med gave him his kilt, and he took it and worked with numb fingers and diminished balance to put it on.

A door opened. He looked up at Sagot. "Sagot," he said; he was very careful to be polite. Duun would hit him if he was rude to the meds, and he was desperate. He made his voice ever so calm and courteous, and stood as easily as he could. "Sagot, they think I ought to go to bed here and I'd much rather go to my own and sleep. Please get me home, Sagot."

Sagot looked at him with her thin mouth all taut. A long while she stood there. "All right," Sagot said. "Call his guard and call Duun and tell him we're coming back." Sagot came and took Thorn's arm, wound her thin, fragile forearm about his and locked both her hands on his, and he walked with her, out of that room.

"We'll wait here a moment," she said in the other room; and stood there with him, holding to his arm. In a moment the door opened and the guard was there who walked with him everywhere. Ogot was his name. He said little, but he was a pleasant man; he was Duun's, and if Ogot had taken him to this place and never told him, perhaps Ogot had not known half as much as Sagot had. Ogot looked worried to see him, and Thorn felt ashamed to be so helpless.

"It's all right," Sagot said, "they've just given him a little sedative; we'll walk slowly. The boy wants to go home now. Come on, Thorn."

He was not in his bed, he was lying on cushions on the riser that touched the main room wall, the windows showed branches lashing in the rain, glass spotted and distorted with water. The audio played thunder and rain-sound. Lightning flashed. The air-conditioning wafted moist, cool air and the smell of woods in rain. He lay against the cushions in the room he knew (but the walls always changed) and blinked. He knew those trees, the one that bent, the crooked limb, the rocks, the way one could climb—

"Here." Duun sat down on the riser and took a cup

and poured him tea. "It's got aghos in it, don't spit it: you could use the calories."

He took it in one hand and sipped at it. The spice was sickly sweet, but it tasted better than his mouth did. He blinked at Duun. His neck was stiff; he had been sleeping wrong.

"That's good," Duun said. "I moved you in here."

"Carried me?" He remembered bed; remembered Duun rousing him once and making him drink.

"I still can."

"Duun, they—"

"Hush."

Thorn caught his breath. So he had been about to embarrass himself. (You have a need, Thorn.) He felt drained and placid now after the storm before. The illusory rain spattered the windows. "That's Sheon, isn't it?"

"I saved that image. I had it done about a year ago. I thought I'd use it someday."

(Some special day. Today? Is it a gift? To make up for the other thing?)

"More tea?" Come on. I want you to wake up now. We're going to have a round in the gym this afternoon."

"You'll kill me."

"I'll go easy, minnow." Duun's face staring at him, half good, half bad, with that forever mocking smile. "You'll manage."

(Is he happy with me now? Was it a test I passed?) "Duun, they had me—"

Duun lifted his right hand, the single finger. Silence, that meant. (I don't want you to talk.)

"They—"

"It didn't happen."

"Dammit, it—"

"It didn't happen. Hush."

Thorn's pulse picked up. He lay there staring at Duun's scarred face, at the unblinking stare. His heart thumped against his ribs. (What are you doing to me? What are you doing to me, Duun-hatani?)

*   *   *

"You're slow, Thorn. Slow. Speed!"

Thorn tried. He spun and lost his centering, dived backward to save himself as the capped knife crossed his belly: he felt the touch of it, spun away and brought his blade up in defense at what followed. Time, Duun called, and hunkered down. Thorn sat down and wiped his face.

"I'm off. I'll get it back."

"You'll go on practicing," Duun said.

"What—'go on'?" (Has something changed? What's wrong?) *Go on* had the sound of finality.

"Three mornings of a five you'll have your study. Every other day you'll go back to that room. It's another kind of study."

"Duun—"

"—which we won't talk about."

"Duun, I can't!"

"Can't?"

Thorn flinched. He clenched his arms about his knees. "Have you? Have you been through it?"

"We won't talk about it. Every other day you'll face that. You'll know you're going to face it; and you'll walk in on your own and be polite with the meds. This is the only time I'm going to tell you this. If you truly begin to suffer they'll put you down to once a five-day. But that's something the meds will decide for medical reasons, not your untutored whims."

"Forever? For the rest of my life?"

Duun hesitated. Duun rarely hesitated in answers, though he might stop to consider. In this, the pause was minute and Duun frowned. "It's a test, minnow. You're not going to fail it, hear? I'm not going to tell you how long it lasts. You're not going to bring the matter through that door. Next time you'll sleep it off in the medical section. When you can walk home on your own you'll do it; and you'll walk in at whatever hour and say, Hello, Duun, I'm home, what are we going to do?—the way you do every day. Sagot was soft and let you do as you pleased, and I should have sent you back right then and not coddled you. Life's not likely to coddle you."

"Neither are the meds, Duun! It *hurt,* it—I don't know how to handle it, Duun, give me some help, for the gods' sakes tell me how I ought to handle it!"

"Accept it. With dignity. Embrace it. With all the strength and cleverness you've got."

"Did I fail today?"

"No," Duun said. "No, you did marvelously well. You can be proud of yourself. You've made a lot of people happy with you, people you've not met. But we won't talk about it anymore. You'll come home and you won't have to talk about it; we'll do everything we always do. I think you'll be glad of that."

"You won't shout at me."

A second time Duun looked taken aback, and that was rarer still. "No, minnow, I won't shout at you."

XI

"Good morning," Sagot said.

Thorn walked across the sand the length of the room to where Sagot sat, as she had sat the first time he saw her. Reprise. He walked to the riser facing hers and sat down on the edge, feet dangling, hands locked in his lap. Sagot's face was a stranger's face, withholding everything behind the eyes, an aged, white-dusted mask.

"How are you, Thorn?"

(As if we started over.) "I'm fine, Sagot. Duun says I have to go back there tomorrow. Is it going to be the same?"

"I can't discuss it, Thorn."

He sat there a moment. "I want to know, Sagot. What are they doing?"

"I can't discuss it. Can we get to our lessons?"

"Will you go with me tomorrow?" (Please, Sagot.)

A long silence. "I don't think I can really make much difference. They won't let me bring you home; they're going to insist you stay there; they think they woke you up too fast. They weren't happy at all about my taking you out of there; you were on your feet and you were being reasonable—" Sagot's mouth puckered in humor. "—but a drunk hatani's not to argue with. Tomorrow you'll know what to expect and you won't argue with the meds, all right?"

"I know. I'd still like for you to stay."

"Thorn—"

"Don't talk to Duun about it. I know he'd say no. Just do it, Sagot. I don't trust the meds. I've never liked them."

"I'll be there." Sagot smoothed the heavy fabric of her kilt and rested her hands on her ankles. "Let's talk about the weather—like atmosphere. Like the interaction of the oceans and air masses. When I was at the north pole, that was back in '87, I flew up there, but I went out on this exploration ship, *Uffu Non* was its name. Ask me about the hothonin some time—"

"What are hothonin?"

"It's this kind of fish, about shonun size. They catch birds. That's right. They have this white spot on their heads which looks like a small fast-swimming fish when they run just below the surface; a bird dives down, the hothun dives up—*snap,* no bird. See what assumptions do? Anyway, we put out of Eor port and headed out to sea—"

"He's still sane," Duun said. Ellud faced him, hands on knees, in the normal clutter of Ellud's desk. Duun sat opposite, in the accustomed place. "Let's not push it, Ellud."

"I'm not pushing it," Ellud said. "Council's pushing me. *Betan's* surfaced. She's alive."

Duun let his face relax in his surprise. "That's no good news. Where?"

"She's in seclusion. Shbit's got her, of course, in his house. That's the report that's gotten to me, via a councillor who talked to a councillor who talked with her. Don't go in there, Duun. For the gods' sake, don't try it at this point. Everything's going our way and Shbit's got nothing but a failed agent."

"The bureau agents must be in Shbit's bed if they're sure what he *hasn't* got. I don't like their complacency. Tell them that."

"Stay out of it, Duun, Gods, you go after Shbit and you could blow this whole thing into the public eye again, and gods know we've been there too often as it is. The Council's riding even just now. The appropriations keep coming."

"I know when Shbit will move. Shbit doesn't know it yet." Duun decided on the tea and poured himself a cup.

"One has to suppose he restrains Betan; but I'd rather not suppose at all. What's the report from Gatog? Any details?"

"They've got the problem solved. It turned out to be a software glitch. They took each other out."

Duun frowned. "I figured. False alarm, then. Dammit, Ellud. Those ears go down again and we'll have councillors in the trees."

"It could be worse."

"Believe me, I never quite forgot that." Duun picked up the cup with two fingers of his right hand and turned it with his left, feeling the incised design, natural clay, the costly happenstance of obu art, which was like Ellud, both clever and lacking plan. The paradoxes of the man confounded him lifelong. "I want to see the reports on Shbit. I want to know when he breathes in and how long he holds it. To the second, Ellud, tell your agents that."

". . . in 1582 the first reactor went on line in toghon province—"

". . . in 1582 the Dsonan League established the international council. The immediate motivation was the drought which occurs in cycles in Thogan and which in that year had created considerable hardship on the seventeen million who inhabited the region stretching from—"

". . . in 1593 the first satellite was launched from the Dardimuur coast—"

(Satellite?)

". . . in 1698 Botan no Gelad became the first shonun into space."

"Sagot." Thorn's heart beat very fast. He looked up from his monitor at a placid, aged face. "Sagot, we're in space."

"I was a little girl when Nagin walked on the moon. I remember my oldest brother coming and bringing me to the television and telling me that was the moon and shonun were walking on it. Nagin and Ghotisin and Sar. I went outside in the dark—it was spring and it was a clear night; I looked up at the moon and tried to see where they were, but of course I couldn't. I stared and stared and my brother came out and stood beside me. 'I'll go up there someday,' he said. He did. He flew all the way to Dothog and he walked on another world. He sent me a picture of him standing there in front of a sea of red dunes, you can't tell it's him, of course, the suit's big and cumbersome, and the sun-visor's down, but I know it's him. I still have it."

(Machines in the dark. Things spinning.)

("The world's wide, minnow, wider than you know.")

"Can I see it? Can I *meet* your brother?"

"He's dead. He died, oh, forty years ago. He had an equipment failure, out on the Yuon desert, on Dothog. Air ran out. I've got the picture, though. I'll bring it."

"I'm sorry, Sagot."

"Child, you grieve and you get over things. I just remember my brother now, not the end of him, just the living. You know the shuttleport, just outside Dsonan? You can feel the ships take off. You can hear them when they come in, like thunder, even through the walls—"

"Is *that* that sound?" ("Duun, what's that?" "I don't know, buildings have a lot of sounds. Mind on your business, minnow.")

"—about every five-day. They carry cargo up to the station, pick up what the station makes, medicines and such, and bring it back down. There's still the Dothog base, it's quite a little town now, all domes and connecting tunnels. All scientists. About once a year you can get a tour out from the station, but it's horrendously expensive, the kind of thing only the rich can afford and too rough to please most of that sort, but they still have a few visitors. I've dreamed about it, I'd like to go, but it takes a year each way; and something always comes up. I don't know—" Sagot looked at her hands and looked up. "I think, I think deep down I'm superstitious about it, I think my brother's still there, still climbing about over the dunes and enjoying himself, but if I went there it'd be just a place, I'd see the town all grown up and the damn tourists and I'd go out in the desert and he wouldn't be there. Then he'd be dead for me, really dead—oh, gods. I'm sorry, boy, the old woman talks on and on. You wanted to ask me about space."

"Have you been there?"

"I've been up to the station. It's a barren kind of place, all tubes and tunnels—"

(Tunnels. Metal tunnels. Going on and on, bending up when you walk them—)

"—and one part of it looks a lot like all the other parts. And strangely enough you don't really get to see the stars much. You can see them from the shuttle if you get up front—they let you do that. It's beautiful. The world's beautiful. Haven't you seen it in pictures?"

(The dark globe with the fire coming over it, the spinning place—)

"No, of course you haven't. I've got this marvelous window-tape. I bought it on the station. It's the earth from space. I think I can find a copy for you. You get to watch the sun come up over and over again round the curve of the world; you get to see all the seas and the clouds all swirled—"

"He's coming round—he's coming round. Hold the injection. He's coming out of it."

"That jolted him. *Something* happened."

"Quiet. He can hear. Let's get him out of here."

"Do you hear us, Thorn? Move your hand if you hear us."

"Aaaaaaaaiiiiii!"

It was his voice. Thorn was the one screaming. He came fighting up out of the dark, and dark was about him, stars aglow in giddy distance.

Light blazed, white and awful; he flung himself out of bed blind and hit the wall with his back before he saw Duun in the doorway, against the dark of the hall, Duun naked from his sleep and staring at him. "Are you all right, Thorn?"

Thorn leaned against the cold surface at his back. His limbs began to shake in aborted reaction. "I'm sorry, Duun."

Duun kept on staring at him. Duun's ears were back.

Thorn peeled himself off the wall. The windows were sunrise now, sun coming up over grasslands. Duun had disrupted the timer. The air-conditioner wafted grass-scent, dewy and cold. Thorn shivered again, feeling the draft on his skin. Bedclothes made a trail over the side of the bed and onto the sand, the route his flight had taken.

"It was a nightmare," Thorn said. "I dreamed. . . . " (Faces. Sounds.) He began to shake again. "Faces like *mine*, Duun—they didn't make me up!"

Duun said nothing. His face had that masklike look that it had when he was not going to say anything.

"Did they?" Thorn persisted.

"Who said they didn't make the *tapes* up?"

"Don't do this to me, Duun!"

"You don't sound sleepy. You want a cup of tea, a bit to eat?"

Thorn surrendered. Duun was being kind. Duun was leading him off again. Thorn knew the tricks. He ripped the sandy bedclothes loose and threw them down on the floor. The bed wanted turning and thumping anyway, and the blankets could use washing. Duun had left the door and left it open. Thorn pulled the bin open in the side of the riser and took out yesterday's clothes, but it was before baths and he had to dress again before class.

Duun was in the kitchen when he came in, setting the teapot on the riser. "Sobasi?"

"It's all right." The microwave was busy. It went off and Thorn pulled the plates out and set them on the table. (Faces. Faces. The station. Ships coming and going. Dots and symbols. Chemistry. The value of *pi*. Numbers.) Thorn sat down and swung his legs about, crossed; Duun did the same and poured tea for himself. "I drink too much of this stuff," Duun said, "it ruins my sleep."

"So do I. Duun, can we talk about it—once?"

Duun's ears went flat.

"Dammit, please!"

Duun held out the teapot to him with a bland look on his face. "One question. I'll listen to it. Only one, Harashatani. You don't have to ask it now if you want to think about it. Snap judgment's never good."

Thorn took the teapot, composed his face and poured. (I hate him. I hate him. He hasn't got a nerve in his body.) "I'll tell you when I ask it: I don't want you taking the first question I ask and claiming that lets you off. Have you got a lover?"

(Got him.) Duun's ears flicked; the eyes dilated and contracted. "Was that the nightmare?"

"No. I'm just curious."

"None now. A companion for a while. I sent her off." Duun filled his mouth and swallowed.

"Why?"

(Another strike. I hadn't thought that.) "She would have wanted marriage eventually. I didn't."

"How old are you?"

"Minnow, when you started this, we were talking about one question. Is this all pertinent?"

"You were onto me yesterday because I always take the defensive; attack sometimes, you said. I realize I do that even outside the gym. So I'm attacking. Do you think you're old?"

Duun grinned. "You'll go too far pretty soon, Harashatani, and I'll call this game. Do you think I'm old?"

"What was your solution for the government?"

"To make you hatani. Which I've done."

"Why didn't you want me to learn about the world the way it is?"

"You have now, haven't you?" Duun shrugged. (Gods, not a flicker.) "It never came up; too much of Sheon and too little of the world. When we came here—two years early, and not quite my planning, I might remind you—" (Counterattack and hit.) "You were pretty badly shaken, if you'll recall, and you knew too damn much you were unusual." (Hit again. Gods! he's got no mercy.) "What was I going to do? Throw the world at you in a day? Listen, minnow, I had a problem on my hands, I had a boy to bring up without newscasts, without pictures of cities, without any hint what went on outside Sheon's woods, because any photograph with people in it was going to show a smart young lad that people all look a lot like me and none of them like you. I had to educate you without educating you, if you see the problem, because I didn't want you to suffer with your difference. I wanted to give you a childhood, and I gave you the best one I knew: I gave you mine."

(He's working on me. He's telling the truth. What *was* the experiment? They're not done with it. It's still going on.) Thorn felt sweat gather in the folds of his knees and beneath his arms.

"You have to admit," Duun said, "the last two years there's been a lot poured into your head. A lot of facts. You've come from the past to the present. I'll tell you: when I started I didn't know what your mental capacity might be, whether it was normal, you understand. I didn't know whether I *could* do what I planned. I had to know that before I let anyone else set hands on you . . . whether you could be hatani. Remember Ehonin's daughter."

"Why is it important—to have me be hatani?"

"Is that your question?"

"I told you I would say when it was my question."

"Well, I'll tell you that one someday."

"This is my question: Why do the things they make me see have the station in them and why is the station full of people like me?"

"That's two questions."

"It's one. A hatani ought to see the unity."

"Well, I'll treat it as one. The station isn't, it's full of ordinary people, and I told you the truth, you're unique. Probably the tests are making you dream in strange ways; it's got psychological implications I'm sure the meds are interested in."

"The experiment's still going on, isn't it?" (Gods, he's twisted me up again. Everything. Everything's an illusion, like the windows.) "Isn't it, Duun?"

"That's still another question. I'm not going to answer that. I told you I didn't want to bring the matter through the door; I'd think you'd be glad of a place where people didn't take your mind apart and play games with what you know."

"Gods, tell me where that *is!*"

Duun smiled; or maybe it was the scar. "Eat. You

woke me up. You can damn well eat the breakfast you made me cook."

"It's a language, Sagot. Why don't they just tell me that?"

"Hush. I can't talk about it."

"What are they doing to me?"

"Thorn, there's no way I can discuss it. Please."

"I ache when I get out of there. I feel like someone's taken me and twisted me inside out. I see things in my sleep. I've had the windows changed. It was stars. I'd wake up and not know where I was and I felt like I was falling, like the sleep-falling, only worse. It's woods now, and sometimes Sheon's woods in the rain, I can't sleep without that. I wish they'd change that awful desert picture in the lab."

"It's meant to be restful."

"There's too much sky in it. It's dead. I dream of a place like that and I don't like it."

"I'll ask them to change it. I'm sure they will. They really try to be good to you, you know that."

"They hate me."

"Boy, they're professionals. They have to be cold. Their minds are busy thinking what to do and they're like all professionals, they get to handling people just like they push their buttons and expect things to work. They forget there's a person attached to that leg and that arm because they're looking down into their minds seeing on a different level, like how the veins and nerves run. On that level your body's just a map with pathways going here and there, and I'm afraid they're on those tracks without much thinking that somewhere up that network there's a skull with a brain in it and a very anxious young man living there and watching and listening to what they're saying to each other."

(Sagot, you're redirecting. I know that trick. I'm a boy between two crafty adults and they keep me off my balance all the time. I get tired of fighting the storm. I just want to sink down and quit sometimes.)

"I'm thinking about killing myself."

Panic. Sagot looked at him in shock. Thorn grinned and ached inside.

"I was joking. You're very good at getting me off the subject. I thought I'd do it too."

"Don't joke about a thing like that, boy. I had a husband do that on me. I don't think it's funny at all."

"Don't tell me about your husband! You're doing it to me again! I won't listen to you!" He flung himself off the riser and stalked across the sand, headed out. Sagot was silent behind him. He got as far as the outside door, in the room with the vase and branch; and the door was locked. He hit the switch. Hammered on the door. "Open it up! I want out of here!"

There was no escape. Eventually he had to go back (as Sagot planned) into the room. But he sat down on the last riser and folded up his legs and studied the veins on his hands and ankles, which were distended in anger. Maps. Pathways. Sagot's husband *had* probably killed himself, she was not making it up. She was sitting up there with an ungratefully rude boy sulking in front of her and he had struck at her in a hatani way. He had hit Cloen. He had hit Sagot. Both times he had perverted what he knew.

He got up finally, and walked up and sat down in front of Sagot. "You can shout at me, Sagot. Please."

"I don't need to."

(Hit. Deft and killing as Duun's wit when he was crossed.) Thorn flinched inside. "Forgive me, Sagot. Sagot, don't hate me."

"Wicked boy. By guile and redirection. I can tell you're Duun's handiwork. Back to the meds, are we?"

"Just don't tell me they don't. I can read bodies; I can read eyes, Sagot. They hate me and they're afraid of me and they made me what I am. Is that reasonable of them?"

"Maybe it's the hatani they're afraid of. Did you think of that? People don't like being read. A hatani stops at your door, you give that hatani food, a place to sleep, and you start thinking over every move you make because you know you're being read, constantly, every tiny move. It would take a very stupid person or a very innocent one to relax with a hatani under his roof."

"A hatani doesn't judge if he's not asked to. Sometimes not even then. Why should they worry?"

"Guilt. Everyone's guilty of something. A hatani makes you know what you're guilty of."

"Even hatani are guilty, Sagot."

"But they cover it. They know how not to be read, don't they? If they really try. Sometimes they don't." Sagot got up and came and sat down next to him, put her arm around him. "Sometimes they don't want to, do they? Come on, lean on me, I won't tell anyone."

"Tell me about the test, Sagot."

"Wicked lad." Her hand pressed his shoulder, close to his neck, and made him nervous. He shrugged and she slipped it to the middle of his back. "You have a hatani mind, all right. You're growing up."

"I hear words, Sagot, sounds run in my head and I hear words in them."

"What do they say, these words?"

"They tell me hello, they want something, I can't tell what, they talk about the sun and the earth, they talk about math and chemistry, oxygen, they say, and carbon, over and over, and they talk nonsense, the elements, the reactions inside the sun, the lifecycle of stars—"

Sagot's arm had gone tense. He turned and looked at her at close range, saw her eyes dilate and contract. "Did I just scare you?" Thorn asked.

"Go on talking."

"I'm not supposed to talk to you about it. You keep telling me that."

"You can tell me about this. Go on."

"There isn't anything more. I can't remember anything else. I see that desert place and a place like a space station, I see the earth in space with the sun coming up, and faces—faces like mine, I see the space station full of them, I see people like me coming and going and talking to each other—sometimes they're mad, and I can read them if I can't figure out what they're saying, one wants something and she's a woman—Duun says I imagine it, but I'd never imagine a thing like that, her mouth is all red and her hair is long and her eyes are all painted round the edges: she wants something very bad and she's angry with a man but he's sorry and they go on meeting in this place, these places where people eat and have clothes, clothes for people with no hair, and she's shaped like—'' He shaped the image of fullness of his chest. (White all white, and large and strange-looking.) "And finally—there are a lot of people that come and go—she goes off with this other man and they go into his bedroom and they love each other, but it isn't love, she doesn't even like him, and he's mad about that, maybe about something else; then she leaves and she goes and finds the first man but he's about to go somewhere and he doesn't want to talk to her. Her eyes run. He goes away. She goes to this place where people eat and she's very unhappy. Then he walks through the door and he comes over to sit with her, but not on ordinary furniture, on these legged things, all the furniture's like that. She's pretending she's not glad to see him, she keeps eating. He knows she's pretending and he says something and they look at each other and say something about going somewhere, and then it stops and I don't know where they went.''

Sagot took his face between her hands and he was so lost he let her. She pulled his face down to her level and washed his eyes with her tongue, which made him feel strange and loved, even as old as Sagot was.

"Is that what I'm supposed to see?"

She let him go. "Go home. I'll call Ogot."

"What am I supposed to see? Is it over? Am I through with that?"

"I don't know. Go home."

XII

Ellud paced the floor and flung his arms out: "I can't cover this!"

"You don't have to." Duun stayed seated. "I'm taking him this afternoon. I'll want the copter on the roof, I'll want the plane at Trusa, no slip-ups; take one off the line. I'll take it myself."

"Gods, your license is expired. I won't have it. You don't fly these damn things nowadays, the damn computers do. I'll get you a pilot." Ellud threw that out and lost his case.

"Do that. One hour. I'm headed out." Duun went for the door.

"They'll have my post, they'll move the minute you're clear of the roof, I'll have councillors at this door."

"Watch Shbit, that's all. I'll get him back for you."

"The Guild won't take him!"

"Is that hope they will or hope they won't?"

Ellud stood there with his mouth open. Duun left.

Thorn hurried; he had a bundle under his arm that was a change of clothes, his and Duun's and Duun's gray cloak, wrapped around things they needed from the bath and tied with a cord; he had new winter-clothes on, quilted coat, baggy trousers, quilted boots: so did Duun, striding along beside him to the elevator.

"Where are we going, Duun?" Half protest and half question, third time posed. (Have I broken some rule, have I made Duun mad?) But he could not read Duun now, except that there were secrets and Duun was in a great hurry to get him out—(Outside?) He had not worn pants and coat since Sheon, in the coldest weather. Had never worn boots. It was only the beginning of fall.)

(He knows what I told Sagot. I've done something wrong! We're running again, like we ran from Sheon—men with guns, people are hunting us— But that's crazy. They wouldn't. I haven't talked to anyone I shouldn't, I haven't done anything—)

(Have I?)

The elevator door opened. Duun went through last and used a card to operate it. The elevator shot up and up, past all the floors between them and the roof.

The door whisked open in the cupola. Beyond the windows was true sky, gray cloud, a copter with its blades turning. Guards were waiting there to open the door for them and the wind skirled in with bitter chill. "Head down!" Duun yelled at him and ran, ducking low when he got near the copter. Thorn remembered that, ran, with the wind of the blades burning his face. He kept low until he reached the copter, and clambered in like Duun did, as fast as he could, flung himself into the seat and started fastening straps. (Like the simulator. But this isn't. This is real.) The copter upped power and surged upward with a vengeance. The tops of Dsonan's tall buildings spun dizzily into view, the deep chasms of rail-courses and maintenance-ways, the distant port with the gray light shining off the water beneath a smear of clouds.

"We're going to the airport," Duun told him, shouting in his ear. "We've got a plane waiting for us."

Thorn looked at Duun with question available to be read. Pleading.

"We're going up to Avenen," Duun shouted at him. "The Guild headquarters. You'd better settle your mind on this trip, minnow. As many hatani as they can muster are going to be coming in there and you're going to have to do it this time or not at all. There won't be a second chance.'

"For *what?*"

"To get you Guild protection, that's what."

                    *   *   *

They ran from the copter to a building and shed their quilted winter gear for suits that hugged the body. Attendants impersonal as the meds worked at fastenings, jerking at them, two at a time, rough in their frantic haste: masks next, that dangled about their necks, and helmets with a microphone inside. "Run," Duun said then, bending to snatch up the baggage, and they ran, out the door attendants held open for them, into a thunderous noisy building open at either end, where a plane sat with its fans at idle, a dip-nosed machine with stubby backswept wings. "This thing uses a runway," Duun yelled over the noise. "We're going to roll out from here—go round behind the wing, there's a ladder."

There was, pushed up against the plane. The canopy was up. Duun tossed the baggage to a guard, scrambled up the ladder and Thorn hit the treads behind him, hampered by the suit that restrained his limbs, panting when he reached the wing surface and crawled over the side close on Duun's tail. There was a pilot and co-pilot and two more seats in back in a cockpit that hardly looked big enough for the seats up front: Duun trod on one seat and dropped into place in the second, grabbed complicated belts and fastened them, and Thorn slid into the one beside him—belts like the simulator. Plug-ins for the mask hoses between their legs: Duun showed him and rammed it home. "Communications switch," Duun's voice came over the speaker over his ear, and Duun turned a face unrecognizable in an insectlike mask to show him the three way sliding switch and button on the side. The canopy was sliding forward with a whine of hydraulics. The pilot turned his head and made some signal with an uplifted hand to Duun and Duun made one back. The pilot turned around but the co-pilot was handling things: the fans picked up and the plane began to roll out of the building, faster and faster under open, overcast sky, the tires bumping on uneven pavings, the Dsonan skyline to their left unreal as a city window-view.

Faster still. They swung out onto a long expanse of concrete and the engine whine increased. The force slammed them back as the plane made its run and thundered out over the river, pulled a sharp bank and showed river for a long dizzy moment until the pilot decided to fly rightwise up again.

"Gods," Thorn said. His heart raced as clouds shredded past and still the climb kept up. (Why this fast? Why this sudden? What's Duun up to?) "How fast can this plane go?"

"Mach two plus if it has to. It's a courier plane—armed, in case you should wonder. And in case you should wonder again, yes, there's a reason. It's problems on the ground I'm worried about. I don't expect trouble, but there's that remote chance. There's a remote chance of trouble even up here. There's a ghota unit over in Hoguni province that's got one of these and I'm worried where its orders come from."

"Ghota? Aren't they guards?"

"Hired. Warrior guild. One of two. The kosan and the ghota. Our friends up front are kosanin. They take one service for life. Ghotanin rent themselves out; you don't trust them until you know how long their contract's for and whether you're the only one paying them. Like one-year wives. They're always hunting for their next advantage. Kosanin won't serve with them. That's why they're in separate units."

"Duun-hatani, I might not know enough!"

"Whatever you do don't lie and don't flinch. No one ever knows enough. That's all I can tell you now. Two rules. A third. Remember Sheon. Remember the knife on your pillow. Remember the pebble-game. But always be polite."

They came screaming in at a runway that jutted out into the sea, braked in a straining effort, and turned sharper than seemed likely toward another collection of buildings and aircraft of all sizes, most small.

And none sleek as their own. "Well," Duun said, "no one's beat us here except the locals and the happen-bys."

Thorn looked, searching. There were insignia on most of the craft. Some were striped and most were white. A copter waited, rotors turning. "Is that ours?"

"We'll hope it is." Duun's hand gripped his, painfully hard. "Hear me. From here on there will be no mistakes, Haras-hatani."

A massive building spread across the land beyond the airport. They had it in sight as they came in, a flat sprawl unlike other buildings Thorn knew. Gray stone. Hatani gray. The guild-hall.

Avenen.

The plane stopped. Engine-sound dwindled. A vehicle whisked up and towed a ladder into place. The canopy slid back, admitting chill wind.

Duun pitched their baggage out into an attendant's hands, climbed out and Thorn followed in haste. (Think, think, watch these attendants, watch everything.)

(Is it all some test? Did Duun lie? Are there really ghotanin after us and would they come here?)

Duun recovered the bundle of their belongings and headed for the copter. Thorn ran at his heels, mask flapping and the suit impairing his movements. (Watch these people. Watch all of them, watch their hands.)

Up the short couple of steps into the copter, the pilot in his place. (Duun's nose is better. He'd smell fear if that man meant trouble, even through all this oil stink.) Thorn fell into his seat beside Duun and belted in as the copter lifted, turned, heaved itself off in its tilted fashion and ground flew along in surreal intimacy after the courier-plane's sun-dazzled altitude. There was only the illusion of speed. It took long minutes to come gliding over the gray walls, over buildings that looked like a dozen architects had quarreled and each changed the plan.

A landing circle came up on a rooftop. There were men standing near it, gray-cloaked, looking up at them as the copter settled.

"They're all right," Duun said. "One thing you can believe: no ghota would wear that color here." The rotors slowed and Duun handed Thorn the baggage and climbed out.

Thorn dropped off the step and followed Duun out

from under the blades. The copter roared off again, pelting them with dust, fluttering the gray cloaks.

Duun took his helmet off and walked with it under his arm. Thorn managed the bundle enough to get his off and the wind caught his hair, cold and unforgiving. He looked at the five standing there to meet them, handsome men, one he thought was a woman, all in their gray cloaks and black kilts; and he and Duun were disheveled and dangling masks and hoses like two animate machines lately disconnected. They gazed at Duun and at him— for the first time, at him who had no like, at blowing hair and his smooth face in all its strangeness, and he could not read what they thought. That before anything else convinced him where he was. No one but Duun could go so unreadable to him until now.

But these could. These great sprawling buildings were full of those who could, every one.

"He's more imposing than the pictures would indicate," Tangan said, a wisp of a man, so old his cheeks were gaunt and even his crest had whitened. The hands clasped in his lap were gaunt and crossed with knife scars, gotten in a youth so long ago it stretched into myth in the Guild, among novices. Duun sat on the white sand which novices had raked into artistic patterns among the five huge rocks which adorned this ancient room. The lights here were electric but that was the only change from the fifth century. Generations of hatani hands had worn these great boulders dark, smoothing them as surely as the river had from which they were taken. Generations of irreverent novices had sat on them and perched there to do their raking, springing from one to the other and (sometimes, novices being the same in every generation) making it a game, leaping and jumping and thrusting at one another with rake handles.

Tangan had caught a certain rebel and oft-warned novice in that game, among others. And Duun had rued it. Four ten-days of cleaning the sand by hand. It shocked him, how much this man had aged.

"I've gotten used to his looks," Duun said.

"Have you?"

Duun met Tangan's guarded stare. "I've had near twenty years."

"Twenty years of power beyond any precedent."

"Sixteen hiding on a mountain, in a woods. Five performing unmentionable tasks which teach any man humility. So does dealing with Dsonan."

"Ah. How is the capital?"

"Carrying news to you is like bringing water to the well."

"How is the capital?"

"There are more ways to cheat on an agreement than they teach here, Tangan-hatani."

"Paradoxically prosperous times. Money. Is that what you see?"

"A lot of new money—paid out in the least educated provinces, to elect fools who'll take orders, who can only see ways to entrench themselves and make sure contracts go to the right companies. Some of these fools are evident, and shrewd countryfolk keep voting them in because the powers in their districts might buy one ten times worse and far more subtle. I tell you we should send one of the novices walking in Elsnuunan and Yoth. Some herder might be passionate enough on some given day to pose us a question. But some of these fools have passed for astute councillors, and protect themselves so well they make and break young politicians on their own."

"Shbit no Lgoth?"

"He will want to challenge."

"He has. His agent is on the way."

Duun smiled softly. "This will be a ghota, I suspect."

"You know this person?"

"Likely we've met."

"You're managing Shbit, then. How well?"

"I could do better. My hours have been occupied. So this man is a danger. I would have removed him arbitrarily but I was crippled by too much power. I could have done too much. So I could do nothing."

"I predicted this."

"I predicted Shbit but I didn't know what his name would be. There was too much money being made. And I was in Sheon wiping noses. Master, you know an answer, maybe: was there another way?"

Long silence. Tangan laced his hands and studied them and looked up. "I saw where you might put us. I thought back over all my years and all the years of the Guild and wondered where the crux was. I think it was when walls were raised. Everything led to this. You put us in a hard place; if we deny him protection we light the fire that will destroy us; if we take him we loose a firestorm. I don't want to contemplate this choice. I'm being frank with you: I ask myself at night how I taught my student that you find yourself capable of this. A hatani ought to have a flaw. A hatani ought to doubt himself enough to have a little guilt of his own. You have none. You burn with too much light, Duun-hatani. You blind me. I can't see whether you're right or wrong. Perhaps it will stop mattering. Perhaps the dark comes next. I confess to trusting you in one thing; I confess to cowardice in this. I didn't believe you'd come here, even when I knew you were training him. Free-hatani would have been my solution."

Duun contemplated a long while. "Master, you say in one breath you predicted my powerlessness; in the next you say you couldn't predict my coming here at the last."

"To infect us with your powerlessness?"

Duun looked up. "Tangan-hatani, in many respects he's a boy like other boys. Remember that."

"Is that your wisdom?"

"Tangan-hatani, if I'm a fire I'm the safer for having had a hearth to burn in."

"Do we make a lamp out of this one and set him on a shelf?"

"You might, but I'd hope it's a damn steady one."

"Keep him here?"

"Set him where you choose. The guild itself is a principal in this solution. So am I. I let you judge."

"We have another choice."

"The guild won't abdicate this."

"Do you predict what the Guild will do?"

"Is that anger, master Tangan?"

"Of course not. It's overweening pride. My student has set us all in a trap. Angmen must have felt pride like that when Chena pulled the guild gates down."

Duun folded his hands in his lap. "You'll handle it."

"Do the scars ache, Duun-hatani? You were such an agile student."

(Strike and draw.) "I have my ways of compensating, Tangan-hatani. You taught me patience, after all."

Thorn searched the room they gave him: it was a comfortable one, all bare wood and aged stone. A fire of real wood burned in the hearth: he had not had that comfort since Sheon, and it might have lured him at once to warm himself there. They gave him water with the assurance it was safe; they gave his meat and cheese with a confection of preserved beanberries. They gave him a bed of furs, and the sand on the floor was white and fine and deep, newly baked and arranged in meticulous spirals. In the next room a hot bath was waiting, milky with aromatics and soothing oils. They smiled at him, hatani smiles, neither false nor true.

And he searched the place, hunting pebbles. There were none. He was thirsty after the long flight and the running. His limbs were chafed and sweaty from the flight suit. He had set their baggage on the wooden riser that was also the bureau. "Is that gray cloak yours?" a hatani had asked, watching while he unfolded these things. "No," Thorn had said with a clear-eyed stare, knowing that they knew whose it was. "It must be Duun's," that hatani said. "It is," Thorn said back. "Give me his belongings," the hatani said then; "I'll put them in his room."

Thorn had smiled then, as certainly as he could. "I'd be a fool to disobey him; forgive me, hatani: when he blames you, tell him it was my fault. In my inexperience I couldn't tell what to do, so I followed his orders."

Another hatani had come up beside him then and

reached out his hand. "Please, visitor: let me at least put these things away for you."

"No," Thorn had said, turning the hand with a slow move of his own. "No, hatani. Forgive me."

That hatani drew back. "No one will trouble you till morning, visitor," the other said. They closed the door behind them.

(It can't be that easy. There's another trick.)

Thorn searched for it. He stripped off the suit, down to his small-kilt. He investigated the food, breaking up the cheese and tearing the meat apart. He drained the tub. He turned out the bed. He searched the closet and pulled out the bureau drawer to look at the space behind it. He racked his brain then. (Even the furniture could hide something.) So he probed the boards of the closet, he investigated the toilet and the bathtub riser, and the sink.

The faucet was dry. That was one thing amiss. He felt into it and found nothing. (Damn. *Something's* wrong there. Maybe it's to prevent my drinking that and not the pitcher.) He tried to move even the tub and the bed and the big riser near it. He investigated the walls.

And finally, he knelt down in the corner near the door and began to move the deep sand.

He found the small panel in the stone beneath when he had shifted half the sand in the room. He was panting by then. He wiped at his face with a dry and dusty arm. (No.) He remembered Sagot's fish and the bird. Duun laying his pebble on the table beside the teapot. (Trust nothing.)

He got his dress kilt and pried up the panel with his thumbnail through the cloth. He laid it back. There was a pebble in a small recess. He went to the bureau, got his razor from his kit and a square of tissue. And with that he raked the pebble out and wrapped it in tissue, replaced the lid and contemplated the long wave of sand which wanted redistributing.

("Be polite.") Perhaps it extended to leaving the room in order.

And then another thought came creeping into his mind. ("Snap. No bird. See what assumptions do?")

(Fish and bird. Pebble and pot.)

(Is there any assurance there's no second stone?)

Half the room remained. (And—gods—how much time? It might be in the sand. I can't move it except by hand.)

He put the one stone securely in his belt and started scooping the rest of the sand away.

The other secret well was in the far corner. There was no third. He stared at a great mound of sand over by the door and went and cleared the plate of the mangled food, and with the plate scooped and scattered sand as quickly as he could. His back and arms ached; his knees were raw, for all that he had tried to pad them with his spare clothing in his crawling about. His hands were abraded of their calluses, all the protection he acquired on them. He was thirsty and thanked the gods he had had breakfast at least, for he would not touch the food. (There might be a pebble in the source vessel, not even in this room. How could I trust it? And the sink. *Something's* wrong. Do I fail if I don't use the safe things? I'm sweaty. I smell awful. I *can't* go to any interview smelling like this. I look like this and now I have to offend their noses too. And I've used the only change of clothes I had.)

(Use Duun's? Gods, no.)

(What time is it?)

Thorn threw sand and spread it, waded into it and kicked it as level as he could with his feet and tried to think. He stood panting, returned to the bath and worked at the sink plumbing until his hands bled. Nothing budged it, and he sat on the cold tiles with his legs going numb. (It's not going to give. It's just the pitcher they want me to use, that's all.) And his mouth was dry, his throat raw with dust and exertion. (I've won. There were two pebbles. I've got them both. I won't drink the water, I won't eat the food; I won't sleep in the bed.)

(The mattress. Is there a rule about not breaking things?)

(In Duun's game we never did.)

(His rules. He'd have taught me. He'd have done it right.)

He heaved himself up off the tiles, limped in to the warm sand in front of the fire and sank down there, gritty and sweaty and chilled. (Gods, at least I can use the razor and the lotion I brought. That smells good. Maybe it will cover some of my stink.)

(I daren't sleep. They promised no one would bother me. I daren't believe that either.)

He felt after the pebbles in his belt and took out his prizes, never touching them with his fingers. They lay in the tissue, each unique, one with a white vein, the other white with a black. (Would someone ever cheat?)

(Fool!)

He looked at the fire, the abundant embers in the grate.

He went to the table and got the pitcher and poured it out on the coals. A great hissing of steam rose up and there was still a vivid glow in the coals.

(Oh, damn, damn, *damn!* The bath I drained. The water that won't run.)

He took the pitcher to the bath and tried the taps again, got down on his knees and dipped out all the water in the toilet with his hands: it filled the pitcher once.

The coals had livened again when he got back. He poured the water on and got the platter and poured sand on, waited a while and scooped some of it out with the plattter. There was still heat. There had been a metal grate beneath the logs. The coals lay at a forearm's depth in sand.

(How much time? O gods, I daren't wait for this.)

He cast the top sand away. He got down to the coals and used his razor again to rake them onto the platter, to turn them and examine them. Bit by bit the collection in the bathroom grew; and he got down to the deeper coals and into the heat. There was a metal grate. He got that out using his flight helmet for a hook. He moved more coals, and heat cracked the plate in two. He used the larger piece and raked more gingerly. His hands blistered now. The pain was a new encounter every time he reached in; everything he held was hot. The shard broke again and one by one the pieces he used broke to smaller and smaller shards. He abandoned his taking the coals to the bath, he only slid them out onto the sand and examined them and reached back for more. He set his knee on a hot ember and tears blurred his eyes, ran on his face and dried.

From far down in the coals, he scooped out a small black ember which was too regular and too smooth. He rolled it in the sand to cool it and scratched it with his razor. It was a pebble.

He wrapped it with the rest and never flinched at the heat. (Should I stop hunting?)

He kept going, to the last. Off to the side of the hearth, beneath old ash, he found a metal trap, and pried that open with his razor. He burned himself again getting out the small stone at the bottom. But he rolled it into the tissue too, and gingerly searched what little ash was left until he was sure there were no more.

He sat down then, slumped with his arms on his knees until he had rested. And then he began to pick the grate and the dead coals up and restore them to the fireplace.

The door opened when he was in the middle of this task. The hatani who had put him into the room were back. They looked about the room.

One walked into the bath and came back again, and Thorn got to his feet.

"Come with us," the first hatani said.

Thorn took his sooty kilt and wrapped it about himself, then started gathering up all the rest of his and Duun's belongings, every one.

"Visitor," the other said, "it's clear you're not leaving, from the condition of this room. There's no need to pack."

"Please." Thorn wrapped Duun's cloak and change of clothing in his flight suit, which, with the cloak, was the only thing left unsoiled. He gathered his razor off the floor and put it in the helmet along with the lotion bottles.

"Oh, don't be a fool!" the other said. "They'll laugh at you in the hall. You're going to meet master Tangan, with all the hatani in the house! You can't drag all that stuff in!"

"I never got to give Duun his cloak. I don't know. I might lose these things. I'll let him tell me what to do."

"Come on, then, fool. But I warn you they'll laugh. Gods—you're filthy. Do you want a change of clothes? I can lend you some."

"Thank you. I'll ask Duun when I see him."

The other gestured at the open door.

The corridor gave way to an open hall, a pit sided with many steps; and gray-cloaked hatani sat on those steps, hundreds of them. The floor was sanded and swirled with raking. There were great boulders on the sand. On each of them a hatani sat.

At the bottom of the steps in front of him stood Duun, the only one without a cloak. Duun lifted his chin slightly and Thorn walked down the steps, his escort behind him.

"You brought my cloak," Duun said. "Have they touched it at all?"

"No, Duun-hatani."

Duun held out his hand and took it and put it on. Duun extended his hand toward the farthest of the rocks. "The last is master Tangen."

Thorn walked down and across the sand, along the narrow path the hatani on the boulders had walked, like the form of a tree. He heard others walk behind him. He stopped in front of the farthest. His belongings were still in his arms.

"You may set those things down." master Tangan said, and lifted his hand in that way Duun had which meant a thing could be trusted. "You will stand." Duun came and stood near him. The two who had brought him stood on the other side. Thorn set his belongings on the ground in front of him.

"You are untidy, young man," Tangan said. "Is this a way to come to this hall?"

"Forgive me, master Tangan."

"Was there something amiss with the room?"

Thorn hesitated. It seemed the right question. He reached into his belt and drew out the tissue. He unfolded it and showed the pebbles. His burns hurt and his sooty hands bled onto the tissue, shaking in spite of all he could do. (Were they all? Did I miss one?)

"Did he drink the water?"

"The pitcher was empty," one of his escorts said.

"Did he eat the food?"

"The food was crumbled," the other said.

"There was a pebble in the pitcher from which that pitcher was poured. There was a pebble in the plate from which that plate was served. Did you drink or eat?"

"No, master Tangan. I poured the water on the fire. I didn't eat. I didn't touch my hand to my mouth after touching the food."

"How can I know this is the truth?"

At first it seemed an accusation. Then it occurred to him it was another question. "You're hatani, master Tangan. If I couldn't find a trick like that you could read me too."

A moment of silence, all about the room. "Did you bathe?"

"No, master Tangan."

"That seems evident."

He was too weary. He only stared up at Tangan, still holding the pebbles.

"What did you do with the water?"

"I let it out, master Tangan, hunting for pebbles."

"Was there one?"

"Not in that tub."

"Lay the pebbles that you found on the sand one by one."

Thorn bent and slipped them from the tissue one at a time. At the third there was a stirring in the seats; at the fourth a greater stirring. He straightened and looked up at the old, old man.

"Four is unusual," master Tangan said simply. "Two beyond the food and water would have passed you.

That's the first test. The second is myself. Tell me the worst thing you ever did."

Almost Thorn let his face react. And stopped himself. He thought a moment. (Losing Sheon? But that wasn't from knowledge. That was my ignorance. That blames Duun.) "I shouted at my teacher Sagot, master Tangan. Yesterday."

"Have you stolen?"

"Only from Duun."

There was another stirring in the seats.

"Have you lied?"

"Sometimes."

"Have you killed anyone?"

"No, master Tangan."

"Have you used your skill in a wrong way?"

He shut his eyes. And opened them. It was easy to count. "Three times, master Tangan. When I shouted at Sagot and when I hit another student and when I threatened him."

"You're very fast on that answer. Aren't there more?"

Thorn thought again. "I've quarreled with Duun."

"So have I, visitor." A mild ripple of laughter went about the hall. Beside him Duun ducked his head. The master's face never changed. "We have a case in the guild. One member claims a knife another claims. How will you resolve it?"

Thorn bit his lip. Panic rushed through him. (It's a wrong question. There's no answer. Dare I say that?) He found himself shivering in the chill. "Master Tangan, there aren't any such hatani in the guild, who would quarrel over property."

"We have another case. Two sisters marry a man for a one-year each in succession. But no sooner has the first marriage been consummated than the man divorces that wife and marries a third for a three-year. How will you judge?"

"Master Tangan, how do they make the question?"

"The first sister says: Judge between me and my sister and that woman."

(Not the man.)

"That's not a hatani matter, master Tangan. They ought to go to the magistrate."

"They persist. They make the same request."

"Where is their property?"

"They have a house and shop from their father and mother. The man is living and working with the new wife in a property he owns. The new wife is tanun-guild."

"Let them go live in their own house and find a new husband."

"Explain."

"The women want this man more than he wants them and they hate the new wife. They could never share with her."

Master Tangan lifted a hand. Beckoned to someone. Thorn resisted the impulse to turn, but he heard someone walking up. More than one.

"One more case," Master Tangan said. "Look at this woman."

Thorn turned and his heart jolted.

It was Betan. Betan, in a pale blue kilt, a dark blue cloak, with her hands folding before her and her ears laid flat. Her scent reached him on a waft of wind. It was still flowers.

(O Betan.) Exhaustion battered at him. (Hatani after all?)

Her face betrayed nothing.

"Look at me," Master Tangan said. "This woman accuses you of assaulting her. Of using your persuasion to seduce her and when she saw you naked and knew your physical difference would harm her, she tried to get away, and you used your skill to restrain her until Duun no Lughn intervened. She asks a hatani judgment of me."

(*Was* that what she thought? Was that what I did?)

"What do you say?"

"I—was in a room alone with her. Everything she says could be true."

"Duun-hatani, you were a witness."

"I came in and this woman ran out," Duun said. "I

ordered her to leave. I witnessed an embrace in which the woman struggled and broke free."

"As you came in."

"Yes, master Tangan."

"What else did you observe?"

"Anger on my student's part, toward me. He said: 'I wish you had come later.' The woman said nothing. Later my student said. 'I wanted to love her.' I explained the differences would have harmed her."

"He had no knowledge of this?"

"It's possible he didn't understand."

"Did you?"

"No. Yes." Thorn struggled for his composure. "I pushed her back, master Tangan. She smelled afraid and I pushed her back."

"Away from you."

"He's lying," Betan said. "He's hatani and he's lying with a straight face."

"What do you ask for him?"

"Send him back to Dsonan. Don't let him in the guild."

"What do you ask for her, visitor?"

"I think it's a trap," Thorn said. "I think this is another test and she's hatani."

"Why do you say that?"

"She moves like one."

"You're wrong, young man. She's not hatani, free or guilded."

"She's ghota," Duun said. "Or I'm blind. And she's a fool to come here."

Betan stood there. (Ghota?) Thorn stared at her. He had expected men with guns. (Betan? Ghota?)

"This is my judgment," Tangan said. "Leave this house. I'll not begin a guild war. You have half an hour to reach the airport. Take my warning seriously."

Betan turned on her heel and walked, carefully, up the track past the hatani on the boulders, up the steps at the end of the hall. Thorn trembled, but it was cold; it was the burns. Where Betan had been, where part of his youth had been, was cold inside.

"One more question," Tangan said.

"Master?" Thorn turned and looked up at the old man on the rock.

"What have you done today that you take the most pride in?"

Thorn blinked. It betrayed him and he was chagrined, but his eyes stung and his knees wobbled under him. "Getting Duun's cloak here."

There was laughter, all round the room, stinging laughter, hoarse and harsh.

"It's a novice's trick," master Tangan said. His face relaxed and kindness came through. "Novices who grow up in the guild house never get caught by that, except the first day they arrive. But you weren't told. And you honor your teacher. They laugh because you found four pebbles besides the water and the food. That's very rare. I do fault you on letting the water out. But you made it up the hard way. Those burns will scar, young man. I think you should get them treated before we send you back."

(I've lost, then.)

"You're apprenticed to Duun no Lughn for as long as Duun sees fit. Beyond that point you'll do as you see fit. You have the wisdom to refrain from judgment where you have no knowledge. That's very important. Be gentle. Be merciful. Give true judgments. All other rules of the guild flow from these. A free-hatani judges and the guild will not involve itself. When you judge, the guild will shed blood to back you. Always remember that, Haras-hatani."

"Yes, master Tangan." And for a moment the master's face let him see past another barrier. (This is a worried man. The hatani up there see it now. They were startled into laughter. There is anger in this room.) He slid his glance toward Duun and saw the other half of that expression. (They know something. No. Duun knows and master Tangan discovers it.)

"Take him and get those burns looked to, Duun-hatani."

XIII

"Take care of him," Duun said in leaving him. These were hatani meds, who took Thorn's clothes and made him stand on a plastic grating and rest his hands on tables on either side for them to work on. Two more meds with soap and a small clear water hose started with his hair and washed him on down with sponges: gray water spattered down and swirled away into the white plastic grate, smoke and sand, and the knee stung and throbbed, but their touch was quick and gentle. The meds washed his hands too, but in a different way, with greater care. "This will be cold," one said: something smelled pungent and likely to hurt; it hit his burned right hand with a shock that seemed for a moment to go to the bone, as the med sprayed a clear liquid on. But numbness followed, or the cessation of pain. It was so great a change Thorn knew then how much pain he had been in. The washing went on, and they did the other hand. The right they immersed in something gelatinous; and immersed again in something else, and that hardened to a shiny plasticity while one dried his hair and another saw to his knee and bandaged it. Their touch was kind. So was their manner. "Please, could I have a drink?" Thorn said, meaning from the hose when they could spare a moment. He had wet his lips while they rinsed his hair and face, but was thirsty again. The one drying his hair left off and brought him a cup of water, holding it for him to drink because they were working on his hands. Thorn looked into this man's eyes and saw nothing but kindness.

"You ought to go to bed," the med said who worked on his right hand, "but we understand otherwise. That's finished now. Carry the elbows bent as much as you can, don't close the hands or lift anything, hear, till the gel peels."

But the one working on his left hand finished and drew him by the elbow over to ordinary ground. Another brought a flight suit and a helmet, his own, Thorn thought dizzily, because he had scarred one earpiece. They took it up and began to put it on him with as much efficiency as they had used on his wounds.

(So we're going back.) The meds in Dsonan would take him then and lay him on a table and mutter dark things while they poked and pried into what these meds had done, and they would hurt.

There would be the tapes again. Nothing would have changed. Thorn shivered while they were seeing to the fastenings, and one stopped and felt of the pulse in his neck. "Go straight to bed when you get to Dsonan," the man said.

"We can't give him anything," another said, and looked worried, not the way the meds at home looked, but gentle. "We don't dare. Hope to the gods he doesn't react to the gel." A pat on Thorn's shoulder. "Are you sick at your stomach?"

"No, not very."

They went on with their pulling and tugging. The suit grew tighter. "Damn. He can't manage the helmet."

(Why this haste? What's wrong? Why were they worried? Ghotanin? They let Betan go. Did she get to the airport? Did she go?) The thought of Betan dying afflicted him with pain. (Even if she's my enemy. She was brave to come here.)

"There." A last tug. "That's right. Hold the helmet in your arm, don't use your hands. Call Duun, someone."

"He's outside."

"Thank you," Thorn said, looking at them. He meant it. And one of them opened the door and called Duun in. Duun was in his flightsuit again and had a gray cloth bag with black straps slung over his shoulder, and his helmet in that arm.

"He'll manage, will he?" Duun asked.

"Take care of him," a med said. And to Thorn: "Keep the arms bent. All right? Good-bye."

That was all, then, Duun waited by the door, threw one look past him at the meds as if to thank them, and let Thorn out into the hall. Hatani came and went, none in their gray cloaks now. Most looked to have business on their minds and some looked to be in haste. Many looked at him and Duun as they passed.

(They don't hate me.) Thorn was used to that special look people had when he walked in on them. Even Elanhen. Even Sphitti. Especially Cloen and especially the meds. And Betan in the hall just now. (Their faces don't show it, maybe.)

(But they're hatani. They *know* me. They know me, inside, past the skin and the eyes and the way I look, that I'm like them. *True judgment,* master Tangan called it. Hatani judgment.) Thorn felt his throat swell and his eyes sting. (I want to know these people. I want to stay here—just a day or two, just that, I want to talk to them and be with them, and live here all my life.)

There was one hall after another, and at last stairs leading up to the roof. Duun stopped here and took him by the arms to make him look at him.

"Betan made the port. She took off and they're tracking her. The radar net shows another pair of ghota aircraft just left the ground at Moghtan. The kosan guild is putting planes up from Dsonan."

Thorn blinked, trying to take this in. (For me. For my being here. That's impossible.) He felt numb. "What's Betan up to?"

"She won't get through to the guild. Missiles ring this place. Hatani are headed for Ellud and Sagot this moment, to protect them. And others whose lives might be in question."

Colder and colder. The numbness reached Thorn's heart. "We've got to get there!"

"Others are doing that job. We've got another one." Duun let go Thorn's left arm and pulled him up the stairs in haste. "The first part of it is getting you out of here."

*   *   *

It was no easy matter getting into the plane. Duun shoved up from behind the way they had gotten into the copter and Thorn clambered over the rim and into the cockpit. The skin on his knee tore as he tumbled into the seat, wriggled in and groped as best he could for straps; Duun fell in beside him and snatched the buckle from him, jammed it together, took his connections and rammed those into the sockets before he saw to himself. The engines were roaring, pushing them into motion, and the canopy was sliding forward overhead. Pilot and co-pilot were ambiguous creatures of plastic and metal, moving thin arms to flip switches in the interval of the seats. The plane picked up speed, swung out onto the runway and straightened itself into a run that slammed them back into the seats.

Wisps of clouds poured past; the sun chased reflections across the cockpit and the plane came about and kept on with the sun on its right wing.

"We're going to pick up our escort in a few minutes," a thin voice came over the speaker in the helmet. The pilot or co-pilot was talking on their channel. "They'll meet us at Delga."

Duun acknowledged that. The voice came again. "We've just got word. We've got ghota craft headed our way. Our escort's going to intercept. Planes are in the air at Homaan. Council's going into session now."

Thorn leaned his head against the cushioned seat and stared ahead of him at the milky glare of light, the black, surreal figures of the pilots. There was no world but this, no past or future. He hung motionless above the earth while the sky rushed faster and faster at them and small voices from the ground spoke to the pilots (who themselves could do nothing) and told them that the world was in chaos. Duun spoke of missiles. Of intercepts. Of aircraft which would be lifting from one city and another around the world, across seas and continents. People down there were looking up in fear at planes they could not see, expecting missiles to fall on them. Children standing on that brown rock at Sheon, next to the bent tree, would look up and wave at white trails in the sky.

("See us, here we are! Hello!")—while dreadful missiles roared off in fire and smoke.

(This can't be happening.)

(There is no *can't,* minnow.)

"Someone's on intercept with us." The pilot's voice again. "Bearing 45 low."

"From the sea," Duun said. "That's Betan. I figured. Hang on, minnow."

The plane turned in flight. Pressure dragged at them, pulled at jaws and eyes and bowels and Thorn's nose ran; there was a pounding in his ears. The plane rocked. They went into a steep bank. (We're going to crash. We were hit.) Thorn rolled his head against the seat as his heart went wild and the sun spun up again and over the right wing.

"That's a miss on their side, a hit on ours. It's down."

(What are they talking about? The other plane? Betan?)

The milky light surrounded them again, implacable. On a screen a tiny point of light went out and Betan no longer existed, a plane scattered itself in shards and fragments, lives went out— ("That's a miss on their side, a hit on ours.") Their own plane had fired. That had been that shaking. And Betan was dead in a moment, with all her courage and her skill. ("It's down.")

"Betan," Duun said, "headed out over the sea and came back again. Points to her. She might have won it right then."

"She's dead."

There was a silence for a moment. The sky was incredibly smooth. Surreal again.

"There's a man named Shbit," Duun said. "A councillor. You know Dallen Oil? You remember your companies?"

"Yes."

"Well, they're not only oil, they're a lot of things. Energy, trade, manufacture. They've got a lot of power in Council. They saw it slipping. They got Shbit elected: one of their own. Shbit wanted you transferred out of Ellud's wing and into one where things are more accessible— where you'd be more—public. Where politics could benefit by controversy. Where I could be weakened. They can't overthrow a hatani judgment. But they can undermine it. They can come at you from so many sides you can't track them all. Shbit tried that. He had a few ghotanin in his employ. Personal guards. They're ordinary as rain in private service. He had a few free-hatani he knew where to reach back home. A few kosanin, gods help them. And the fool got Betan past a fool of a personnel supervisor, the security chief, the division chief, Ellud—gods, five years ago; while we were still at Sheon. Brightest young security officer Ellud had. She ought to have been."

"Elanhen and Sphitti and Cloen—"

"Security as well. Sphitti's a free-citizen, son of a woman I know. Elanhen and Cloen from the station: kosanin. Damn good kids. Betan; free-citizen, career security. So they said. They left out pertinent details in her case."

The smoothness continued. The milky light never varied. To one side and the other cold terms like *intercept* flew on radios; ("It's down. . . .") Lives ended. Beyond illusion-forests in city windows missile silos opened like flowers to the sun.

". . . Betan knew we were succeeding. That was what tipped the balance. She had help, gods know; all of Shbit's resources, forged records. She made a foul-up of it even so—a free-ghota might be that careless. But she wasn't working for Shbit. She meant to foul things up. Kill you if she could. Doublecross Shbit. I know it was a possibility. I took my time settling that affair and it was damn near too much time, while I was working on those tapes."

"You—"

"While you were out. Daily. Constantly. Never mind that. I'd spread myself too far; I'd hastened things, and my time was occupied; and I was held to law. I traced Betan as far as Shbit. When I learned she'd surfaced again in Shbit's keeping and stayed alive—*then* I knew either Shbit himself was ghota or Shbit was being worked by one. I saw the pattern."

Thorn turned his face from the sun a second time and

looked at Duun, at a face rendered faceless by the mask, sun reflecting on plastic eyeshields.

"Betan," Duun said, distant through the speaker, "may have been aimed all her life for what she did. Guild-service. A special kind of ghota. Gods know what the ghotanin had been feeding Shbit for information out of the department. Shbit was up against the ghota guild and totally outmatched . . . playing their moves against me and thinking they were his. Even Dallen Company. I can't say I didn't expect guild trouble. But there was law, again—I was trying to keep from destroying the Council's autonomy. Dammit, they gave me too much. I let Shbit live because I knew he was a trigger I could pull, one the ghota would respond to. There's a spy in Ellud's office *I've* let stay. Sagot's mine."

(Something's still faithful in this world. O Sagot, one bit of truth.)

". . . And you did what we'd been waiting for."

"What did I do? That *tape*? That damned stupid *tape*? The numbers and the pictures?"

"You survived it. You survived it, minnow, and you read it. And the meds would know what you knew in one more day—and the instant they knew, that unstopped leak would send the news straight to our enemies; while Ellud wouldn't want to let you leave the building—I could overrule him, but he could have fought me on it and fouled things up beyond recovery. He's a good man; and honest; and he always wants more time than the opposition gives him. Some things I couldn't even tell Tangan himself. Like guild war. Like the fact I'd pulled the trigger."

"This Shbit sent Betan when he knew we'd left the city."

"You're catching onto it. He gave a ghota a courier plane and never suspected she'd been hired by her own guild to be hired by him. He had to give her a ghota crew: no kosan would fly her to us."

"Why come *here* for the gods' sake?"

"She couldn't overtake us. For Shbit—she was supposed to go in and wail and howl and put on a good act.

Disgrace you. Keep you out of the guild. Create scandal.
For the ghota—she was to walk in there just the way she
did and deliver a message from her guild. You read Tangan. He wouldn't bend. That's clear to you and me—but
ghotanin have a guiding belief that everything can be
bought if you set the terms up right; she walked in there
and saw she hadn't the right coin . . . by her way of
looking at it. It was clear when she said keep you out
the way she did she wasn't talking for Shbit. Tangan
knew it then. Read what she was and knew what I'd
done to him and knew why. And forgave us both." Duun
was silent for a long while.

And men and women died for them, would be dying,
now, in planes which darted and fired missiles no one
saw except on screens.

(Damn you, Duun. Is even this a maneuver?)

"I liked him," Thorn said at last. "I liked Tangan,
Duun."

"I didn't betray him. I gave him the power he needed.
I set him free. Do you understand?"

"To stop the ghota?"

"To back what I do. Don't you understand it yet, minnow? You will." Static sputtered, Duun's hand at the
side of his mask clicking the other channel in. "How are
we doing?"

"Dsonan's screen's going to drop in a minute to let us
through," the pilot's voice came to them. "It's hot up
ahead. Two missile strikes got to the base. The Third
Wing's going to throw everything they've got at them
while we get in, sey Duun."

"Gods save them," Duun muttered. "Gods save us all.
Do it right, Manan."

"Damn sure trying."

Thorn eased over to look out the canopy as best he
could. There was no sight of anything beyond their wings,
beyond the pitiless sun and the endless sky.

Static snapped again. "Not to make you nervous, minnow," Duun said, "but what that means is Dsonan's key-
ing its missile defenses down to give us a window to get
in, and don't ask me what happens if something glitches.

Kosanin are moving to be sure nothing gets through that gap for the five critical minutes it's going to take us to get through that screen. Then it goes up behind us. When we get on the ground we get over that side and off that wing: and it's going to be hotter than hell. You go down that wing edge and jump once I'm down. I'll steady you in landing. Don't think about anything, just run for that shuttle pad and go."

"Shuttle?"

"Tallest thing you'll see in front of you."

"I know what it looks like! Where are we going?"

"Station."

Static snapped. The nose of the plane dipped in a dive. Altitude traded for speed.

("Mach two plus if it has to.")

Thorn trembled. There was pain, pain from his burns, from warmth; he gasped at the sluggish thin feed of the mask and his nose and throat and eyes were raw. Sweat ran on him. There was a high strange sound, a sense that quivered through his bones and bowels like elemental fear. (I'm scared, Duun; Duun, I don't want to die like this—)

There was a blur ahead of them, the first substance there had been, a shadow in front of them, a blaze of light.

(That's ground coming up, that's the river—O gods, that's ground, the city—)

Pressure began, a constriction of his limbs, the pain again—the world tilted violently and became half earth and sky split vertically, flipped straight again as Thorn felt the straining of the straps. (They'll break, I'll go up and into the canopy, I can't hold on—)

Then another force slammed in, and they were losing speed. One ear failed to pop, reached a painful point and pressure went on and on in acute agony that made one fabric with other things.

Smoke on the horizon. Smoke palling the city in the one direction, a gray blur to either side.

A runway ribboned out of the forward perspective, a straight pale line ahead. The plane came in knife-straight, sank on its haunches in a long jarring rush before the thunder of the reversing engines made headway against their speed. More speed down. More. Tires squealed and the jets roared again as a gantry loomed up, a shuttle poised like a white tower against the smoke-stained sky. On the horizon a red sun burst and swelled and faded. Another, burning bright.

Closer and closer. The plane jolted and thumped and rocked over uneven pavement; there was a truck coming toward them. The plane's canopy retracted and metal stank, pinging and popping with heat. Duun reached and yanked connections as the engines whined down; popped Thorn's belt and his own, stood up and vaulted the side. Thorn scrambled up on the seat, flinched at heat and saw Duun spring from the wing's back edge to the truckbed and go to one knee as he landed; Thorn rolled over the side and hit the wing as Duun got up, strode once on a yielding surface and leapt for the truckbed and Duun's arms.

Duun and he both went down, rolled, and the truck lurched into motion, leaving the plane dwindling behind. On the horizon more suns burst, and one flowered in the sky and faded in a smudge of smoke.

Duun held onto him. Thorn trembled, felt Duun unfasten his mask for him and let him fill his lungs with cold gasps of air. Duun clenched him the tighter as the truck whined and jolted and the gantry towered into view, white girders against the smoke-ravaged sky. It braked. "Out," Duun said, and helped him balance as he got up, vaulted the rear of the truck to the ground and was there to steady him when his feet hit the pavement.

"Come on. *Run!*" Duun dragged him for the gantry, for the white wall that was a shuttle fin. There was an elevator, its door open, and a woman who motioned at them hurry, hurry, in a violence like an oath. They made it in: the woman shut the door and moved a bar-switch that set them moving up. The whole elevator reeked of their suits and sweat and fear, and Thorn staggered as it lifted. Duun's hand met his chest. "Hold on, dammit, Thorn! Hold on!"

Thorn locked his knees, leaned on the wall with his forearm. Girders whipped past the window in a blur; then the woman jammed down the switch and the car slammed to a stop. The door opened, showing them a thick-walled open hatch.

"Come on," Duun said, and shoved Thorn into it and followed. Thorn looked back in distress as explosions came like distant thunder.

Still outside, the woman swung the hatch shut, disappearing in a diminishing crescent of the murky sunlight. Thump. (What about her?) The world seemed an unsafe place, no place to leave alone. But Duun spun him about and all but threw him into a seat in this cubbyhole of a place, one of three seats built flat on this dimly lighted floor.

"Belt in," Duun said, and Thorn groped for belts as Duun fell into his seat and got them, fastened them for him and got his own helmet off. Duun hugged it to his breast and pushed a button on the arm of the seat. "We're set, we're set back here."

"Understand you clear."

Thorn stripped his helmet off with his wrists; Duun helped him, bent and stowed it in a bin in the floor beside his seat. The lid latched and echoed hollowly. Thorn lay there breathing in great gasps while Duun secured his own belts. "They're waiting on the attendant to get down the escape route," Duun said, his own head back, his eyes shut. "Driver of that truck's got to get out too."

"What about the plane?"

"Maran and Koga—they're headed out and over to Drenn. Refuel and up again. It's their wing that's taking the beating out there. They'll have a window—ours: they've got to take that missile screen down again for us to clear this port."

(People are dying. Everywhere those shells go off. All those people—)

A thunder began to grow. (They're hitting close to us.) Sweat flooded Thorn's body in a sickly sense of doom; then the sound went to his bones and the force came down on him, dizzying and all-encompassing. Another thunder began, pieces of the ship rattling, as if it was all coming apart. (We won't make it, we won't make it—some missile will stop us.)

The weight grew, pressing him down into the couch.

They were leaving the world. Everything. There was void ahead, incomprehensible and without end.

(I looked up at the moon and tried to see where they were, but of course I couldn't.)

(The world's wide, minnow, wider than you know.)

(The world's beautiful. Haven't you seen it in pictures?)

XIV

There was peace, eerie peace and stillness, in which moving cost little and breathing cost far less. A gentle air touched Thorn's face and a breeze stirred against his cheek.

Duun floated above him, balanced crazily on one arm that gripped the back of the seat. Thorn blinked, and Duun freed him of the restraints. A little move of Thorn's arm against the seat freed him from the cushion.

"We're up," Thorn murmured. "We're up."

"Where the worlds spin, yes. You can be easy awhile, minnow. It's a great ocean you've come to. It's easy to move and easy to move too far." Duun grinned at him. (Can he smile after all that? Can he be happy? Can anyone ever, after that?)

Duun pulled gently at his wrist— "Keep your arm stiff. Never mind, don't try to hold." The fastenings of the flightsuit gave way. Duun's own suit drifted in pieces, loosed at chest and wrists and ankles. Duun worked him free: torque set them spinning and they drifted together while the cabin revolved slowly about them.

Freedom, then, Thorn drifted, shut his eyes in exhaustion, half-slitted them to watch Duun come and go through a hole he had not seen before. A hatch had opened above them. In the lazy spin Thorn caught sight of white light, of shonun bodies that drifted to and fro about some business. Duun went up to that place and sailed down again like some graceful diver. Duun's ears were up; his eyes were lively and bright.

(He knows this, he knows all of it, he's been this way more than once.)

"Where are we going, Duun?"

"Hush. Rest. People are busy."

"What's happened to the world?"

"It's still there. Fighting's centered mostly now around the shuttleports and Avenen and Suunviden, but it's dying down now—now that we're away and there's not a damn thing they can do about it."

"Why did we do it? Where are we going?"

"Why, why, and why? There's a shower on board. I'm going to use it. When I have I'm going to tape some plastic around those hands of yours and make you pleasanter company." Duun drifted off from him. Thorn twisted in midair and saw him disappear down yet another hole. Thorn tried to maneuver himself, spun and brought up against the cushions, remembering only at the last moment not to use his hands; he rebounded helplessly and drifted, waiting.

A vacuum went on in the shower and Thorn watched the water droplets run in clinging trails until they were gone and the lamp dried him. He elbowed the latch and drifted out again, turned once in midair in slow revolution before Duun snagged him and wrapped a plain blue kilt about him, tugged the self-belt about his waist with a touch familiar years ago, exactly the snugness, exactly the way Duun had done it then—Thorn looked into Duun's face from a grownup angle, met him eye-to-eye when Duun finished with the small pat on the side he had given him when he was small. Time went backward and forward, spun like the room.

"Follow me," Duun said, trod on the cabinet wall and drifted upward with unerring grace through the narrow hatch.

Thorn kicked off, angled his body with what grace he could manage and sailed through in Duun's wake, followed him again, up into a light, into the mind and heart of the shuttle where crew came and went.

They stared—(they shocked; they want to be polite; they don't know whether to stare or not, whether staring's honest or only rude.) Duun drifted on and stopped and Thorn imitated his move, ignoring the stares— (The world in flames. They *ought* to hate me. I don't blame them. I was born for it.) And he floated strangely free, taking all their blame, ignoring their eyes on his smooth pale skin, suffering Duun's grip on his arm that drew him toward the window.

The bright blue world—was there. Its fires were invisible. The perspective denied everything—the fires became one more illusion beyond a window; his life shrank to invisible scale, lived out on a mountain and in a city whose burning could not even stain the clouds.

He stared and stared, and the tears beaded in his eyes until his blinking drove them. He wiped his eyes and a droplet floated free from his fingertip, perfect, a wobbling orb like the world in space.

"Do you love it?" Duun asked. "Do you love it, minnow?"

"Yes," Thorn said when he could say anything at all. He wiped his eyes again. "It's still there."

"So long as you aren't on it," Duun said, and it was truth; he had seen it. Thorn's chest ached. He put out a hand and touched the window and the world.

The ship left the world, while they belted in below. The engines kicked them hard and long.

Thorn shut his eyes. I can't sleep, I can never sleep, he told himself, but the strength ebbed put of him and he felt the pain reminding him of what he was and what it cost, constantly, like the beats of his heart. "Drink," Duun said, and fed him something through a straw that he wanted no more of after the first sip. "Drink it." Again, in that voice that had drilled him all his life, and it left no choice. Thorn drank, and slept; and when he woke Duun slept by his side—his unscarred side toward him, that side that gave its own illusions, of what Duun had been before.

Thorn shut his eyes again. (Is Sagot alive? Did Manan and the other pilot live? The guild—did the missiles defend it?)

(Children standing on the rock at Sheon, seeing red

suns bloom on their horizons. Smoke palls the sky. Thunder shakes the ground.)

(In the halls at Dsonen people run in confusion, not knowing where to go.)

The sun whirls past the canopy and men like great insects manage the controls. The plane hangs in the sky and time stops. The war goes on in a moment frozen forever, all war, all time.

Sagot sits in her lonely hall. There is thunder. She sits frail and imposing at the end of that room, waiting in front of all the empty desks.

A shuttle flies in place and the universe rushes past it, sweeping the world out of its reach.

There were mundane things. There had to be: there were bodily needs, and Thorn cared stubbornly for himself, once Duun had shown him how things worked; there was a breakfast of sorts, and Thorn found his hands a little less painful. Crew came drifting through their compartment in the urge of like necessities and coming back again. There was still the surreal about it, like the drifting course they took, a leisurely pace, a slowness like a dream.

"Where are we going, Duun?"

"Gatog."

"Is that the station?" Thorn had never heard it called that.

"It's one of them." Duun said.

(*Is* there more than one?) Sagot's teaching developed cracks, fractured in doubts. (Is no truth entire?)

"We had a report," Duun said, "the ghotanin have sent a messenger to Tangan offering to talk. The kosan guild refused at first, but they're going to relent."

"Is that part of your solution?" Thorn asked. His mind worked again. Duun looked at him with that closed hatani stare to match what Thorn gave him.

"Balance is," Duun said. "It was never my intention to destroy the ghota."

"They call you *sey* Duun."

"It's a courtesy these days."

"You led kosanin?"

"Once."

No more than that. Duun would not be led.

More of sleep and meals and bodies. The gel on his hands began to peel. The crew grew familiar: Ghindi, Spart, Mogannen, Weig. Half-names. Pet-names. But it was enough. Duun knew them and talked with them in quiet tones, and talked sometimes with voices on the radio from one end or the other of their journey.

None of it concerned Thorn. And everything did. He eavesdropped in mortal dread and caught nothing but city names and Gatog's name and jargon after that.

Intercept, Thorn heard once, and his heart delayed a beat. He looked Duun's way and kept looking Duun's way when Duun stopped the conversation.

"Minnow," Duun said to him, drifting toward Thorn. And nodded to him that he ought to follow.

Duun drifted down into the place they slept in and came to a graceful stop. Thorn reached with his foot and a half-healed hand and did almost as well. "Are there ghotanin here?" Thorn asked.

"Maybe there are," Duun said. "They're not our job to fight."

"Is it a game?" Thorn asked in anger. "Am I supposed to discover what we're going to? Where I am? *Isn't it over, Duun?*"

Duun looked at him in a strange, distant way. "It's only beginning. It's not the right question, Haras-hatani. None of those is the right question."

Thorn grew very still inside.

"Think on it." Duun said. "Tell me when you know."

The void that had sped past him, about him, shrank to a single familiar dimension.

("Again," Duun said, standing over him on the sand. *"Again."*)

Thorn sucked in a breath and stared at Duun as Duun pushed off and soared up through the lighted hatchway like some sleek gray man-sized fish.

(He's been waiting for me. Where have I been? Where has my mind been? It was *pity* he felt for me.)

(He *belongs* here. This is his element, like Sheon; and the city-tower and the guild-hall never were.)

Thorn pushed off and extended his body the way Duun had, with the same grace, conscious of it. He came up into the light of the crew-compartment, found his touch-point with one sure motion and drifted to the counter-hold he sought, there where he could see Duun and the others.

They were receiving and sending messages again. Duun listened and answered in that jargon again which made little sense. "Is it custom," Thorn asked when there was a lull, "to talk like that; or have we enemies up here?"

"Is that your question?" Duun asked.

"I'll tell you when I ask it." Thorn held to the counter and felt the sensitivity of his burns. "If this is an ocean, this minnow had better learn to swim. He should have learned days ago."

Duun looked at him and slanted his ears back in an expression Thorn had seen a thousand times. "There are enemies. The same as we met on earth. The companies who maintain factories and mines up here use ghotanin for guards. And some of them have ships. Not like the shuttle. The shuttle's not built for what we're doing. Ships are moving, some friendly, some not. We've burned all the fuel we have getting out of earth's pull. It wasn't a scheduled launch. It was the reserve shuttle we used. One's always kept launch-ready: the companies like their schedules kept. And getting it powered up without letting Shbit and the ghotanin trace that order to me—that took some work."

(You knew it all in advance, then. Dammit, Duun—)

Duun might have smiled; on the ruined side such motions were ambiguous and made him deceptive to read. It might have been a grimace. "Right now," Duun said, "we're on course for Gatog. It lies some distance out. We're not capable of stopping, of course. But that's not a great problem. A miner's already moving into line to be on that course a few weeks hence, a simple salvage job. If nothing intervenes. We're moving very slowly. Our enemies are closing at ten times our speed. We have no weapons. Those ships do. Fortunately so do our friends. It's a very touchy business, minnow, hour by hour. A ship spends fuel; the other side does; each move changes the intercept point and the schedule. We're the only fixed quantity because we *can't* maneuver, no more than a world or a moon. We just sail on. And hour by hour those ships out there burn a little, figure, discover what the enemy's doing, refigure, maneuver and do another burn. Faster and faster. It depends on how willing crews are to die, and at what point they commit themselves. For the nearest of our friends the earth is close to the infinity point: they were never built to land, and if they overspend on fuel they'll not have the capacity to do the necessary vector change and get back again: the gravity well is just that, a treacherous slope, and a ship that spends everything can find itself going downhill. For our enemies, the infinity point *is* infinity—or some star a hundred years away. And someone could eventually fetch them back. They don't need to be as brave. Or as careful."

"What will our friends do?"

"Some of them are hatani."

"They'll do what they have to, then." The guild house. The laughter which no longer sounded cruel, but innocent and brave. (They didn't know then they were in such close danger. Even hatani failed to read it. They saw the ghota; they knew trouble had come in, but they couldn't know it all.) "Are they armed?"

"Yes."

Thorn looked about him, at the crew who worked so unceasingly, who talked calmly over the radio and sometimes joked with each other or did whimsical things, like sailing a morsel of food toward a fellow crew member for that one to catch. "These are brave people," Thorn said, as if he stood at the foot of some great mountain. It was that kind of awe, making him quiet inside. He thought of Manan and his co-pilot, the plane runnning ahead of the maelstrom the shuttle would kick up. The woman at the shuttle hatchway, sealing them in, staying in the shattered world.

Sagot kissing him good-bye.

Tangan accepting an old student's betrayal of him and giving kindness to one more incoming boy.

Tears filled his eyes and he wiped at them and found Duun looking at him. "I'm sorry, Duun. I don't know why I do that."

"Don't you know by now I can't?" Duun asked him.

Thorn stared at him with the streaks drying on his face.

"Duun," Weig said. And Duun went to see what Weig wanted.

"We're down to twenty hours," Weig said.

There was suit drill. "If we get hit, at least there's some chance." Duun said, and opened that long locker which hugged one side of the bridge, where spacesuits nestled one behind the other like embryos in a womb. Duun pulled one out and shoved it at him, fastenings all undone. "Try it."

Thorn tucked up and got his feet inserted, struggling with the rest. Duun showed him once how to do the fastenings, then made him do it over and over again until his hands hurt. Duun showed him how the backpacks fit against the rear of the seats, and how an automation on the seat back would bring the helmet down and release it in his grip. "So you don't have to sit in that damn rig for hours," Duun said, and showed him the air connectors to the shuttle's own emergency supply, and how to disconnect and use the backpack. "Helmet first, then disconnect and you've got air enough in the suit to get to the pack and get it started." Duun made him work it all again and again until he was exhausted.

"Sleep awhile," Duun said then. "You'll need it."

It amazed Thorn that Duun could do that so readily, anchored to his couch down in their own compartment; and most of all that up above in the activity and bright light of the bridge, Ghindi and Spart tethered themselves in a corner by the closets and went to an honest and quick sleep, while Weig and Mogannen kept computing changes. Thorn tethered himself beside Duun and tried, succeeded at least in resting; but the plane got into his half-dreams; so did the flight; and Betan.

Then he unclipped and sailed up to the bridge to discover Ghindi and Spart at work and the other two asleep. The computer ticked away. Thorn came gingerly closer off the overhead, hanging upside down over Ghindi's post and a little back so that he could see the screen.

Ghindi turned her chair around and looked up. She had that look people had when they came face-to-face with him; and then she banished it for one he could not well read. Exhaustion. Sadness. Was it love? It made no sense. He tumbled over and righted himself with a move of his hand that helped him turn. Perhaps the look made more sense right-side up.

"I'm sorry," Thorn said, meaning for bothering her in her work. He wanted to go and hide himself below before Duun found out.

She started at him, bewildered. They were both tired and a little crazed. They could not make sense to each other. "We'll get you there," she said.

(To Gatog?) Thorn was dismayed. He showed it like a child. Less seemed dishonest toward Ghindi. "Are you kosan?" he asked. He remembered the pilots.

"Tanun," Ghindi named her guild. *Tanun,* seafarers. It seemed appropriate to him.

"Ghindi," Spart said from his computers. "We've got another burn from *Kandurn.*"

Ghindi turned as if Thorn had fallen suddenly from her world. "We're getting short, aren't we?"

"We're getting short. I think we'd better get Weig and Mogannen up."

Thorn began to turn, found purchase with his foot and dived for the downward hatch, sailed through into that dim light and tumbled to hit a wall and stop. "Duun. They're calling the crew up. It sounds like we're short of time."

Duun moved in his drifting and looked at him. "How short?"

"I don't know. I don't know how to tell, except there's some good bit less time than we had, forty minutes one time and now they've had another burn."

Duun touched bottom and shot up like a swimmer for the light. Thorn touched and followed.

Mogannen and Weig were getting into spacesuits. There were three spare seats at one counter that could be powered back from it and locked. Duun did that with the two of them that were assigned to them when they were on the bridge. "When matters get to it," Duun said. "Suit up now."

All very calm. The routine of the bridge went on, except the suiting. Spart and Ghindi took their turn and got back into their seats. Duun drifted loose, suited, helmetless. The waiting became tedium. Thorn's heart once beating in panic could not sustain it. Panic ebbed down to long vexation. He wanted a drink of water. If he did that he might regret it. In such small indignities the worst moments proceeded. Thoughts of itches inaccessible. His own sweat inside the suit, gathered and undispersed. He hung in midair, watching the viewpoint for want of other distraction in this slow creeping of time and the beep of incoming messages droning methodically about the insane business of ghotanin who wished to kill them. Ships had begun to overcommit. Calm voices reported the facts and called it things like zero-return and no-turnaround.

(Strangely enough you don't get to see the stars much. You can see from the shuttle if you get up front. . . . It's beautiful.)

A star brightened while he watched, brightened and brightened, and his heart slammed into rapid beats. "Duun! Weig!" It began to be a sphere.

"Get to that seat!" Duun yelled, and shot that way himself. Thorn dived, caught the back of one and hauled himself into it by the armrest, reached for the furled restraints and started fastening them. He looked up, ahead of them where the star had vanished. "Where is it?" They had not turned, could not have turned: the shuttle had nothing left.

"Helmet," Duun said. Thorn pushed the button on the

armrest, pulled up the connnecting hose and communications plug and inserted them as the helmet came down. He locked it in place, selected the third communications channel. One was unified and two was crew-only, three was non-crew. Himself and Duun. He could hear his breathing, could hear Duun's, and it was steadier than his own.

(O gods, how do people get used to this?)

There was another star. All in silence. Only the breathing sounds, the faraway noises of the shuttle's operations that were everywhere ambient, but dimmed by the helmets.

He switched channels, heard the crew talking and the messages coming in. The sweat gathered on his body and his arm was going to sleep until he shifted it. ("Damn suits never fit," Duun had said.) It was better than the flightsuit. Looser.

(Another star. Are those missiles or are those ships? Are those ships dying?)

The crew-talk made no sense to him, full of codes. He cut third channel in. "Duun, what's happening?"

"They're within range of each other. And of us, with far less accuracy. The hatani have headed them off. Outmaneuvered them, if they don't let one get past. If they do they'll never get a second chance and we can't stop it."

The flashes went on. Thorn shut his eyes and opened them again, wishing he dared take the helmet off. The air was cold and stung his throat and nose and eyes.

"That's *Ganngein*," Weig's voice broke in on third channel "They got them all. We've got debris on intersect. That's all."

"How's *Ganngein*?" Duun asked.

A pause. "Zero-return. So's *Nonnent*. *Ganngein* wishes us well and says they'll stay in contact. They're trying to determine their numbers now; they've been skewed."

"Can't the station send something out?" Thorn asked. "Couldn't earth?"

"Station's in ghota hands," Duun said. "Unfortunately. Hatani there were too few. But there's no ship at the station now—Hatani got that, thank the gods, or ghotanin'd have overhauled us from behind. It was the ghota outliers that hit us up ahead. Station's got one shuttle left; earth has a few. But a shuttle can't stop *Ganngein*. Not a question of slowing down that mass, which they couldn't in the first place. Just of catching them in a docking maneuver. They can't match those speeds even to get the crew off."

(Sphitti's voice: "Here's an application now. If you were drifting in mid-air—no friction and no gravity—)

("You can't.")

("Say that you could.")

(Angles and lines on a schoolroom screen—)

There was a long time that the crew and the doomed ships talked, business only.

"That's it," Thorn heard one say. "We're going to hit the well—looks like three days on. It could be worse. Like four."

"We hear you," Weig said. There was sorrow in his voice. Thorn listened and stared at the points of light. His arm and his leg were numb. No one moved to take off the suits. *Debris on intersect.* He remembered that. The other two ships talked awhile. There was no better news.

(This is more dreadful than the planes. This silence. This inevitability of ships that meet that fast, with distances that take days. For Betan it was quick. These men and women will have time to talk and eat and sleep and wake three times before they hit the ground. Before they skim through the well and get caught and dragged in.)

". . . we think," *Nonnent* said, "we think we may have the angle to transit. We don't know yet."

"We'll miss your company then," *Ganngein* said.

A long pause. "Yes, we hear that." Quickly, from *Nonnent*.

"Don't be embarrassed about it. This isn't a trip we want to share."

Hatani. Or tanun guild.

There was long silence. Eventually there began to be

a hole in space, small at first, that grew and ate the stars. "Something's out there, Duun. Isn't it?"

"Dust," Duun said. "Particles. We won't use the lights. We're conserving all the power we've got and we can't dodge it anyway."

(How long can it take us? What if a mostly whole ship were in our path?)

(Fool's question, Thorn.)

Wait and wait and wait. All the stars were gone. The ships talked now and again. They talked about the cloud.

Static began. Transmission broke up. A noise penetrated the helmet, a distant hammer blow. Another. The sounds accelerated to a battering. It stopped.

"We're still in it." Weig said. "This is going—uhh!"

The shock rang through the structure and up through the deck. Thorn clenched his gloved hands on the armrests and forgot the pain. Silence a time.

"Clipped the left wing," Mogannen said. "We've got a little spin now. Don't—"

Another shock. Shock after shock. Silence then. An occasional strike, none large.

(Pieces of the ghotanin. Or of one of our own. We're flying through dead ships. Dead. Bodies. Or bits of them. Blood out there would freeze like snow.)

The stars came back. "Hey!" Weig shouted. "We're through!"

(For me. For me and Duun, the dead back on earth. *Ganngein* and *Nonnent*. Ghota and hatani ships.)

"There's a ship out there," Spart said, and Thorn's heart stopped. "It's *Deva*. It's going to serve as pickup. It's about nine hours down."

"Thank the gods," Mogannen said.

"We go out to it," Duun explained. "They can't stop our spin to pick us up. We're easier to manage in suits."

Deva shone a light for them. The shuttle turned slowly, wedge-shaped shadow against the sun. Debris trailed from one wing edge, and from the tail. A touch came at his leg and Duun snagged him, maneuvered and got him by the hand. Near them three became a chain. One of them was still loose but in no danger. *Deva*'s beacon brightened among the stars, a white and blinding sun.

Deva was not so fine inside as the shuttle—was all bare metal and plastics; but it had shonunin in it. It had welcome.

"Duun-hatani," the captain said.

"You're a good sight, Ivogi-tanun," said Duun.

Thorn held his helmet in his hands. He saw the others' looks, the crew who stood gazing at him. As they might look at some strange fish they had hauled up in their nets.

"This is Haras," Duun said. "Hatani guild."

"We heard," Ivogi-tanun said.

XV

There was silence from *Ganngein* now. For four days. Static obscured *Nonnent*'s voice. Earth spoke in code, and *Deva* had no facilities. Gatog spoke back, constantly; and that was coded too, even when it was *Deva*'s code. Machines read it out. There was seldom a voice, until the last, when Gatog began to shine in *Deva*'s viewport like a scatter of jewels.

(It seemed sinister till we saw it. It's like an ornament. Why is it out here?) "Duun, what is this place?"

Duun was silent. Thorn trembled, looking at it from the place on the bridge where Ivogi-tanun called them. It was foolish. Perhaps it was all the other shocks. But there seemed no other destination. Earth and Gatog spoke in some hieratic tongue past them, sharing secrets; and earth had drunk down *Ganngein*—"Gods," the last transmission had been, or it had sounded like that. Then static from *Nonnent* too. "They're behind the earth," Duun said. They expected transmission to pick up again. But they never found it, though *Deva* asked Gatog. "We've lost it too," Gatog said, one of the few uncoded transmissions they had gotten from this secretive place.

(Can silence be worth so much here, so far from earth?)

The lights shone against the stars, white and gold, a cluster here and removed from it, another.

"Five minutes to braking," Ivogi said; and: "Go aft," Duun said. *Deva* had no spare seats for six passengers. They had to brace themselves in a narrow place where *Deva* had provision for passengers during maneuvering:

there was no viewport there, and nothing more than padding. Thorn went with them. Duun did not.

But Duun came for him after the hard burn. "We're going to suit up to cross," Duun said.

It was a cold place, *Deva,* gray and smelling of chilled metal and electrics and their own bodies and their own food. But *Deva* was a known place, and Thorn looked over it while he fastened up his suit. He did these things for himself and looked at *Deva* and thought of Sheon's woods, and the hearthside. His mind leapt from one to the other. From that to the glittering lights.

(Duun, I'm afraid. I want the world again, Duun, I want to go home. I knew things there; but I go from one thing to the other, and you change, Duun, you go away from me, you talk with Weig, you talk with Ivogi, you talk a language I don't understand and you've lost interest in me. You go farther away.)

(Don't look at me like that. Don't think about leaving me. I can read you, Duun, and it scares me.)

"Good-bye," Ivogi said, and *Deva*'s hatch spat them out as impersonally as it had taken them in.

Thorn's hand froze on the maneuvering gun in all that unforgiving dark. He drifted. His eyes jerked wildly from light to light to light—a great dish suspended, building-wide, or close to them; his eyes refused perspective. A web of metal stretching to insane thinness in the distance, dotted with brilliant lights. "Gatog," Duun said, a voice gone strange with the speaker. "That's the great ear, that dish. It listens. So does another, considerably across the solar system. Out in Dothog orbit."

(What does it listen to?) But Thorn could not ask any question. His soul was numb, battered with too many answers. Duun dragged at him and turned him, and aimed him at another *down* with such a shift in perspective his sense of balance sent terror through him.

A great pit yawned, all lit in green: it went down a vast rotating shaft to a core; and his peripheral vision formed it as the hub of a vast wheel.

Yet another turn, and Weig and the others were there, their backs to them, their faces toward a great lighted scaffolding prisoning something from which the lights could not utterly remove the darkness—it looked older than the shining girders which embraced it: a cylinder of metal no longer bright.

"That's a ship," Duun said. "*The* ship."

Thorn said nothing. He hung there, lost, held only by Duun's hand. He had no more wish to be inside, wherever *inside* was, than to hang here forever in the blaze of these lights. (Is this the place? Is this what cost so much? Do I go beyond this place or is this the stopping-point for us? Duun, Duun, is this your solution?)

Duun held him by the hand and dived down (or up) into the well, which was green as Sheon's leaves. The walls spun and turned about them.

In the heart of the well in the hub, was a hatch that flowered with gold light. They came into it, and Weig and the others did.

Then it closed and delivered them to another chamber with several metal poles in it and a sign that told them where *down* was. Duun grabbed a pole holding onto Thorn; Mogannen and Chindi did; Spart and Weig took the other; there came a great shock that made them sway and then rise.

"Hang on," Duun said when Thorn grabbed the pole for himself. "It does it one more time. We're bound for the rim."

It was like a ship moving; *down* began to feel alarmingly sideways, and the cylinder seemed slowly to change its pitch before it jolted into contact and the door opened.

There were attendants, men and women wearing ordinary kilts, all white; Duun pulled his helmet off and Thorn did so with the rest.

(Look your fill. Stare at me.) Thorn kept his eyes from them and handed the helmet to a woman he never looked at. "Sey Duun," a man said, "they'd like to see you in the office."

"They'll have to come to me," Duun said. He peeled his suit off, sat down and removed the boots. One attendant started to touch the baggage and Thorn moved and stepped on the strap. The attendant changed his mind. And Duun smiled with the twisted side. It was right. After drifting so long Thorn knew something, if only so small a thing. They did not touch him and they did not touch Duun and they kept their hands off the baggage.

Weig and his crew took their leave. "Duun-hatani," Weig said, nothing else. He seemed moved. "Weig-tanun," Duun said. "Appeal to me if things don't go right." And Duun gave a twisted smile: "Not all my solutions are so cursed difficult."

"I'll remember," Weig said, and took his crew away; but Ghindi looked back once, and Thorn paused.

"Come on," Duun said, standing up. Theirs was another door, that opened narrowly.

(Tubes. The spinning place. Tubes and people like me—)

But there were no such people. Thorn picked up the baggage and followed Duun, along the deserted corridor which bent upward and brought them to another room.

Hatani waited for them there, three of them; Thorn saw the gray cloaks and felt profound relief. "Tagot, Desuuran, Egin," Duun said. "Haras."

There were courtesies. Thorn bowed, looked up into careful hatani faces which did not intrude their passions into anyone's view. He held the baggage with hands to which the last shreds of the gel still clung, and it was as if he had stood in a battering gale of others' feelings, others' fears; others' needs—and found a sudden calm.

"We'll rest," Duun said.

"Duun-hatani. Haras." Tagot's hand indicated the way, and he walked with them, the others at their backs, and that order was all settled with the slightest of signs that left no doubt Duun would let them at his back. Thorn slung the carry strap to his shoulder and walked a little at Duun's heel, rumpled and with his knee abraded raw again, with the red scars of burns on his hands, his hair loose and tending to fall into his eyes; but so was Duun scarred; but so was Duun's silver hide stained dark with sweat at his shoulders and the small of his back.

(Have we found a place, finally? Hatani live here. Is this a place we won't be driven from?)

They passed doors; they rode down two levels in an elevator; they walked down a bowed hallway that might have been the city tower in some distorted mirror.

They opened one door; a hatani waited there in a short hall and opened yet another for them, on a large bare-floored room to which they had to step, as if it were all one riser on which other risers were built. The walls were barren and white. An elder hatani waited here. "Your rooms are safe," that hatani said, and walked out, quietly, economically, with everything said that needed saying.

"Food, bath, bed," Duun said. Thorn set the baggage down and Duun opened it and took out his cloak. It wrapped another one. "This is yours." Duun laid it on the riser. "When you need it."

Thorn looked at it and looked at Duun. And Duun walked away, himself in search of those things he had named.

It was not, ultimately, safe: Duun knew this. There were always, where shonunin existed, ways to corrupt and ways to strike at a target. The ghotanin had thought at Gatog One they had chosen the most vulnerable target in the shuttle; at Gatog Two the fight was likely to be closer to the station itself, but ghotanin might change their minds and divert their attention here. Dallen Company was not funding them anymore. There was a likelihood they would try to hold the earth station now, and stalemate Tangen, who with kosan and tanun allies held the shuttleports and the earth-based controls of satellite defense. No great number would get into space in those few shuttles. Space was out of reach for most of earth now, perhaps for years and years, and the earth-station would be deprived of ships, if ghotanin risked the few they had left still outside the zone of the conflict.

Duun padded into the darkened bedroom, taking no great care for quiet; and exhausted as Thorn was the boy likely waked. "It's Duun," Duun said. "Go on sleeping.

"I've business to take care of. Hatani are at every entrance to this place and I know them. Go on sleeping."

Thorn stirred in the bed, turned on his back and looked up at him in the twilight. Thorn smelled mostly of soap now. He had scrubbed and shaved. "You'll be back."

"Oh, yes." (So he perceives something.) "Deep sleep, Thorn: you can do that here. With them outside. Relax."

Duun left and closed the door this time.

Duun was back and there were visitors. "Who?" Thorn asked Duun at breakfast. "People who want to see you," Duun said, looking at him across the unfamiliar table in a guarded, critical way. "Finish your breakfast and make yourself presentable. I don't want to be ashamed."

Thorn laid down his plate in front of his ankles and put the spoon in it. "No, finish," Duun said. "You have time. You've lost weight."

"I never liked this." It was the green mince that was on his plate every day at home. It tasted like the fish oil that was in his pills when as a child he had bitten down on one. "My stomach's queasy as it is."

"Do people worry you?"

(Do you have a need, minnow?)

"Their faces shout at me," Thorn said. It was the best way he could explain it.

Duun looked at him, still as a pond in winter. "Too many needs coming at you, is it, Haras-hatani?"

"Duun, how is earth? Have you heard?"

(He doesn't want that question. He doesn't want it at all.)

"Sagot wishes you well," Duun said.

(He's lying, surely he's lying, his face is so good at it.) But it looked like truth. (Sagot in her room, Sagot waiting for me—O gods, I want to go home, Duun!)

"I'm glad," Thorn said. "Tell her that from me."

"I'll relay that. Eat your breakfast."

Thorn turned on the riser and put his feet off, missing the teapot.

"Thorn."

Thorn stopped; it was reflex.

"Wear your cloak," Duun said.

They were mostly old, the visitors, two very old, with the pale mask of age on them: one was hatani and another kosan guild. There were a scattering of shonunin of middle years, one with the dark crest of the Bigon; one with the silver-tip of the icy isle of Soghai: Thorn had heard of such people and never seen one. It was a woman, a hatani, and she was the most beautiful woman he had ever seen. Sogasi, Duun named her, and Thorn stored away that name the way he stored the names of the others, in their sequence and their guilds, which were hatani and tanun and kosan. The tanun gazed at him with that frankness he had seen in Ghindi and Weig and the others; the kosan with something of dread and longing. The hatani shielded him from such things and he was grateful.

The visitors never spoke to him. Few even looked him directly in the eyes, but the hatani did. (Thank you, Thorn sent to them in a little relaxing of his face, and got that message in return, the mere flicker of the muscle above an eye.) "We'll talk later," the old kosan said to Duun. "Tell him we're glad to have seen him," a tanun said, and Thorn was even gladder of the hatani cloak that gave him some protection, that lent him something to be besides smooth-skinned and different in their eyes. "Thank you," Thorn said softly for himself, without a hint of pain. "It was a long trip, Voegi-tanun. I wish others could have made it here."

He shocked them somehow; he intruded himself with politenesses he thought were right and at least were true, and refused to care whether they spat on him or thanked him. He had missed saying that to Ghindi and Weig; to the woman at the hatch; to the pilots and to Sagot. He frightened Voegi. (That man was not supposed to talk to me, and now he thinks he did something his guild will disapprove.) Tanunin shouted everything in their movements, the little step back, Voegi's drawing near his senior with a worried backslant of his ears. The other

tanunin moved and made vague bows and showed every
sign of leaving; the kosanin were more definite. The eldest hatani looked at Duun and got his dismissal. So the
hatani turned and showed the others out.

"What was that about?" Thorn asked.

"Take a walk with me," Duun said.

They passed through a huge room, after many halls,
where a handful of workers in white, body-covering garments labored over terminals in their laps. It was all
computers, row upon row of mostly empty risers. The
few workers that were there turned in curiosity and
stared in shock, and one by one began to get up. "Stay
seated," Duun said. His quiet voice went to the walls of
that vast place, stopping all such movement. And more
quietly still: "This is the control center. Nothing's coming
in now: this is all housekeeping."

"What do they do here?" Thorn asked, since questions
seemed invited.

"They monitor the equipment." Duun brought him to
the nearest corner of the room and used a card to open
an elevator door: it was the sort they had ridden into the
wheel. Thorn seized on the nearest support pole as the
door shut; and they both held on.

"Where are we going?" Thorn asked. Duun's reti-
cences maddened him. (But what would I know if he
told me? He can't tell me. He can only pose me riddles
and let me get there as best I can.)

"To the future," Duun said. (Truth and untruth.) The
elevator shifted and the strongest force was the grip of
their hands on the pole, while other forces seemed more
and more ambiguous. "You've seen the earth, from its
simplest to its most complex. Its past, its present; you're
in Gatog, do you see no paradox?"

"I'm helpless, Duun. Am I supposed to see?"

"Change is your world. Flux and shift."

"Will we go home again?"

"Is that your question?"

The car shifted yet again, a violent sway, and seemed
to have changed direction. Thorn clenched the pole and

looked at the control panel and back to Duun. "We passed the core," Duun said. "Now we're going out again."

"Why did they make me, Duun?"

Duun met his eyes belatedly. There was dreadful amusement on Duun's face. The scarred mouth tautened on that side. "Is that the question? I'm answering it."

"In this place?" Thorn's heart sped. Panic afflicted him. "Is this where I come from? *This?*"

"I'll show you something. We're almost there."

(I don't want to see. Stop it, Duun. Duun, *tell* me, don't show me anything!)

The car slowed again, turned, slammed home. The door opened on another room much like the last, but all the risers were vacant, their in-built monitors dark. Thorn walked out into it in Duun's wake. The floors were bare and cold as all floors in this place. Like a ship. Like a laboratory. No foot left traces. There was no record of passage, no hint of time or change: it afflicted him. There were windows. Duun touched a wall-switch and they came alive clear across the far wall, showing the lights, the girders, the strange shapes that were Gatog.

"Quite a sight, isn't it?" Duun said. "Don't you see discrepancies?" Duun walked to a counter and pushed a button.

Sounds began, static-filled, a sputtering crackle. ". . . stop . . ." a voice said; it *was* a voice. ". . . you . . . world . . ."

(Gods. Gods. The tapes.)

Duun pushed another button. (One beep. A word. Two. Word. . . .) Thorn came as far as the console and leaned on it beside Duun. His heart slammed against his ribs. "It comes from here."

Duun cut all the sound. The silence was numbing. Duun walked away, up the aisle toward the illusion of the windows and Thorn followed, on the trackless floor and stopped when the windows were all the view. Duun lifted his arm and pointed. "That's what the ear picks up. It listens, minnow, it's turned beyond this solar system. What does it say to us?"

"Numbers." Thorn looked and lost all sense of up and down. The vision reeled among lights and Gatog's shape and the occasional bright stars, and Duun a gray-cloaked shadow against that bottomless void. "It talks about the stars, the elements— Stop playing games, Duun! What's sending it?"

"People." Duun turned toward him. "People like you, minnow."

The room was very still. There had never been such a voice. There was nowhere such a voice. The windows were illusion and the world was.

"No, Duun."

"Do you know differently?"

"Dammit, Duun—*don't do this to me!*"

"You wanted your answer. There's one more question. Do you want to ask it?"

"What am I?"

"Ah." Duun walked to the window rim, eclipsing a light. "You're a genetic code. So am I. Yours is different."

"I'm not shonun?"

"Oh, gods, minnow, you've known that for years." Duun faced him, twilight shadow against the glare, gray against the void. "You just didn't know what else you could be. The world held all your possibilities. I created you. A code into an egg, not the first trial; there were thousands of tries till the meds got the right of it. A technology had to be built: we had the most of it, our own doing; but you were a special problem. And you— were the success. They brought you to me: they didn't want to. They'd labored so hard to have you. Do you believe me, minnow? Am I telling the truth?"

"I don't know, Duun." Thorn wanted to sit down. He wanted to go somewhere. There was no refuge, on this floor, beneath these windows.

"It is the truth," Duun said. "The ear picks up those messages. Perhaps there's something in the pathways of the brain; perhaps it's knowing one's own face; perhaps both these things. You duplicate the sounds on the tapes perfectly; no shonun can manage all those consonants—

no shonun could read the faces on that tape—except maybe myself; except Sagot sometimes. You taught me. You taught me your reflexes and your inmost feelings; and when we gave you the vocabulary we've been able to guess for ourselves—perhaps it's pathways, gods know—you began to handle it. That's what you were made for."

"To live here? To work with *this?*"

"It doesn't appeal to you?"

"Duun—take me home. O gods, take me home again."

"Haras. Don't break down on me. You haven't come this far to beg me like a child."

Thorn came over to the window and turned his back to it. It took the sight away. It put light on Duun's face and hid his own. "Don't play me tricks. I can't—" (*Can't, minnow?*) There was silence.

"The transmissions come at regular intervals," Duun said in a calm, still voice. "They repeat, mostly. What do they say?"

"I told you what they said."

"You encourage me."

"To what?" Thorn looked up at the window; perspective destroyed the illusion, made it only glare and dark, meaningless. He flinched from it and looked back. "Is that why they're afraid of me?"

"I took an alien, I held it, fed it, warmed it—it was small, but it would grow. I took it up on a mountain and lived with it alone. I slept under one roof with it, I made it angry, I encouraged it and pushed it and I had nightmares, minnow, I dreamed that it might turn on me. There were times I held it that my flesh crawled; I did these things."

(Duun—o gods, Duun—) It was beyond hurt.

". . . I was more than fair with it. I gave it everything I had to give; I went from step to step. I made it shonun. I taught it; argued with it; discovered its mind and step by step I gave it everything I knew how to teach. Every chance. You grew up shonun. No one knew what to expect. When I told Ellud I would make you hatani he was appalled. When the world knew—there was near panic.

No matter. It never reached you. When I told Ellud I would bring you to the guild—well, hatani was bad enough: their judgments were limited. But to put you in the guild— That was earthquake. And you won it. You won Tangen. You did it all, minnow."

"Do you love me, Duun?"

(Thrust and evade.) Duun's scarred ear twitched and he smiled. There was sorrow in it and satisfaction. "That's a hatani question."

"I was taught by the best."

(Second attack.) Duun's mouth tautened on the scarred side. "Let me tell you a story, minnow."

"Is it a good one?"

"It's how I lost the fingers. You've always wondered, haven't you? —I thought you had. No one asks the questions of their relatives that they really want to know— after they grow up. And they never discover the good questions until it's far too personal to ask."

"Was it my fault?"

"Ah. I got through your guard."

"Tell me the story, Duun."

"We were rank beginners—I'm sure Sagot told you most of this: tanun guild took us into space, just the merest foothold. The moon. A station. The companies moved in. We had scientific bases here and there. Hatani guild, ghota, tanun—kosan here and there; not many. A lot of ordinary folk, doing what ordinary folk do— making money, mostly; or learning things. The world fared pretty well in those days. Then a ship turned up." Duun's face lifted slightly, a gesture toward the window, toward the lights. "The one out there."

"Not shonun," Thorn said.

"Not shonun. It was pretty badly battered when I first saw it. It's not clear what happened at first: it scared the hell out of the Dothog mission and someone started shooting, it's not clear which side. They were ghotanin, of course. There wasn't much left to question to fix responsibility. But the ship didn't leave the solar system then—too heavily damaged. It moved off, faster than anyone wanted to believe; ghotanin and kosanin chased that thing where they could—we could at least tell each other where it was heading. And for the next two years we chased that ship and battered at it. We. Tangen sent me up. I wasn't chief of the mission then, but I survived longer. We battered away at it; we lost ships. Its maneuvers got slower. We knew it was transmitting. We knew it was transmitting to someone outside the solar system, and we finally silenced that. We chewed away at it and finally we got it at a speed we could match. We boarded. There was one of them still alive. We tried to take him that way. That was my mistake." Duun lifted the maimed hand, palm outward. "He got all the rest of us. One blast. I got through it and got to him. I killed him. We found out later the ship was rigged in a way that might have destroyed it. But he never did that. We found four others frozen in vacuum. And this one. Maybe he was crazy by then. Maybe he thought he could live a little longer. Maybe he was afraid to use that last trick. But I got back; we hauled that ship in with all it contained.

"It changed the world, Thorn. Until that time we thought we were alone. And this thing was a nightmare. Two years. Two years of throwing everything we had at it and it was five of these people. Just five. They nearly wrecked the world. They cost us—O gods. Nothing was the same. And there was panic. They came to me, the Council did. I was very famous then. It was those first days: we'd stopped it damn close to the earth. That was why we fought like that, and why it cost so much. The Council asked me to do something: Tangan had refused them. Hatani judgment? I asked them. Is that what you want? We'll give you anything, they said, any help. All our backing. I told them they were fools. They had all the provinces hammering at their doors demanding action, they had the companies, they had the guilds all pulling in different directions, and kosan and ghota at odds. You've been out there, they said; give us a solution. And I took them up on it." Duun motioned to the window. "I knew there were transmissions that went out from that ship while we hunted it. I thought there might be answers we couldn't hear. I called in scientists. I or-

dered Gatog built. I ordered that ship studied. I ordered
it duplicated if we could. I ordered you—created. You're
him, Thorn; you're the man on the ship. Born from his
blood, his cells. You *are* my enemy. I made you over
again. You are my war, my way to fight a war we didn't
know how to fight. You're my answer. I knew what you
would look like—what you will look like, in another ten-
year. I knew what you'd grow into—physically. But now
I know what I killed. What he might have been. If he
were my son."

Thorn shut his eyes. There were tears. ("Don't you
know by now I can't?") They ran when he blinked and
shattered Duun's image when he looked at Duun again.
"You're maneuvering me."

"I'm hatani. Of course. I always have been. I told
you that."

"The way you maneuvered Tangan. Gods—why?
What do you want?"

"You're the world's long nightmare. A bad dream.
Everything earth has gone to build Gatog, to build that
other ship— You understand what it is to jump that far
that fast in industry? New materials, new processes, new
physics—new fears and new money and all that goes with
it. Politics. Companies. A world that had just reached
out into space—and all of a sudden—discoveries that
shatter it. Energies that, gods help us—we're still unrav-
eling, technologies with potentials we're not ready to
cope with, with all that means. We didn't know, when
that ship transmitted, how long we had before an answer
might come. We know now that ship came from a star
nine light-years out. That's when the first message
came—nine years after that ship first transmitted. We
don't know how fast the ship traveled. We're beginning
to understand that. It's fast. It's very fast. Translight. I
was naïve at first. I imagined we had years—half of a
century—to get here. Duplicate the ship. Teach them a
lesson. Send the kosan guild to deal with them and hatani
to settle matters. We know a lot more now—what the
cost of a ship like that is when you have to develop each
part and joint as a new technology; the social cost of

changes. It's made us rich. It's made us capable of blowing ourselves to hell. The tapes, minnow, the tapes—we salvaged off the ship. The machine that runs them, the drug that we found with them. A whole new category of drugs; a new vice. Gods, I had to be so careful with you. Every substance, every damn plant you touched—drove the meds crazy. Livhl you could take; sjuuna and mara; dsuikin, never—"

("Try this, minnow, try it on your tongue, never swallow first-off—")

"—you tolerate most things; we tolerate most of yours. Thank the gods that's so, or you'd have lived in virtual isolation."

(Sheon, the leaves moving in the summer wind, green and fragrant—)

(The stinging smell of lugh-flowers on the long road down from home to exile—)

"Am I the only one, am I all, Duun?"

"Yes. There was argument on that point. A lot of it. All they could see was the tapes; read the tapes; if he doesn't live, if he should meet with accident. . . . But there was only one of me, minnow; and I had to teach you, my way; learn from you, my way. If you'd been in isolation, I would have been too. We were bound together. To make you what you are took me, and it took those tapes, minnow— Some of them, gods know, may be simple entertainment for the crew—the one that was the key. There are others. The audio you heard—that's from Gatog. The messages come regularly. You know what I imagine they say? 'Here we are. You killed our messenger.' But I don't know what they say after that. I don't know how long they'll wait. They know we've got a ship. They know whatever that pilot told them. 'They're killing me. I can't leave. They're poor primitives. They're not worth much. But look out for them.' "

"You think they're going to attack."

"I planned to be capable of coming to them—whatever they're doing. But the way that ship works—the way they think it works— We guess wrong and we might lose Gatog. We might lose everything. The irony is, minnow, we can push it out to some safe distance and try—but we'd be flying that ship with no knowledge how to do it. Even if it works. And we can't start that kind of engine near anything else. And not from a standing start, they tell me. The awful truth is we don't know the last things. We don't know how to fly it. If we did we could have saved *Ganngein* and *Nonnent*. It's that fast—even inside a solar system. Outside—gods help us, we don't know."

"Am I supposed to do something about this?" Thorn trembled, a brief convulsion. "Am I what the ghota want to stop?"

"There are three kinds of people I've found: those who think the universe is good, those who believe it's corrupt, and those who don't want to think about it any more than they can help. I prefer the first two. The last can be hired by anybody. Dallen Company wants you stopped because they're scared of you: so do others; the ghota are just damn scared of your being hatani and not theirs, and of more and more knowledge in hatani hands and not theirs. They're dying and they know it. The world can't afford them anymore. It can't afford ignorance. The tanun, the kosau guilds—you're their hope."

"To do what? *Fly* that ship?"

"I don't know. Maybe. Someday. What would you do?"

"O gods.

"*Now* you know what you're for."

"Don't ask me this! Duun—"

"Haras-hatani, what will you do?"

Thorn walked off across the floor, raised his hands to his head, dropped them. There were no thoughts. Nothing but a tumbling of images. (The boulders in the sand, each with a hatani. Tangan's aged mask and Sagot's blurred. Manan's impersonal voice: "That's a miss on their side, a hit on ours. It's down." *Ganngein*'s: "This isn't a trip we want to share.")

He looked back at Duun. At a quiet shadow against the vast illusion of the windows.

"Well?" Duun asked.

"I'm not even eighteen years old!"

"I didn't say it was all in your lap. You're not responsible for the ghota. You're not to blame for the world's foolishness; but it's burning, Haras-hatani. And maybe that eighteen years is all the world is going to have. What will you do to stop it?"

(Go back to earth? How could I stop it? Who would hear me? Hatani. Tanun guild; kosanin would hear Duun.)

(A room with a bed, a bath, a fire, and hidden tricks. What is my room? This place. This world. How do I put out the fire but with my bare hands? Am I twice a fool?)

(*Now* you know what you're for.)

Thorn looked about him, the windows, the glittering sprawl of Gatog; the computer banks. (The ghotanin are afraid of something. This. Of its use.)

(The tapes. The voices.)

"I see," Thorn said. "You already know what you want me to do. You think you know. You wonder what I think. Pathways? Is that it?"

"Maybe just the hope of something better. Tell me your solution."

"The ship transmitted. Did the message go out translight?"

"No. Lightspeed."

"The pilot knew they wouldn't be in time then. He wasn't asking them to save him."

"No. There was no hope of that. So what did he want, hatani?"

"How can I know? *You* taught me."

"Perhaps you can't. A great deal of you is shonun."

"But the messages started nine years later. They say, 'hello; here we are.' And they go on saying it. And he said: I'm dying; they're killing me and they have such little ships.' They *know* we can't come to them. Don't they?"

"They've known at least since that message got to them, seven years, nine years after he was dead. And nine years after that attack on their ship their first messages came to us. And still come."

"How long have you been getting them now? Five years?"

"Near seven."

Thorn shut his eyes a moment. Opened them. "People should have been relieved."

"Some were. Some were simply reminded. Others said the ship wasn't really translight, that nothing could do that, that the message was a trick and timed to take us off our guard: that ships would be arriving sublight. And soon. And they hired the ghota, who saw only money and a chance to stop the hatani guild from getting control of the war they believed would come. The war they've already started."

"To see who meets those ships."

"That, yes."

"Is it so simple, then? The ship out there could transmit."

"Even simpler. Gatog can."

"They wouldn't hear me for nine years!"

"But then earth would know there's no stopping it. No undoing the messages once we've started sending. And we can hold here at Gatog indefinitely. We can stand off the ghotanin, and it won't take much more than that nine years for ships from the other side to get here if they hear us: some think so, at least. One year, two, at the rate that ship might go. They might have been here years ago—if we're right about that speed. They might come tomorrow. They may be waiting for their answer. We had no way to read them—until now. When they come, whatever they intend, you'll be here. Safe. A voice like theirs. Perhaps they'll remember their pilot when they see you. Perhaps they'll wonder. Maybe they'll begin thinking and hesitate at whatever they plan. Gods know, in ten years maybe we'll have learned to fly that ship."

"Does the earth have to bleed that long?"

"Maybe it does. Or maybe when earth knows what your solution is a lot of people will stop and think about it. Remember you're hatani. Of the Guild. That's some-

thing the world understands. That's part of my solution
too. When the panic dies, shonunin will remember the
Guild passed you. They'll know it's a true judgment."

"No one likes a hatani under his roof. Sagot told me
so."

"Yes, and you've been near eighteen years under
theirs. It's true. People begin searching themselves for
guilt. They imagine judgment on their sins. They know
you read them. They see your face and they know you
read them. Even I, minnow. I killed you once, remember.
Conscience is dreadful company."

"Duun." Thorn walked back to him, slowly, on the
trackless floor; Thorn reached out his hand, slowly,
slowly, and touched Duun's face, the scarred side. "So
you know I could," Thorn said. And took his hand away.

There was quiet in the room. Technicians stood about
the walls, hatani, tanunin and kosanin. "Sit by me,"
Thorn said, and Duun settled down in the seat beside
him. Thorn hesitated over the keys, checked this and
that. He spoke, quietly, steadily into the microphone and
it went out, starting the long journey messages would
take each day. Minutes to the earth and hours to Gatog
Two and Dothog; nine years to another star. Duun's skin
tightened. He had heard that voice, speaking that language, for two years before they silenced it the first time;
doubtless others had the same reaction. It would create
new panic on earth, in the station. Perhaps *Nonnent*
would hear it in their lonely journey, if they had waited
to hear it, and know that they had won.

There was a translation. Thorn read that out, which
was only for their solar system. ("I'll have to keep working with the tapes," Thorn had said, for there were the
originals at Gatog: there were written documents. They
had a vast library of them here; and other tapes. Thorn
dreaded it; Duun knew how much. Thorn had heard that
voice too, twin of his own, in its rage and agony. But
the computers built more and more complex fields. They
had certainty on some words. They had broken the al-

phabet. They worked out the phonics and that study branched and multiplied, on a strange story of strange people a hatani had learned to read.)

"The message is," Thorn said: *"I am Haras. One. Two. Three. I am Haras. Star G. Oxygen. Carbon. I am Haras. I hear you. The world is the earth. The star is the sun. I am a man. Hello."*

SERPENT'S
REACH

"HYDRI REACH: QUARANTINED. Approach permitted only along approved lanes. SEE: Istra."

—*Nav. Man.*

"HYDRI REACH: CLASSIFIED: Apply XenBureau for information."

—*Encyclopaedia Xenologica*

"HYDRI STARS: quarantined region. For applicable regulations, consult Cor. Jur. Hum. XXXVII 91.2. Native species of alpha Hydri III include at least one sapient species, majat, first contacted by probe Celia in 2223. Successful contact with majat was not made until Delia probe followed in 2229, and majat space was eventually opened to very limited contact under terms of the Hydri Treaty of 2235, with a single designated trade point at the station of beta Hydri II, locally called Istra.

"The entire region is under internal regulation, assumed to be a majat-human cooperation, and it is thus excluded from Alliance law. Alliance citizens are cautioned that treaties do not extend to protection of Alliance citizens or property in violation of quarantined space, and that Alliance law prohibits the passage of any ship, or person, alien or human, from said zone of quarantine into Alliance space, with the exception of licensed commerce up to the permitted contact point at Istra, by carefully monitored lanes. The Alliance will use extreme force to prevent any such intrusion into or out of quarantine. For specific regulations of import

and export, consult ATR 189.9 and supplements. The nature of the internal government is entirely a matter of speculation, but it is supposed on some evidence that the seat of government is alpha Hydri III, locally called Cerdin, and that this government has remained relatively stable during the several centuries of its establishment . . .

"Majat are reported to have rejected emphatically all human contact except the trading company initially introduced by Delia probe. The Kontrin company is currently assumed to be the government of the human inhabitants. Population of the mission was originally augmented by importation of human ova, and external observation indicates that colonization has been effected on several worlds other than Cerdin and Istra within the quarantine zone.

"Principal exports are: biocomp softwares, medical preparations, fibers, and the substance known as lifejewels, all of which are unique to the zone and of majat manufacture; principal imports are metals, luxury foodstuffs, construction machinery, electronics, art objects."

—*XenBureau Eph. Xen. 2301*

"MAJAT: all information classified."

—*XenBureau Eph. Xen. 2301*

"The fact is . . . we've become dependent. We can't get the materials elsewhere. We can't duplicate them."

—*report, EconBureau, classified*

"Advise you take whatever opportunities exist to establish onworld observation at Istra, even to clandestine operations. Accurate information is of utmost importance."

—*classified document, AlSec*

BOOK ONE

i

If it was anywhere possible to be a child in the Family, it was possible at Kethiuy, on Cerdin. There were few visitors, no imminent hazards. The estate sat not so very far from the City and from Alpha's old hall, but its hills and its unique occupation kept it isolated from most of Family politics. It had its lake and its fields, its garden of candletrees that rose like feathery spires among its fourteen domes; and round about its valley sat the hives, which sent their members to and from Kethiuy. All majat who would deal with Men dealt through Kethiuy, which fended one hive from another and kept peace, the peculiar talent of the Meth-marens, that sept and House of the Family which held the land. Fields extended in one direction, both human-owned and majat-owned; labs rambled off in the other; warehoused in yet a third, where azi, cloned men, gathered and tallied the wealth of hive trade and the products of the lab and the computers, which were the greatest part of that trade. Kethiuy was town as much as House; it was self-contained and tranquil, almost changeless in the terms of its owners, for Kontrin measured their lives in decades more than years, and the rare children licensed to replace the dead had no doubt what they must be and what the order of the world was.

Raen amused herself, clipping leaves from the dayvine with short, neat shots; the wind blew and made it more difficult, and she gauged her fire meticulously, needle-beamed. She was fifteen; she had carried the little gun clipped to her belt since she had turned twelve. Being Kontrin, and potentially immortal, she had still come into this world because a certain close kinsman had died of carelessness; she wished her own replacement to be long in coming. She was a skilled marksman; one of the amusements available to her was gambling, and she currently had a bet with a third cousin involving the target range.

Marksmanship, gambling, running the hedges into the fields to watch the azi at work, or back again in Kethiuy, sunk in the oblivion of deepstudy or studying the lab comps until she could make the machines yield her up communication with the alien majat . . . such things filled her days, one very like the other. She did not play; there were years ahead for that, when the prospect of immortality began to pall and the years needed amusements to speed them past. Her present business was to learn, to gather skills that would protect that long life. The elaborate pleasures with which her elders amused themselves were not yet for her, although she looked on such with a stirring of interest. She sat on her hillside and picked an extraordinary succession of leaves off the waving vine with quick, fine shots, and reckoned that she would put in her required time at the comp board and be through by dinner, leaving the evening free for boating on Kethiuy's lake . . . too hot during the day: the water cast back the white-hot sky with such glare one could not even look on it unvisored; but by night what lived in it came up from the bottom, and boats skimmed the black surface like firebugs, trolling for the fish that offered rare treat for Kethiuy's tables. Other valleys had game, and even domestic herds, but no creature but man stayed in Kethiuy, between the hives. None could.

Raen a Sul hant Meth-maren. She was a long-boned and rangy fifteen, having likely all her height. Ilit blood mixed with Meth-maren had contributed that length of limb; and Meth-maren blood, her aquiline features. She bore a pattern on her right hand, chitinous and glittering, living in her flesh: her identity, her pledge to the hives, such as all Kontrin bore. This sign a majat could read, whose eyes could read nothing of human features. Betas went unmarked. Azi bore a tiny tattoo. The Kontrin brand was in living jewels, and she bore it for the distinction it was.

The tendril fell last, burned through. She clipped the gun to her belt and smoothly rose, pulled up the hood of her sunsuit and adjusted the visor to protect her eyes before leaving the shade. She took the long way, at the fringe of the woods, being in no particular haste: it was cooler and less steep, and nothing awaited her but studies.

A droning intruded on her attention. She looked about, and up. Aircraft passing were not unusual: Kethiuy lake was a convenient marker for anyone sight-navigating to the northern estates.

But these were low, two of them, and coming in.

Visitors. Her spirits soared. No comp this afternoon. She veered from the lab-ward course and strode off down the slope with its rocks and thread-bushes, tacking from one to the other point of the steep face with reckless abandon, reckoning of entertainments and a general cancellation of lessons.

Something skittered back in the hedge. She came to an instant halt and set her hand on her pistol: no fear of beasts, but of men, of anything that would skulk and hide.

Majat.

She picked out the shadowed form in the slatted leaves, perplexed to find it there. It was motionless in its guard-stance, half again as tall as she; faceted eyes flickered with the slightest of turns of its head. Almost she called to it, reckoning it some Worker strayed from the labs down below: sometimes their eyes betrayed them and, muddled with lab-chemicals, they lost their direction. But it should not have strayed this far.

The head turned farther, squaring to her: no Worker . . . she saw that clearly. The jaws were massive, the head armored.

She could not see its emblems, to what hive it belonged, and human eyes could not see its color. It hunched down, an assemblage of projecting points and leathery limbs, in the latticed play of sun and shade . . . a Warrior, and not to be approached. Sometimes Warriors came, to look down on Kethiuy for whatever their blind eyes could perceive, and then departed, keeping their own secrets. She wished she could see the badges: it might be any of the four hives, while it was only gentle blues and greens who dealt with Kethiuy—the trade of reds and golds channeled through greens. A red or gold was enormously dangerous.

Nor was it alone. Others rose up, slowly, slowly, three, four. Fear knotted in her belly—which was irrational, she insisted to herself: in all Kethiuy's history, no majat had harmed any within the valley.

"You're on Kethiuy land," she said, lifting the hand that identified her to their eyes. "Go back. Go back."

It stared a moment, then backed: badgeless, she saw in her amazement. It lowered its body in token of agreement; she hoped that was its intent. She stood her ground, alert for any shift, any diversion. Her heart was pounding. Never in the labs had she been alone with them, and the sight of this huge Warrior and its fellows moving to her order was incredible to her.

"Hive-master," it hissed, and sidled off through the brush with sudden and blinding speed. Its companions joined it in retreat.

Hive-master. The bitterness penetrated even majat voice. *Hive-friends,* the majat in the labs were always wont to say, touching with delicacy, bowing with seeming sincerity.

Down the hill a beating of engines announced a landing; Raen still waited, scanning the hedges all about before she started away. *Never turn your back on one;* she had heard it all her life, even from those who worked closest with the hives: majat moved too quickly, and a scratch even from a Worker was dangerous.

She edged backward, judged it finally safe to look away and to start to run . . . but she looked now and again over her shoulder.

And the aircraft were on the ground, the circular

washes of air flattening the grassed near the gates, next the lakeshore.

A bell rang, advising all the House that strangers had come. Raen cast a last look back, finding the majat had fled entirely, and jogged along toward the landing spot.

The colors on the aircraft were red striped with green, which were the colors of the House of Thon, friends of Sul sept of the Meth-marens. Men and women were disembarking as the engines died down; the gates were open and Meth-marens were coming out to meet the visitors, most without sunsuits, so abrupt was this arrival and so welcome were any of Thon.

The cloaks on the foremost were Thon; and there was the white and yellow of Yalt among them, likewise welcome. But then from the aircraft came visitors in the red-circled black of Hald; and Meth-maren blue, with black border, not Sul-sept white.

Ruil-sept of the Meth-marens, with Hald beside them. Raen stopped dead. So did others. The welcome lost all its warmth. Save under friendly Thon colors, neither Ruil nor Hald would have dared set foot here.

But after some delay, her kinsmen stepped aside and let them pass the gates. The aircraft disgorged more Thon and Yalt, but there were now no welcomes at all; and something else they produced—a score of azi, sunsuited and visored and anonymous.

Armed azi. Raen stared at them in disbelief, nervously skirting round the area of the landing; she sought the gates with several backward glances, angry to the depth of her small experience of Ruil, the Meth-marens' left-hand line. Ruil had come for trouble; and the guard-azi were Ruil's arrogant show, she was sure of it. Thon would have no reason.

She put on a certain arrogance as she walked in the gates. Sul-sept azi closed them securely after her, leaving the intruder-azi outside in the heat. She wished sunstroke on them and sullenly made her way into the House, the whole day spoiled.

ii

It was a lasting strangeness to see Ruil-sept's black among the white-bordered Sul cloaks—and as much so to see Hald red-and-black; and incredible to find them admitted to the dining hall; where House councils and dinners took place simultaneously.

Raen sat next her mother and found security in her— Morel, her mother, who had gotten her of an Ilit who himself was bloodkin to Thon; she wondered if any of these present were distant relatives. If it were so, her mother, who would know, said nothing, and deepstudy had given her no clues.

Grandfather headed the table . . . more than grandfather, but that was shortest, eldest of Meth-marens, *the* Meth-maren, who was gray-haired and bent with the decades that he had lived, five hundred passes of Cerdin about its sun: eldest of all Sul-sept, of Ruil too, so that they had to respect him. Raen regarded him with awe, seldom now as he came out of his seclusion in westwing, rarely to venture into domestic concerns, more often to Council down at Alpha, where he wielded the power of a considerable bloc of votes. Meth-marens, unlike other Houses whose members were scattered from world to world across the Reach, stayed close to home, to Kethiuy. Of the twenty-seven Houses and fifty-eight septs within those Houses that composed the Family, Methmaren Sul was the only one whose duties rarely took him elsewhere, away from Cerdin and the hives. The Family's post was here, between the hives and Men, while Meth-maren Ruil hovered about the area of Alpha and guested where they could, Houseless since the split.

Hald remembered that day, that Meth-maren and Meth-maren had fought. Hald had bled for it, sheltering Ruil assassins; and it was a powerful persuasion that brought Halds and both septs of Meth-maren again under the same roof.

It had taken all the influence of Thon and Yalt together to persuade Grandfather to accept this gathering, Halds and the divided Meth-marens at the same dinner table, carefully separated by Thons and Yalts. It needed a certain bravado on the part of Halds and Ruils to eat and drink what Sul gave them.

Raen herself felt her stomach unsettled, and she declined when the serving-azi brought the next elaborate dish. "Coffee," she said, and the azi Mev whispered the order at once to one of his fellows: it arrived instantly, for she was eldest's great-granddaughter's daughter in direct descent, and there was in the House a hierarchy of inheritance. She was to a certain extent pampered, and to another, burdened, for the sake of that birthright. It mandated her presence at table tonight in the first place, and made it necessary to mix with her elders, most of whom had resentment for the fact. She tried to bear herself with her mother's studied disdain for the proceedings, but there was a Ruil across the table, cousin Bron, and she avoided his eyes when possible: they were hot and insolent.

"We hope for a reconciliation," the Thon elder was saying, at the other end of the table. He had risen, to begin what he had come to say. "Meth-maren, will you let Ruil speak here? Or would you prefer intermediaries still?"

"You're going to say," Grandfather intoned in his reedy voice, "that we should take in this left-hand branch of ours. It diverged of its own accord. It's not welcome in Kethiuy. It's trouble to us, and the hives avoid it. Ruil-sept alienated them, and that wasn't our doing. This is hive territory. Those who can't live under those terms can't live here."

"Our talents," said Tel Ruil Meth-maren, "lie with other hives, the ones Sul can't manage."

"Reds and golds." Grandfather's chin wobbled with his anger. "You deceive yourself, Tel a Ruil. They've no love of humankind, least of all of Ruil. I know you've had red contacts. It's rumored. I know what you're up to and why you've gone to the trouble of drawing Thon and Yalt into this. Your plans to build on Kethiuy lake are unacceptable."

"You're head of House," Tel said. He had an unfortunate voice, nasal and whining. "You ought to be impartial to sept, eldest. But you carry on feuds from before any of the rest of us were born. Maybe Sul sept feels some jealousy—that Ruil can handle the two hives Sul can't touch. They've come to us, not we to them. They preferred us. Thon saw; Thon will witness it. All within the Pact. Red-hive has promised us its cooperation if we can secure that holding near its lands, on the lake. We've come *asking,* eldest. That's all. Asking."

"We support the request," the Thon said.

"Yalt agrees," said the other eldest. "It's good sense, Meth-maren, to end this quarrel, and to get some good out of it."

"And does Hald ask the same?"

There was silence. Raen sat still, her heart pounding.

The Hald eldest rose. "We have a certain involvement here, Meth-maren. The old feud has gone on beyond its usefulness. If it's settled now, then we have to be involved, or the Meth-marens will have peace and we'll have none. We're willing to forget the past. Understand that."

"You're here to stand up with Ruil."

"Obligation, Meth-maren."

They did not say friendship. Raen herself did not miss that implication, and there was a space of silence while Ruil glowered.

"We have opportunities," the Hald said further, "that ought not to be neglected."

"At least talk on the matter," siaid Yalt "We ask you to do that."

"No," some of the House muttered. But Eldest did not refuse. His old eyes wandered over them all, and finally he nodded.

Raen's mother swore softly. "Leave," she said to Raen. And when Raen looked at her in offense: "Go on."

Others, even adult and senior, were being dismissed from what was becoming elder council. There was no objection possible. She kissed her mother's cheek, pressed her hand, and sullenly made her retreat among the others, younger folk under thirty and third- and fourth-rank elders, inconsiderable in council.

There was a muttering gathering in the hall just outside, her cousins no happier than she with what was toward.

No peace, she heard. *Not with Ruil.*

And: *Reds and golds,* she heard, reminding her of the hillside and the meeting which had diverted her. She had told no one of that. She was too arrogant to contribute that meaningless fragment to the general turmoil in the hall. She skirted the vicinities of her chattering cousins, male and female, and brushed off the attentions of an azi, walked the corridor in a fit of irritation—both at being cast out and at reckoning what Ruil-sept proposed. Kethiuy lake belonged to Sul-sept, beautiful and pristine. Sul had cared to keep the shores as they were, had labored to make the boat-launches as inconspicuous as possible, to keep all evidence of man out of view. Ruil wanted a site which would obtrude into their sight, to plant themselves right where Sul must constantly look at them and reckon with them. This business of reds and golds: this was surely something Ruil had concocted to obtain backing from other Houses. There was no possibility that they could do what they claimed, interceding with the wild hives.

Lies. Outright lies.

She shrugged past the azi at the door and sought the cool, clean air of the porch. She filled her lungs with it, looking out into the dark where the candletrees framed Kethiuy lake; and the ugly aircraft sat in her view, gleaming with lights.

Armed azi, as if this were some frontier holding. She was indignant at their presence, and no little uneasy by reason of it.

A step sounded by her. She saw three men, the one nearest in Hald's dark Color. She froze, recalling herself unarmed, having come from the table. Childish pride held her from the flight prudence dictated.

It was a tall man who faced her. She stared up at him with her back to the door and the light from the slit windows giving her a better look at him: mid-thirties, beta-reckoning; on a Kontrin, that could be anywhere between thirty and three hundred. The face was gaunt and grim: Pol Hald, she recognized him suddenly, with the *déjà vu* of deepstudy. The two with him, she did not know.

And Pol was trouble. He had lost kin to Meth-marens. He was also reputed frivolous, a libertine, a jester, a player of pranks. She could not connect that report with that gaunt face until quite suddenly he grinned at her and shed half a dozen apparent years.

"Good evening, little Meth-maren."

"Good evening yourself, Pol Hald."

"What, should I know your name?"

She lifted her head a degree higher. "I'm not in your studytapes *yet,* ser Hald. My name is Raen."

"Tand and Morn," he said with a shrug at the kinsmen at his back, the one young and boyish, the other lean-faced and much like himself, like enough for full kin. His grin did not fade. He reached out with complete affrontery and touched her under the chin. "Raen. I'll remember that."

She took a step backward, feeling a rush of blood to her face. She had no experience to deal with such a move, and the embarrassment became rage. "And who sent you out here, skulking round the windows?"

"We're set to watch the aircraft, little Meth-maren. To be sure Meth-maren hospitality is what it should be."

She did not like the sound of that, and turned abruptly, seized the door handle, afraid for the instant that they would stop her; but they made no move to do so, and she delayed to glower resentment at them, determined to make it clear she was not being chased off her own doorstep. "I seem to have left my gun inside," she said. "I usually carry it for pests."

Pol's gaunt face went serious then, quite, quite sober.

"Good evening, Meth-maren," he said.

She opened the door and went in, into the safe light, among her own kin.

iii

There was the drone of an engine toward dawn. Aircraft taking off, Raen thought, turning in her bed and burrowing into the pillows. The talk down in the dining hall had gone on and on, sometimes loudly enough to be heard outside the doors, generally not. The gathering in the hall outside had drifted off at last toward duties or pleasures: there was a certain lack of law in the House, younger men and lesser elders piqued by their exclusion, seeking to make clear their displeasure. A few became drunk. A few turned to bizarre amusements, and the azi maid who had bedded herself down in Raen's room had fled here in panic.

Lia had taken her in, Lia her own azi, a female nearing her fatal fortieth year. Raen blinked and looked at Lia, who had fallen asleep in a chair by the door, while the fugitive maid had curled up on a pallet in the corner . . . dear old Lia was upset by the commotion in the House, and had surely taken that uncomfortable post out of worry for her security.

Love. That was Lia, whose ample arms had sheltered her all her fifteen years. Her mother was authority, was beauty, was affection and safety, but Lia was love, lab-bred for motherhood, sterile though azi were.

And she could not slip past such a guard. She tried to rise and dress in silence enough, but Lia wakened and began to fuss over her, choosing her clothes with care, wakening the sleeping maid to draw a bath and make the bed, supervising every detail. Raen bore this, for impatient as she was to learn how things stood downstairs, she had infinite patience with Lia, who could be hurt by refusal. Lia was thirty-nine. There remained only this last year, before whatever defect was bred into her, killed her. Raen knew this with great regret, though she was not sure that Lia knew her own age. She would on no account make a day of Lia's life unhappy; and on no account would she let Lia know the reason of her attitude.

It's part of growing up, her mother had told her. *The*

price of immortality. Azi and betas come and go, the azi
quickest of all. We all love them when we're young. When
one loses one's nurse, one begins to learn what we are,
and what they are; and that's a valuable lesson, Raen.
Learn to enjoy, and to say goodbye.

Lia offered her the cloak of Color, and she decided it
was proper to wear it; she fastened it and let Lia adjust
it, then walked to the window, where the first light of
dawn showed the landing.

One aircraft still remained. It was not over.

She went out into the corridor and down, past the
council room where a few of her elder cousins and rela-
tions lounged disconsolately. They were not in the mood
to brief a fifteen-year-old, be she heir-line or not; she
sensed that and listened, heard voices still talking inside.

She shook her head in disgust and walked on, thinking
of breakfast, though she rarely ate that meal. Lessons, at
least, were still suspended, but she would have traded a
week of holidays to have Ruil and their friends out of
Sul's vicinity. She recalled the three Halds and wondered
whether they were still occupying the porch.

They were not. She stood on the porch with her hands
on her hips and breathed deeply. The area was clear and
the azi were heading out to fields as they did every morning. A golden light touched the candletrees and the hedges
at this most beautiful hour, before alpha Hydri showed
its true face and scorched the heavens.

There was only the single aircraft befouling the land-
scape.

And then she saw movement at the corner of the
house.

An azi, sunsuited at this hour.

"What are you doing there?" she shouted at him. And
then she saw shadows skittering in a living wave across
the lawn, tall, stiltlike forms moving with eye-blurring
speed.

She whirled, face to face with an armed azi, and
cried out.

BOOK TWO

i

Raen stumbled, skidded, came to a halt against a projecting rock. Pain shot through her side. The cloth clung there. The burn had broken open; moisture soaked her clothing. She felt of it and brought away reddened fingers, wiped a smear on the rock which had stopped her, fingers trembling. She kept climbing.

She looked back from time to time, on the lowlands, the forest, the lake, on all the deceptive peace of Kethiuy's valley, while her breath came short and balance nigh failed her on the rocks. They were all dead down there, all her kin: all, all dead—Ruil sept held Kethiuy for its own, and Sul-sept bodies were everywhere. Only her own was missing from the tally, and that from no act of wit, nothing of credit: burned, she had fallen, and the bushes by the porch had sheltered her.

They were all dead, and she was dying.

There was no relief from the sun up here; it burned in a sky white with heat, blistered exposed skin, threatened blindness despite her cloak that she had wrapped about her face. Stones burned her hands and heated the thin soles of her boots. Her eyes streamed tears, seared by the dryness and the glare. Her chance for shelter was long past, at the beginning of the climb. If Ruil sought her, they would find her. She left a trail for any groundsearch they might care to make, smeared on the rocks from her hands and her side. And from the air, Ruil might well manage heat-sensors for night tracking. There was no hope of shaking them if they wanted her.

She kept running, climbing, all the same, because there was no going back, because it was less her Ruil cousins she feared than red-hive, the living wave that had poured over her into Kethiuy, spurred feet trampling her among the bushes, deadly jaws clashing. There were deaths and deaths, and she had seen them in plenty in recent hours, but those dealt by majat were crudest, and majat trackers were those she most feared, swift beyond any hope of escape.

A second fall; this time she sprawled full length, and from this impact she was slow in rising. Her hands shook now as in ague, and there was skin gone from her palms and her knees and elbows, cloth torn. Thirst and the blinding heat of the rocks were more painful than the abrasions, but even those miseries were devoured by the pain that stitched her side. She drew breath with difficulty, reaching for support to hold her on her feet.

She was running again. She could not remember how, but she faced a climb, and her mind was forced to work again. She used hands as well as feet, and managed it, slowly, tottering on the brink, slipping, gaining another body's length. There had been other refuges, the woods, the road toward the City. She had chosen wrong. Her mother, her uncles—they would have done otherwise, would have tried for the City. She had made a panic choice, the hills, hide-and-seek in the rocks, the high places, hard ground for their vehicles. But most of all the hills were blue-hive territory, old neighbors. Red-hive would not readily venture *their* borders, not for all Ruil's urging.

Panic choice. There was no help up here, nothing human, no way down, no way back. She knew what she had done to herself, and the tears that ran down her face were of rage as well as the heat.

There was another gap in her memory, and then a bald hill swam in her sight. Here was the boundary, the point-past-which-not for any human. Majat trails ran through the gap, converging here. Raen caught her breath and felt her way along the rocks and down, into the shadows, set her feet on that well-worn track and looked about her, at tilted, tumbled rocks, flinching from the white sky.

Here was the refuge. No one would come here rashly; no one would likely take the trouble and the risk. It was a private place, for the private business of dying, and she knew it finally, that dying was what she had left to do. She had only to sit down and rest a while, while the blood kept leaking from her side and the sun baked her brain. Of pain there could be no more to endure. It had reached the top of the curve, and lessened even from standing still; there was only the need to wait. Her mother, eldest, her kinsmen and her azi . . . there was no grieving for them: their pain was done. Hers was not.

Balance failed her. She moved to save herself, fearing the fall, and that move led to the next step and the next. Her vision went out for a moment, and panic and failing balance drove her stumbling and reaching for the rocks which she remembered ahead. She hit them hip-high, braced herself, recovered a blurred vision of daylight and kept moving downhill. It was a little death, that dark, that blindness; the real one was coming, deeper and larger, and already the heat of the sun seemed less. She fled it, fighting each dark space that sent her staggering and reeling from point to point.

Thorns ripped her arm and her clothing. She recoiled and fought past the edge of the obstacle, blinked her eyes clear. She knew the meaning of the hedge, knew that here was the place she must stop, must. Her frightened body kept moving with its own logic, heedless of dangers; her mind observed from a distance, carried along helplessly, confused . . . and suddenly, in grim rage, found a focus.

The pact of Family had failed; it was murdered, with her mother, Grandfather, her kin . . . slaughtered by Ruil and Hald.

There was an older Pact, that which was grafted into the very flesh of her wounded hand, chitinous and part of her, living jewels.

She was Kontrin, of the Family which ruled the Hydri stars, which had won of majat the rights of settlement and trade, the serpent-emblemed Family, which lived where other humans would not; she was Meth-maren, hive-friend.

A great many fears diminished in her. There was a place to go, a thing to do, a means to make Ruil suffer. Her mother smiled grimly in her mind, encouraging her: *Revenge is next only to winning.* Raen's mouth set in a rictus between gasp and grin, seeking air, a little more life, and someone else's death.

The blacknesses came more frequently now, and she hurled herself from rock to rock, tumbling from one winding turn to the next, fending off thorns with her chitin-shielded right hand . . . majat barriers, these ancient hedges.

"I'm from Kethiuy!" she shouted at the grayness which hazed her senses, the cold that numbed the pain and threatened her with losing. "Blue-hive! I'm Raen Meth-maren! *Kethiuy!*"

The black edges closed on her sight.

She thrust herself toward the next hedge, and heard rocks shift and rattle above her, stones which she had not stirred.

They were all about her, tall leathery shapes, hazy shadows, shimmering with jewels in the blinding sun.

"Go back," one said, a baritone harmony of pipes. "Go back!"

She saw the dark opening in the earth, and held her bleeding side, flinging herself into a last, frantic effort. She could not feel her legs under her. There was no more heat nor cold, nor up nor down nor color. Her body hit stone. Her wounded hand slicked wetly across it and the gray itself went out.

ii

Workers tugged and arranged to satisfaction, careful not to further damage the fragile structure, delicate as new eggs. Worker palps busily gnawed away the ruined clothing, laved off the foul outsider smells and cleaned the spilled life fluids from body and limbs. Warriors still milled about the vestibule, disturbed by the invasion, seeking directions. Confusion reigned throughout the sector.

A Worker took the essence of the problem and circled its companions, squealed a short burst of orders to clear the trafficway, and scurried off. Worker was already in contact with Mother, after that subliminal fashion which pervaded the hive, but that kind of communication was not sufficient for details. There was need of direct report.

Other Workers delayed it briefly, chance encounters in the dark corridors. *Human-in-hive,* they scented, among other things of life-fluids and injury. Alarm spread. Warriors would be moving; Workers would be throwing up barricades, sealing tunnels. Worker kept traveling, original and most accurate carrier, and obsessed with urgency. Its personal alarm was chiefly distress for the untidiness, a vague sense of higher things out of control and therefore threatening the whole hive: chaos was already loosed and worse might follow.

Dim glow of fungi and the sweet scent of Mother pervaded the inmost halls, near the Chamber. Worker passed others, Egg-bearers—touched, smelled, conveyed the alarm which sent them hastening away. A Warrior shouldered past, bluff and hasty, returning from its own inquiry. Its message was of sense to Warriors. Worker rejected it, although it bore upon its own, and scurried on, forelimbs tucked, into the Presence.

Mother sat in a heaving mass of Drones and attendants. The smell was magnetic, delirious. Worker came to Her in ecstasy, opened its palps and offered taste and scent, receiving in turn.

Mother thought. The shifts of chemistry swirled dazzlingly through Worker's senses. She spoke at the same time, sound which occasionally ascended to the timbre of human names. Communication wove constantly between the two levels, intricate interplay of sound and taste.

Heal it, the decision came, complex with the chemicals necessary to the performance of this task. *Feed it. This is of Kethiuy hive, the young queen Raen. Workers of blue-hive have encountered her before. I taste injury, abundant life-fluids. Warriors report red-hive intrusion in the Kethiuy area. Accept this intruder.*

Queen. The scent touched off reactions in the chemistry of Worker, terrifying changes—communicated also to the Drones, who shifted uneasily and sought touch. The hive-mind was one. Worker was one complex unit of it. Mother was a master-unit, the key, which made sense of all the gatherings. Others moved closer, compelled by the intimation of understandings, Workers and Drones and Foragers and Warriors, each sharing this intelligence and feeding into it in its own way.

Kethiuy. That was a Drone, who Remembered, which was a function of Drones. Images followed, of the land before and after the human hive called Kethiuy had been built . . . domes, one at first, and then others, and trees growing up among them. Blue-hive's memory was as long as its members were brief: a billion years the memories went back, and the specific memory of Kethiuy saw the hills rise and the lake form and drain several times, and form again. Drone-memory extended even back into hives older than Kethiuy's hills, into days of dimmer and dimmer intelligence; but these memories were not at issue: humans were brief upon the earth, only the last several hundreds of years. The hive sorted, comprehended, knew Sul-sept of Meth-maren hive and all its issue, its bitter rivalry with Ruil and Ruil's allies. Human thought: intelligence served by peculiar senses, a few more than the hives possessed, a few less, and contained by single bodies. The concept still troubled the hive, the idea that individual death could extinguish an intelligence. It was still only dimly grasped. Mother in particular put it forward, the impending death of an irreplaceable intelligence.

Queen, Worker insisted, perturbed.

Dying, another Worker added, with an implication of untidiness.

No rival, Mother reassured the hive, but distress persisted strongly in her taste, permeating all consciousness. *We perceive that red-hive is massing in the vicinity of*

*Kethiuy; golds are stirring; and now there is a human
injured, perhaps others as well. We have not enough information. Red-hive is involved where red-hive does not belong. Red-hive has a taste of hostilities, of strange contacts,
human contacts. The Pact is at issue. Feed Kethiuy's
young queen. Heal her. She is no threat to me. She is
important to the hive. She contains information. She is an
intelligence and contains memory. Tend. Heal.*

Worker departed, one part of the Mind, bent on action. Others raced off on their own missions, impelled
by their own understandings of what Mother had said,
reactions peculiar to their own chemistries and functions.

Then the Mind did a very difficult thing, and lied to
itself.

Mother directed certain three Warriors, who rushed
from the Chamber and from the hive and out into the
heat of the day. Beyond the thorn-hedges, beyond the
safe boundary of the hills, they stopped, and began pur-
posely to alter their internal chemistry, breaking down
all the orderly complex of their knowledge, past and
present.

The hive lost them, for they were then mad.

They died, wandering inevitably into red-hive ambush
in the valley, and red-hive could only believe the lie
which it read in the chemistry of the slaughtered blues,
that blue-hive had tasted the death of the young queen
of Kethiuy hive, that no such survivor existed.

iii

"What is this?" Lian muttered, looking about him at
the Council, the many-Colored representatives who settled into place beneath the serpent emblem of the Kontrin. Suddenly there were new faces, new arrangements
of seating. His blurred vision sought friends, sought old
allies. The eldest Hald was gone; a younger man sat in
his place. There was of the blue of Meth-maren . . . the
black-bordered cloak of a Ruil; of several of the oldest
septs and Houses . . . no sign, or younger strangers wear-

ing their Colors. Lian, Eldest of the Family and first in
Council, looked about him, hands trembling; and, having
almost risen—he sank down again.

He began to count, and took reckoning what manner
of change had come on the Family in these chaotic days.
Some of the House eldests looked at him across the
room, glances carrying question and appeal: he had always opened the sessions . . . seven hundred years in the
Council of Humans on Cerdin, the assembly of the
twenty-seven Houses of the Family.

"Uncle," said Terent of Welz-Kaen. "Eldest?"

Lian turned his face away, hating the cowardice which
must now be the better part of common sense. Assassins
had been planted. A purge had been carried out with
extreme efficiency, not at one point, but at many. One
had no idea where matters stood now, or what the count
of votes would be on a challenge. There was something
new shaped or shaping, dangerous to all who stood too
tall in the Family. One did well now to wait and hear
others' decisions.

Lian felt his age, an incredible weight on him, memory
which confused one with too many alternatives, too much
of wisdom, experience heaped on experience, which always counselled . . . *wait and learn.*

"Eldest!" the Malind elder called aloud, dared rise
from her seat, marking herself among dissenters. "You
will open the session?"

The whole hall was waiting. He declined with a gesture, hand trembling uncontrollably. There was a sudden
murmur of surmise in the hall, dismay from many. He
looked last on Moth, aged Moth, seeming older than he
in her face and her brittle movements, but she was half
a century younger. Her pale eyes met his, shrouded in
wrinkles.

She bowed her head, having taken count as well as he;
her hands occupied themselves with some minute adjustment in the trim of her robes.

Of those who had come first into the Reach, first humans among majat, there had been few survivors. Even
immortality did not stand well against ambition.

This morning, in Council, there were fewer survivors still; and new powers had risen, who had waited a century in patience.

The new Hald rose, bowed ironically, and began to speak, setting forth the changes that were already made.

iv

Raen lived.

She discovered this fact slowly, in great pain, and on the verge of madness.

That she was Meth-maren, and therefore no stranger to majat at close quarters . . . this saved her sanity. She was naked. She was blind, in absolute darkness, and disoriented. She suffered the constant touches of the Workers the length of her body, wetness which worked ceaselessly on her raw wounds, and over all her skin and hair; an endless trickle of moisture and food was delivered from their mandibles to her mouth. Their bodies shifted above and about her, invisible in the dark, with touch of bristles and grip of chelae or mandibles. They hovered, never stepping on her, and their ceaseless humming numbed her ears as the dark numbed her eyes.

She was within the hive. No Kontrin had ever gone within a hive, not since the first days. The Pact forbade. But the blues, the peaceful blues, so long Kethiuy's good neighbors—had not cast her out. Tears squeezed from her eyes. A Worker sipped them instantly, caressing her face with feather-touches of its palps. She moved, and the humming at once grew louder, ominous. They would not permit her to stir. Raw touches on her wounds were constant. She flinched and cried out in agony, and they hovered yet closer, never putting full weight on her, but hindering each movement. The struggle, the needed coordination, grew too much. She hurt, and surrendered to it, finding a constant level for the pain, which finally merged with the sound and the sense of touch. There was neither past nor future; grief and fear were swallowed up in the moment, which stretched endlessly, circular.

She was aware of Mother. There was a Presence within the hive which sent Workers scurrying on this mission and that, to touch her and depart again in haste. In her delirium she imagined that she sensed the touches of this mind, that she was aware of things unseen, the movements in countless blind passages, the logic of the hive. She was cared for. The dark was endless, the touches at her body ceaseless, the sound only slowly varying, which was like deafness, and the touches became numbness. It was, for a long time, too difficult to think and too hard to struggle.

But from the latest sleep she wakened with a sense of desperation.

"Worker," she said into the numbing sound, on a delicate balance of returning strength and diminishing sanity. "Help. Help me." Her voice was unused, her ears so long assaulted by majat-song that human words sounded alien in her hearing. "Worker, tell Mother that I want to speak with her. Take me to her. Now."

"No," said the Worker. It sucked up more air and expelled it through chambers, creating the illusion, if not the intonations of human voice. Other sound fell away, Workers pausing to listen. Worker harmonized with itself as it spoke, the chambers all working in intricate combination. "Unnecessary. Mother knows your condition, knows all necessary things."

"Mother doesn't know what I intend."

"Tell. Tell this-unit."

"Revenge."

Palps swept her face, her mouth, her body, picking up Scent. Worker could not comprehend. Majat individually had their limits. A Worker was not the proper channel for an emotional message and Raen knew it, manipulated the Worker with confusion. She had been cautioned against it from infancy, Workers going in and out of the labs, near at hand: *never play games with them.* Again and again she had heard the dangers of disoriented majat. It might call Warriors.

It drew back abruptly: she suddenly missed that particular touch. Others filled the gap, constantly feeling at limbs and body.

"It's gone for Mother?"

"Yes," one said. "Mother."

She stared at the blind dark, hard-breathing, euphoric with her success. She moved her hand with difficulty past the hindering limbs and palps of Workers, felt of her wounds, which were slick with jelly . . . tested her strength, moving her limbs.

"Are there," she asked, "azi within call?"

"Mother must call azi."

"I shall stand," she declared, rationally, firmly, and began to do so.

Workers assisted. Palps and chelae caressed her naked limbs and urged her, perhaps sensing new steadiness, conscious direction of her movements. Leathery bodies, chitin-studded, pushed at her. She trusted them, despite the possibility of pain. Their knowledge of balance and leverage was instinctive, none truer. With their support she stood, dizzied, and felt about her in the featureless dark. The floor of the chamber was uneven. Up and down seemed confused in the blackness. Her ears were still numbed by their voices; her hands met jointed palps and the hard spines of chelae. The Workers moved with her, never overbalancing her, supporting her with unfailing delicacy as she sought a few steps.

"Take me to Mother," she said.

The song grew harsh and ominous. "Queen-threat," one translated. Others took up the words.

They feared for Mother. That was understandable: she was female, and of females, the hive held only one. They continued to groom her, wishing to feed her, to placate her. She turned from their offerings, distressing them further. She was in pain and her legs trembled under her. The burn on her side had opened in the exertion of rising. They tended this, keeping it moist, and she could not fend them from it. The touches on raw flesh were familiar agony. She had time to reckon what might come of an intruding female, that there would be no welcome:

she refused to think it. Mother must control all that happened here. Mother had tolerated her this far.

Then Worker must have returned; she reckoned so from the commotion that had broken out in the direction of the principal draft. "Bring," a voice fluted, human language, of courtesy. "Mother permits."

Raen went toward the voice, guided by delicate touches of bristling forelimbs, feeling to one side and the other in the blackness, following the currents of moving air. The tunnels were wide and high . . . must be, to afford passage to the tall Warriors. And once, when the right-hand wall vanished suddenly at a steep climb, she fell, in great pain, her body abraded by the hard earth. Workers chittered alarm and lifted her at once, steadied her more carefully as she climbed. The air began to be close and warm. Sweat ran on her bare skin, and distressed the Workers, who tried frantically both to walk and to remove the untidy moisture.

The tunnel seemed all at once defined, the first light her unused eyes had perceived in uncounted days. It was the only proof she had had that she was not blind, and yet it was so very faint she doubted that she perceived it at all . . . circle patterns, oblong and irregular patterns. She realized with a surge of joy that she *was* seeing, realized the shapes for apertures, opening onto a faint greenish phosphorescence, in which majat shadows stalked, bipedal, deceptively human in some poses, like men in ornate armor. Raen hastened, misjudged, almost lost her senses in the warmth and closeness of this place. She gained her balance again, aided and supported into the Presence.

She filled the Chamber. Raen hung in the grip of the Workers, awed by the sight of Her, whose presence dominated the hive, whose mind was the center of the Mind. *She* was the one, if there was any single individual in the hive, with whom they of Kethiuy had so long dealt . . . the legends of all her childhood, living and surrounded by the seething mass of Her Drones, a Scene of fever-dreams, males glittering with the chitinous wealth of the hive.

Air stirred audibly, intaken.

"You are so *small*," Mother said. Raen flinched, for the timbre of it made the very walls quiver, and vibrated in Raen's bones.

"You are beautiful," Raen answered, and felt it. Tears started from her eyes . . . awe, and pain at once.

It pleased Mother. The auditory palps swept forward. Mother inclined Her great head and sought touch. The chelae drew her close. Mother tasted her tears with a brush of the palps.

"Salt," said Mother.

"Yes."

"You are healed."

"I will be, soon."

The huge head rotated a few degrees on its circular jointing. "Scouts report Kethiuy closed to them. This has never happened since the hills have stood. We have killed a red-hive Worker on Kethiuy's borders. Young queen, majat Workers do not enter an area until Warriors have secured it. We tasted it in traces of greens, of golds, recent in red-hive memory. Of humans. Of life fluids. Greens deal with golds and avoid us. Why?"

Raen shook her head, terrified. Her mind began to function in human terms. Majat were still in the valley, when the Pact dictated restrictions. Red-hive. Ruil's allies. The whole Family might have risen against Ruil; it had not; it had agreed, and red-hive remained. She forgot the other questions, ignored logic. Reason could not be on her side. "I'll take Kethiuy back again," she said, knowing that it was mad. "I'll get it back."

"Revenge," Mother said.

"Yes. Revenge. Yes."

More air sighed into Mother's reservoirs. "Since before humans were known, blue-hive has held this hill. Humans came, We majat killed the first. Then we understood. We understood stars and machines and humans. One Family at last we permitted, all, all, red-hive, blue, green, gold . . . one human ship to come among us, one human hive. One ship, which brought the eggs of other humans. We were deceived so. Yet we accepted this. We permit Kontrin-hive to trade and breed and build, instead of all other humans. We permit Kontrin-hive to keep order, and to keep all other humans out. So we have grown, majat hives and Kontrin. We have gained metals, and azi, and consciousness of things invisible; we have enlarged our hives and sent out new queens beneath other suns. Azi work for us with their human eyes and their human hands, and trade gives us food, much food. We can support more numbers than was so in many cycles. We have ridden Kontrin ships to Meron and to Andra and Kalind and Istra, making new extensions of the Mind. We have been pleased in this exchange. We have gained awareness far surpassing times before humans. Your hives have multiplied and prospered, and increased nourishment for ours. But suddenly you fragment yourselves, and now you fragment us. Suddenly there is division. Suddenly there is nest-war among humans; this has been before: we have seen. But now there is nest-war threatened among majat, as it has not been since times before humans. We are confused. We reach out to gather the Mind and we have grown too wide; the worlds are too far and the ships are too slow to help us. We do not gain synthesis. We failed to foresee, and now we are blind. Aid me, Kethiuy-hive. Why are these things happening? What will happen now?''

Drones sang, and moved, a tide of life about Mother. The Drone voices shrilled, much of the song too high for human ears; sound drowned words, drowned thought, grated through bone.

"Mother!" Raen cried. "I don't know. I don't know. But whatever is going on in the Family, we can stop them, blue-hive could stop them!"

Air sighed. Mother heaved Herself lower, and breathed a bass note that made silence. "Kethiuy-queen, Kethiuy-queen—is it possible that our two species have overbred? What is the proper density of your population, young queen? Have you reached some critical level, which humans did not foresee? Or perhaps the equation for both our species is altered by some complex factors of our association. This should not have happened yet. We reach for synthesis and do not obtain it. Where is human synthesis? Have you the answer?"

"No." Raen shivered in the battering sound of Mother's voice, conscious of her own inexperience . . . of that of all men with majat. She reached in the utmost irreverence and touched the scent-patches below the compound eyes, imprinting herself as her kinsman would do with majat Workers, establishing friendship. Mother suffered this without anger, though the jaws might have closed at any instant, though the Drones were disturbed and disturbance ran through all the others. "Mother, Mother, listen to me. Kethiuy was blue-hive's friend, we always were, and I need help. They've killed—everyone. Everyone but me. They think they've won. Ruil sept has brought red-hive in with them. And do you think that Ruil will ever send them away again, or even that they know how? No, they're not going away. Ever. Red-hive will always be in Kethiuy, in our valley, and the Family isn't going to stop them or they would have done something by now."

"This seems an accurate estimation."

"I can take it back. If blue-hive helped me, I could take it back again."

Mother lifted up Her head, mandibles clashing. While She considered, She brought half a dozen new lives into the world. Workers snatched these up and carried them away. Drones groomed Her, uttering soft, distressed pipings, that shrilled away into higher ranges.

"It is very dangerous," Mother said. "Intervention violates the Pact. It adds confusions. And you have no translation computers. Without precise instruction, Warriors and humans cannot cooperate."

"I can *show* them. They can work that way. I can guide them. Some know Kethiuy, don't they? They've been there. And the others can follow them."

Mother hesitated. Again the head rotated slightly. "You are right, young queen, but I suspect you are right for the wrong reasons. All, all Warriors know Kethiuy.

We do not fully understand how your thoughts proceed. But you can serve as nexus. Yes. Possible. Great risk, but possible."

"I can't yet. A few days, a few days, and then I'll be able to try. I'll need a gun, azi, Warriors. Then we can take Kethiuy back. Kethiuy's azi will join the fight when they have orders. Revenge, Mother! And blue-hive can come and go in Kethiuy when they please."

There was again long thought. Air sucked in, gusted out, sucked in again, and the songs of the attendants rose and fell. "I breed Warriors," She said. "This aspect of the hive is needful in these circumstances." While She spoke, She produced several more eggs. "I cannot breed azi. The azi will be irrevocable losses. There can be only one attempt on Kethiuy. Blue-hive has deceived red-hive concerning your presence here. Your death was reported. Warriors went out unMinded in this cause. But Warriors who go with you into Kethiuy cannot go unMinded; they could not then remember their mission or focus properly. There are reds full-circle of Kethiuy. Once you meet them and once blue-hive Warriors have fallen, you cannot retreat here. Taste will betray your existence here to red-hive and they will come here very quickly, for we have admitted a human to the inner hive, and there is strong sentiment against this practice. Therefore we will be fighting both here and there, which will require all our Warriors engaged at once. If we lose many Warriors in this action, we will face further attack from red-hive and others without sufficient time for new to hatch. Tell me, Kethiuy-queen, is this the best action? Perhaps you could find Drones and reestablish elsewhere with better prospect. You could produce Warriors of your own, young queen. You could buy azi. You could make a new hive."

Raen looked up into the great moiré-patterned eyes, in which she existed only as a pattern of warmth. "Red-hive is breeding Warriors too, won't that be so? If they've been expecting to attack Kethiuy, then they'll have been breeding toward it for a long time. Years. What when they come farther than they have? You need

Kethiuy in Sul-sept control. If you wait . . . if you wait, you won't have time to breed enough Warriors, and red-hive—" She caught her breath, for she suddenly sensed what key to use, the essentially honest character of the blues. "Red-hive killed humans, killed Meth-marens, against the Pact. Ruil may have led them to it, but red-hive did it, they chose to do it. Do you want them for neighbors forever, Mother? And your Warriors—do they know the ways into Kethiuy that they can't see? I do. I can get them inside, now. I can get Warriors inside. It doesn't matter how many reds are guarding the doors if blues once get in. And I know I can get you that far."

There was silence.

"Yes," Mother said finally. *"Yes."*

A haze flooded over Raen's eyes, blurring greenish radiance and majat shadows, and the glitter of the Drones. She thought that she would fall, and she must not, must not show weakness before Mother, throwing all she had won in doubt. She touched the chelae, drew back, not knowing what rituals the majat observed with Her. None hindered her going. None seemed offended. She sought the tunnel out of the Chamber. The fungus-glow was like the retinal memory of light, and in this direction lay the dark, circles, holes in the light, into which she entered, losing suddenly all use of her eyes. The air hummed with Worker songs, the deeper songs of Warriors and the high voices of the Drones. She met bristly touches in the dark.

Workers swarmed and circled her, guided, caressed, sought her lips, to know her mind, though human chemistry was chaos to them. Perhaps the scent of Mother lingered. She did not flinch, but touched them in turn, delirious with triumph. They were the substance of her dreams and her nightmares, the majat, the power under-earth, native here where men were newcomers. She had touched the Mother who had lived under the hill since before she was born, and Mother had permitted it. She was Kontrin, of the Family, and the pattern grafted to her right hand was the power of the hives, which Kethiuy had always understood, more than all others of the Family—

hive-friends. She laughed, bewildering the Workers, even while her senses began to fail.

V

Chairs moved; the group settled. A female azi, engineered for functions which had nothing to do with household labor, passed round the long table setting out drinks and beaming dutifully at each.

Eron Thel patted her leg, whispered a dismissal—she was his, as was the summer house in the Altrin highlands—and ignored her familiar charms as she left, although more than one of the men regarded her retreat. He was pleased by this, pleased by the obvious attention of the others to their surroundings. The objects which decorated the meeting room were unique, gathered from worlds even outside the Reach, and met with gratifying admiration . . . nothing of awe; the envy of kinsmen in the Family was difficult to rouse, but they looked, and approved.

Awe: that was for what entered the room now, the majat Warrior who took up guard by the door. That was power. Yls Ren-barant, Del Hald, certain others . . . they were accustomed to the near presence of majat; so was Tel a Ruil, well-accustomed—but familiarity did not remove the dread of such a creature, the sense that with it, invisible, were countless others, the awareness of the hive.

"Are you sure of the majat?" the Hald asked. "It remembers, even if it can't understand."

"It carries messages only to its hive," Eron said, "and its hive has some necessary part in this meeting, cousin, a very central part, as it happens." He beckoned to it, gave a low whistle, and it came, sank down beside the table, towering among them, incapable of the chairs. It was a living recorder; it received messages; it contained one. "Red-hive," Eron explained, "is standing guard at a number of critical posts, on these grounds and elsewhere. Incorruptible guards. Far better than ordinary security.

Their desires are . . . not in rivalry with ours. Quite the contrary." He opened the plastic-bound agenda before him, and the others anxiously did the same. They were a mixed group, his own comrades, and some of the older representatives, selected ones . . . thankful to have been exempted from the general purge . . . grateful—Eron laughed inwardly, while gazing solemnly at the page before him—to have been admitted to this private meeting, the place of power where Council decisions were to be pre-arranged. He folded both hands on the agenda, smiled and leaned forward with a confidential warmth: it was a skill of his, to persuade. He practiced it consciously, foreknowing agreement. He was handsome, with the inbred good looks of all the Kontrin; he looked thirty: the real answer was two centuriest above that, and that was true of most present, save a few of the Halds. He had grace, a matter most Kontrin neglected, content with power; he knew the use of it, and by it moved others. He was spokesman for the inner circle, for Hald and Ren-barant and Ruil Meth-maren. He meant to be more than that.

"Item one: widening the access permitted by the Pact. There has been too severe a restriction between ourselves and the hives." He reached, horrifying some of the older representatives, and laid a hand on the Warrior's thorax. It suffered this placidly, in waiting pose. "We have learned things earlier generations didn't know. The old restrictions have served their purpose. They were protective; they prevented misunderstandings. But—both majat and humans have adjusted to close contact. New realities are upon us. New cooperations are possible; Red-hive in particular has been responsive to this feeling. They are interested in much closer cooperation. So are golds, through their medium."

"Azi." The deep baritone harmonies of the Warrior vibrated even through the table surface. The elder faces at the end of the table were stark with dread. Eron watched them and not the Warrior, reckoning their every reaction. "We widen the hives," the Warrior said. "We protect human hives, for payment in goods. We need more fields, irrigation, more food, more azi. You can give these things. Red-hive and Kontrin—" More air hissed into the chambers. "—are *compatible*. We group now without the translation computers. We have found understanding, identification, *synthesis*. We taste . . . mutual desire."

That was awe. Eron saw it and smiled, a grim, taut smile, that melted into a friendlier one. "The power of the hives. Kontrin power, cousins. Human space shuts us *out*. Kontrin policy has limited our growth, limited our numbers, limited beta generation growth, limited the breeding of their azi. Colonized worlds throughout the Reach are fixed at the level of population reached four centuries ago. Our whole philosophy has been *containment* within the Reach. We have all acquiesced in a situation which was arranged for us . . . in the theory that humans and majat can't cooperate. But we can. We don't have to exist within these limits. We don't have to go on living under these restrictions. Item number one in the program before you is essential: widening access permitted by the Pact. Your affirmative vote is vastly important. Majat will be willing to assist us on more than the Worker level. We already have Warriors accessible to our direction, at this moment; and possibly, possibly, my dear cousins—Drones. The key to the biologic computer that is the hive. *That* kind of cooperation, humans working directly with what has made the hives unaided by machines . . . capable of the most complex order of operations. *That* kind of power, joined to our own: majat holistic comprehension, joined to human senses, human imagination, human insights. A new order. We aren't talking now about remaining bound by old limits. We don't have to settle for *containment* any longer."

No one moved. Eyes were fixed on him, naked, full of speculations.

No, more than speculation: it was fact; they had made it fact. This, here, in this room, was the reality of the Council. Decisions were being shaped here, and no one objected—no one, staring into the glittering eyes of the red Warrior—objected. At this end of the long table, in the hands of the Thels, the Meth-marens, the Renbarants and the Holds . . . rested authority; and the others would go into the Council hall and vote as they were told, fearing for themselves what had been wrought elsewhere.

And perhaps . . . perhaps conceiving ambitions of their own. The old order had been stagnant, centuries without change; change confronted them. *Possibilities* confronted them. Some would want a share of that.

"Second item," Eron said, not needing to look down. "A proposal for expansion of the azi breeding programs. The farms on Istra . . . have applied for expansion of their industry, repeatedly denied under the old regime. The proposal before Council grants that license . . . with compensations for past denials. The facilities on Istra and elsewhere can be quadrupled, an eighteen-year program of expansion easily correlated with the majat's eighteen-year cycle of increase. The hives can be paid . . . in azi; and the population of the Reach can be readjusted.

"Third item, cousins: authorization to beta governments for a ten percent increase in birth permits. The supervisory levels of industry and agriculture must increase in proportion to other increases.

"Fourth: licensing of Kontrin births pegged to the same ten percent. There has already been attrition; there may be more.

"Fifth: formal dissolution of certain septs and allotment of their Colors and privileges to other septs within those Houses. This merely regularizes certain changes already made."

There was laughter from the left side of the room, against the wall, where some of the younger generation sat. Eron looked, as many did. It was Pol Hald who extended his long legs and smirked to himself, ignoring his great-uncle's scowl.

"Questions?" Eron asked, trying to recapture the attention of those at the table. "Debate?"

There was none offered.

"We trust," Tel a Ruil said, "in your votes. Votes will be remembered."

Meth-maren arrogance. Eron scanned faces for reactions, as vexed in Ruil's bald threat as he had been in Pol's mistimed laughter. The elders took both in silence.

Glass smashed, rattled across the tiled floor. Eron looked rage at Pol Hald, who was poised in the careful act, hand open, his drink streamered across the floor. Eron started to his feet, thought better of it, and was grateful for the timely hand of Yls Ren-barant, urging him otherwise; and for Del Hald, who heaved his own bulk about from the table to rebuke his grandnephew.

Meth-marens and Halds: that hate was old and deep, and lately aggravated. Pol's act was that of a clown, a mime, pricking at Family pomposities, more actor than the azi-performers. The poised hand flourished a retraction, buried itself beneath a folded arm. *Sorry,* the lips shaped, elaborate mockery.

Tel Ruil was hard-breathing, face flushed. Ren-barant calmed him too, a slight touch, a warning. Tand Hald and Pol's cousin Morn both looked aside, embarrassed and wishing to disassociate themselves. Eron scanned the lot of them, smiled in his best manner, leaned back. Tel a Ruil relaxed with a similar effort. The small knot of oldest Houses at the end of the table was a skittish group, apt to bolt; those faces did not relax.

Eron relaxed entirely, and kept smiling, all cordiality. "We've begun a smooth transition. That has its difficulties, to be sure, but the advantages of keeping to a quiet schedule are obvious. There is the absolute necessity of keeping a calm face toward the betas and toward the Outside. You understand that. You understand what benefits there are for all of us. We have energies that are only grief to us, so long as we're pent within these outmoded limits. Those talents can be of service. Is there any debate on agenda issues?

"Are we agreed without it, then?"

Heads nodded, even those at the end of the table.

"Why don't we," Eron suggested then, "move on into the bar, and handle this in a more . . . informal atmosphere. Take your drinks with you if you like. We'll talk there . . . about issues."

There was a relieved muttering, ready agreement. The

air held a slightly easier feeling, and chairs went back, men and women moving out in twos and threes, talking in low voices—avoiding the majat Warrior, whose head rotated slightly, betraying life.

Eron cast an urgent scowl at Del Hald, and a grimmer one at Pol and his two companions, who tarried in the seats against the wall, no more anxious to quit the room than their elders. Ros Hald and his several daughters delayed too, the whole clutch of Halds banded for defense.

But Del wilted under Eron's steady gaze, turned to Pol as he rose and caught at Pol's arm. Pol evaded his hand, cast his great-uncle a mocking look . . . son of a third niece to Del and Ros, was Pol: orphan from early years, Del's fosterling, and willing enough to put Del in command of Hald—but Del could not control him, had never controlled him. Pol was an irritant the Family bore and generally laughed at, for his irritation was to the Halds as often as any . . . and others enjoyed that.

Pol rose, with his cousins.

"The essence of humor," said Eron coldly, "is subtlty."

"Why, then, you are very serious, cousin." And seizing young Tand by the arm, Pol left for the bar, self-pleased, laughing. Morn followed in their wake, his grim face once turned back to Eron with no pleasure at all.

Eron expelled a short breath and looked on Del. The eldest Hald's lips were set in a thin line. "He's a hazard," Eron said. "Someone has to make sure of him. He can do us hurt."

"He should go somewhere," Yls said softly to Del, "where he can find full occupation for his humor. Meron, perhaps. Wouldn't that satisfy him?"

"He goes," the Hald said in a thin voice. "Morn goes with him. I understand you."

"A temporary matter," Eron said, and clapped his hand to the Hald's shoulder, pressed it as they walked toward the bar, Ros and his daughters trailing them. "My affection for the fellow. You understand. I don't want trouble right now. We can't afford it. Older heads have to manage this."

And when matters were more settled, Eron thought, Pol might come to some distant and inconspicuous end. Pol's wit was not all turned to humor . . . a child of the last great purge, Pol a Ren hant Hald, and participant in a more recent one, when Meth-marens had done some little damage. Pol Hald and Morn: Pol whose jokes were infamous, and Morn who never laughed—they were both quite apt to treacheries.

Eron thought this, and smiled his engaging smile, among others who held their drinks and smiled most earnestly . . . anxious folk, appropriately grateful to be invited here, admitted to the society of power.

With the Halds and the Meth-marens, the Ren-barants and other key elders here, with Thon and Yalt decimated, and their bloc decimated . . . this gathering and the blocs they represented constituted the majority, not only of raw power on Cerdin, but of votes to sway all the Reach.

vi

"Night," said a Worker.

Raen had sensed it. She had learned the movements and rhythms of the hive which said that this was so: the increase of the traffic coming in, the subtle shifts of air-currents, the different songs. Inside the hive, the blackness was always the same. She had wished a piece of the fungus to provide light, and Workers had brought it, establishing it on the wall of the chamber that was hers. By this she proved to herself that her eyes still functioned, and gave them limits against which to work. But that was only for comfort. She had learned to see with touch, with the variations of the constant song of the hive; and to understand majat vision. *Beautiful, beautiful,* they called her, entranced with the colors of her warmth. *You are the colors of all the hives,* the attendants told her, *blue and green and gold and red, ever-changing; but your limb is always blue-hive.*

Her hand, covered with blue-hive chitin: they were

endlessly fascinated by that, which was a secret toward
which majat had contributed. Kontrin genetic science and
majat biochemistry . . . the two in complement had
spawned all the life of the Reach. Majat were capable of
analyses and syntheses of enormous range and sensitivity,
capable of sampling and altering substances as naturally
as humans flexed limbs, a partnership invaluable to Kontrin labs. But the hive, she realized, the hive had never
directly participated. The majat Workers who came into
the labs to stay were always isolated from Workers of
the hive, lest their chemical muddle impress the hive and
disturb it. They never returned, but clung forlornly to
human company and direction, dependent on it, patterned to the few humans who dared touch them: seldom
resting, sleepless, they would work until their energy
burned them out. Afterward, humans must dispose of
the corpses: no majat would.

My being here is a danger to the Mind, she thought
suddenly, with a deep pang of conscience. *Maybe my
coming here has done what they've always feared, shifted
their chemistry and affected them. Perhaps I've trapped
them.*

There were azi, human Workers . . . the majat lived
closely with those, unaffected by chemical disturbance.

Are they? she wondered; and then, more terrifyingly:
Am I?

The song deafened, quivered in the marrow of the
bones. Mother began it, and the Workers carried it, and
the Warriors added their own baritone counterpoint,
alien to their own species, the killer portion of the partitioned hive-mind. Drones sang but rarely . . . or perhaps,
like much of majat language, the Drone songs were seldom in human range.

Raen rose, walked, tested the strength of her limbs.
They had given her cloth of majat spinning, gossamer,
the pale web of egg-sheaths. She did not wear it, for it
disturbed them that she muted her colors, and nakedness
no longer disturbed her. But she considered it now.

"I am ready," she decided. Workers touched her and
scurried off, bearing that message.

A Warrior arrived. She informed it directly of her plans, and it hurried off.

Soon came the azi . . . humans, marginally so, though majat did not reckon them as such. Lab-bred, sterile, though with the outward attributes of gender, they served the hives as the Workers did, with hands more agile and wits more suited to dealing with humans, the new appurtenances the hives had taken on when they began to associate with humans, a new and necessary fragment of the hive-mind. Betas made them, and sold them to other betas . . . and to Kontrin, who sold them to the hives, shortlived clones of beta cells.

They came, bearing blue lights hardly brighter than the illusory fungus, and gathered about her, perhaps bewildered by the chitin on her hand, the realization that she was Kontrin, though naked as they, and within the hive. They were not bred fighters, these particular azi, but they were clever and quick, bright-eyed and anxious to serve. They were much prized by majat and must know their worth in the hive, but they were a little mad. Azi who dwelled among majat tended to be.

"We're going outside," Raen told them. "You'll carry weapons and take my orders."

"Yes," they said, voices overlapping, song-toned, inflectionless as those of the majat. There was a certain horror in these strangest of the azi. They came here younger than azi were generally sold; they acquired majat habits. They touched her, confirming her in their minds. She returned the touches, and gathered up the clothing she had been given. She wrapped it round and tied it here and there. It had a strange feel, light as it was, the reminder of a world and a life outside.

A Warrior came then, sat down, glittering in the azi-lights, chitinous head and powerful jaws a fantasy of jewel-shards. It offered her a pistol. It carried weapons of its own, besides the array nature had provided it: these items too majat prized, status for Warriors . . . empty symbols: humans had believed so. Raen took up the offered gun, found it shaped to a human hand. The cold, heavy object quickly warmed to her grip, and she took keen pleasure in the solidity of it: power, power to make Ruil pay.

"Azi-weapon," Warrior said. "Shall we arm azi?"

"Yes." She thrust her free hand against its scent-patches, reaching between the huge jaws. "Are you ready?"

A song hummed from Warrior. Others appeared, shifting from unseen tunnels into the meager light. They bore weapons, some belted to their leathery bodies; others went to the azi. The azi's human eyes were intense with something other than humanity. They grinned, filled with excitement.

"Come," she bade them.

Her word had Mother's authority behind it, the consensus of the hive. They moved, all of them, down the tunnels. Other Warriors joined them, a great following of bodies strangely silent now, songs stilled. They went in total blackness, azi-lights left behind.

Then they reached the cool air of the vestibule, and poured out under the night sky. Raen shivered in the wind and blinked, awed to find the stars again, to realize the brilliance of the night.

Warriors gathered silently about her, touching, seeking motive and direction. She was nexus, binding-unit for this portion of the Mind. She started away, barefoot and agile among the rocks.

vii

Starlight glistened on the lake, and bright artificial lights danced wetly at the farther shore, where Sul had never put lights. Raen stopped on the last rocky shelf above the woods and snatched a look at sights to which majat eyes were all but blind. For the first time her wounds hurt, her breath came short. Kethiuy-by-the-waters.

Home.

She felt more grief than she had yet felt. She had been out of human reference; and now the deaths became real to her again. Mother, cousins, friends . . . all ashes by now. Ruil would have spared no one, least of all eldest, so that there would be no possibility of challenge to their claim. Even yet the Family had made no move to intervene: Ruil still held here, or the hive would have known, would have told her. Red-hive remained here: of that they were sure.

Bile rose in her throat, bitter hate. She swallowed at it, and wiped her eyes with the back of her left hand, the gun clenched in her chitined right.

"Meth-maren," Warrior urged her. She scrambled down, reckless on the rocks, half-blind. Her limbs trembled with the strain, but Warrior caught her, its stilt-limbs strong and sure, a single downward stride spanning several of hers, joints bracing easily at extensions impossible for human limbs: its muscles attached to endo- and exoskeletons. Azi too swarmed back up the rocks and took her arms, helping her, handing her down to other Warriors, who urged her on in their turn Worker-fashion: most adaptable of majat, the Warriors, capable of independent judgment and generalized functions.

"This way," she bade them, choosing her way through the forest, along paths she knew. They went with hardly a crack of brush, walking as fast as she could run.

Red Warrior. It started from cover in the thickets and misjudged its capacity for flight. Blues sped after it, brought it down and bit it. The group of combatants locked into statuelike quiet for a few moments, blue bowed over their enemy, mandibles locked with majat patience. Then the head came free, and blue Warriors came to life and stalked ahead, some on the trail and some off, passing taste in weaving contacts, one to the other.

"Strong red force," Warrior said to Raen, and nervously touched palps to her mouth as they walked, a curious backward dance in the act. It interpreted aloud what taste should have told her, a mere breathing of resonances. "Ruil humans. No sense of alarm. They do not expect attack."

The blue Warriors were elated; their movements were exaggerated, full of excess energy. Some darted back, urging on those who lagged; a dark flood of bodies in their wake tumbled down the rocks and through the trees. The azi, touching each other and grinning with joy, would have loped ahead. Raen distrusted their good sense and hissed at them to hold back. She was hurrying as much as she could. Her side hurt anew. Her bare feet were torn by the rocks and the thorns. She ignored the pain; she had felt ·worse. An increasing fear gripped her stomach.

I'm too slow, she thought in one moment of panic. *I'm holding them back too long.* And in another: *There are grown men down there, used to killing; there are guard-azi, bred for fighting. What am I doing here?* But they were not expecting attack: the blues read so; and they would not be expecting majat. She looked about her at her companions, at creatures whose very instincts were specialized toward killing, and drank in their enthusiasm, that was madness.

They were nearing the end of the woods, where there were only thickets and thorn-hedges. "Hurry," Warrior urged her, seizing her painfully by the arm. Majat were not like men, who respected a leader: hive-mind was one. She pressed a hand to her throbbing side and started to run, spending the strength she had saved.

There were ways she knew, paths she had run in other days, shortcuts azi workers took to the fields; places where the hedges were thin. She ran them, dodging this way and that with agility that only the azi matched in this tangle. A wall loomed up, the barrier to the inner gardens by the labs, no obstacle to the Warriors, who living-chained their way up and made a way for the azi. Azi swarmed over, tugging and pulling at her to help her after, climbing over their naked and sweating bodies. She made it. The chain undid itself. The last Warrior came over, a stilt-limbed prodigy of balance and strength, pulled by its fellows.

They were pleased with the operation. Mandibles scissored with rapid excitement. Suddenly they broke and raced like a black flood in the dark, majat and azi, moving with incredible rapidity.

More red-hivers. Bodies tangled on the lawn, rolled; the wave-front blunted itself, knotted in places of resistance. There were crashings in the shrubbery, the booming alarm of Warriors, flares of weapons. Raen froze in shadow, panic-stricken, everything she had planned slipping control. Then she adjusted her grip on her gun, swallowed air and ran, to do what she had come to do.

A Warrior appeared by her, and another, half a dozen more, and some of the azi. She raced for the main door, for an area visibly guarded by red-hive. Fire laced about them, and from them. Warriors beside her fell, twitching, uttering squeals from their resonance chambers. In sanity, she would have panicked. There was nothing to do now but keep running for the door . . . too far now to retreat. She reached the door and Warriors tangled in combat about her. She burned the mechanism, and struggled with the door; azi and then a Warrior used their strength to move it. Azi and Warriors flooded behind her as she raced into Kethiuy's halls.

"Exits all covered," Warrior breathed beside her; and then she realized where all the others had gone—majat strategy, efficient and sudden. The main corridor of the central dome lay vacant before her . . . what had been home. Rage hammered in her in time to her pulse.

Suddenly, far off down the wings, there was crashing and shrilling of alarms, from every point of the building: blue-hivers were in. A domestic azi darted from cover, terrified, darted back again, up the stairs—and screamed and fell under a rush of majat down them.

Red-hivers. Raen whipped the gun to target and fired, breaking up their formation, even while blue-hive swarmed after them.

There were human cries. Doors broke open from westwing: Ruils burst from that cover with a handful of blues on their heels. Raen left majat to majat, steadied her pistol on new targets and fired, careful shots as ever in practice, at the weapon's limits of speed. Her eyes stayed clear. Time slowed. They fell, one after the other, young and old, perhaps not believing what they saw. Their faces were set in horror and hers in a rigid grin.

Then a baritone piping assailed her ears and the blues in all parts of the corridor signaled each other in booming panic, regrouping to signals she could not read. From eastwing came others, reds, golds, a horde of armed azi.

Raen stood and fired, coldly desperate, not seeing how to retreat. Some of the Kethiuy azi and the surviving blues attempted to rally to her, but fire cut them down and a rush of majat came over them.

Warrior fell almost at her feet, decapitated. The limbs continued to struggle, nearly taking her off her feet. Naked azi sprawled dead about her. She spun then, catching her balance, and tried to run, for there was no other hope. The blues, such as survived, were in full flight.

Something crashed down on her, crushing weight.

viii

A second time Raen lay quietly and waited to live or die; but this time the walls were stark white and chrome, and the frightened azi who tended her kept their eyes down and said nothing.

That was well enough. There was nothing she particularly wanted to hear. She was not in Kethiuy. That told her something. Drugs hazed her senses, keeping her from wishing anything very strongly.

This continued for what seemed days. There were meals. She was fed, being unable to feed herself. She was moved, bothered for this and the other necessity. She said nothing in all this time, and from the azi there was no word.

But finally the drugs were gone, and she waked with a majat guard in the room.

Red-hive. She recognized the badges, the marks they wore for humans, who could not see their colors. Red-hive Warrior.

She knew then that she had lost, lost more than Kethiuy.

The majat gave her clothing, gray, without Color. She

put it on, and found the close feeling of it utterly strange. She sat afterward with her hands in her lap, on the edge of the bed, staring at the wall. The majat guard did not move and would not move while she did not.

There was shock attendant on regaining the human world; there were realizations of what she had lost and what she had become. She was very thin. Her limbs still hurt, although she bore scars only on her side. She held her right hand clenched in her left, feeling the beaded surface of the chitin which was her identity: Raen, Sulsept, Meth-maren, Kontrin. They gave her gray to wear, and not her Color. There was no way to remove the other distinction save by massive scarring. A scale lost would regrow. She had heard of Kontrin deprived of identity, mutilated by assassins, or by Council order. That prospect frightened her, more than she was willing to show. It was all she had left to lose. She was fifteen, going on sixteen. She was mortally afraid.

It was a very long time before the call she anticipated came.

She went with the azi guards, unresisting.

ix

They were the authority of the Family, the available heads of the twenty-seven holdings and the fifty-odd subgrants, with their outworld branches. They wore the Colors of House and sept, and glittered with chitinous armor . . . ornament, little protection, for most was for right-arm only; and weapons in Council were outlawed. Old men and old women inside, although the faces did not make it evident . . . Raen scanned the half-circular array, the amphitheater of Council, herself in the low center, and realized with mixed feelings that no one present wore Kethiuy blue. She saw Kahn, once the youngest in Council; at seventy-two, senior of assassin-ravaged Beln sept of the Ilit; he looked thirty. There was Moth, who showed her age most, incredibly wrinkled and fragile . . . going soon, the Family surmised. She was beyond her six hundredth year and her hair was completely silver and thinning. And Lian, Eldest of Family . . . to him Raen looked with a sudden access of hope; Lian still alive, uncle Lian, who at seven hundred had been immune from assassination perhaps because the Family grew curious how long a Kontrin could live and remain sane. Lian was one of the originals, old as the establishment of humans on Cerdin, first in Council.

And he had had friendship with Grandfather. Raen had known him from her infancy, a guest in her home, who had noticed her at Grandfather's feet. She tried desperately now to meet his eyes, hoping that about him still gathered some power to help her; but she could not. He nodded away in his own thoughts, placid, seeming elsewhere, and simply old, as betas grew old. She stared past him at the others then, altogether out of hope.

There were Eron Thel and Yls Ren-barant, allies, some of Ruil's friends. Sul had detested them. And there were others of that ilk. She had deepstudied the whole Council and all the Houses of greatest import to Sul Meth-maren, so that she knew every name and face and the manners and history of them: but the faces she should have seen were not there, and others wore their Colors. There were new representatives for Yalt and Thon, young faces. Her skin went cold as she reckoned what must have happened throughout the Family—many, many Kethiuys, in so short a time. New men had come into power everywhere, on Cerdin and elsewhere, a new party in power, and from it only Ruil Meth-maren was missing.

Eron Thel rose, touched his microphone to activate it, looked at Council in general, sweeping the banks of seats.

"Matter before the Council," he said, "the custody of the minor child Raen a Sul Meth-maren."

"I am my own keeper," Raen shouted, and Eron turned slowly to stare at her, in the silence, the consent of all the others. Of a sudden she realized in whose keeping she was intended to be, and what that keeping might be. The thought closed on her throat, making words impossible.

"That you tried to be," Eron Thel said, his voice echoing from the speakers. "You succeeded in wiping out
Ruil-sept. All perished, down to the youngest, by your
action. *Child* may be a misnomer in your case; some have
argued to that effect. If you held the Meth-maren House,
you would have to answer for its actions; and I don't
think you'd want that, would you? Council means to consider your age. You'd be wise to remember that."

"I am *the* Meth-maren," she shouted back at him.

Eron looked elsewhere, signaled. Lights dimmed.
Screens central to the room leaped into life. There was
Kethiuy. Raen's heart beat painfully, foreknowing in this
prepared show something meant to hurt her. *I shall not,*
she kept thinking, *I shall not please them.*

There was the garden, by the labs. Bodies lay in neat
rows. The scene came closer, and she recognized them
for the azi of Kethiuy, most merely workers, inoffensive
and innocent of threat to any, face after face, all of them
slaughtered and laid out for inspection, one body upon
another. The line went on and on, hundreds of them,
most strange to her, for she had not known all who
worked the fields; but there was Lia, there were others,
and those faces suddenly appearing struck at her heart.
She feared they would show her the bodies of her kin
next, but they should have been long cremated and beyond such indignities. She hoped that this was so.

The scene shifted to the hills. Majat swarmed everywhere, reds, greens, golds. She saw blue-hivers dead. The
lens approached the very vestibule of blue-hive. There
were white objects cast about the entry, eggs, their fragile
wrappings torn, half-formed majat exposed to the air.
Blue-hive bodies were stacked in a tangle of stilt limbs,
Workers as well as Warriors, and naked human limbs
among them, dead azi.

Then Kethiuy again. Fire went up from it. Walls crumbled in great heat. Candletrees went up in spurts of flame.

The screen dimmed; the lights of the room brightened.
Raen stood still. Her face was dry, cold as the center
of her.

"You can see," said Eron, "Meth-maren's holding is

abolished. It has no adult membership, no property, no vote."

Raen shrugged, jaw set, not trusting her voice. This was something in which her protests meant nothing. She was Kontrin, well-versed in the techniques of assassination and the exigencies of politics; and reckoned well her probable future in the hands of an enemy House. She had deepstudied the history of the Family. She knew the adjustments that necessarily followed a purge, knew that even elders of sensitive conscience would raise no objection now, not for so slight a cause as herself, who could not repay. She continued to focus on the empty screen, wishing a weapon in hand, one last chance, perceiving her enemies more than Ruil alone.

There was another stirring, from a quarter she had not expected. She did look. It was old Moth, who had been an ornament in Council for years, representative of little Eft-sept of the Tern, silent whatever happened, siding with any majority, sleeping through many a session.

"There has been no vote," Moth said.

"But there was," said Eron. "Moth, you must have been napping." There was laughter, obedient, from all Eron's partisans, and it had many voices.

Suddenly Eldest rose, Lian, leaning on the rail. He was not the joke that Moth was. There was quiet. "There was no vote," he repeated. No one laughed. "Evidently, Thel, you have counted your numbers and decided a vote of the full Council would be superfluous." Lian looked toward Raen, blear-eyed, his face working to focus. "Raen a Sul hant Meth-maren. My apologies and condolences, from the Family."

"Sit down, Eldest," said Eron.

The old man briefly pressed Moth's hand, and Moth left her place and descended the steps toward the center where Raen stood. She had difficulty with her robes and the steps, and tottered as she walked. There was displeasure voiced, but no one moved to help or to stop her.

"Procedures," Moth said over the speakers, when she had gained the floor and faced them. "There are procedures. You have not followed them."

"I will tell you something," said Eldest from his place above. He activated his microphone. "It's a dangerous precedent, this destruction of a House, this . . . assumption of consent. I've lived since the first ship came into the Reach, and I'll tell you this: I saw early that men couldn't live here without being corrupted."

"Sit down," someone shouted at him.

"The hives," Eldest said, "had a wealth to be taken; but humanity and the hive-mind weren't compatible. A probe came down on Cerdin; it came into red-hive possession, the crew held captive, such of them as survived. *Celia* probe. The hives gained knowledge. There was *Delia,* then, that got through. Back in human space there was talk about sterilizing Cerdin before the plague could spread. But suddenly the hives changed their attitude. They wanted trade, wanted us, wanted—one ship, they said: one hive for humans, and the Reach set aside for themselves."

There was sullen silence. Moth touched Raen's sleeve, pressed her wrist with a soft-fleshed hand. Someone else started to his feet, a Delt; Yls Ren-barant stopped him. The silence continued, deadly. Lian looked about him, uncertainly, and pursed his lips.

"We tricked them." Lian's voice, quavering, resumed. "We brought in human eggs and the equipment to handle them. Half a billion eggs, all ready to grow. And we set up where this building stands, and we set up our labs and we started breeding while our one ship made its trade runs and the others of us who had skill at communication developed agreements with the hives." His voice grew stronger. "Now do you suppose, fellow Councillors, that the hives didn't know by then what we were about? Of course they saw. But the human animal is a mystery to them, and we kept it that way. They saw a hive-structure. They saw an increasing number of young and a growing social order which well-agreed with their own pattern. We planned it that way. They still had no idea what a non-collective intelligence was, or what it could do. Just one large hive, this of ours, all one mind. They knew better, perhaps, in theory. But the pattern of their own thinking wouldn't let them interpret what they saw.

"When they began to learn, we frightened them with our differences. Frightened them most with the concept of dying. They locked into our chemistry and understood the process, worked out a cure for old age. They had finally gained the dimmest notion, you see, of what our individuality *is*. The hives are millions of years old. Do you reckon why the majat were worried about our dying? Because among majat, there are only four persons . . . red, green, gold, and blue. Those are their units of individuality. These *persons* have worked out how to deal with each other over millions of years. They're accustomed to stability, to memory, to eternity. How could they deal with a series of short-lived humans? So they cured death . . . for some of us, for those of us fortunate enough to be born Kontrin. The beta generations, the product of our cargo of eggs . . . they go on dying at the human rate, but we live forever. Economic ruin, if there were many of us. So even we Kontrin kill each other off from time to time. The majat used to find that shocking.

"But now things will change, won't they? You've gotten red-hive Warriors to kill Kontrin; blue-hive has admitted a human. Things change. Now the majat have taken another vast leap of understanding. And one of the four entities which has lived on Cerdin for millions of years—is on the verge of extinction. Not beyond recall: majat have more respect for life than we do, after their fashion. But you persuaded them to kill an immortal intelligence, knowingly. Several of them. And one day you may live to see the reward of that. Thanks to majat science, some of you may live to see it.

"Seven hundred years we've thrived here and across the Reach. The lot of you have all you could possibly need. The betas take care of the labor and the trade; and the betas, the betas, dear friends, discovered the best thing of all, discovered what the hives really prize: they trade in humanity, altered humanity, gene-tampered humanity, humanity that can't reproduce itself, that self-destructs at forty, for economic convenience. So even the betas don't have to do physical labor; they just breed azi and balance supply and demand. And the barrier to the Outside holds firm, so that the whole Reach and all it produces is ours—including the betas and the azi. None of us tries the barrier.

"Ever been out that far, to the edge? I have. In seven hundred years a man has time to do everything of interest. Ugly worlds. Nothing like Cerdin. But we've established hives that far out, extensions of our four entities here . . . or whole new personalities. Has anyone ever asked them? We've entered into a strange new relationship with our alien hosts; we've become ultimately involved in their reproductive process . . . indispensable to them. Without metals, majat could never have left Cerdin. They have no eyes to see the stars, just their own sun, their own sun-warmed earth. But we've changed that. Even majat don't have to work much, not the way they used to seven hundred years ago. But they thrive. And their numbers increase. And back here at Alpha, this Council, this wise . . . expert Council . . . makes ultimate decisions about population levels, and how many of us can be born, and where; and how many betas; and where betas can be licensed to produce azi, and when azi levels have to be reduced. Humanity's brain, are we not, doing for our kind what the queens do for the hives? And in that process, we've grown *different,* my young friends.

"I was here. I was here from the beginning, and I've watched the change. I'm from Outside. I remember. You . . . you've studied this in your tapes, you young ones of a century or so, you Council newcomers. I'm an old man and I'm delaying things. You think you know it all, having been born here, in the Reach, in a new age you think an old Outsider can't understand. But I'm going to go on telling you, because you need to remember it. Because the majat will tell you that a hive that has lost its memory, that has . . . unMinded itself . . . is headed for extinction.

"Do you know that no ship from Outside has ever tried to reach Cerdin? Ever, since *Delia?* We're quarantined. They're all around us, Outside. Human space. These few little stars . . . are an island in a human sea. But you don't see them trying to come in. Ever wonder why?

"They don't want the majat, my friends. They want what the majat produce, the chitin-jewels, the biotics, the softwares. Humans from Outside meet the betas and the azi at Istra station, and they will pay for those goods, pay whatever they must. They cost us little and Outsiders value them beyond price. But they don't want the majat. They don't want hives in their space.

"And above all, they don't want us. Alpha Hydri, the Serpent's Eye. Off limits by treaty. And no one wants in. No one wants in."

"Get to the point," Eron said.

Slowly Lian turned, and stared at Eron. There was quiet, anticipation. And suddenly outcries erupted, people throwing themselves from seats. A bolt flew from Moth's hand to Eron, and the man fell. Raen flung herself to the back wall, expecting more fire, eyes scanning wildly for weapons on the other side.

"When you practice assassination," Lian said, while Moth held the weapon on Eron's friend Yls, "recall that Moth and I are oldest."

Yls died. Men and women screamed and tried to bolt their seats. Moth continued to fire. There were bodies everywhere, on the floor, draped over seats, over the rail, in the aisles. At last she stopped, and the half of the Council that remained alive huddled against the door.

"Resume your seats," Lian said.

Slowly, cowed, they did so. Moth still had her weapon in hand.

"Now," said Lian, "the matter of a vote."

Someone was sick. The stench of burning was in the hall. Raen clenched her arms about her and shivered.

"Raen a Sul hant Meth-maren," Lian said.

"Sir."

"You may go. I think that it would be advisable to leave Cerdin and seek some House in obscurity. You have outlived all your enemies. Count that fortune enough for a lifetime. I don't think it wise that you shelter with another House on Cerdin; you could too easily become a cause, and the Family has seen enough of that."

"Sir," she began to protest.

"There's no reason to detain you for proceedings. The vote is only a formality. Kethiuy is gone; that is a fact over which Council has no control. You broke the Pact and involved majat. The ones principally involved are dead; their influence is ended. Your own judgment in what you've done was that of a child, and under compulsion. You refuse guardianship; I daresay you are competent to survive without it. So I charge you this, Raen a Sul: avoid majat hereafter. You are given all the privileges of majority, and if you cross Council's notice again, it will be under those conditions. You are free to go, with that understanding. I suggest Meron. Council liaison there will be sympathetic. I have an old estate there that you can use. You won't be without friends or advice."

"I don't need it."

It was out of bitterness she said it. She saw Lian's mouth go to a taut line, and reckoned that she should not have refused; but it was not in her nature to bend. She looked on Moth, looked on Eldest, and turned, walked, with difficulty, to the door and her freedom.

She did not stop, nor look back, nor shed the tears that urged at her. They dried quickly. She knew the passages from the Old Hall at Alpha to the beta City. She carried nothing, but the clothes she had been given and the identity on her hand.

Leave Cerdin: she would, for there was nothing on Cerdin she wanted.

X

The betas of the City were shocked, alarmed that a Kontrin appeared alone among them, with bodyguards. Perhaps they had some apprehension of trouble, having heard of the decimation of Kontrin Houses, and of bluehive, and therefore feared to involve themselves in her affairs; but they had no means to refuse.

She bought medical care, and drugs for the pain; she

slept a time in a public lodging, and recovered herself. She bought clothing and weapons, and engaged a shuttle up to station, where she hired a ship with the credit of the Family—the most extravagant she could find. She was moody and the beta crew avoided her.

That was the first journey.

It brought her to Meron. She did not take Eldest's offer, but bought a house and lived there on the endless credit which the chitin-pattern of her right hand signified. There were Halds onworld: her interest pricked at that . . . Pol and Morn; she stirred to care again. Plotting their assassinations and guarding against her own occupied her time . . . until Pol and Morn turned up boldly on her doorstep, and Pol swept her a mocking curtsy.

Pol Hald. She had passed her sixteenth birthday; he was unchanged, whatever age he really was. He stared her up and down and she looked at him, and at Morn, who stood at his shoulder; and she realized with a chill that her gun was on safety in its belt-clip; she could not possibly be quick enough.

"Your operation is entirely too elaborate," Pol said, grinning at her. "But well-thought, little Meth-maren. I applaud your zeal . . . and your precocious cleverness. Please call them off."

She fairly shook with rage, but fear chilled her mind to clarity. Of a sudden she saw the reaction to take with this man, and grinned. "I shall," she said. "Thank you for the courtesy, Pol Hald."

"What self-possession you have, Meth-maren."

"Shall I leave Meron?"

"Stay," he said, and laughed, with a flourish of his chitined hand. "You have what Ruil never had: a sense of balance. I know neither of us would be safe under those terms. There'd be a new plot by suppertime."

She regarded them through slit lids. "Then you leave Meron."

He laughed outright, brushed past her, into her home. Morn followed.

She thumbed the safety off her gun and stared at them, watching their hands. Pol folded his arms and nodded a gesture to his cousin. "Go on," he said, "Morn. You've no interests here."

Morn surveyed her up and down, his gaunt face untouched by any emotion. Without a word he strode to the door and closed it behind him.

And Pol settled in the nearest chair and folded his arms, extended his long legs before him. His death's-head face quirked into an engaging smile.

He ate the dinner she served him; they sat across the table from one another: he made a proposal which she declined, and laughed rather regretfully when she did so. Pol's humor was infamous, and infectious; and he hazarded his life on it now. She refrained from poisoning him; he refrained from using whatever weapons he surely carried on his person. They laughed at each other, and she bade him good night.

He and she turned up at the same social events thereafter, in the busy winter season of Kontrin society on Meron. They smiled at each other with the warmth of old friends, amused at the comment that caused. But they never met in private.

And eventually there was an attempt on her life.

It happened on Meron, a year after Pol and Morn had taken themselves elsewhere, in separate directions, Morn to Cerdin and Pol to Andra. It happened in the night, on another Kontrin's estate, a Delt, Col a Helim, who was her current, but not exclusive interest. She was twenty-one. Col died. She did not. None came back from that attempt, but they were azi who had done it, and their past was wiped, their tattoos burned away. She swore off Delts, suspecting something local and involving a rival, and moved and engaged a small estate on Silak.

Word reached her there that Lian had died . . . asassination, and no one knew now how long he would have lived, so the longest human life in the Reach reached no natural conclusion and Kontrin everywhere had been frustrated. The attempted coup was a failure, and the assassins all died miserably, the penalty of failure and the revenge of Kontrin who had considered Lian's long life a talisman of luck, an example of their own immortality.

Moth held Eldest's place, first in Council. The Council thus remained much as it had been, and Raen took no interest in its affairs . . . took no interest in the present for anything political. There was no more Kethiuy, although the nightmares lingered. She was mildly amused in one respect, for she reckoned at last that the attempt on her had been connected to Lian's impending fall; but that had failed, the conspirators (Thel and some lesser Houses) decimated, and matters were settled again. The Family knew where she was at all times, and if she had been of continuing importance to any cause, someone would have attempted to enlist her or to assassinate her in the fear that she belonged to some other cause. Neither happened. The remnant of the House of Thon on Cerdin established itself as the new liaison with the hives. Raen settled again on Meron and, when she heard how Thon had usurped the post with the hives, she pursued vices in considerable variety and nuance and gained a name in Meron society. She was twenty-four.

She had her privileges: those never failed; and she had no lack of anything money could buy. She amused herself, sometimes within Kontrin society and sometimes in moody withdrawal from all contact. She looked on betas and azi with the disdain of her birth, which was natural, and her tedious lifespan, which was (since Lian's assassination) indefinite, and her power, which was among betas as fearsome as it was negligible where she would have desired to apply it.

She had as her current interest Hal a Norn hant Ilit, a remote and seldom-social member of the House most involved in Meron's banking; she reckoned he might be a direct relative, and tried to jog his memory which of his kinsmen Morel a Sul Meth-maren had had for a lover, but he avowed it was several, and she went frustrated. He was frustrating in other ways, but he was a useful shelter, and they had some common interests; few could argue comp theory with him, or for that matter, cared to: she did, and for all the vast disparity in their ages (he was in his third century) and in outlook, he avowed himself increasingly infatuated.

She found herself increasingly uncomfortable, and began, as gently as possible, to break that entanglement, coming out of her isolation into the society he hated; a part of that society was his grandnephew Gen.

In all of this, there was a certain leisure.

The order which Moth maintained in Council and in the Reach was a calm one, and a prosperous one, and no one on Cerdin or off seemed energetic enough to seek Moth's life: it seemed superfluous, for no one expected that life to extend much longer. What enemies Moth had were evidently determined to outwait her, and that meant a surface peace, whatever built up beneath. Raen reckoned with Moth in power she might even have gone home to Cerdin, had she asked. She simply declined to make the request, which required on the one hand a humility toward Council she had never acquired; and on the other, faith that Moth would survive long enough for her to entrench herself among friends: she did not think so. And more than all other reasons, she simply refused to face the ruin at Kethiuy; there was nothing there for her.

On Meron, there was.

Then strife erupted among majat on Meron, reds and greens and blues at odds. Golds took shelter and stayed out of sight. Reds strayed into the passages of the City on Meron, terrifying betas and occasioning several deaths in panicked crowds. A Kontrin estate or two suffered minor damage.

Raen quitted Meron then, having lost the four azi who had served her the last several years.

The four azi, dying in their sleep, did not suffer. Raen did, of bitter anger. It gave her temporary motivation, settling with the erstwhile Ilit lover who had let red-hivers into the estate; but that was arranged with disappointing lack of difficulty; and afterward she was tormented with doubt, whether Hal Ilit had had choice in the matter. Blue-hive, she heard, skirmished with the others and retreated, sealed into its hill again, while reds came and went where they would: Thons came from Cerdin to try to persuade them back into quiet.

There was similar disturbance on Andra, and Raen was there, . . . attempted last of all to contact blue-hive directly, but it evaded her, and sealed itself in, while other hives walked Andran streets with impunity.

She was thirty-four. It had been nineteen years since Kethiuy, since Cerdin.

She began, obsessively, to practice certain skills she had let fall in recent years. She withdrew entirely unto herself, and ceased to mourn for the past.

Even for Kethiuy, which was the last thing she had loved.

She was utterly Kontrin, as Moth was, as Lian had been, as all her elders were. She had come of age.

"She's on Kalind," Pol said.

Moth regarded him and his two kinsmen with placid eyes.

"She can be removed," Morn said.

Moth shook her head. "Not yet."

"Eldest—" Tand leaned on her desk, facing her with a lack of respect not uncommon in Halds, not uncommon in his generation. "Blue-hive has been astir on Meron; she was there; and on Andra; she was there; and on Kalind; she is there now. The indications are that she's directly involved, contrary to all conditions and advice. She's broken with all her old contacts."

"She's learned good taste," said Pol. He smiled lazily, leaned back in his chair, folded his slim hands on his belly. "And about time."

Morn fixed him with a burning look. Pol shrugged, made a loose gesture, rose and bowed an ironic goodbye. The door closed behind him.

"She's involved," Tand said.

Moth failed to be excited. Tand finally took the point and stood back, folded his hands behind him, silent as Morn.

"You are trying to urge me to something," Moth said.

"We had thought in your good interests, in those of the Family—there was some urgency."

"You are called here simply to inform me, Tand Hald. Your advice is occasionally of great value. I do listen."

Tand bowed his head, courtesy.

Bastard, she thought. *Eager for advancement however it comes fastest and safest. You hate my guts. And, Morn— yours too.*

"Other observations?" she asked.

"We're waiting," Morn said, "for instructions in the case."

Moth shrugged. "Simply observe. That's all I want."

"Why so much patience with this one?"

Moth shrugged a second time. "She's the last of a House; the daughter of an old, old friend. Maybe it's sentiment."

Morn took that for the irony it was and stopped asking questions.

"Simply watch," she said. "And, Tand—don't provoke anything. Don't create a situation."

Tand took his leave, quietly. Morn followed.

Moth settled in her chair, hands folded, dreaming into the colored lights that flowed in the table surface.

BOOK THREE

i

There was, in the salon of the *Andra's Jewel,* an unaccustomed silence. Normally the first main-evening of a voyage would have seen the salon crowded with wealthy beta passengers, each smartly turned out in expensive innerworld fashions, tongues soon loosened with drink and the nervousness with which these folk, the wealthy of several worlds, greeted their departure from Kalind station. There were corporation executives and higher supervisors, and a scattering of professionals of various fields dressed to mingle with the rich and idle, estate-holders, of whom there were several.

This night there were drinks poured: azi servants passed busily from table to table, the only movement made. The fashionable people sat fixed in their places, venturing furtive glances across the salon.

They were the elite, the powers and movers of beta society, these folk. But they found themselves suddenly in the regard of another aristocracy altogether.

She was Kontrin. The aquiline face was the type of all the inbred line, male or female, in one of its infinite variations. Her gray cloak and bodysuit and boots were for the street, not the society of the salon, elegant as they were. It was possible that they masked armor . . . more than possible that they concealed weapons. The chitinous implants which covered the back of her right hand were identification beyond any doubt, and the pattern held unlimited credit in intercomp, in any system of the Reach . . . unlimited credit: the money for which wealthy betas strove was only a shadow of such entitlement.

She smiled at them across the room, a cold and cynical gesture, and the elite of the salon of *Andra's Jewel* tried to look elsewhere, tried to pursue their important conversations in low voices and to ignore the reality which sat in that corner of empty tables. Suddenly they were uncomfortable even with the azi servants who passed among them bearing drinks . . . cloned men, decorative creations of their own labs, as they themselves had been sprawned wholesale out of the Kontrin's, seven hundred years past. Proximity to the azi became suddenly . . . *comparison.*

The party died early. Couples and groups drifted out, which movement became a general and hasty flow toward the doors.

Kont' Raen a Sul watched them go, and in cynical humor, turned and met the eyes of the azi servant who stood nearest. Slowly all movement of the azi in the salon ceased. The servant stood, held in that gaze.

"Do you play Sej?" she asked.

The azi nodded fearfully. Sej was an amusement common throughout the Reach, in lower and rougher places. It was a dicing game, half chance and some part skill.

"Find the pieces."

The azi, pale of face, went among his companions and found one who had the set. He activated the gaming function of the table for score-keeping, and laid the three wands and the pair of dice on the table.

"Sit down," said Kont' Raen.

He did so, sweating. He was young, several years advanced into the service for which he existed. He had been engineered for pleasing appearance and for intelligence, to serve the passengers. He had no education beyond that duty, save what rumor fed him and what he observed of the betas who passed through the salon. The smooth courtesy which he had deepstudied in his training gave him now the means to function. Other azi stood about, stricken by his misfortune, morbidly curious.

"What's your name?" she asked.

"Jim," he said. It was the one choice of his life, the one thing he had personally decided, out of a range of names which belonged to azi. Only azi used it, and a few of the crew. He was vastly disturbed at his loss of anonymity.

"What stakes?" she asked, gathering up the wands.

He stared at her. He had nothing, being property of the line, but his name and his existence.

She looked down and rolled the wands between her hands, the one glittering with chitin, and infinite power. "It will be a long voyage. I shall be bored. Suppose that we make wager not on one game, but on the tally of games." She laid the wands down under her right hand. "If you win, I'll buy you free of Andra lines and give you ten thousand credits for every game you've won. Ten rounds an evening, as many evenings as there are in my voyage. But you must win the series to collect: it's only on the total of games, our wager."

He blinked, the sweat running into his eyes. Freedom and wealth: he could live out his life unthreatened, even in idleness. It was a prize beyond calculation, and not the sort of luck any azi had. He swallowed hard and reckoned what kind of wager he might have to return.

"But if I win," she continued, "I shall buy your contract for myself." She smiled suddenly, a bleak and dead smile. "Play to win, Jim."

She offered him first cast. He took up the wands. The azi in the salon settled silently, watching.

He lost the first evening, four to six.

ii

A small, tense company gathered in the stateroom of the ASPAK Corporation executive. There were other such gatherings, private parties. The salon was still under occupation on this third evening. No one ventured there any longer save during the day. There remained available of course the lower deck lounge, where the second-class passengers gathered; but they were not willing to descend to that society, not under the circumstances. Their collective pride had suffered enough.

"Maybe she's going to Andra," someone suggested. "A short trip . . . perhaps some bizarre humor . . ."

The Andran executive looked distressed at that idea. Kontrin never traveled commercial; they engaged ships of their own, a class of luxury unimaginable to the society of *Andra's Jewel,* and separate. Impatience, near destination . . . even the possibility of assassins and the need to get offworld by the first available ship: the surmise made sense. But Andran affairs did not want a Kontrin feud: there was trouble enough without that. This one . . . this Kontrin, did things no Kontrin had ever done, and might do others as unpredictable. Worse, the name Raen a Sul stirred at some vague memory, seldom as names were ever exchanged between Kontrin and men . . . *Men* . . . *Beta* was not a term men used of themselves.

This one had been on Andra, and might be returning. Majat were where they ought not to be, and suddenly Kontrin were among them. Until lately it had been possible to ignore Kontrin doings entirely; a man could live years and not so much as see one; and now one came into their midst.

"There's a rumor—" someone else said, and cleared her throat, "there's a rumor there's a majat aboard."

Another swore, and there was a moment's silence, nervous glances. It was possible. Majat traveled, rarely, but they traveled. If it were so, it would be somewhere isolate, sinking into dormancy for the duration of the flight Majat parted from the hive became disoriented, dangerous: this one would have awakened long enough to have performed its mission, whatever it was, and to secure passage home—function assigned it by the hive. So long, it might remain sane, having clear purpose and a goal in sight. Thereafter, it must sleep, awakening only in proximity to its hive.

There were horror tales of majat awakening prematurely on a ship; and majat horror tales were current on Andra, on Kalind, on Meron, unreasoning actions, killings of humans. But the commercial lines could no more refuse a majat than they could have refused the Kontrin. It was a question of ownership, of the origins of power in the Reach, and some questions it was not good to raise.

Silence rested heavily on the gathering, which sat uncomfortably on thinly padded furniture in an anteroom designed for smaller companies. Ice rattled in glasses. The executive cleared his throat.

"Kontrin don't travel alone," he said. "There are always bodyguards. Where are they?"

"Maybe they're . . . some of us," a Kalinder suggested. "I'd be careful what I said."

No one moved. No one looked at anyone else. No Kontrin had ever done such a thing as this one had done: they feared assassination obsessively, guarding the immortality which distinguished their class as surely as did the chitin-patterns. That was another cause by which men found it difficult to accept the presence of a Kontrin, for her lifespan was to theirs far longer than theirs was to that of the azi they created. Men were likewise designated for mortality, as surely as the Kontrin had engineered themselves otherwise, and kept that gift from others. It was the calculated economy of the Reach. Only the owners continued. Men were to the Kontrin . . . a renewable resource.

Someone proposed more drinks. They played loud music and talked in whispers, only to those they knew well, and eventually this party too died.

There were other gatherings in days after, in small number, by twos and by threes. Some stayed entirely in their staterooms, fearing the nameless threat of meetings in the corridors, unnerved by what was happening on worlds throughout the Reach. If there was a majat aboard, no one wanted to find it.

The game continued in the salon. Jim's luck improved. He was whining, thirty-seven to thirty-three. The other azi's eyes followed the fall of the wands and the dice as if their own fortunes were hazarded there.

The next evening the balance tilted again, forty to forty.

iii

Andra's Jewel jumped and made slow progress to
Andra station. Ten grateful first-class passengers disembarked and the Kontrin did not. The majority of lower-
deck passengers left; more arrived, short-termers, for
Jim, and three first-class, bound for Meron. The game in
the salon stood at eighty-four and eighty-six.

The *Jewel* crept outward in real-space, for Jim; again
for Sitan and the barrenness of Orthan's moons; made
jump, for glittering Meron. Such passengers who remained, initiates of the original company, were dismayed
that the Kontrin did not leave at Meron: there had even
been wagers on it. The occupation of the salon continued
uninterrupted.

The score stood at two hundred forty-two to two hundred forty-eight.

"Do you want to retire?" Kont' Raen asked when the
game stood even. "I've had my enjoyment of this. I give
you the chance."

Jim shook his head. He had fought his way this far.
Hope existed in him; he had never held much hope,
until now.

Kont' Raen laughed and won the next hand.

"You should have taken it," an azi said to Jim that
night. "Kontrin don't sell their azi when they're done
with them. They terminate them, whatever their age. It's
their law."

Jim shrugged. He had heard so already. Everyone had
had to tell him so. He worked the dice in his clenched
hand and sat down on the matting of the azi quarters.
He cast them again and again obsessively, trying the
combinations as if some magic could change them. He
no longer had duties on the ship. The Kontrin had
marked his fatigue and bought him free of duties. He
was no longer subject to ration: if he wanted more than
his meals, he did not have to rely on tips to buy that
extra. He seldom chose to go beyond ration, all the same,
save once or twice when he had been far ahead and his
appetite improved. He cast the dice now, against some

vague superstition formed of these empty days. He played himself, to test his run of luck.

He could not have quit, the game unfinished, could not go back to the others, to being one of them, and exist without knowing what he had given up. He would always think that he might have been free and rich. That would always torment him. The Kontrin had sensed this, and therefore she had laughed. Even he could understand the irony.

iv

Andra's Jewel reached Silak and docked. *Ship will continue to Istra,* the message flashed to the three passengers who should have disembarked there with the others, to seek connections further. So grand a ship as *Andra's Jewel* did not make out-planet runs with her staterooms empty. But the passengers who had packed, unpacked, with the desperate fear that they would do better to disembark anyway and seek other transportation, however long they had to wait. A few more passengers boarded. The *Jewel* voyaged out, ghostly in her emptiness.

"It's the Kontrin," the ITAK envoy whispered to his wife. "She's going to Istra."

The woman, his partner-in-office, said nothing, but glanced anxiously at the intercom and its blank screen, as if this might be carried to other ears.

"What other answer?" The Istran shaped the words with his lips, soundlessly. "And why would they come in person? In *person,* after all?"

The woman regarded him in dread. Their mission to Meron, dismal failure, had been calamity enough. It was their misfortune that they had chosen the *Jewel* for their intermediate link to Silak—tempted by the one brief extravagance of their lives, compensation for their humiliation on Meron. They were executives in a world corporation; they had attempted to travel a few days in the grand style of their inner-world counterparts, once, *once,* to enjoy such things, foreseeing ruin awaiting them on Istra. "We should have gotten off this ship at Silak," she said, "while we had the chance. There's only Pedra now, and no regular lines from there. We should have gotten off. Now it's impossible she wouldn't take notice of it. She surely knows we're Istran."

"I don't see," he said, "how she could be involved with us. I don't. She's from *before* Meron. Unless—while we were stalled on Meron—some message went through to Cerdin. I asked the azi where she boarded. They said Kalind. That's only one jump from Cerdin."

"You shouldn't have asked the azi."

"It was a casual question."

"It was dangerous."

"It was—"

"Hush! not so loud."

They both looked at the intercom, uncomfortable in its cyclopsic presence. "It's not live," he said.

"I think she owns this ship," the woman said. "That's why there aren't any guards visible. The whole crew, the azi—"

"That's insane."

"What else, then? What else makes sense?"

He shook his head. Nothing did.

v

They reached barren Pedra, and took on a straggle of lower-deck passengers, who gaped in awe at the splendor of the accommodations. Nothing the size of the *Jewel* had ever docked at Pedra. There were no upper-deck passengers: one departed here, but none boarded.

The game stood at four hundred eighteen to four hundred twelve. Bets had spread among the free crew. Some of them came and watched as the azi's lead increased to thirteen. It was the widest the game had ever been spread.

"Your luck is incredible," the Kontrin said. "Do you want to quit?"

"I can't," Jim said.

The Kontrin nodded slowly, and ordered drinks for them both.

Andra's Jewel made out from sunless Pedra and jumped again. They were in Istran space, beta Hydri two, snake's-tail, the Outside's contact point with the Reach.

There were, after the disorientation of jump, a handful of days remaining.

The game stood at four hundred fifty-nine to four hundred fifty-one. Midway through the evening it was four hundred sixty-two to four hundred fifty-three, and there was still a deep frown on the face of Kont' Raen. She cast the wands governing aspect of the dice. They turned up star, star, and black. The aspects were marginally favorable. With black involved, she could have declined the hand and cancelled it, passing the wands to Jim for a new throw. She simply declined the first cast of the dice. The azi threw six and she threw twelve: she won the star and it took next star automatically: twenty-four. The azi declined first throw on the deadly black. She threw four; the azi threw twelve. The azi had won black, cancelling his points in the game. A low breath hissed from the gallery.

"Do you concede?" Kont' Raen asked.

Jim shook his head. He was tired; his position in this game was all but hopeless: her score was ninety-eight; his was zero . . . but it was his option, and he never conceded any game, no matter how long and wearing. Neither did she. She inclined her head in respect to his tenacity and yielded him the wands. His control of the hand, should black turn up, afforded him a marginal chance of breaking her score.

And suddenly there was a disturbance at the door.

Two passengers stood there, male and female, betas. The azi of the salon, so long without visitors to serve of evenings, took an instant to react. Then they hurried about preparing chairs and a table for the pair, taking their order for drinks.

The game continued. Jim threw two ships and a star. He won the ships and had twenty; Raen won the star and took game.

"Four hundred fifty-four," she said quietly, "to your four hundred fifty-two."

Jim nodded.

"Take first throw."

He shook his head; one could refuse a courtesy. She gathered up the wands.

A chair moved. One of the passengers was coming over to them. Raen hesitated in her cast and then looked aside in annoyance, the wands still in her hand.

"I am ser Merek Eln," the man said, and gestured back to the woman who had also risen. "Sera Parn Kest, my wife."

Raen inclined her head as if this were of great moment to her. The betas seemed to miss the irony. "Kont' Raen a Sul." And with cold courtesy. "Grace to you both."

"Are you . . . bound for Istra?"

Raen smiled, though coldly. "Is there anything more remote?"

Merek Eln blinked and swallowed. "The ship must surely start its return there. Istra is the edge of the Reach."

"Then that must be where I am bound."

"We . . . are in ITAK, Istran Trade . . ."

". . . Association, Kontrin-licensed. Yes. I'm familiar with the registered corporations."

"We offer our assistance, our—hospitality."

Raen looked him up and down, and sera Kest also. She let the silence continue. "How kind," she said at last. "I've never had such an offer. Perhaps I'll take advantage of it. I don't believe there are other Kontrin on Istra."

"No," Eln said faintly. "Kontrin, if you would care to discuss the matter which brings you here—"

"I don't."

"We might . . . assist you."

"You aren't listening, ser Merek Eln. I assure you, I have no interests in ITAK matters."

"Yet you chose Istra."

"Not I."

The man blinked, confused.

"I didn't divert the ship," Raen said.

"If we can be of service—"

"You've offered me your hospitality. I've said that I shall consider it. For the moment, as you see, I'm engaged. I have four games yet to go this evening. Perhaps you'll care to watch." She turned her back on ser Merek Eln and sera Kest, looked at Jim, who waited quietly. Azi were accustomed to immobility when not pursuing orders. "What do you know of Istra?" she asked him.

"It's a hive world. A contact point with Outside. Their sun is beta Hydri."

"*The* contact point. I don't recall any Kontrin going there recently. I knew one who did, once. But surely there are some amusements to be had there."

"I don't know," Jim said very faintly, quieter in the presence of the Istrans than he had been since the beginning. "I belong to Andra Lines. My knowledge doesn't extend beyond the range of my ship."

"Do these folk make you nervous? I'll ask them to leave if you like."

"Please, no," Jim said hoarsely. Raen shrugged and made the cast.

It came up three stars. She took first throw. Twelve. Jim made his: two. Raen gathered thirty-six points. Jim took up the wands as if they were venomed, threw three whites. Raen won the dicing and automatically took game.

"Your luck has hit a sudden downward turn," Raen said, gathering up the three wands. She passed them to him. "But there's still margin. We're at four hundred fifty-five to your four hundred sixty-two."

He lost all but the last game, setting the tally at four hundred sixty-three to four hundred fifty-seven. His margin was down to six.

He was sweating profusely. Raen ordered a drink for them each, and Jim took a great swallow of his, all the while staring at a blank corner of the room, meeting no one's eyes.

"These folk do make you uncomfortable," she said. "But if you win—why, then you'll be out among them, free and very wealthy. Perhaps wealthier than they. Do you think of that?''

He took yet another drink and gave no answer. Sweat broke and ran at his temple.

"How many games yet remain?" she asked.

"We dock three days from now."

"With time in the evening for a set?"

He shook his head. This was to his advantage. He still had his lead.

"Twenty games, then." She glanced at the Istrans, gestured them to seats on opposite sides of her table, between him and her. Their faces blanched. There was rage there, and offense. They came, and sat down. "Do you want to play a round for amusement?" she asked Jim.

"I would rather not," he said. "I'm superstitious."

Azi served them, all four. Jim stared at the area of the table between his hands.

"It's been a long voyage," Kont' Raen said. "Yet the society in the salon has been pleasant. What brings you out from Istra and back, serfi?"

"Trade," Kest said.

"Ah."

"Kontrin—" Merek Eln said. She looked at him. He moistened his lips and shifted his weight in his chair. "Kontrin, there's been some disturbance on Istra. Matters are still in a state of flux. Doubtless—doubtless you've had some report of these affairs."

She shrugged. "I've kept much to myself of late. So trade took you off Istra."

There was a hesitation, a decision. Merek Eln went pale, wiped at his face. "The need for funds," he confided. His voice was hardly more than a hoarse whisper. "There has been hardship on Istra. There's been fighting in some places. Sabotage. One has to be careful about associations. If you've brought forces—"

"You expect too much of me," Kont' Raen said. "I'm here on holiday. That is my profession."

This was irony even they understood as such.

They said nothing. Kont' Raen sipped at her drink and finished it. Then she rose and left the table, and Jim excused himself hastily and withdrew among the azi who served.

The thought occurred to him, not for the first time, that Kont' Raen was simply insane.

He thought that if she gave him the chance now to withdraw from the wager, he would take it, serve the ship to the end of his days, content in his fate.

He lost two points of his margin the next evening. The tally stood at four hundred sixty-seven to four hundred sixty-three.

There was no sleep that night. Tomorrow evening was the last round. No one in the azi quarters offered to speak to him. The others sat apart, as if he had a contagion. It was the same when one approached termination. If he won, they would hate him; if he lost, he would only confirm what they believed, the luck that made them what they were. He crouched on his mat in a corner of the compartment, tucked his knees up to his chin and bowed his head, counting the interminable moments of the final hours.

vi

Jim was at the table early as usual, waiting with the wands and the dice. The Istrans arrived. Other azi served them, while even beta crew arrived in the salon to watch the last games. The whole ship was shut down to skeleton crew, and those necessary posts were linked in by monitor.

Jim looked at the table surface rather than face the stares of free men who owned his contract, who had come to watch the show. They would not own it after this night, one way or the other.

There were light steps in the corridor, toward the door. He looked up, saw Kont' Raen coming toward him. He rose, of respect, the same ritual as every evening. Azi set drinks on the table, as every evening.

She was seated, and he resumed his chair.

What others did in the room now he neither knew nor

cared. She cast the dice for the first throw; he did, and
won the right to begin.

He won the first game. She won the next. The sigh of
breath was audible all about the salon.

The third game was hers, and the fourth and fifth.

"Rest?" she asked. He wiped at the sweat that gathered on his upper lip and shook his head. He won the
sixth and lost the seventh and eighth.

"Four sixty-nine to four sixty-nine," she said. Her eyes
glittered with excitement. She ordered ice, and paused
for a drink of water. Jim drained his glass and wiped his
face with his chilled hand. The cooling did not seem
enough in the salon. People were crowded all about
them. He asked for another drink, sipped it.

"Your stakes are greater," she said. "I cede first
throw."

He accepted the wands. Suddenly he trusted nothing,
no generosity of hers. He trusted none present. Of all
the bets which had been made on the azi deck, he was
sure now how they had been laid. The looks as the Kontrin tore away his lead let that be known . . . who had
bet on him, and who against. Some of those against, he
had believed liked him.

He cast. Nothing showed but black and white; he declined and she cast: the same. It was a slow game, careful.
At twenty-four he threw a black . . . chose to play the
throw against her thirty-six, and won not only the pair
of ships, but also the black, wiping out his score. His
hands began to sweat. He played more conservatively
then, built up his score and declined the next black,
dreading black in her hand, which did not show. He
reached eighty-eight. She held seventy-two, and swept up
a trio of stars to take the ninth game.

It stood at four hundred sixty-nine to four hundred
seventy, her favor.

"What do you propose if we tie?" she asked.

"An eleventh game," he said hoarsely. Only then did
it occur to him that he might have proposed cancellation
of bets. She nodded, accepting him at his word. He must
win tenth to force an eleventh.

She gathered up the wands. The living chitin on the back of her hand shone like jewels. The wands spilled across the table, white, white, white.

Game, for the winner.

She offered him the dice. She led; the courtesy was mandated by the custom of the game. His hand was sweating; he wiped it on his chest, took the dice again, and cast: six.

She took up the cubes for her own turn, threw.

Seven.

"Game," she said.

There was silence. Then those in the room cheered . . . save the azi, who faded back, reminded that escape was not for their kind. Jim blinked, and fought for breath. He began to shiver and could not stop.

Kont' Raen gathered up the wands and, one by one, broke them. Then she leaned back in her chair and slowly finished her drink. Quiet was restored in the room. Officers and azi remembered that they had duties elsewhere. Only the Istran couple remained.

"Out," she said.

The couple hesitated, indignant, determined for a moment to stand their ground. Then they thought better of it and left. The door closed. Jim stared at the table. An azi never looked directly at anyone.

There was a long silence.

"Finish your drink," she said. He did so; he had wanted it, and had not known whether he dared. "I thank you," she said quietly. "You have relieved my boredom, and few have ever done that."

He looked up at her, suicidal in his mood. He had been pushed far. The same desperation which had kept him from withdrawing from the game still possessed him.

"You could have dropped out," she reminded him.

"I could have won."

"Of course."

He took a last swallow from his glass, mostly icemelt, and set it down. The thought occurred to him again that the Kontrin was quite, quite mad, and that out of whim she might order his termination when they docked. She evidently traveled alone. Perhaps she preferred it that way. He was lost in the motivations of Kontrin. He had been created to serve the ships of Andra Lines. He knew nothing else.

She walked over and took the bottle from the Istrans' table, examined the label critically and poured again, for him and for her. The incongruity of the action made him sure that she was mad. There should have been fresh glasses, no ice. He winced inwardly, and realized that such concerns now were ridiculous. He drank; she did, in bizarre celebration.

"None of them," she said, with a shrug at all the empty tables and chairs, the memories of departed passengers, "none of them could dice with a Kontrin, Not one." She grinned and laughed, and the grin faded to a solemn expression. She lifted the glass to him, ironic salute. "Your contract is already purchased. Ever borne arms?"

He shook his head, appalled. He had never touched a weapon, seldom even seen one.

She laughed and set the glass down.

And rose.

"Come," she said.

Later, high in the upper decks and the luxury of the Kontrin's staterooms, it came to what he thought it might.

BOOK FOUR

i

"Commercial," Moth muttered, and steepled her wrinkled hands, staring at them to the exclusion of the several heads of Houses who surrounded her. She laughed softly, contemplating the reports of chaos strewn in a line across the Reach.

"I fear," said Cen Moran, "I lack your perception of humor in the matter. This involves Istra, and the hives, and the surviving Meth-maren. I see nothing whatsoever of humor affordable in the combination."

"Kill her," said Ros Hald.

Moth turned a chill stare on him, and he fell silent. "Why? For trespass? I don't recall that visiting Istra is grounds for such extreme measures."

"It's a sensitive area, Istra."

"Yes. Isn't it."

The Hald broke eye contact. Moth did not miss that fact, but glanced instead at Moran and the others, raised querulous brows. "I think some Kontrin presence there might be salutary, provided it's discreet and sensible. The Meth-maren's presence is usually quiet toward non-Kontrin."

"A hive-world," said Moran, "another hive-world, and critical."

"The only hive-world," said Moth, "without Kontrin permanently resident. We've barred ourselves from that . . . sensitive . . . contact point, at least by custom. Depressing as Istra is reputed to be, I suspect we simply lack enthusiasm for the necessary privations. But majat

don't seem to mind being there, do they? In my long
memory, only Lian had the interest to visit the place
after the beta City was set down there—and that was
very long ago. Maybe we should reconsider. Maybe
we've created a blind spot in our intelligence. Reports
from Istra are scant. Perhaps a Kontrin should be there.
It surely couldn't hurt their economy."

"But," said Kahn a Beln, "*this* Kontrin, Eldest?
There's been trouble across the Reach. And the Meth-
maren, of the hive-masters—of *that* House—the simplest
prediction would tell us. . . ."

"We will let her alone," Moth said.

"If it were put to a vote," said Moran, "that sentiment
would not carry. Thon would be the logical choice, trust-
worthy. The Meth-maren, no."

Moth looked at him steadily. A measure would have to
be written up formally: some one of them would have to
put his name on it as proponent. Someone would have
to risk his personal influence and the well-being of his
agents. She did not estimate that Moran quite meant it
as an ultimatum: he was simply kin to the ineffectual
Thons. There were more meaningful, more inflammatory
issues on which opposition could rise. When challenge
came, if it came in the Council at all, it would not be
like this, on a directive for assassination; such things did
not make good rallying points. Assassinations were usually managed by House or executive order, quietly and
without embarrassments.

"Let her alone," Moth said, "for now."

There was a small and sullen silence at the table. Talk
began quietly, drifted to other matters. There were excuses made early, departures in small groups. Moth
watched them, and noted who left with whom, and reckoned that not a few of them were plotting her demise.

And after me, she thought with a taut, hateful smile,
let it come.

She spread upon the table the reports which had occupied the committee, all the various problems with which
the Council had to deal: over-breeding of azi, population
stresses and economic distress among underemployed

betas, turmoil in the hives, killings of greens and the lately-recovered blues by reds and golds on Cerdin. The Thon House, hive-liaisons in the place of Meth-marens, proved ineffectual: the reports skirted that fact and covered truth with verbiage.

And, persistently, reports that reds sought out Kontrin and made gifts, trespassed boundaries, turned up in beta areas.

There was a proposal put forward by the House of Ilit and the econbureau that this surplus be consumed by the modest ship-building industry of Pedra. It gathered support; it was very possible that it would pass. It would alleviate conditions that created discontent on several worlds.

Moth studied it, frowning—remembered to push a button, to summon the young man waiting—and sat leaning her mouth against her curled hand and staring moodishly at the persuasive statistics on the graphs. The Hald entered; she was still pursuing her train of thought, and let him stand, the while she read and gnawed at her finger.

At last she shifted the reports into three stacks and then into one, and put atop it a dry monograph entitled *Breeding Patterns among the Hives*.

"Commercial," she chuckled again, to the listening walls, and looked up sharply at young Tand Hald. "Kill her, you would say too. I've heard that Hald point of view until my ears ache. You're nothing if not consistent. Where's Morn?"

Tand Hald shrugged, stared at her quite directly. "I'm sure I don't know, Eldest."

"Pol with him?"

"I'm sure I don't know that either. Not when I left him."

"Where did you part with them?"

"Meron." He failed to flinch. The eyes remained steady. "Pol involved himself with amusements there. Morn went his own way; I went mine. No one controls them."

She gazed at him steadily, broke contact after a moment. "You want her taken out."

"I give the best advice I have."

"Why are you so apprehensive of this one subject? Personal grudge?"

"No. Surely your agent who watches your other agents would have turned up any personal bias in this."

She laughed softly at the impertinence. The youngest Hald had been with her too long, too closely. She was not diverted. "But why then? What interference has she ever attempted in Family business? She's never made an economic ripple; she only—*travels,* from time to time."

"Is she your agent?" Tand asked, a question which had taken him five years to ask.

"No," Moth said very softly. "But I protect her as if she were. She is, after a remote fashion. Why do you fear her so, Tand?"

"Because she's atypical. And random. And a survivor. She ought to have grudges. She never exercises them . . . save once, but that was direct retaliation. She never pursues the old ones."

"Ah."

"Now she's chosen a place where there's potential for serious harm. There are Outsiders directly available; there are hives, and no one to watch her, only betas. Her going there has purpose."

"Do you think so? She always seems to proceed by indirection."

"I believe there is reason."

"Perhaps there is. Yet in all these years, she's never reached back to Cerdin."

"It was a mistake to have let her live in the first place."

"The Family has searched for cause against her ever since she left Cerdin. We've found none; she's given none."

"So she's intelligent, and dangerous."

Moth laughed again, and the laughter died and she sorted absently through the reports, shifting them into disorder. "How long do majat live?"

"Eighteen years for the average individual." Tand seemed vaguely annoyed by this extraneity. "Longer for queens."

"No. How long do majat live?"

"The hives are immortal."

"That is the correct answer. How long is that?"

"They calculate—millions of years."

"How long have we been watching them, Tand?"

The young man shifted his weight and his eyes went to the floor and the walls and elsewhere in his impatience. "About—six, seven hundred years."

"How long would a cycle take—in the lifespan of an immortal organism?"

"What kind of cycle? Eldest, I'm afraid I don't see what you're aiming at."

"Yes. We don't, do we? We lose our memories with death. Individually. Our records record . . . only what we once perceived as important, at a given hour, under given circumstances. The Drones remember . . . everything."

Tand shook his head. A sweat had broken out on his face. "I wish you would be clear, Eldest."

"I wish I had a long enough record at hand. Don't you see that things have changed? No, of course not. You're only a third of a century old yourself. I'm only six hundred and a half. And what is that? What is that experience worth? The Pact used to keep the hives out of human affairs. Now reds and golds . . . mingle with us, even with betas. Hives are at war . . . on Cerdin, Meron, Andra, Kalind . . . On Kalind, it's blues and greens against red. On Andra, and Cerdin, it's blues and greens against red and gold. On Meron, it's blues against reds and greens, and gold is in hiding."

"And Istra—"

"One can't predict, can one?"

"I don't understand what you're trying to say, Eldest."

"Until you do—spread the word among the Houses that Moth still has her faculties. That killing me would be very unwise."

"The matter," Tand said tentatively, "the matter is Raen a Sul, Eldest."

"Yes, it is, isn't it?" Moth shook her head. Blinked. At nigh seven hundred, the brain grew unreliable, too full of information. There were syntheses which verged on prophecy, cross-connections too full of subtle intervening data. Her hands shook uncontrollably with the effort of tracing down these interloping items. Self-analysis. Of all processes, that was hardest, to know why the data interconnected. Her eyes hurt. Her hands could not feel the papers they handled. She became aware that Tand had been speaking further.

"Go away," she said abruptly.

He went.

She watched him go, without doubt now: her death was planned.

ii

The azi had settled finally, his world redefined. He slept as if the luxury of the upper deck staterooms were no novelty at all. Raen gathered herself up quietly, slipped past the safety web which shrouded the wide bed, and stretched, beginning now to think of departure, of the disposition of personal items scattered through the suite during the months of voyaging.

Now there was the azi . . . help or burden: she had not yet decided which. She had second thoughts of her mad venture, almost changed her mind even on this morning, as often of mornings she had had doubts.

She put it from her mind, refused to think of more than the present day; that was her solution to such thoughts, at least for the hour, at least to pass that tedious time of waiting and solitude. The voyage itself had promised to be unendurable; and it was done; there had even been moments of highest enjoyment, moments worth living, too rare to let finality turn them sour. She refused to let it happen—yawned and stretched in deliberate self-controlled luxury—went blindly to the console and keyed a double breakfast into the foodservice channel.

A red light blinked back at her at once, Security advisement. Her pulse jolted; she keyed three, which was the channel reserved for ship's emergencies and notices.

MAJAT PASSENGER HAS AWAKENED. PLEASE VACATE VICINITY OF SECTOR #31.

On schedule—alarm to the ship, none to her. She punched in communications. "This is 512. I advise you take extraordinary care in emergency in 31. This is not a Worker. Please acknowledge."

They did so. She cut them off, rubbed her eyes and sought the shower, her social duty fulfilled.

The touch of warm water and the smell of soap: some things even the prospect of eternity could not diminish. Water slid over a body which bore only faint scars for all that was past, spare of flesh despite all her public self-indulgences. She endured heat enough to make her heart speed, generating a cloud of comfortable steam within the cabinet, combed her hair and punched the dry circulation into operation.

Dry, combed, composed, she hauled a sheet out of storage, wound into it and ventured the chill air of the outer rooms, back to the console with a new object in mind.

Jim's papers were on the desk. She flicked through them, keyed in ship's store with a few requests for display. Samples in simulacrum flashed onto the screen, accurate representation of his body-type with one and another suit. She indicated approval for several and put them on her account, selected a traveling case from the same source, along with an assortment of necessary personal items and a few of jewelry.

Doing so amused her. She anticipated his delight. But after the screens went dark and the only pleasant necessity of the morning had been cared for, she sat still on the bench and faced the prospect of Istra itself, of other things, in a sudden dark mood which had some origin in a morning headache.

Perhaps it was overmuch of drink the night before. She had certainly overindulged.

Perhaps it was the azi, who had a melancholy about him which touched strongly at her own.

She bestirred herself finally and dressed . . . plain, beige garments, close-fitting. And, which she had not done on the ship, she put on the sleeve-armor, which was simple ostentation. Light, jewel-toned chitin strung on the lightest of filaments, it ran from the living jewels of her right hand to her collar: the beauty of it pleased her, and the day wanted some ceremony, after such long voyaging.

She laughed bitterly, staring back at the replacement of her fortunes, who slept, still oblivious, and thought her all-powerful. Where it regarded a ship like *Andra's Jewel*, this was surely so.

There were several cloaks among her belongings. She took out the beige one, and intended to put it on, to hide the sleeve armor, as it would hide the weapons she carried constantly when she left the stateroom. But it went back into the locker, the beige cloak; she fingered another, that was blue, white-bordered, forbidden.

Even to have it was defiance of the Family. In almost two decades no one had worn that Color.

She did now, in the consciousness of isolation—quiet, furtive defiance; let some beta make inquiry, let some description and name be sent back to Council: at least let it be accurate, so that had they had missed all other signals, they might read this one, clear beyond all doubt. She shrugged it on, fastened it, looked back again at the azi.

Jim had worked himself into the farthest corner of the large bed, into the angle of the two walls, limbs tucked, fetal position. He had done it before, also in sleep. It was somewhat disconcerting, that defensive tactic; she had thought he had relaxed beyond it.

"Wake up," she called sharply. "Jim. Wake up."

He moved, disorganized for the moment, then untucked and sat up within the webbing. He rubbed at his eyes, wincing at what was likely a headache to match hers. He looked strangely lost, as if he had misplaced something essential this morning, perhaps himself.

He wanted time, she decided. She paid him no further attention, reckoning that the best thing. He stirred out after a moment, gathered up his clothes from the floor and went to the bath. There was long running of water, then the hum of the shower fans.

Cleanly, Raen thought with approval. She keyed in the Operations channel and sank into a comfortable chair to wait, feet propped, listening to chatter, watching the screen with the mild interest of one who had been herself many times at the controls of a ship on station approach. The meticulous procedures and precautions of the big commercial liner were typically beta, fussy and over-cautious . . . but neither was putting a ship of this size into station berth a process forgiving of little errors. They would spend an amazing amount of time working in, nothing left to visual estimation.

Channel five afforded view of their destination: this was what she had been looking to see. There was the faint dot of the station, due to grow rapidly larger over the next few hours . . . and Istra, a bluish disc as yet without definition. On the upper quarter screen, filtered, was beta Hydri itself, the Serpent's Tail, a malevolent brilliance which forecast less than paradise on Istra's surface.

Two major continents, two ports onworld, a great deal of desert covering those two continents. The weather patterns of Istra bestowed rain in a serpentine belt, low on one continent and coastally on the other, storms breaking on an incredible mountain ridge which created wetlands coastward, and one of the most regrettable desolations of the Reach on the far side. The rainfall patterns never varied, not during all human occupancy. Such life as Istra supported before humans and majat came had never ascended to sapience . . . and such as dimly knew better had retreated from the vicinity of majat and humans both.

She had deepstudied Istra, and knew it with what information the tapes had to give. It was not populous. The onworld industry was agriculture, and that was sufficient for self-support: the Family had never thought it wise to turn its most prosperous face to the Outside. The world was merely support for the station, that was the real Istra: the agglomeration of docks and warehouses swinging in orbit about Istra was the largest man-made structure in the Reach, the channel for all trade which passed in and out.

It was a sight worth seeing if one were out this far. She meant to do so. But it was also true that facilities at this famous station were primitive and that ships other than freighters did not come here. It was actually possible to strand oneself in such a place, if she let the *Jewel* go.

She went bleakly sober, staring at the screen with greater and greater conviction that she should stay aboard the *Jewel*, ride her home again to the heart of the Reach, where a Kontrin belonged. Other acts of irritation she had committed, but this was something of quite different aspect. She had accomplished part of her purpose simply by coming this far.

The Family knew by now where she was; it was impossible that they had not noticed.

An infinite lifespan, and enforced idleness, enforced uselessness, enforced solitude: it was a torment in which any variance was momentous, in which the prospect of change was paralyzing. It might have taken her. The Family had planned that it should, that finally, it would take her.

Her lips tautened in a hateful smile. She was still sane, a marginal sanity, she reckoned. That she was here—at the Edge—was a triumph of will.

The blue light began to blink in the overhead: room service. She rose and started for the door, remembered that she had not yet clipped her gun to her belt and paused to do so.

It was, after all, only two of the azi, bringing breakfast and the purchases from the store. She admitted them, and stood by the open door while they set breakfast on the table and laid the packages on the bench, a considerable stack of them.

To take such a breakfast, from uncontrolled sources . . . was a calculated risk, a roll of the dice with advantageous odds here in the *Jewel*'s closed environment; but stakes all the same greater than she had hazarded in the salon. Accepting the packages was such a risk. The voyage, unguarded, among strangers, was a monumental one. Or taking an azi such as Jim: the tiny triangle tattooed under his eye was real, the serial number tattooed on his shoulder was likewise, and both faded with age as they should be; that eliminated one possibility . . . but not the chance that someone could have corrupted him with programs involving murder. Such risks provided daily diversion— necessary chances; one regarded them as that or went insane from the stress. One gambled. She smiled as the two bowed, their duties done; and over-tipped them extravagantly—another self-indulgence: the delight in their faces gave her vicarious pleasure. She was excited with the purchases she had made for Jim, anxious for his reaction. His melancholy was a challenge . . . simpler, perhaps, and more accessible than her own.

"Jim," she called, "come out here."

He came, half-dressed in his own uniform, his hair a little disordered, his skin still flushed from the heat of the shower. She offered the packages to him, and he was somewhat overwhelmed, it seemed, with the abundance of things.

He sat down and looked through the smaller packages, fingered the plastic-wrapped clothing and the fine suede boots, the traveling case. One small box held a watch, a very expensive one. He touched the face of it, closed the box again and set it aside. No smile touched his face, no hint of pleasure, but rather blankness . . . bewilderment.

"They ought to fit," she said, when he failed of the happiness she had hoped for. She shrugged, defeated, finding him a greater challenge than she had thought. "Breakfast is cooling. Hurry up."

He came to the table then, stood waiting for her to sit down. His precise courtesy irritated her, for it was mechanical; but she said nothing, and took her place, let him adjust her chair. He sat down after, gathered up his fork after she had picked up hers, and took his first bite only after she did. He ate without once looking at her. Still, she persuaded herself, he was remarkably adaptable. Limited sensitivity, the betas insisted of the azi they created, justifying what might otherwise have seemed abuses. She had not understood that when she was a child: there had been Lia, who had loved her; and she had loved Lia. But it was true that azi did not react to things in the way of born-men, and that there were, among them, no more Lias, never one that she had found.

Genetically determined insensitivity? she wondered, staring at Jim. She refused to believe it. Kontrin geneticists had never worked in terms so ill-defined as the ego and the emotions: and, Meth-maren, she knew the labs better than most. No, there had to be specific biological changes, unless betas knew something Kontrin did not, and she refused to believe that: there had to be something, some single, simple alteration, unaided by majat.

Less sensitivity to physical pain? She could conceive how that might be done, and it would have psychological consequences . . . advantageous, within limits. The biological self-destruct inbuilt in azi evidenced some beta expertise with gene-tampering.

Jim intrigued her suddenly, in that monomaniac way that she filled her days, even important ones, with distractions. She found herself thinking of home, and of comforts, and of Lia's human warmth; and ordinarily she would have stopped herself at this point, dead-stopped, but that there was a distance possible this day, in this place, and she felt, suddenly, that life owed her something of comfort, some last self-indulgence, some . . .

And there the thoughts *did* stop. She turned them cold, and made the question merely intellectual, and useful, the matter of gaining knowledge. Jim was a puzzle, one fit for the time—not easy. She had the strange realization that they were a puzzle she had never wondered about, the azi—a presence too useful and ordinary to question; as she wore clothing, and never perceived the technical skills involved in its making, until she had chanced to desire a cloak made, and had stirred herself to visit a place that might manage it. She had discovered by that, a marvelous workshop of threads and colors and ma-

chines, and an old beta who handmade things for the joy
of them, who found pleasure in the chance to work with
rare majat silk. There was behind the production of the
cloth an entire chain of ancient arts, which had quite
awed her—at distance: there were gifts and gifts, and
hers was not creative.

It was that manner of insight with the azi, had been
so from the first night of the game, although it was only
now she realized why the game had mattered: she had
filled her time with it, and gained occupation—anesthetic
for the mind, such occupations, a near-at-hand focus, a
work of art to analyze and understand.

The highest one, perhaps. Weaving, sculpting, the com-
posing of poetry—what more than this, that Kontrin left
betas to practice? They made men.

His face was surely not unique: there would be others
identical to him, at various ages, scattered across the vicinity of Andra. They would be high types, as he was:
technicians, house-officers, supervisors, foremen, guards,
entertainers—the latter a euphemism on jaded Meron,
where anything could be done; a great many of his doubles were likely majat azi, for majat prized cleverness.
That he was also pleasant decoration to an establishment
would not occur to the majat, whose eyes could not determine that, but it obviously occurred to Andra Lines.
All the serving-azi were of that very expensive class, although no two of them were alike. Obviously they were
to please the passengers in capacities outside the Salon,
and Jim seemed to have had some experience of such
duties. It was wasteful, as the elaborate decor of the ship
was wasteful and extravagant, to settle the most sensitive
and capable of azi to tasks far beneath their mental capacity. But that was typical of beta-ish ostentation: if
one could pay, one bought and displayed, even if it was
completely senseless.

Jim finished his breakfast and sat, staring at the plate
between his hands, probably unsure what to do next, but
looking distressingly like a machine out of program.

Many, many azi *were* machinelike, incapable of even
basic function when diverted from their precise series of

duties, or taken from the specific house or factory to
which they belonged. A few even went catatonic and had
to be terminated if they could not be shocked out of it
and retrained. But Jim, had he won the wager, could
have passed for beta . . . save for the tattoo; he was
capable of living on his own: he was of that order, as
mentally alert as any born-man.

Lia had been such.

Jim looked up finally, perhaps conscious of her concentration on him. There was again that sadness . . . the
same that she had met in the night, a deep and unreach-
able melancholy, the same that had faced her mirrorwise
across the gaming table: suspicion, perhaps, that some
games were not for winning, even if they had to be
played out.

"You don't ask questions," she said.

He still did not.

"We're going to Istra," she said.

"I'll leave with you, then."

That sounded like a question. She realized the drift of
his previous thoughts, and leaned back, still studying him.
"Yes. You should be well-accustomed to traveling, oughtn't
you? Haven't you ever wanted to go downworld? I should
think you might have had some curiosity about the ports
this ship touches."

He nodded, with an infinitesimal brightening of the eyes.

"You can buy," she said, "whatever you like. My resources ceased to amuse me . . . long ago. I pass the
curse on to you: anything you want, any extravagance.
There would have been a limit to your funds had you
won. But with me, there's none. There are hazards to
my company; there are compensations too. If there's anything on this ship you've ever wanted to have, you're
free to buy it."

That only seemed to confuse him. He had seen betas
come and go, richly dressed, ordering fine food and in-
dulging in ship-board pleasures: the limit of his experience in avarice, no doubt. Any beta so invited could have
imagined something at once.

"Why don't you go change again?" she suggested.

"You don't belong in ship's uniform any longer. See how the clothes suit you. Then you might think about packing. We'll be docked by noon. I have some business to attend, but when it's done, then we'll amuse ourselves, have a look at the world, commit a few extravagances, see if there's not some society to disarrange. Go on, go on with you."

He looked no less confused, but he rose from table and turned to the bench to sort through the packaged clothing. He spilled a stack onto the floor, gathered it up again, only to spill another, clumsiness that was not like him. He knelt and collected everything into groups, hesitating in his movements, finally made his selections and restored order. The sight disturbed her, hit her like a blow to the stomach. Azi. Motor confusion, brought on by too much strangeness, too many changes at once. She held her tongue. A sticking-point in the clockwork: it was like that. Intervention would make it worse.

She thought of Lia, and pushed Lia out of her mind.

He went off with his armful of packages, into the bedroom.

She became aware of subdued chatter from the viewer, and rose to cut it off. Depression returned the more forcefully, the more she tried to ignore it.

I could apply to Cerdin, she thought *I could beg Moth and Council for shelter. I could go on living, among Kontrin, home again. All I have to do is bow to Council.*

That was always, she reckoned, all it required. And she would not, not now.

She started about her own packing, opening lockers and chests in search of forgotten items.

The room lights flared red suddenly, the whole suite bathed in the warning glow.

"Sera?" Jim was out of the bath in an instant, his voice plaintive with alarm.

Raen crossed the room in four strides and punched in the emergency channel, foreknowing.

MAJAT PASSENGER, the screen read, NOW MOVING. SECTION 50 PLEASE SECURE YOUR DOORS

AND REMAIN INSIDE. PLEASE CALL STATION 3 IF YOU FEEL YOU NEED ASSISTANCE.

She punched 3. "Security, this is 512. I've noticed your alarm. Would you kindly key us out? Thank you."

Room light went normal white again. Jim still hovered in the doorway, looking frightened.

She checked the gun, clipped it again to her belt beneath her cloak. "Majat hibernate in flight," she told him. "They shed when they wake. The skin's still soft. Instinct—inevitably drives them for daylight when they've shed; the gravitational arrangement on this ship, you see, the upper decks . . . no attack, just natural behavior. Best just to let it wander. It's slightly deaf in this state; the auditory palps are soft . . . eyes none too keen either. Not to be trifled with. I'm going out to see to it. You can stay here if you like. Not many folk care to be around them."

"Do you want me to come?"

It was not enthusiasm, but willingness. She detected no panic, and nodded. "If you'll make no move without advice. The hazard is minor."

"You and the majat—are together?"

"A hazard of my company. I warned you. Their vicinity affects some people. I hope you're immune."

She opened the door and went out into the corridor, where the lights were still red.

Jim followed before the door shut. "Lock it," she said, pleased that he had come. "Always lock things behind me."

The sweat of fear was already glistening on his face, but he punched the lock into operation and stayed with her as she headed down the corridor.

iii

Corridor 50 was next the lifts and the emergency shafts. Raen reckoned well enough how a blind majat could have arrived on fifth level: tunnels were natural for it.

And it was there, huddled against a section-door at

the farther end of the corridor, a tall hulk of folded limbs and fantastical chitinous protuberances. It glistened in the red light, slick with new skin, bewildered by the barriers that had closed before it.

"Quite blind to most of its surroundings," she said to Jim, and the majat's palps were not all that soft. It caught sound and turned, mandibles moving in great agitation. It was a Warrior, hatchling-naked and weaponless.

"Stand here by the corner," Raen said to Jim. "Step round it if it turns ugly. Never try a long run: no human can outrace a Warrior. Its vision, you see, is entirely thermal, and dependent on contrasts of heat; put something cold and solid between yourself and it, and it's lost you. It doesn't see this corridor in anything like our vision: it sees us, maybe . . . or places where metal is warmed by underlying machinery, or by the touch of a hand. Never touch a wall or a surface with your bare skin if you're trying to elude one. And they not only detect scent: they read it."

The auditory palps still moved, perceiving sound, but at this range, perhaps, unable to distinguish it. Seated, it suddenly heaved itself up on two leathery legs, towering against the overhead. It boomed a warning note.

Raen walked forward slowly, flung back her cloak, held up both her hands, backs outward.

Air sucked in, an audible gust.

"Kontrin," it said in deep harmonies. "Blue-hive Kontrin."

"Blue-hive Warrior." She spoke distinctly, a little loudly, for its sake.

"Yes," it sighed, blowing air from its chambers. "Yess." Auditory palps swept decisively forward, like a human relaxing to listen. It lowered its erect body, forelimbs tucked, the whole eloquent of vast relief, trust. There was pathos in the action, sense-deprived as the Warrior was. Something welled up in her, a feeling she had pursued from world to world and not captured until now.

"I knew that a blue had taken this ship," she said. "I came."

It started forward in evident intent to touch, stopped abruptly. Air pulsed in and out, thumping with the force of its expulsion. The sound became words. "Other. Other. Other."

She realized the fix of its dimmed vision and looked back, where Jim waited by the corner.

"Only an azi, Warrior. Mine, my-hive. Don't be concerned for it."

It hesitated, then stalked up to her, bowed itself, seeking touch. She lifted both her hands to its scent-patches. It absorbed this. Then it bowed further, and in a gesture very like a human kiss, opened its mandibles wide and touched the false chelae to her lips. The venomed spike was very close, the jaws gaping on either side. The wrong taste would snap them shut on reflex, and unlike another Warrior, she had no chitinous defense but the sleeve-armor. Yet the taste was sweet; it gently received taste from her.

"No resolution," it said. "From? From?"

"Cerdin," she said. "Once."

"Queen." The analysis proceeded in its body, and it drew back, mandibles clashing in distress. "I taste familiarity. I taste danger."

"I am Raen a Sul. Raen a Sul hant Meth-maren."

It went rigid. Even the mandibles ceased to move. A Warrior alone, it comprehended only Warrior-memories, whatever the complexities its body might carry for others to read.

"Danger," it concluded helplessly. Auditory palps swung forward and back. "Recently waked." It gave warning of its own disorganization, still trusting, but it retreated. The mandibles began to work again in visible distress.

"Warrior, you have reached Istra. Is this not the place for which blue-hive intended you?"

"Yesss." It scuttled farther back from her, into the corner next the door. "Forbidden. Forbidden. Forbidden."

She stayed where she was. Warriors were often laconic and disjointed in conversation, but this one seemed mortally confused. It crouched down, limbs tucked; and cornered, it might spring at the least advance. "Warrior," she said, "I have helped you. If I were not aboard, this ship might have been—stopped. An accident might have happened to you-unit in your sleep. This was not the case. Before you were hatched, I was in blue-hive Cerdin, within the hive. You are Kalind blue, but is there no memory in Kalind, of Meth-marens? Before you left Cerdin, you knew us, Meth-maren-hive, hive-friends. There was a hill, a lake by a place called Kethiuy. We spoke—for all human hives."

"Warrior," it reminded her; it could not be expected to Remember. But the auditory palps were strained forward, and the mandibles worked rapidly. "Meth-maren hive. Meth-maren. Meth-maren. Kethiuy. Hive-friends. First-humans, Meth-marens. Yessss. Warrior-memory holds Meth-marens."

"Yes," she said. She held out her hands, offering touch, should it accept. There was no queen to advise Warrior, no Drones to Remember for it: she had it snared, almost, almost, and tried not to betray the anxiety in her. It had no means to know how other blues had eluded her. It was going to Istra, as blues had attempted other worlds; but this one, this sending would get through. *She* saw to it, though blue-hive elsewhere had fled her and met disaster, had voyaged and never wakened, or perished in ambush. This one lived, at the one world where she had a chance of protecting it.

As the one world where there was no one of the Family to stop her or forbid her access to the hives.

"Warrior. You were sent to Istra. True?"

"True."

"Our purposes coincide, it may be. Tell me. Why have you come here? What message do you carry?"

It held its silence, thinking, perhaps. It was a new generation, this Warrior; eighteen years was the time of a new generation for its kind . . . all across the Reach, a new generation of blue-hive, quiet within its separate hills—blues withdrawn, while greens came to the labs managed by Thons, performed as always, abided by the Pact under Thon direction.

Until last year.

"Why have you come?" Raen asked.

It eased forward again, wary. The fix of her head was not toward her, but beyond. It turned the head then, rotating it on its circular joints. "Azi. Meth-maren azi."

It wanted touch. Majat called it Grouping, the need to be emotionally sure of others. Jim remained where she had left him, red-dyed in the light. "My azi," Raen confirmed, her heart beating rapidly. "Jim. Jim, come to me, slowly."

He could break and run. She stood in Warrior's way, and perhaps, only perhaps she could restrain Warrior from the kill if Jim set him off. But Jim left his corner and came, stopped at yet a little distance, as if suddenly paralyzed. Warrior shifted forward, the matter of three strides that Raen could not match, and leaned over him.

Jim had simply shut his eyes in panic. Raen reached him, caught his arm, shocked him out of it. "Touch," she told him. "You must touch it." And when he did not move with propriety, reaching instead to the thorax, Raen took his right hand in hers, guided it between the jaws to Warrior's offered scent-patches. The huge Warrior, only minimally sane, bent lower, jaws wide, touched false chelae to Jim's lips, taking taste as well as scent. Jim's face broke out in sweat: this too Warrior tasted, sweeping it from his brow with the delicate bristles of the false chelae.

"Trust it," Raen whispered into his ear, yet gripping his arm. "Stand still, stand still; blues will never harm you once this Warrior has reported on Istra. It can't recognize faces, but it knows the taste now. Maybe it can even distinguish you from your duplicates; I'd imagine it can."

She let go. Warrior had perceptibly calmed. It touched at Jim, touched her.

"Blue-hive," it murmured, deep baritone. And then with a distressed waving of its palps: "Danger."

"There is danger everywhere for blues." Raen offered her right hand to its mandibles, willful hazard, comforting gesture. "Hive-friend. Do you also bear taste of reds? Of Kethiuy? Of killing?"

Mandibles clashed as her hand withdrew; jaws snicked, strongly enough to decapitate human or majat. "Killing," it moaned from its chambers, deep harmony. "Red-hive, killings, yess."

"I was there, on Cerdin, when reds killed blues. Does Kalind blue remember that? Messengers went out from Cerdin then. Surely some got through. Some must have lived."

"Not-clear. Drone-function."

"But you know Cerdin."

"Cerdin." It sucked air and expelled it softly. "Yess. Cerdin. First-hive. This-unit does not make full understanding. This-unit will report. Blue queen of Istra will interpret. Queen will understand."

"Surely she will."

"This-unit will not see Kalind again. This-unit is cut off. I can carry this message no farther than the Istran queen. Then I must unMind."

"Perhaps the Istran queen will take you instead, Warrior, and change that instruction."

"This-unit hopes."

"This-unit also hopes, Warrior."

Palps caressed her face with great tenderness. Truly neuter, Warrior had no concept of any function but duty; yet majat units could feel some sentiment on their own, and Warriors were—very slightly—egocentric.

She laid her hand on its forelimb. "What brings you here? What message, Warrior? Answer me."

The great armored head rotated in that gesture that had so many nuances to majat vision. "This-unit does not know; I taste *of revenge,* Kethiuy-queen."

It was complex, then, locked within its body-chemistry; it gave her Warrior-reading only, and the Warrior-mind conceived it as revenge. A chill ran over her skin, an echo of things past.

"I have known you before, Warrior."

"Warrior memory," it confirmed, and touched at her, touched at them both. "Meth-maren. Yesss. Not all Kontrin are friends. Trust you. Trust you, Kethiuy-queen."

A message had gotten through, eighteen, nineteen

years ago. Warrior was with her. She touched it, her hand trembling.

"We will be docking soon, Warrior. You must secure yourself for your own protection, and not trouble these beta humans. They are no harm, no harm to you."

"Yes," it agreed. It reared up and looked about, head rotating half this way and half that. "Lost," it complained. "Human-hive. Lost."

"Come," she bade it, and brought it to a security panel, took its right chela and touched it to the emergency grip. It clenched it, secure then as a human safely belted. "You must stay here, Warrior. Let your skin dry. You've come high enough. Hold and wait, and harm no human who doesn't threaten you. I'll come for you when it's time."

"Lost. This-unit must find Istra blue."

She stroked the sensitive side-palps, reckoning what a complex and fearful task Warrior faced, with no sun overhead, encased in one cold metal structure after another on its way. Majat did not easily comprehend that it was not all one sun and all one world. It had entrusted itself to betas for hire, hoping it was given right directions, set on the right ship; and blue messengers faced other obstacles, for Kontrin discouraged their traveling, and accidents befell one after the other. "I will guide you," she told it "Stay. Wait for me."

"Blue-hive," it breathed, bowed under the pleasurable caress. Jaws clashed. "I wait. Yesss."

"My-chamber is twelfth door beyond the turning-left, as you face."

"This-unit guards."

"Yes," she agreed, touched the palps and drew back. The halls were cold; its processes were slow: it was all too willing now to sink down and rest. She thought of bidding it instead to her own suite, but there was Jim, who stood against the wall in a seeming state of shock. She soothed it a last time with her hand, turned away and took Jim with her, trusting it would be safe; indeed, no one would likely venture that hall, and if someone would have harmed it, of those aboard, that would have been done while it slept, helpless—not now.

This messenger would get through.

Is this the best action? the Mother of Cerdin had asked. Among majat there were no children, only eggs, and adults. Mother had asked a human for advice, and a child had answered: Mother had not known.

It was wise that humans had been forbidden the hive, direct access to queens, to Drones, to the Mind. She abhorred now what she was doing, imprinting Warrior, while it was unadvised by any queen.

That imprint would enter Istran blues, as truth, as true as Warrior's legitimate message.

It was her key to the hives.

iv

Jim exited the bath, whiter than he had been. He had lost the breakfast, and decided on another prolonged bath. Now, wrapped in a bathsheet, he flung himself belly-down on the wide bed and showed no disposition to move.

Raen bent over him, touched his damp shoulders. "You're sure you're all right? You didn't let it scratch you, did you?"

"All right," he echoed indistinctly. She decided that he was, and that the kindest thing she could do at the moment was to let him lie. He was still overheated from the water. She pulled a corner of the bedclothes loose and flung it over him, shrugged and walked back to her own business.

She packed, settling everything with precision into her several cases—scuffed and battered from much use, that luggage—but it contained so well the things she would not give up, from world to world. Most that she had bought on the ship she thought of leaving; and then she decided otherwise and simply jammed things in the more tightly: Istra did not promise their equal.

To all of it she added the fifth and sixth cases, the deep-study apparatus and her precious tapes; she never trusted a strange apparatus, and the tapes—the tapes she kept much beyond their usefulness for casual knowledge, some for pleasure, some for sentiment, a few for reference. And there were half a dozen that Council would be aghast to know existed in duplicate; but Hal Ilit had admitted her within his security, and never seen beyond his own self-indulgence, his own vanity, not even in dying. She counted the tapes through, making sure everything was in its slot, nothing lost, nothing left to assumption.

And she would have taken the refuge deepstudy offered for an hour now, having finished all else: it was the best antidote for unpleasantness. But Jim was there, and she did not mean to make the Ilit's mistake: under deepstudy, one was utterly helpless, and she would not, would never accept sinking into that state in another's presence, even an azi's. She paced the suite in boredom, and finally, sure beyond doubt that there remained nothing to do, she sat down and keyed in the viewer, one of the entertainment channels.

Beta dramas, trivial and depressing . . . worse, when one knew the deliberate psych-sets which had gone into training their lab-born ancestors: work to succeed, succeed to be idle, consume, consume, consume, consumption is status. It worked, economically: on it, the entire economy of the Reach thrived; but it made excruciatingly boring drama. She keyed in docking operations, and found more interest simply in watching the station spin nearer, the abstract shift of light and shadow across its planes.

She heard a sound from the other room. Jim was up and about. She listened for him to head for the bath again in distress, but he did not, and she decided that he had recovered. She heard a great deal of walking back and forth, the crumbling of plastics, and finally the click of a suitcase closing. She looked round the side of the chair and saw him, dressed in conservative street clothes, setting his case beside her several.

He could indeed have been beta, or even Kontrin: he

was tall. But he was a little too fair; and there was the minute tattoo beneath the right eye.

"You look very fine, Jim."

He glanced down, seeming embarrassed. "I thank you, sera."

"Formalities are hardly appropriate in private." She spun the chair about from the viewer and looked up at him. "You're all right, then."

He nodded. "I'm sorry," he said almost inaudibly.

"You didn't panic; you stood your ground. Sit down."

He did so, on the bench against the wall, still slightly pale.

"Meth-maren," she said, "is not a well-loved name among Kontrin. And sooner or later someone will make an attempt on my life." She opened her right hand, palm down. "The chitin grafted there is blue-hive; blue-hive and the Meth-marens met a common misfortune two decades ago. Warrior and I have something in common, you see. And listen to me: I once had a few azi in my employ. Somehow a gate was left unlocked and red-hive majat got in. I sleep lightly. The azi didn't. The room was no pretty sight, I may tell you. But an azi who would walk with me out mere into the hall . . . might have been of some use to me that night."

"On the ship—" He always spoke in a hushed voice, and the more so now. "We have security procedures. I understand them."

"Do they teach you about self-defense?"

A slight shake of the head.

"They just tell you about locks and accesses and fire procedures."

A diffident nod.

"Well, that's far better than nothing. Hear this: you must guard my belongings and things that I'll use and places that I'll come back to, with far more care than you use guarding me. I take care of myself, you see, and most of my enemies wouldn't go for a head-on attack on me if there were an easier way; no, they'd go for something I'd use, or for an unlocked door. You understand what I'm talking about."

"Yes, sera."

"We're docking in an hour or so. You could save confusion by getting a baggage cart up here. I really don't think azi are going to be safe coming up here, not past Warrior out there. But it wouldn't hurt you, not if you let it touch you and identify, you understand. No more than it would me. You have the nerve for it?"

He nodded.

"Jim, perhaps we may stay together a long time."

He stood up, stopped. "Nineteen years," he said. And when she gave him a puzzled frown: "I'm twenty-one," he said, with the faintest quirk of a smile.

Azi humor. He would live to forty. A feeling came on her the like of which only the blues had stirred in many years. She recalled Lia, and the gentle azi of her childhood: their dead faces returned with a shock; and the slaughter, and the burning . . . She flinched from it. "I value loyalty," she said, turning away.

He was gone for a considerable time. She began to pace the room, realized that she was doing it and stopped, thought of going after him, hated to show her anxiety among betas.

At last the blue light winked in the overhead and she hurried to open the door, stood back to admit him and the cart.

"No trouble?" she asked him. Jim shook his head with a little touch of self-satisfaction and began at once putting the baggage on.

He finished, and settled, lacking anything else to do; she sat, watching their approach to station. Their berth was in sight; the station was by now a seemingly stationary sprawl extending off the screen on both sides, an amazing structure, as vast as rumor promised.

And ships, ships of remarkable design, linked to their berths—freighters, as bizarre in shape as they needed to be, never landing, only needing the capability to link to station umbilicals and grapples; the only standard of construction was the docking mechanism, the same dimensions from the tiniest personal craft to the most massive liner.

A ship was easing out as they came in, slowly, slowly, an aged freighter. The symbols it bore were unlike any sigil or company emblem in Raen's memory; and then she realized it for the round Sol emblem. A thrill went through her.

An Outsider ship.

A visitor from beyond the Reach. It drifted like a dream image, passed them, vanished into the *Jewel*'s own shadow.

"Outsider," she said aloud. "Jim, look, look—a third one at berth is the same design."

Jim said nothing, but he regarded the image intently, with awe on his face.

"The Edge," Raen said. "We've reached the Edge."

V

Merek Eln's hands trembled. He folded his arms and paced, and looked from time to time at Parn Kest.

"We'd better call in," he said. "There's time enough."

"With a majat involved—" she objected. "A majat! How long can the thing have been aboard?"

"It's with *her*. Has to be." He looked toward the door with an inward shudder, thinking of the majat stalking the corridors at liberty, half-sane from its dormancy. The Kontrin had at least calmed the creature: the emergency channel had said so, and thanked her, whether or not the Kontrin cared for anyone's gratitude. But worse could go wrong than had. They had been long away from Istra, half a year removed from the situation there, long removed from the last message.

He stepped suddenly to the console.

"Merek," Parn said, rising, and caught his arm. Sweat stood on her face; it did on his. Her hand fell away. She said nothing. Their cover no longer served to protect them. There was no more guarantee of safety, even in coming home.

He sat down at the console and keyed in the communications channel. Communications was fully occupied with the flow of docking instructions; a message would have to go Priority, at high cost.

Communications wanted financial information beyond ordinary credit; it accepted a string of numbers and codes to bounce back through worldbank, and finally a chain of numbers which was the destination of the message, ITAK company representative on-station.

GO, it flashed.

Merek keyed response. NOTIFY MAIN OFFICE MERON MISSION INBOUND. URGENT ITAK ON STATION MEET US AT GATE WITH SECURITY. AWAIT REPLY WITH DEEP DISTRESS.

There was the necessary long delay.

"You shouldn't have mentioned Meron," Parn said at his shoulder. "You shouldn't have. Not on a public channel."

"Do you want to do this?"

"I wouldn't have called."

"And there wouldn't have been anyone to meet us but maybe—maybe some of the office staff; and maybe things have changed on the station. I want our own security out there."

He mopped at his face, recalling codes. DEEP: that was trouble; and DISTRESS at the end of any message meant majat. He dared not talk of Kontrin. One had no idea where their agents might be placed.

ITAK REPRESENTATIVE WILL BE AT GATE, the reply flashed back. DEEP DISTRESS UNDERSTOOD. OUR APOLOGIES.

It was the right code, neatly delivered. Merek bit at his lip and keyed receipt of the message.

ITAK took care of its people, if ITAK had the chance to move first. And if other messages had been sent, from the Kontrin or another agency, surely it was best to have broken cover and asked for help.

Parn took his hand in hers, put her arm about his

shoulders. He was not sure that he had done the right thing; Parn herself had disagreed. But if some message had gone ahead, if the ship had even done something so innocent as flash its tiny passenger list ahead, then it was necessary to be sure that among those gathered to meet the *Jewel,* ITAK would be chiefest.

vi

"Warrior," Raen called softly.

It stirred, let go its hold on the emergency grip.

"Warrior, we are docked now. It's Raen Meth-maren." She came and touched it, and it must touch in return, and examine Jim as well, swift gestures.

"Yes," it said, having Grouped.

"Jim." Raen gestured at the nearby lift. Jim maneuvered the baggage cart in, pressed himself against the inside wall as Warrior eased in, and Raen followed.

The doors sealed, and the lift moved. The air grew very close very quickly with the sealed system and the big majat's breathing. Warrior smelled of something dry and strange, like old paper. The chitin, still wet-looking from shedding, was dry now; where Warrior had broken his old shell, the ship's crew might find a treasure-trove . . . none of the Drone-jewels, of course, but material which still had value in ornament: so the hive paid a bonus on its passage. Warrior regarded them both, mildly distressed as the lift reoriented itself; the great head rotated quizzically: compound eyes made moiré patterns under the light, shifting bands of color buried in jewel-shard armor.

It was beautiful. Raen stroked its palps to soothe it, and softly it sang for her, Warrior-song.

"Hear it?" Raen asked, looking at Jim. "The hives are full of such sound. Humans rarely hear it."

Again the lift shifted itself to a new alignment, hissed to a stop. The doors opened for them. Azi on duty fled back, giving them and their tall companion whatever room they wanted.

There was the hatch, and a wafting of the cold, strange air of Istra station, dark spaces and glaring lights. Crew waited to bid them farewell, a changeless formality: so they had surely wished every passenger departing over the long voyage; but there was the strained look of dementia in their eyes and behind their smiles. *Andra's Jewel* could go home now, to safe and friendly space, to ordinary passengers, and her staterooms would fill again with beta-folk, who never thought of Kontrin or majat save at distance.

Raen lingered to shake hands with each, and laughed. Their hands were moist and cold, and their fingers avoided the chitin on her hand where they could.

"Safe voyage," she wished them one and all.

"Safe voyage," Warrior breathed, incapable of humor.

No one offered to help them down the ramp. Jim managed the baggage, struggling with the cart which they had tacitly appropriated. They boarded the conveyer and rode it down.

There at the bottom of the ramp stood the Istran pair, inside the security barriers, with a clutch of business types and three others who might be azi, but not domestics: guards. Raen moved her hand within her cloak, rested it by her gun, calculating which she might remove first if she had to . . . simple reflex. Her hand rested comfortably there.

The moving ramp delivered them down, and there was view of a drab, businesslike vastness, none of the chrome and glitter of Meron, none of the growing plants of Kalind, or the cosmopolitan grandeur of Cerdin station. This station wasted nothing on display, no expensive shielded viewports. It was all dark machinery and automata, bare joinings and cables and every service-point in sight and reach of hands. It was a trade-station, not for the delight of tourists, but for the businesslike reception of freight. Conveyers laced overhead; transport chutes and dark corridors led away into narrow confinements; azi moved here and there, drab, gray-clad men, unsmiling in their fixation on duty.

Raen inhaled the grimness of it and looked leftward,

third berth down, hoping for exotic sights of Outsiders, but all docks looked alike, vast ramps, dwarfing humans, places shrouded in tangles of lines and obscured by machinery. A few human figures moved there, too far to distinguish, tantalizing in their possibilities. And she could not delay to investigate them.

"Lost," Warrior complained, touching nervously at her. The air was cold, almost cold enough to make breath frost. Warrior was almost blind in such a place, and would grow rapidly sluggish.

And the Istrans came forward, further distressing it. Raen reached lefthanded to comfort it, and gave Merek Eln a forbidding stare.

"I'd keep my distance," she said.

Ser Merek Eln did stop, with all his companions. His face was ashen. He looked at the tall majat and at her, and swallowed thickly.

"My party is here," he said. "We have a shuttle engaged. Would you consider joining us on our trip down Kont' Raen? I . . . would still like to talk with you."

She was frankly amazed. This little man, this beta, came offering favors, and had the courage to approach a majat doing it. "My companions would make that rather crowded, ser."

"We have accommodation enough, if you would."

"Beta," Warrior intoned. "Beta human." It moved forward in one stride, to touch the strange human who offered it favors, and Raen put up her hand at once, touched a sensitive auditory palp, restraining Warrior. It endured this indignity, fretting.

Merek Eln had not fled. It was possibly the worst moment of his life, but he stood still. Her respect for him markedly increased.

"Ser," she said, "our presence here must be very important to you personally."

"Please," he said in a low voice. "Please. Now. The station is not a secure place to be standing in the open. ITAK can offer you security. We can talk on the way down. It's urgent."

All her instincts rebelled at this: it was dangerous, ridiculously dangerous, to accept local entanglements without looking into all sides of the matter.

But she nodded, and walked with them. Jim followed. Warrior stalked beside, statuary in slow motion, trying to hold to human pace.

Their course took them along the dock, nearer and nearer the Outsider berth.

Raen tried not even to glance much that way: it distracted her from the general survey of the area, which her eyes made constantly, nervously. But there were Outsiders; she knew they must be such, by their strange clothing and their business near that berth.

"Are such onworld too?" she asked. "Do they come down-world?"

"There's a ground-based trade mission," Kest said.

That cheered her. She could bear it no longer, and stopped and stared at a group of men near them on the dock . . . plainly dressed, doing azi-work. She wondered whether they were true men or what they were. They stopped their work and stood upright and gaped . . . more at the majat, surely, than at her.

From Outside. From the wide, free Outside, where men existed such as Kontrin had once been. Until now, Outsiders had seen only the shadows of Kontrin; she wondered if they knew—what betas were, or if they had the least comprehension of Kontrin, or realized what she was.

"Sera," Eln said anxiously. "Please. Please."

She turned from the strangers, reckoning the open places about them, the chance of ambush. Warrior touched her anxiously, seeking reassurance. She followed the Eln-Kests at what pace they wanted to set, uncertain whether they were evading possible assassins or walking among them.

BOOK FIVE

i

"The old woman has something in mind," Tand said. "I don't like it."

The elder Hald walked a space with his grandnephew, paused to pull a dead bloom from the nightflower. Neighboring leaves shrank at the touch and remained furled a moment, then relaxed. "Something concrete?"

"Hive-reports. Stacks of them. Statistics. She may be aiming something at Thon. I don't know. I can't determine."

The elder looked about at Tand, his heart laboring with the heavy persistence of dread. Tand was outside the informed circles of the movement. There were many things of which Tand remained ignorant: must. Where Tand stood, it was not good that he know . . . near as he was to the old woman's hand. If the blow fell, all that he knew could be in Moth's hands in hours. "What kind of statistics? Involving azi?"

"Among others. She's asking for more data on Istra. She's . . . amused by the Meth-maren. So she gives out. But here's the matter: she muttered something after the committee left. About the Meth-maren serving her interests . . . conscious or unconscious on the Meth-maren's part, I don't know. I asked her flatly was the Meth-maren her agent. She denied it and then hedged with that."

The Hald dropped the dry petals, his pulse no calmer. "The Meth-maren is becoming a persistent irritant."

"Another attempt on her—might be advisable."

The Hald pulled off a frond. Others furled tightly, remained so, twice offended. He began to strip the soft part off the skeleton of the veins. It left a sharp smell in the air. "Tand, go back to the Old Hall. You shouldn't stay here tonight."

"Now?"

"Now."

One of Tand's virtues was his adaptability. The Hald pulled another frond and stripped it, trusting that there would not be the least hesitation in Tand, from the garden walk to the front gate to the City. He heard him walk away, a door close.

His steps would be covered, cloaked in innocence . . . a supposed venture in the City; and back to Alpha, and Old Hall. There were those who would readily lie for him.

The Hald wiped his hand and walked the other path, up to other levels of the Hald residence at Ehlvillon, to eastwing, to other resources.

A pattern was shaping.

On Istra . . . things had long been safe from Council inspection. Communications had been carefully channeled through Meron, screened thoroughly before transmission farther.

He walked the halls of paneling and stone, into the shielded area of the house comp, leaned above it and sent a message that consisted of banalities. There was no acknowledgment at the other end.

But three hours later, a little late for callers, an aircraft set down on the Hald grounds, ruffling the waters of the ornamental pond.

The Hald went out to meet it, and walked arm in arm with the man who had come in, paused by the pool in the dark, fed the sleepy old mudsnake which denned there. It gulped down bits of bread, being the omnivore it was, its double-hinged jaws opening and clamping again into a fat sullenness.

"Nigh as old as the house," the Hald said of it.

Arl Ren-barant stood with folded arms. The Hald stood up and the mudsnake snapped, then levered itself off the bank and eased into the black waters, making a little wake as it curled away.

"Some old business," said the Hald, "has surfaced again. I'm beginning to think it never left at all. We've been very careless in yielding to Eldest's wishes in this case. I'm less and less convinced it's a matter of whim with her."

"The Meth-maren?" Ren-barant frowned and shook his head. "Not so easy to do it now. She's completely random, a nuisance. If it were really worth the risk—"

The Hald looked at him sharply. "Random. So what happened on Meron?"

"A personal quarrel, left over from the first attempt. Gen and Hal have become a cause with the Ilits. It was unfortunate."

"And on Kalind."

"Hive-matter, but she wasn't in it. Blues have settled again. Reds seem to be content enough."

"Yes. The Meth-maren's gone. Meron's damaged and Kalind isn't unscathed. Attention rests where it doesn't suit us. The old hive-master's talent . . . Arl, we have an enemy. A very dangerous one."

"She hardly made a secret of her going to Istra. Why make so much commotion of it, if she's not as mad as we've reckoned? A private ship could have reached there in a direct jump. She could have had time to work . . ."

"The whole Council noticed, didn't they? It was bizarre enough that it caught the curiosity of the whole Council. Attention focused where we don't need it focused at all."

Ren-barant's face was stark, his arms tightly clenched. "Cold sane, you think."

"As you and I are. As Moth is. I have news, Arl. There was a majat on that liner when it left Kalind. We haven't discovered yet how far it went, whether all the way with her or whether it got off earlier."

"Blue messenger?"

"We don't know yet. Blue or green is a good bet."

Ren-barant swore. "Thon was supposed to have that cut off."

"Majat paid the passage," the Hald said. "Betas can't tell them apart. The Meth-maren boarded at the last moment . . . special shuttle, a great deal of noise about it. We knew about her very quickly. Use of her credit was obvious, at least the size of the transaction and the recipient, which was Andra Lines, through one of their sub-agents. But the majat paid in jewels, cash transaction, freighted up dormant and inconspicuous . . . a special payment to someone, I'll warrant. Cash. No direct record to our banks. No tracing. We still can't be sure how much was actually paid: probably a great deal went into the left hand while the right was making records; but the Meth-maren was right there, using vast amounts of credit, very visible. We didn't find out about the majat until our agents started asking questions among departing passengers. Betas won't volunteer that kind of gossip. But the whole operation, that a hive could bypass our surveillance and do it so completely, so long—"

"The Thons do nothing. Maybe we'd better ask some questions about the quality of that support."

"She's Meth-maren; the Thon hive-masters have no influence with the blues. And Council can vote Thon the post; they can't make them competent in it. Anyone can handle reds. The test is whether Thon can control the blues. I think Thon is beyond the level of their competency, for all their assurances to us. The Meth-maren's running escort for majat; she outwitted Thon, and she's made Council look toward Istra. The old woman, Arl, the old woman is collecting statistics; she's taking interest again; there's a chance she's taken interest for longer than we've known."

The Ren-barant hissed softly between his teeth.

"There's more," the Hald said. "The old woman dropped a word about the Meth-maren being—*useful*. Useful. And that with her sudden preoccupation with statistics. Istran statistics. The Pedra bill is coming up. We'd better be ready, before the old woman hits us with a public surprise. Istra's vulnerable."

"Someone had better get out there, then."

"I've moved on that days ago." And at the Ren-barant's sudden, apprehensive stare. "*That* matter is on its way to being solved. It's not the Meth-maren I'm talking about."

"Yes," the Ren-barant said after a moment. "I can see that."

"Tand's next to her. He stays, no breath of doubt near him. The organization has to be firmed up, made ready on the instant. You know the program. You know the contacts. I put it on you. I daren't. I've gone as far as I can."

The Ren-barant nodded grimly. They began to part company. Suddenly the Ren-barant stopped in his tracks and looked back. "There's more than one way for Moth to use the Meth-maren. To provoke enemies into following the wrong lead."

Ros Hald stared at him, finally nodded. It was the kind of convolution of which Moth had long proved capable. "We've counted on time to take care of our problems. That's been a very serious mistake. Both of them have to be cared for—simultaneously."

The mudsnake surfaced again, hopeful. The Hald tossed it the rest of the morsel: sullen jaws snapped. It waited for more. None came. It slipped away again under the black waters and rippled away.

ii

The Istran shuttle was an appalling relic. There was little enough concession to comfort in the station, but there was less in the tight confines of the vessel which would take them down to surface. Only the upholstery was new, a token attempt at renovation. Raen surveyed the machinery with some curiosity, glanced critically into the cockpit, where pilot and co-pilot were checking charts and bickering.

The Istrans had settled in, all nine of them, Merek Eln and Parn Kest, the several business types and their azi guard. Warrior had taken up position in the rear of the aisle, the only space sufficient for its comfort and that of the betas. It closed both chelae about the braces of the rearmost seats, quite secure, and froze into the statue-like patience of its kind.

Jim came up the ramp, and after some little perplexity, secured the whole carrier into storage behind the Eln-Kest's modest luggage, . . . forced the door closed. Raen let him take his seat first, next the sealed viewport, then settled in after, opposite Merek Eln, and fastened the belts. Her pulse raced, considering the company they kept and the museum-piece in which they were about to hurtle into atmosphere.

"This is quite remarkable," she said to Jim, thinking that Meron in all its decadent and hazardous entertainments had never offered anything quite like Istran transport.

Jim looked less elated with the experience, but his eyes flickered with interest over all the strangeness, . . . not fear, but a feverish intensity, as if he were attempting to absorb everything at once and deal with it. His hands trembled so when he adjusted his belts that he had trouble joining them.

The co-pilot stopped the argument with the pilot long enough to come back and check the door seal, went forward again. The pilot gave warning. The vessel disengaged from its lock and went through the stomach-wrenching sequence of intermittent weightlessness and reorientation under power as they threaded their way out of their berth. The noise, unbaffled, was incredible.

"Kontrin," Merek Eln shouted, leaning in his seat.

"Explanations?" Raen asked.

"We are very grateful—"

"Please. Just the explanation."

Merek Eln swallowed heavily. They were in complete weightlessness, their slight wallowing swiftly corrected. The noise died away save for the circulation fans. Istra showed crescent-shaped on the forward screen, more than filling it; the station showed on the aft screen. They were falling into the world's night side, as Raen judged it.

"We are very glad you decided to accept transport with us," Eln said. "We are quite concerned for your safety at Istra, onstation and onworld. There's been some difficulty, some disturbance. Perhaps you have heard."

Raen shrugged. There were rumors of unrest, here and elsewhere, of crises; of things more serious . . . she earnestly wished she knew.

"You were," Merek Eln said, "perhaps sent here for that reason."

She made a slight gesture of the eyes back toward Warrior. "You might ask it concerning its motives."

That struck a moment of silence.

"Kontrin," said sera Kest, leaning forward from the seat behind. "For whatever reasons you've come here—you must realize there's a hazard. The station is too wide, too difficult to monitor. In Newhope, on Istra, at least we can provide you security."

"Sera—are we being abducted?"

The faces about her were suddenly stark with apprehension.

"Kontrin," said Merek Eln, "you are being humorous; we wish we could persuade you to consider seriously what hazards are possible here."

"Ser, sera, so long as you persist in trying to tell me only fragments of the situation, I see no reason to take a serious tone with you. You've been out to Meron. You're coming home. Your domestic problems are evidently serious and violent, but your manner indicates to me that you would much rather I were not here."

There was a considerable space of silence. Fear was thick in the air.

"There has been some violence," said one of the others. "The station is particularly vulnerable to sabotage and such acts. We fear it. We have sent appeals. None were answered."

"The Family ignored them. Is that your meaning?"

"Yes," said another after a moment.

"That is remarkable, seri. And what agency do you suspect to be the source of your difficulty?"

No one answered.

"Dare I guess," said Raen, "that you suspect that the source of your troubles *is* the Family?"

There was yet no answer, only the evidence of perspiration on beta faces.

"Or the hives?"

No one moved. Not an eye blinked.

"You would not be advised to take any action against me, seri. The Family is not monolithic. Quite the contrary. Be reassured: I am ignorant; you can try to deceive me. What brought the two of you to Meron?"

"We—have loans outstanding from MIMAK there. We hoped for some material assistance . . ."

"We hoped," Parn Kest interrupted brusquely, "to establish innerworlds contacts—to help us past this wall of silence. We need relief . . . in taxes, in trade; we were ignored, appeal after appeal. And we hoped to work out a temporary agreement with MIMAK, against the hope of some relief. Grain. Grain and food. Kontrin—we're supporting farms and estates which can't possibly make profit. We're at a crisis. We were given license for increase in population, our own and azi, and the figures doubled our own. We thought future adjustment would take care of that. But the crisis is on us, and no one listens. Majat absorb some of the excess. That market is all that keeps us from economic collapse. But food . . . food for all that population . . . And the day we can't feed the hives . . . Kont' Raen, agriculture and azi are our livelihood. Newhope and Newport and the station . . . and the majat . . . derive their food from the estates; but it's consumed by the azi who work them. There are workers enough to cover the estates' needs four times over. There's panic out there. The estates are armed camps."

"We were told when we came in," Eln said in a faint voice, "that ITAK has been able to confiscate azi off some of the smaller estates. But there's no way to take them by force from the larger. We can't legally dispose of those contracts, by sale or by termination. There has to be Kontrin—"

"—license for transfer or adjustment," Raen finished. "Or for termination without medical cause. I know our policies rather thoroughly, ser Eln."

"And therefore you can't export and you can't terminate."

"Or feed them indefinitely, Kontrin. Or feed them. The economics of the farms insist on a certain number of azi to the allotted land area. Someone . . . *erred*."

Eln's lips trembled, having said so. It was for a beta, great daring.

"And the occasion for violence against the station?"

"It hasn't happened yet," one of the others said.

"But you fear that it will. Why?"

"The corporations are blamed for the situation on the estates. Estate-owners are hardly able to comprehend any other—at fault."

There was another silence, deep and long.

"You'll be glad to know, seri, that there are means to get a message off this world, one that would be heard on Cerdin. I might do it. But there are solutions short of that. Perhaps better ones." She thought then of Jim, and laid a hand on his knee, leaning toward him. "You are hearing things which aren't for retelling . . . to anyone."

"I will not," he said, and she believed him, for he looked as if he earnestly wanted to be deaf to this. She turned back to Eln and Kest.

"What measures," she asked them, "*have* the corporations taken?"

No one wanted to meet her eyes, not those two, nor their companions.

"Is there starvation?" she asked.

"We are importing," one of the others said at last a small, flat voice.

Raen looked at him, slowly took his meaning. "Standard channels of trade?"

"All according to license. Foodstuffs are one of the permitted—"

"I know the regulations. You're getting your grain from Outside trade. Outsiders."

"We've held off rationing. We've kept the peace. We're able to feed everyone."

"We've tried to find other alternatives," Merek Eln

said. "We can't find surplus anywhere within the Reach. We can't get it from Inside. We've tried, Kont' Raen."

"Your trip to Meron."

"Part of it, yes. That. A failure."

"Ser Eln, there's one obvious question. If you're buying Outsider grain . . . what do you use to pay for it?"

It was a question perhaps rash to ask, on a beta vessel, surrounded by them, in descent to a wholly beta world.

"Majat," one of the others said hoarsely, with a nervous shift of the eyes in Warrior's direction. "Majat jewels. Soft-wares."

"Kontrin-directed?"

"We—pad out what the Cerdin labs send. Add to the shipments."

"Kontrin-directed?"

"Our own doing," the man beside him said. "Kontrin, it's not forbidden. Other hive-worlds do it."

"I know it's legal; don't cite me regulations."

"We appealed for help. We still abide by the law. We would do nothing that's not according to the law."

According to the law . . . and disruptive of the entire trade balance if done on a large scale: the value of the jewels and the other majat goods was upheld by deliberate scarcity.

"You're giving majat goods to Outsiders to feed a world," Raen said softly. "And what do majat get? Grain? Azi? You have that arrangement with them?"

"Our population," sera Kest said faintly, "even now is not *large*—compared to inner worlds. It's only large for our capacity to produce. Our trade is azi. We hope for Kontrin understanding. For licenses to export."

"And the hives assist you in this crisis—sufficient to feed all the excess of your own population, and the excess of azi, and themselves. Your prices to the majat for grain and azi must be exorbitant, sera Kest."

"They—need the grain. They don't object."

"Do you know," Raen said, ever so softly, "I somehow believe you, sera Kest."

There was a sudden stomach-wrenching shift as the shuttle powered into entry alignment. They were downward bound now, and the majat moved, boomed a protest at this unaccustomed sensation; then it froze again, to the relief of the betas and the guard azi.

"We're doing an unusual entry," Raen observed, feeling the angle.

"We don't cross the High Range. Bad weather."

She looked at the beta who had said that, and for that moment her pulse quickened—a sense that, indeed, she had to accept their truths for the time. She said nothing more, scanning faces.

They were coming in still nightside, at a steeper angle than was going to be comfortable for any reason. There might be quite a bit of buffeting. Jim, unaccustomed to landings even of the best kind, was already looking gray. So were the Eln-Kests.

Two corporations: ITAK onworld and ISPAK, the station and power corporation overhead. ISPAK was a Kontrin agency, that should be in direct link with Cerdin. So were all stations. They were too sensitive, holding all a world's licensed defense; and in any situation of contest, ISPAK could shut Istra down, depriving it of power. With any choice for a base of operations, ITAK onworld was not the best one, not unless the stakes were about to go very high indeed.

No licenses, no answer to appeals: the link to Cerdin should have had an answer through their own station. No relief from taxes; other worlds had such adjustments, in the presence of Kontrin. Universal credit was skimmed directly off the tax; majat were covered after the same fashion as Kontrin when they dealt through Kontrin credit; but they could, because they were producers of goods, trade directly in cash, which Kontrin in effect could not. Throughout the system, through the network of stations and intercomp, the constant-transmission arteries which linked all the Reach, there were complex formulae of adjustment and licensing, the whole system held in exact and delicate balance. A world could not function without that continual flow of information through station, to Cerdin.

Only Istra was supporting a burden it could not bear,

while inner worlds as well were swollen with increased populations, with no agricultural surpluses anywhere to be had. Council turned a deaf ear to protests, after readjusting population on a world where arable land was scarce.

And the azi-cycle from lab to contract was eighteen years, less for majat-sale.

Nineteen years, and Council had closed its eyes, deafened itself to protests, talked vaguely about new industry. Population pressure was allowed to build, after seven hundred years of licensed precision, every force in meticulous balance.

She watched the screen for a time, the back of her right hand to her lips, the chitin rough against them.

Blue-hive, blue-hive messenger, hives in direct trade with betas—and a world drowning in azi, as all the Reach was beginning to feel the pressure—a forecast for other worlds, while Council turned a deaf ear to cries for help.

Moth still ruled. That had to be true, that Moth still dominated Council. The Reach would have quaked at Moth's demise.

What ARE you doing? she wondered toward Moth.

And put on a smile like putting on a new garment . . . and looked toward ser Eln and sera Kest, enjoying their unease at that shift of mood. "I seem to recall that you invited me to be your guest. Suppose that I accept."

"You are welcome," Kest said hoarsely.

"I shall take the spirit of your hospitality . . . but not as a free gift. My tastes can be very extravagant. I shall pay my own charges. I should expect no private person to bear with me, no private person nor even ITAK. Please permit this."

"You are very kind," said ser Eln, looking vastly relieved. They began to feel their descent. The shuttle, in atmosphere, rode like something wounded, and the engines struggled to slow them, cutting in with jolting bursts. Eventually they reached a reasonable airspeed, and the port shields went back. It was pitch black outside, and lightning flared. They hit turbulence which dampened even Raen's enthusiasm for the uncommon, and dropped through, amazingly close to the ground.

A landing-field glowed, blue-lit, and abruptly they were on it, jolting down to a halt on great blasts of the engines.

They were down, undamaged, moving ponderously up to the terminal, a long on-ground process. Raen looked at Jim, who slowly unclenched his fingers from the arm-rests and drew an extended breath. She grinned at him, and he looked happier, the while the shuttle rocked over the uneven surface. "Luggage," she said softly. "You might as well see to it. And when we're among others, don't for the life of you let someone at it unwatched."

He nodded and scrambled up past her, while one of the guard azi began to see to the Eln-Kests' baggage.

The shuttle pulled finally up to their land berth, and met the exit tube. The pilot and co-pilot, their dispute evidently resolved, left controls and unlatched the exit.

Raen arose, finding the others waiting for her, and glanced back at Warrior, who remained immobile. Cold air flooded in from the exit, and Warrior turned its head hopefully.

"Go first," Raen bade the Istran seri and their azi. They did so in some haste; and Jim pulled the luggage carrier out after the ITAK azi. Raen lifted her right hand and beckoned Warrior to follow her out; the ship's officers scrambled back into the cockpit and hastily closed their door.

The party began to sort themselves into order in the exit tube, the ITAK folk and their armed azi keeping ahead. Raen walked with Jim and Warrior, whose strides were apparent slow motion beside those of humans.

Customs officials were waiting at the end: incredibly, they only stared stupidly at Warrior still coming and proceeded to hold up the ITAK men, stopping the whole party, with Warrior fretting and humming distress. The Eln-Kests and the others began at once producing cards for the agents, who bore ISPAK badges.

It was bizarre. Raen stared at the uniformed officials

for the space of a breath, then thrust her way to them, motioned for the Eln-Kests to move on. There were stunned looks from the officials, even outrage. She made a fist of her right hand and held that in their view.

There was no recognition for an instant: a Kontrin wearing House Color, and a majat Warrior, and these betas simply stared. Of a sudden they began to yield, melted aside, vying for obscurity. "Move!" Raen said to the others, ordering azi, betas and majat with equal rudeness; her nerves were taut-strung; public places were never to her liking, and the dullness of these folk bewildered her.

They entered the concourse, a place surprisingly trafficked . . . AIRPORT, a sign advised, pointing elsewhere, which might explain some of the traffic; a sign advised of a scheduled flight to Newport weekly, and a board displayed scheduled flights to Upcoast, but few walkers had any luggage. It was the stores, Raen decided, the shopping facilities, which might be the major ones for the beta City here. Everywhere the ITAK emblem was prominently displayed, the letters encircled; undercorporations advertising goods and services and selling from small sample-shops all bore the ITAK symbol somewhere on their signs. The faint aroma from restaurants, their busy tables, gave no hint of a world on the brink of rationing and starvation. The goods were on a par with Andra, and nothing indicated scarcity.

Betas, crowds of betas, and nowhere did panic start in that horde. Adults and rare children stared at them and at Warrior . . . stared long and hard, it might be, but there was no panic at such presence. It was insane, that on this world a majat Warrior could be so ignored; or a Kontrin, evident by Color.

They were not sure, she thought suddenly. Downworlders. No one of them had *seen* a Kontrin. They perhaps suspected, but they did not expect, and they were not in a position, these short-lived betas, to recognize a Color banned in innerworlds for two decades. It was even possible that they did not know the Houses by name; they had no reason to: no beta of Istra had to deal with them.

But a majat needed no recognition. Betas elsewhere had died in panic, trampling each other . . . until majat in the streets became ordinary. She had heard that this had happened in places she had left.

Her nape-hairs prickled with an uncommon sense of a whole world amiss. She scanned the displays they passed, the garish advertising that denied economic doom, but most of all she regarded the crowds, free-walking and those standing by counters who turned to look at them.

The hands, the hands: that was her continual worry. And she could not see behind her.

"I read blue-hive," Warrior intoned suddenly. "I must contact."

"Where?" Raen asked. "Explain. Where are you looking? Is there a heat-sign?"

It stopped, froze. Mandibles suddenly worked with frenzied rapidity, and auditory palps swept back, deafening it, like a human stopping his ears. Raen whirled to the fix of its gaze, heard a solitary human shriek taken up by others.

Warriors.

They poured forward out of an intersecting corridor, a dozen of them, almost on them, and the sound they shrilled entered human range, agony to the ears. Blue Warrior moved, scuttled for a counter, and the attackers pursued with blinding speed, more pouring out from another hall, overturning displays of clothing. Men screamed, dashed to the floor by the rush, trying to escape the shop.

Raen had her gun in hand . . . did not even recall drawing; and put a shot where it counted, into the neural complex of the leading Warrior, whirled and took another. She stumbled in her retreat, hit a solid wall, stood there braced and firing.

Reds. Hate improved her aim. Her mind was utterly cold. Three went down, and others swarmed the counter where betas and Warrior scattered in panic. She fired into the attackers and swung left, following Warrior's darting form, into several reds. She took out one, another. Warrior leaped on the third and rolled with it in a tangle of limbs, a squalling of resonance chambers. Raen caught movement out of the tail of her eye and whirled and fired, no longer alone: the azi guards had decided to back her. Betas had lifted no hand against majat, dared not, by their psych-set; but humans were dead out on the floor. One body was almost decapitated by majat jaws. Blood slicked the polished flooring in great smears where majat feet had slipped. Other humans were bitten.

Surviving reds tried to Group; her fire prevented it. She saw other majat crowded in the corner down at the turning, Grouped and thinking. Not reds; they would have come into it. The reds which survived were confused. Azi fire crippled them; Raen sighted with better knowledge of anatomy and finished the job. Blue Warrior was up, excited.

Then came the flare of a weapon from the farther group, several of them. Warrior went down, limbs threshing, air droning from resonance chambers.

"Stop them!" Raen shouted at the azi. The majat charged, ran into their concentrated fire: five, six, seven of them downed. One scuttled off, slipping on the floor, a limb damaged. Two shielded that retreat with their own bodies. They were the sacrifices. Raen took one. The azi butchered the other with their fire.

They were alone, then. Humans lay tangled with dead majat. She looked about her, at majat still convulsing in death-throes: those would go on for some minutes . . . there was no intelligence behind it. Merek Eln and Parn Kest were down, along with their companions from ITAK, and one of the guard azi. Bystanders were dead. A siren began to sound. It was already too late for the victims of bite: they had long since stopped breathing.

Blue Warrior still moved. She left the wall and the two living azi guards and went out into the center of the bloody floor, where Warrior lay, in a seeping of clear majat fluids. She held out her hand and it knew her.

Air sucked into the chambers. Auditory palps extended, trembling.

"Taste," it begged of her.

"Reds didn't get it," she said. "We took them all."

"Yesss."

Someone cried out, down the corridor. More tall shapes had entered, moving in haste: she flung up her hand, forbidding the azi to fire.

"Blues have come," she said. Warrior attempted to rise, but had no control of its limbs. She gave it room, and the blues scattered human medical personnel and what security forces had arrived. They crossed the last interval cautiously, stiff and sidling, until Raen showed her right hand, and they recognized her for blue-hive Kontrin.

Then they came in a rush. Some went at once to the fallen reds, taking taste, booming to each other in majat language, and two bent over Warrior.

Taste passed, long and complex, the mandibles of living and dying locked. Then the first Warrior drew back, seeming disoriented. The second took taste, in that strange semblance of a kiss. Other blues came. Somewhere a human wept, audibly. Medical personnel tried quietly to drag victims away from the area. Raen stood still. A third, a fourth Warrior bent over the fallen Kalind blue. The message was being distributed as far as Warrior's fluids could suffice.

The fifth one breathed something in majat language; Warrior sighed an answer. Then the Istran blue's jaws closed, and Warrior's head rolled free.

"Kontrin," another intoned, facing her.

"I am Raen Meth-maren. Tell your Mother so, Warrior. This-unit was from Kalind. Mother will know. Can you reach your hill safely from here?"

"Yesss. Must go now. Haste."

It turned away. Separate Warriors gathered up the head and body of Warrior, lest other hives read any portion of its message. Grouped, they turned and scuttled out.

Two remained.

One came forward, Istran blue, auditory palps extended in sign of peaceful approach. It bowed itself and opened its mandibles. It was Istra's gift, the fifth Warrior, the one who had tasted and killed. In a sense, it *was* Warrior: the thread continued.

Raen touched its scent-patches, accepted and gave taste in the majat kiss. It backed, disturbed as Warrior had been disturbed; but it had Warrior's knowledge of her, and Grouped, with a delicate touch of the chelae.

"Meth-maren," it breathed. Its fellow came forward, and likewise desired taste; Raen gave it, and saw distress in the working of mandibles and the flutter of palps. It resolved its conflict after a moment, touched at her.

They were hers. They followed, as she crossed the littered floor. The two guard azi were still standing against the wall; no one had claimed them, and they seemed in a state of shock. They had lost their employers. They had failed. Merek Eln and Parn Kest were dead, both bitten. One of the businessmen was decapitated; the others had been bitten. So had the third guard azi, and a number of bystanders.

The luggage carrier had been thrust back into a recess beyond the counter. Raen walked that way, and found Jim, jammed within that recess, sitting with his knees tucked up and both hands clutching a gun set upon them. His face was white; his teeth chattered; he had the gun braced and stable.

Guarding the luggage, as she had told him.

For an instant she hesitated, not knowing what he might do; but he did not fire . . . likely could not fire. She approached him quietly and disengaged the gun from his hands, realized Warrior's presence at her shoulder and bade it and its companion stay back. She knelt, put her hand on Jim's rigid arm.

"We need to get out of here. Come on, Jim."

He nodded. Out of near-catatonia, it was a wonder that he could do that much. She patted his shoulder and waited, and he wiped at his face and began to make small movements toward rising, shaking convulsively.

She thought then of the other two azi, who had been in the shuttle with them, who had heard what was said.

She flung herself to her feet and pushed past Warrior, past the counter.

The two azi stared at her; they had not moved. But by now Security police, betas ITAK-badged, had arrived on the scene, and some of them started gingerly forward.

"You," she said, rounding on the two azi, "belong to me. Is that clear? I'm transferring your contract. The formalities will be taken care of. You say nothing . . . *nothing,* hear me? I'm buying you out only because I don't like terminating azi."

The two seemed to believe her. She turned then and faced the police, who had hesitated at a safe distance—the majat were still near her—and now started forward again.

"There's been enough commotion," she said, turning toward them her hand, that, with her cloak, was identification enough. "This was a hive-matter and that's enough said. It's settled." She walked to Merek Eln's body, bent and took from his pocket the identity card she had seen at customs. There was, as she had expected, an address. It seemed to be in an ITAK executive district. "I want some manner of transport for myself, three azi, our baggage and two Warriors at once; and an armed officer or two for escort, thank you."

Possibly they thought that this had to go through channels; they stood still a moment. But then the senior gave orders to one of the officers, who left, running.

"Chances are," Raen said, "that the matter is confined to the hives; but you'll kindly call and put this number under immediate surveillance. And you can escort us to that vehicle."

The officer looked at the ID, made a call on his belt unit, . . . would have retained the card, but that Raen held out her hand and insisted. She turned, pocketing it, and gestured to the two guard azi to take charge of the baggage. Jim was leaning on the counter, seeming to have recovered himself, although he was still shaken. She returned the gun to him and he hastily put it in his pocket, missing the opening several times in his agitation.

He walked well enough. Warrior and companion stalked along with them, and the shop personnel and the terminal employees and others who had reason to be in the cordoned area stared at them uneasily as they sought the door.

"The car will be there," the senior officer said. "There's an executive from the Board coming out to meet you, Kontrin; we're profoundly embarrassed—"

"My sincere regrets for the next of kin. I want a list of the names and citizen numbers and relatives of those killed. There will be compensation and burial expenses. Relay the information to that address. As for the executive, I'm more interested in settling myself at the moment. There's another call I want you to make. I understand there's an Outsider trade mission in the City. I want someone from that mission . . . I don't care who . . . at that address as quickly as possible."

"Sera—"

"I wouldn't advise you to consult with ITAK on it. Or to fail to do it."

Outer doors opened. She heard the officer behind her speaking urgently on the matter through his belt unit; it would be relayed. An ITAK police personnel transport waited outside, armored officers with rifles ringed about it. Raen kept her hand near her own weapon, trusting no one.

It took time to load baggage in, to have the azi and the two majat settled in the available space in the rear of the transport. "We can find a car," an officer said; Raen shook her head. She did not trust being separated from her belongings. She still feared majat, a sniping shot; their vision could hardly tell one human from another, but they were stirred enough not to care for such niceties.

The majat must go in last. Warrior fretted, nervous at so many humans it must not touch. Raen touched the sensitive palps, held it attentive an instant. "You must not touch the azi in the vehicle, Warrior. Must not frighten them. Trust. Be very still. You-unit tell the other Warrior so."

It boomed answer, protest, perhaps; but it boarded, its partner with it. The officer slammed the door. Raen hurried round and flung herself in beside the driver. A man slammed the door. She set her drawn gun comfortably on her knee in plain sight as they moved out, watching the shadows of the pillars as they whipped past the terminal entry for the exit ramp.

They were clear. She gave the officer driving the address she wanted and relaxed slightly, trying not to think of Warrior and its companion and the azi in the rear, behind the partition, and what misery they were severally undergoing, two Warriors forbidden to touch and three azi pent up with majat in near darkness.

Night-time city whisked past, lines of domes marching out into dark interstices of wild land, asterisk-city, mostly sealed or underground. The flavor of the air was coppery and unpleasant. The stormclouds boiled above them, frequent with lightnings, and a spattering of rain hit the windshields and windows, fragmenting the lights. Then they were underground again, locked into the subway track, whisking in behind a big public carrier. Raen hated these systems, this projectile-fashion passage through public areas; but it was, perhaps, the safest means of travel this night.

Majat hives did not have communication equipment—no links with station—but majat had been ready for them: red-hive, with ambush prepared. Humans had participated in it almost certainly.

And more than Warrior had died: two beta envoys were gone, two who had been in prolonged contact with a Kontrin, who had perhaps talked too much.

She was not about to trust ITAK. She doubted, at least, that they would move against her openly: it might be—if they knew she was alone, that there was not behind her an entire Kontrin sept and House—

But one bluffed. It was all, in fact, that Kontrin had ever been able to do among betas, in one sense—for the armed ships that rested solely in Kontrin hands were inevitably far away when one might need them; but the ships did exist. So did the ultimate knowledge of the psych-sets with which the original beta culture had been created. So did the power to license and embargo, to adjust birth quotas, to readjust any economic fact of a beta's existence, individually or by class.

The beta beside her did not attempt friendliness, did not speak, did not acknowledge her: stark fear. She had seen the reaction elsewhere. She remembered the port, the salon of the ship . . . reckoned what her coming might mean to Istra, which had not seen Kontrin onworld in centuries, many beta lifespans; the veil jerked rudely aside, a whole world subjected to what she had done to the folk of *Andra's Jewel*.

In her present mood, her hand clenched and sweating on the grip of the gun, with the reaction of the ambush finally overtaking her, she little cared.

iii

The car disengaged from the tube-system and nosed up the ramp into a residential circle. It was an area of lighted paving, with space for greenery—or something similar—in the center. A high wall encircled them, gates 41, 42, 43 . . . the rain-spattered windshield showed the glare of more lights, vehicles clustered at the area of 47. A guard let them through the open gate; they eased up the curved drive. Floodlights from the cars had the grounds in garish clarity: twisted tree-forms, dappled trunks and tufts of tiny leaves. The garden was all rocks and spiky plantings, and the house was a white, tiered structure, contiguous with the neighboring houses, so that the whole would form a cantilevered ring, like one vast apartment, each groundlevel with its own walled garden. The driver wove past two obstructing vehicles and stopped the car before a well-lit entry, a portico with uniformed officers aswarm about the door.

Raen opened the door and stepped out, spattered by raindrops, whipped in under the portico, and waited while the driver and another officer opened the rear doors. They retreated in haste, and Warrior one and

Warrior two climbed out, grooming themselves in evident distaste. Jim followed, and the two guard azi . . . unharmed, Raen was glad to see.

"Jim," she said. "You two. Get the luggage out and put it inside the house." She looked then to the officers on the porch and those with her. "Are there occupants?"

"The house has been shut for half a year, Kontrin." A man in civilian clothes edged forward among the others . . . dark-haired, overweight, balding. There was a woman with him, likewise civilian, matched in age, and in corpulence. "Hela Dain," she said. "My husband Elan Prosserty, vice-presidents on the board."

"ITAK is vastly sorry," the man said, "for this reception. Our profound apologies. If we had known you were without sufficient guard . . . You're not injured, Kontrin."

"No." She recalled the gun and slipped it back into its place beneath the cloak. "I'm a guest of the Eln-Kests. Posthumously. I regret the circumstances, but I'll take the hospitality nonetheless. If one of your security people will lodge himself at the front gate . . . outside, if you will . . . to discourage the most obvious intruders, I'll take care of the rest. Kindly come inside. I requested another presence here; have they arrived?"

The Dain-Prossertys made shift to follow her in the wake she cut through the crowd of police and armored guards, into the house, with its stale air and mustiness. Agents were inside likewise, and another group, conspicuous for their white faces and their bizarre dress, four of them.

Outsiders, indeed.

"Kontrin," Hela Dain said with careful deference. "The senior of the trade organization, ser Ab Tallen, and his escort."

Armed. She did not miss that. Tallen was gray-haired, thin, aging. There was one of his young men of strange type, a physiognomy exotic in the Reach. She put out her hand, and Tallen took it without flinching—smiling, his eyes unreadable, cold . . . real. No Kontrin had devised the psych-set behind that face.

"Kont' Raen a Sul hant Meth-maren," she said. "*The*

Meth-maren. A social courtesy, ser Tallen. How kind of you to come."

Tallen did not flinch, though she reckoned the summons as delivered by the police had had no option in it. "An opportunity," he said, "which we were not about to refuse. The fabled Kontrin company."

"The Family, ser. The company has set its mark on things, but those days are past." The Outsider's ignorance dazed her; she was pricked by curiosity, but it was not the time or place, not with betas at her elbow. She turned away, made a nod of courtesy toward the ITAK executives. "How kind of you all to come. I trust the little difficulty has settled itself and that it will stay settled. Would you kindly rid me of this commotion of police, seri? Extend them my thanks. I trust my communication lines are free of devices and such. I trust they have been making sure of that. I shall trust that this is the case. I don't have to tell you how distressed I would be to discover something had slipped their notice. Then I would have to carry on some very *high* inquiries, seri. But I am sure that no one would let such a thing happen."

Fear was stark in their faces. "No," Dain assured her at once. "No," her husband echoed.

"Of course not," she said very softly, put a hand on each of their arms as she turned them for the hall, dismissing them. "I thank you very much . . . *very much* for disarranging yourselves to come out here on such a night. Convey to the board my thanks for their concern, my sorrow for the Eln-Kests and for the damage at the port. And if one of you will contact me tomorrow, I will be very pleased to make that gratitude more substantial; you've done very kindly by me tonight. Such attention to duty should be rewarded. You personally, seri. Would you be very sure of the guards you set at the gate, of their dependability? I always like to know who is accountable. I shall be through with these folk in very short order. Merely a courtesy. I do thank you."

They let themselves be put into the hall; Raen turned back then, hearing them quietly ordering police out.

There was a sudden disturbance; she looked back: the majat were in, stalking back through the house, on their own security check.

She regarded the man Ab Tallen, gave a deprecating shrug. "I shall be staying, ser. I wanted to be sure your mission was informed of that fact. And I shall welcome the chance to talk with you at leisure, as soon as matters are stable here."

"You're of the government, Kont' Raen—"

"Kont' Raen is sufficent address, ser. Kontrin *are* the government, and the population. And is your mission permanent here?"

"We understood that our presence onworld had official—"

"Of course it does. ITAK is competent to extend such an invitation. I have no plans to interfere with that. In fact, I'm quite pleased by it." It was truth, and she let a bright smile to the surface, a conscious weapon. "If I had not asked to see you, you would have had to wonder whether I knew of your presence and how I regarded it. I've told you both beyond possibility of misunderstanding. Now we can both rest tranquil tonight. I'm extremely tired. It's been a very long flight. Will you favor me with a call tomorrow?"

This man was not so easily confused as the Dain-Prossertys. He gave a self-possessed and slight nod of the head, smiled his official smile. "Gladly, Kont' Raen."

She offered her hand. "How many Outsiders are on Istra?"

His hand had grasped hers. There was a very slight reaction at that question. "A varying number." He withdrew the hand in smooth courtesy. "About twenty-two today. Four went up to station at the first of the week. We do come and go with some frequency: our usefulness as trade liaison depends on that freedom."

"I would expect that, ser Tallen. I assure you I've no plans to interfere. Do make the call tomorrow."

"Without fail."

"Ser." She gave a nod of courtesy, dismissal. Tallen read it, returned it with the same thoughtfulness, gathered his small company, and left; the others not without paying their courtesy likewise . . . not guard-types, then. She stared after them with some curiosity as to precisely how authority was ordered among Outsiders, and what strange worlds had sent them, and how much they truly understood.

The police had vacated; there was the sound of cars pulling away outside. The Dain-Prossertys had disappeared. She walked into the hall, the door open on the rain on one side, Jim and the two guard-azi with the baggage on the other. The majat stalked up behind her from another doorway, and stopped, sat down, waiting.

She drew a breath and looked about her, at the house and the azi. It was a comfortable place: execrable taste in furnishings . . . it gave her a little pang of regret for the Eln-Kests, for in its beta-ish way it had a certain warmth, less beauty than Kontrin style, but a feeling of habitation, all the same.

"Stay now, Kontrin-queen?"

She looked at the Warrior who had spoken, the smaller of the two. "Yes. My-hive, this place." She looked at Jim, at the new azi. "You have names, you two?"

"Max," one volunteered; "Merry," the other. They were not doubles. Max was dark-haired and Merry was pale blond, Max brown-eyed and Merry blue. But the heavy-bodied build was the same, the stature the same, the square-jawed faces of the same expression. The eyes told most of them . . . calm, cold, stolid now that their existence was re-ordered. They could recognize threats; they were likely compulsive about locks and security; they would fight with great passion once the holder of their contracts identified the enemy.

"You two will take direction from Jim as well as from me," she told them. "And identify yourselves to the majat: Jim, show them. Warrior, be careful with these azi."

The two Warriors shifted forward in slow-motion, met Jim; auditory palps flicked forward in interest at his taste, Kalind blue's memory. Max and Merry had to be shown, but they bore the close touch of mandibles with more fortitude than betas would have shown: perhaps the ride enclosed with the majat had frightened all the fear out of them.

"That's well done," she said. "There's not a majat won't know you hereafter; you understand that. —Luggage goes upstairs, mine does; the other can go to some room at the back: Jim, see to it. You two help him; and then check out the place and make sure doors are locked and systems aren't rigged in any way." She wiped a finger through the dust on a hall table, rubbed it away. "Seals aren't very efficient. Be thorough. And mind, Kontrin azi have license to fire on any threat: *any* threat, even Kontrin. Go on, go on with you."

They went. She looked at the two majat, who alone remained.

"You remember me," she said.

"Kethiuy-queen," said the larger, reclining its head to her.

That was Warrior's mind.

"Hive-friend," she said. "I brought you Kalind blue, brought Kalind hive's message. Can you read it?"

"Revenge."

"I am blue-hive," she said. "Meth-maren of Cerdin, first-hive. What is the state of things here, Warrior-mind? How did reds know us?"

"Many reds, redsss, redsss. Go here, go there. Redss. Goldss. I kill."

"How did reds know us?"

"Men tell them. Redss pushhh. Much push. I defend, defend. The betas give us grain, azi, much. Grow."

"How did you know to come to the port, Warrior?"

"Mother sendss. I killed red; red tastes of mission, seeks blue, seeks port-direction. I reported and Mother sent me, quick, quick, too late."

It was the collective *I. I* could be any number of individuals.

"But," she said, "you received Kalind blue's message."

"Yesss."

"This-unit," said the other, "is Kethiuy-queen's messenger. Send now. Send."

"Thank Mother," she told it. "Yes. Go."

It scuttled doorward with disturbing rapidity, a rattle of spurred feet on the tiles—was gone, into the dark.

"This-unit," intoned the other, the larger, "guards."

"This-hive is grateful." Raen touched the offered head, stroked the sensitive palps, elicited a humming of pleasure from Warrior. She ceased; it edged away, then stalked out into the rain—no inconvenience for Warrior, rather pleasure: it would walk the grounds tirelessly, needing no sleep, a security system of excellent sensitivity.

She closed and locked the front door, let go a breath of relief. The baggage had disappeared; she heard Jim's voice upstairs, giving orders.

The temperature was uncomfortably high. She wandered through the reception room and the dining room and located the house comp, found it already activated. That was likely the doing of the police, but the potential hazard worried her. With proper staff she would have insisted on a checkout; as it was, she stripped off her cloak and set to work herself, searching for the most likely forms of tampering, first visually and then otherwise. At last she keyed in the air-conditioning.

Failing immediate catastrophe, feeling the waft of cold air from the ducts, she sat down, assured that she could see the door in the reflection of the screen, and ran through the standard house programs from the list conveniently posted by the terminal . . . called up a floor plan, found the usual security system, passive alarm, nothing of personal hazard: betas would not dare.

Then she keyed in citycomp, pulled Merek Eln's ID from her belt and started inquiries. The deaths were already recorded: someone's extreme efficiency. The property reverted to ITAK; the Eln-Kests had not used their license-for-one-child, and while Parn Kest had living relatives, they were not entitled: the house had been in Eln's name. A keyed request purchased the property entire, on her credit.

Human officials, she reflected, might be mildly surprised when citycomp and ITAK records turned that up in the morning. And Parn Kest's effects . . . Merek Eln's too . . . could be shipped to the relatives as soon as it was certain there was no information to be had from them. It was the least courtesy due.

Max and Merry came noisily downstairs, rambled about the lower floor and the garage looking for security faults, finally reported negative.

She turned and looked at them. They seemed tired—might be hungry as well. "Inventory shows canned goods in the kitchen stores. Azi quarters are out across the garden, kitchen out there too. Does that suit you?"

They nodded placidly. She sent them away, and began reckoning time-changes. She and Jim had missed lunch and, she figured, supper, by several hours.

That accounted for some of the tremor in her muscles, she decided, and wandered off to join Max and Merry in their search of kitchen storage. Warrior could make do with sugared water, a treat it would actually relish; Warrior would also, with its peculiar capacities, assure that they were not poisoned.

iv

Jim ate, sparingly and in silence, and showed some relief. It was the first meal he had kept down all day. She noted a shadow about his eyes and a distracted look, much as the crew of the *Jewel* had had at the last.

Notwithstanding, he would have cleared the dishes after . . . his own notion or unbreakable habit, she was not certain. "Leave it," she said. He would not have come upstairs with her, but she stopped and told him to.

Second door to the right atop the stairs, the main bedroom: Jim had set everything there, a delightful room even to a Kontrin's eye, airy furniture, all white and pale green. There was a huge skylight, a bubble rain-spotted and showing the lightnings overhead.

"Dangerous," she said, and not because of the lightnings.

"There are shields," he offered, indicating a switch.

"Leave it. We wouldn't be safe from a Kontrin assassin, but we probably will from the talent Istra could summon on short notice. Let's only hope none of the Family has been energetic enough to precede me here. Where's your luggage?"

"Hall," he said faintly.

"Well, bring it in."

He did so, and set about unpacking his own things with a general air of distress. She recalled him in the terminal, frozen, with the gun locked in his hands. The remarkable thing was that he had had the inclination to seize it in the first place . . . the dead guard, she reckoned, and opportunity and sheer desperation.

He finished, put his case in the closet and stood there by the door, facing her.

"Are you all right?" she asked. "Warrior's outside. Nothing will get past it. No reason to worry on that account."

He nodded slowly, in that perplexed manner he had when he was out of his depth.

"That skylight—doesn't bother you, does it?" The thought struck her that it might, for he was not accustomed to worlds and weather.

He shook his head in the same fashion.

She put her hand on his shoulder, a gesture of comfort as much as other feeling; he touched her in return, and she looked into his face this time cold sober, in stark light. The tattoo was evident. The eyes . . . remained distracted, perplexed. The expression was lacking.

His hand fell when she did not respond, and even then the expression did not vary. He was capable of physical pleasure—more than capable. He felt—at least approval or the lack of it. He suffered shocks . . . and tried to go on responding, as now, when a beta or Kontrin would have acknowleged distress.

"You did well," she said deliberately, watched the response, a little touch of relief.

Limited sensitivity. Suspicion washed over her, answers she did not want. He made appropriate responses, human responses, answered to affection. Some azi could not; likely Max and Merry were too dull for it. But even Jim, she thought suddenly, did not react to stress as a born-man might. She touched him; he touched her. But the responses might as easily be simple tropisms, like turning the face to sunlight, or extending cold hands to warmth. To be approved was better than to be disapproved.

Lia too. Even Lia. Not love, but programs. Psych-sets, less skillfully done than the betas' own.

Beta revenge, she thought, sick to the heart of her. *A grand joke, that we all learn to love them when we're children.*

She hated, for that moment, thoroughly, and touched Jim's face and did not let it show.

And when she was lying with the azi's warmth against her, in Merek Eln's huge bed, she found him—all illusions laid aside—simply a comfortable presence. He was more at ease with her than he had been the first night, an incredible single night ago, on the *Jewel;* he persisted in seeking closeness to her, even deep in sleep, and the fact touched her. Perhaps, whatever he felt, she was his security; and whatever his limitations, he was there, alive—full of, if not genuine humanity, at least comfortable tropisms . . . someone to talk to, a mind off which her thoughts could reflect, a solidity in the dark.

It stopped here; everything stopped here, at the Edge. She lay on her back staring up, her arm intertwined with Jim's. The storm had passed and the stars were clear in the skylight: Achernar's burning eye and all, all the other little lights. The loneliness of the Reach oppressed her as it never had. The day crowded in on her, the Outsider ship ghosting past them in the morning, the presence of them in the house.

What's out there, she wondered, *where men never changed? Or do we all . . . change?*

Perspective shifted treacherously, as if the sky were downward, and she jerked. Jim half-wakened, stirred. "Hush," she said. "Sleep." And he did so, his head against her, seeking warmth.

Tropism.

We created the betas, built all their beliefs; but they

*refused to live as we made them: they had to have azi.
They created them; they cripple them, to make themselves
whole by comparison. Of what did we rob the betas?*

Of what they take from the azi?

She rubbed at Jim's shoulder and wakened him deliberately. He blinked at her in the starlight. "Jim, was there another azi on the *Jewel,* more than one, perhaps, that you would have liked to have here with you?"

He blinked rapidly, perplexed. "No."

"Are you trying to protect them?"

"No."

"There was none, no friend, no—companion, male or female?"

"No."

She considered that desolation a moment, that was as great as her own. "Enemy?"

"No."

"You were, what, four years on that ship, and never had either friend or enemy?"

"No." A placid no, a calm and quiet no, a little puzzled.

She took it for truth, and smoothed his hair aside as Lia had done with her when she was a child, in Kethiuy.

She at least . . . had enemies left.

Jim—had nothing. He and the majat azi, the naked creatures moving with will-o'-the-wisp lights through the tunnels of the hive—were full brothers, no more nor less human.

"I am blue-hive," she whispered to him, moved to things she had never said to any human. "Of the four selves of majat . . . the gentlest, but majat for all that. Sul sept is dead; Meth-maren House is dead. Assassins. I'm blue-hive. That's what I have left.

"There was an old man . . . seven hundred years old. He'd seen Istra, seen the Edge, where Kontrin won't go. Majat came here to live, long ago, but Kontrin wouldn't, only he. And I." She traced the line of his arm, pleased by its angularity, mentally elsewhere. "Nineteen years ago some limits were readjusted; and do you know, they've never been redone. Somone's taken great care that all that not be redone.

"Nineteen years. I've lived on every hive-world of the Reach. I've caused the Family a minimum of difficulty. Not from love, not from love, you understand. Ah, no. There's an old woman in Council. Her name is Moth. She's not dictator in name, but she is. And she doesn't trouble me. She does the nothing she always preferred. And the things let loose nineteen years ago—have all come of age.

"The Houses are waiting. Waiting all this time. Moth will die, one of these days. Then the scramble for power, as the Reach has never seen it."

"Sera—"

"Dangerous listening, yes. Don't call me that. And you have sense enough to keep quiet, don't you? The azi down in the azi quarters . . . are not to be trusted. Never confide in them. Even Warrior knows the difference, knowing you were with me before they were. No, trust Warrior if ever you must trust anything; it can't tell your face from that of any other human, but hail it blue-hive and give it taste or touch, it or any blue. I'll show you tomorrow, show you how to tell the hive-markings apart. You must learn that and show Max and Merry. And if there's ever any doubt of a majat, kill it. I mean it. Death is a minor thing to them. Warrior—always comes back. Only humans don't."

"Why—" From Jim, question was a rarity. "Why did they attack us at the port?"

"I don't know. I think they wanted Warrior."

"Why?"

"Two questions in sequence. Delightful. You're recovering your balance."

"Sera?"

"Raen." She struck him lightly with her fist, an excess of hope. "My name is Raen; call me Raen. You can manage that. You were entirely wasted on the *Jewel*. Handling of arms: everything that pair downstairs can do; and anything else, anything else. You can learn it. You're not incapable of learning. Go back to sleep."

He did not, but lay to this side and that, and finally settled again when she rested her head against his shoulder.

Security.

That, she reckoned, was somewhat mutual.

BOOK SIX

i

The Mother of Istra blue took taste, and heaved herself back, mandibles working. Drones soothed Her, singing in their high voices. She ceased, for a moment, to produce new lives.

"Other-hive." She breathed, and the walls of the Chamber vibrated with the low sound. "Blue-hive. Blue-hive Kontrin. Meth-maren of Cerdin. Kethiuy."

The Drones moved closer, touched. She bowed and offered taste to the foremost, and it to the next, while She gave to a third. Like the motion of wind through grass it passed, and the song grew in its wake. An impulse extraordinarily powerful went out from them; and all through the Hill, activity slowed. Workers and Warriors turned wherever they were, oriented themselves to the Chamber.

In the egg-chamber, frightened Workers, sensing vague alarm, began building a seal for the shafts. Theirs was the only activity. Mother lowered Her head and reached out for the reporting Warrior yet again; and Warrior, knowing fear of Mother for the first time in its existence, locked a second time into Mother's chemistry, suffering the reactions of Her body as the messages swirled through Her fluids.

Others crowded close, seeking understanding.

They could not interpret fully. Each understood after its own kind.

There was impression of a flow of chemistry which had begun many cycles ago, a tiny taste of Cerdin, homeworld. The Mind Remembered. There had been a small hill. The memory went back before there were humans, salt-tasting, quick-perishing; before the little lake had filled; before the hill itself had stood. There were ages, and depths. The Mind reeled in ecstasy, the reinforcement of this ancient memory. There were partings, queens born of eggs ship-sent, hives hurled out to the unseen stars, over distances the Mind comprehended only when majat eyes beheld a new heat source in the heavens, different in pattern and timing and intensity, only when majat calculations reckoned angles and distances and an impression of complexities beyond the comprehension of the Mind, mysticism alien to majat processes.

Vastness, and dark, and cold.

Where the Mind was not.

Death.

At last the Mind had something by which to comprehend death, and finitude of worlds, and time before and after itself. It staggered in such comprehensions, and embraced abstracts.

Finite time, as humans measured it, suddenly acquired meaning.

The Mind understood.

Kalind-mind. There was dazzling taste of it, which had tasted of Andra, and of Meron, which had tasted of Cerdin, a wave starting at Cerdin and rippling outward: violence, and enmity. Destruction. Cerdin. Destruction.

The motion in the hive utterly ceased. Even the egg-tenders froze, paralyzed in the enormity of the vision.

Growth since. Growth, denying death.

Mind reached outward, where there was no contact, for the distances were too far, and synthesis was impossible. There was only the longing, a stirring in the chemistries of the hive.

"Hazard," a Warrior complained, having tasted Kontrin presence, and the slaughter of blues, the murders of messengers.

It could comprehend nothing more; but the hive closed the more tightly.

"She—" Mother began, interpreting across the barriers of type, which was queen-function, while chemistries meshed on other levels, "she is Meth-marn hive. She *is* the hive. She is Kethiuy. Her Workers are late-come, gathered from strange hives. Azi. She tastes of danger, yess. Great hazard, but not hostile to blues. She preserved us the messenger of Kalind. She was on Meron, and Andra; her taste is in those memories. She was *within* the Hill on Cerdin. She has patterned with Warriors, against majat, against humans. Istra-reds . . . taste of hate of her. Cerdin-taste runs in red-memory, taste of humans and death of blues. Great slaughter. Yess. But the entity Raen Meth-maren is blue-hive Kontrin. She has been part of the Mind of Cerdin."

"Queen-threat," a Warrior ventured.

The Drones sang otherwise, Remembering. The Mother of Cerdin blue-hive lived in Kalind blue's message. There was a song that was Kethiuy, and death, abundant death, the beginning of changes, premature.

"Meth-maren," Mother recalled, feeding into the Mind. "First-human. Hive-friend."

Then the message possessed Her, and She poured into the Drones a deep and abiding anger. The Mind reached. Its parts were far-flung, scattered across the invisible gulfs of stars, of time, which had never been of significance. The space existed. Time existed. There was no synthesis possible.

The Drones moved, laved Mother with their palps, increasingly disturbed. They rotated leftward and Mother also moved, drawing from Warriors and Foragers far-ranging on the surface—orienting to the rising sun, not alpha, but beta Hydri, beholding this in the darkness of the Hill.

The Drones searched Memory, rotated farther, seeking resolution. Full circle they came, locked again on the Istran sun. Workers reoriented; Warriors moved.

The circling began again, slow and ponderous. Seldom did Mother move at all. Now twice more the entire hive shifted prime direction, and settled.

A Warrior felt Mother's summons and sought touch.

It locked into Mother's chemistry and quivered its entire
length in the strength of the message it felt. It turned
and ran, breaking from the Dance.

A Worker approached, received taste, and likewise
fled, frantically contacting others as it went.

The Dance fragmented. Workers and Warriors scattered in a frenzy in all directions.

The Drones continued to sing, a broken song, and dis-
sonant. Mother produced no egg. A strange fluid poured
from Her mandibles, and the Workers gathered it and
passed to the egg-tenders, who sang together in consternation.

ii

The house-comp's memory held a flood of messages:
those from the Dain-Prossertys, who had lost no time;
anxious inquiries from the ITAK board in general; from
ISPAK, a courteous greeting and regrets that she had
not stayed in the station; from the police, a requested
list of casualties and next of kin; from forward ITAK
businesses, offers of services and gifts.

Raen dealt with some of them: a formal message of
condolences to the next-of-kin, with authorization for fu-
neral expenses and the sum of ten thousand credits to
each bereaved, to be handled through ITAK; to the
board, general salutations; to the Dain-Prossertys a suggestion that any particular license they desired might be
favorably considered, and suggesting discretion in the
matter.

She ordered printout of further messages and ignored
what might be incoming for the time, choosing a leisurely
breakfast with Jim, the while Max and Merry ate in the
azi quarters, and Warrior enjoyed a liquid delicacy in
the garden—barely visible, Warrior's post, a shady nook
amongst the rocks and spiky plants, a surprise for any
intruders.

A little time she reckoned she might spend in resting;

but postponing meetings with ITAK had hazard, for these folk might act irrationally if they grew too nervous.

There was also the chance that elements of the Family had agents here: more than possible, even that there could have been someone to precede her. In the *Jewel*'s slow voyage there was time for that.

She toyed with the idea of sending Council a salutation from Istra, after two decades of silence and obedience. The hubris of it struck her humor.

But Moth needed no straws added to the weight under which she already tottered. Raen found it not in her present interest to add anything to the instabilities, to aggravate the little tremors which were beginning to run through the Reach. Kontrin could act against her on Istra; but they would not like to, would shudder at the idea of pursuing a feud in the witness of betas, and very much more so here at the window on Outside. No, she thought, there would be for her only the delicate matter of assassination . . . and Moth, as ever, would act on the side of inaction, entropy personified.

No such message would go, she decided, finishing her morning tea. Let them discover the extent of their problem. For herself—she had them; and they had yet to discover it . . . had a place whereon to stand, and, she thought to herself, a curiosity colder and more remote than all her enemies' ambition: to comprehend this little ball of yarn the while she pulled it apart.

To know the betas and the azi and all the shadows the Kontrin cast on the walls of their confinement.

Jim had finished his breakfast, and sat, hands on the table, staring between them at the empty plate. The azi invisibility mode. If he did not move, his calculation seemed to be, then she would cease to notice him and he could not possibly bother her. The amazing thing was that it so often worked. She had seen azi do such things all her life, that purposeful melting into the furnishings of a room, and she had never noticed, until she persisted in sitting at table with one, until she relied on one for company, and conversation, and more than that.

It is something, she thought, *to begin to see.*

She pushed back from the table without a word, seeking her own invisibility, and went off to the computer.

The printout had grown very long during breakfast. She tore it off and scanned it, found overtures from some of the great agricultural cooperatives within ITAK—suggesting urgent and private consultations. Word had indeed spread. Some messages were from ITAK on the other continent, imaginatively called West: that was the Newport operation; simple courtesies, those. Another had come from ISPAK, inviting her up for what it called an urgent conference. A message from ITAK on East acknowledged with gratitude the one she had sent before breakfast and urged her to entertain a board meeting at some convenient time; the signature was one ser Dain, president, and of a sudden she smiled, recalling sera Dain and her husband . . . betas too, had their Family, and she reckoned well how the connections might run in ITAK. Small benefit, then, from corrupting Prosserty: Dain was the name to watch.

And finally there was the one she had hoped for, a courteous greeting from ser Tallen of the trade mission, recalling the night's summons and leaving a number where he might be reached: the address was that of a city guest house . . . considering Newhope, probably the only guest house.

She keyed the same message to all but Tallen. NOTED. I AM PRESENTLY ARRANGING MY SCHEDULE. THANK YOU. R.S.M.-m.

To Tallen: AT TWO, MY RESIDENCE, A BRIEF MEETING. RAEN A SUL.

She cleared that with the police at the gate, lest there be misunderstandings; and reckoned that it would be relayed to ITAK proper.

And a brief call to ITAK registry, bypassing automatic processes: Max and Merry were legally transferred, even offered as a company courtesy; she declined the latter, and paid the modest valuation of the contracts.

Supply: she arranged that, through several local companies . . . ordered items from groceries to hardware in prodigious quantity, notwithstanding borderline shortages. Fruit, grain, and sugar were in unusual proportion on that list . . . distressing, to any curious ITAK agent who investigated.

To the nine neighbors of Executive Circle 4, the same message, sent under the serpent-sigil of the Family: TO MY NEIGHBORS: WITH EXTREME REGRET I MUST STATE THAT AN ATTEMPT ON MY LIFE MAKES NECESSARY CERTAIN DEFENSIVE MEASURES. THIS CIRCLE MAY BE SUBJECT TO HAZARDOUS VISITORS AND ACTIONS ON THE PART OF MY AGENTS MAY NECESSITATE SUDDEN INCURSIONS INTO NEIGHBORING RESIDENCES. I REFUSE RESPONSIBILITY FOR LIVES AND PROPERTY UNDER THESE CIRCUMSTANCES. IF, HOWEVER, YOU WISH TO RELOCATE FOR THE DURATION OF MY STAY ON ISTRA, I SHALL BE HAPPY EITHER TO PURCHASE YOUR RESIDENCE OR TO RENT IT, WITH OR WITHOUT FURNISHINGS. I SHALL MEET ANY REASONABLE PRICE OR RENT WITHOUT ARGUMENT AND OFFER TO BEAR ALL EXPENSES OF TEMPORARY OR PERMANENT RELOCATION IN A COMPARABLE CIRCLE, PLUS 5,000 CREDITS GENERAL COMPENSATION FOR THE INCONVENIENCE. KONT' RAEN A SUL HANT METHMAREN, AT 47. RESPONSE EXPECTED.

Then she settled back, shut her eyes and rested for a few moments . . . set herself forward then, having begun the sequences in her mind.

Kontrin-codes. Kontrin had set up worldcomp and intercomp, and maintained both. There were beta accesses, in a hierarchy of authorizations; there were many more reserved to Kontrin, and some restricted to specific Houses, to those who worked directly with specific aspects of the central computers at Alpha—with the trade banks or the labs or the other separate agencies, which met in Council: the democracy of the Family, the secrecy that kept certain functions for certain Houses, making Council necessary. Meth-marens had had somewhat to do with establishing Alphacomp in the very beginning—

in matters of abstract theory and majat logic, the mathematics of the partitioned hive-mind: translation capacity, biocomp, and the dull mechanics of warehousing and hive-trade; but Ilit had had the abstract interest in economics.

Merely to enter worldcomp or even intercomp, and to touch information of beta's private lives . . . any Kontrin could do that. Trade information was hardly more difficult, for any who knew the very simple codes: locations of foodstuffs, ships in port, licenses and applications for license. It was all very statistical and dull and few Kontrin without direct responsibility for a House's affairs would bestir themselves to care what volume of grain went into a city.

She did. Hal Ilit had realized, perhaps, the extent of her theft from him; perhaps this shame as much as the other had prompted him to turn on her. Certainly it was shame that had prompted him to try to deal with her on his own, a man never experienced in violence.

He had been in most regards, an excellent teacher.

And the Eln-Kests, according to the statistics on record, had not been lying.

There was a periodic clatter in the next room, the rattle of dishes. Jim was probably at the height of happiness, doing what his training prepared him to do. It irritated her. She ordinarily carried on some operations in her mind, and could not to her usual extent, whether through preoccupation or because of the extraneous noise: she posted them to the auxiliary screens and checked them visually.

The rattle of dishes stopped. There was silence for a time. Then it began again, this time the moving of chairs and objects, a great deal of pacing about between.

She threw down the stylus, swore, rose and stalked back to the main rooms. Jim was there, replacing a bit of sculpture on the reception hall table.

"The noise," she said, "is bothering me. I'm trying to work."

He waved a hand at the rooms about him, which were, she saw now, clean, dusted, well-ordered. *Approve,* his look asked, and killed all her anger. It was his whole reason for existence on the *Jewel*.

It was his whole reason for existence anywhere.

She let go her breath and shook her head.

"I beg pardon," he said, in that always-subdued voice.

"Take a few hours off, will you?"

"Yes, sera."

He made no move to go; he expected her to walk away, she realized, being the one with a place to go. She thought of him at breakfast, absolutely still, mental null . . . agony, she thought. It was what the Family had tried to do with her. She could not bear watching it.

"I've a deepstudy unit upstairs," she said. "You know how to use it?"

"Yes, sera."

"If you can't remember, I'm going to make a tape that says nothing but *Raen*. Come on. Come upstairs. I'll see whether you know what you're doing with it."

She led the way; he followed. In the bedroom she gestured at the closet where her baggage was stored, and he pulled the unit out, while she located the 'bin bottle in her cosmetics kit and shook out a single capsule.

He set it up properly, although he seemed puzzled by some of the details of it: units varied. She watched him attach the several leads, and those were right. She gave him the pill, and he swallowed it without water.

"Recreation," she said, and sorted through the second, the brown case, that held the tapes. "You're always free to use the unit. I wish you would, in fact. Any white tape is perfectly all right for you." She looked at him, who sat waiting, looking at her, and reckoned that no azi was capable of going beyond instructions: she had never known one to, not even Lia. Psych-set. They simply could not. "You don't touch the black ones. Understood? If I hand you a black one, that's one thing, but not on your own. You follow that?"

"Yes," he said.

They were black ones that she chose, Kontrin-made. The longest was an artistic piece, participant-drama: a little cultural improvement would not be amiss, she thought. And the short one was *Istra*. She put them in the slot. "You know this machine, do you? You understand the hazards? Make sure the repeat-function never adds up to more than two hours."

He nodded. His eyes were beginning to dilate with the drug. He was not fit for conversation—fumbled after the switch, in token of this. She pushed it for him.

There was delay enough for him to compose himself. He settled back, folded his arms across his belly, eyes glassy. Then the machine began to activate, and it was as if every nerve in his body were severed: the whole body went limp. It was time to leave; the machine was a nuisance without the drug, and she never liked to look at someone undergoing the process—it was not a particularly pretty sight, mouth slack, muscles occasionally twitching to suggestion. She double-checked the timer to be sure: there was a repeat function, that could be turned to suicide—dehydration, a slow death as pleasant or as terrible as the tape in question; it was not engaged, and she turned her back on him and left, closed the door on the unit and its human appendage.

Every tape she had had since she was fifteen was in that box, and some she had recovered in duplicate for sentiment's sake. *If he knew them all,* she thought wistfully, *he might be me.* And then she laughed, to think of things that were not in the tapes, the ugly things, the bitter things.

The laugh died. She leaned against the rail of the stairs and reckoned another thing, that she should not have meddled at all, that she should ravel at other knots that had importance, and let this one alone.

No more than the hives, she thought, and went downstairs.

iii

Ab Tallen brought a different pair with him . . . an older woman named Mara Chung and a middle-aged man named Ben Orrin. Warrior was nervous with their presence: what Warrior could not touch made it entirely nervous, and the police had liked Warrior no better, having the duty of escorting the Outsiders to the safety of the house.

Max served drinks: Jim was still upstairs, and Raen was content with that, for Max managed well enough, playing house-azi. She sipped at hers and watched the Outsiders' eyes, what things drew them, what things seemed of interest.

Max himself was, it seemed. Ser Orrin was injudicious enough to stare at him directly, glanced abruptly at some point on the glass he held when he realized it.

Raen smiled, caught Max's eyes and with a flick of hers, dismissed him to neutrality somewhere behind her. She looked at her guests. "Seri," she murmured, with a gesture of the glass. "Your welcome. Your profound welcome. Be at ease. I plan no traps. I know what you've been doing on Istra. It's of no moment to me. Probably others of the Family find it temporarily convenient. A measure which has prevented difficulties here. How could the Reach complain of that?"

"If you would be clear, Kont' Raen—what interests you do serve, forgive me—we might be on firmer footing."

"Ser Tallen, I am not being subtle at the moment. I am here. I don't choose to see anything of the transactions you've made with Istra. Pursuing that would be of no profit to me, and a great deal of inconvenience. Some interests in the Family would be pleased with what you're doing; others would be outraged; Council would debate it and the outcome would be uncertain, but perhaps unfavorable. Myself, I don't care. The hives are fed. That's a great benefit. Azi aren't starved. That's another. It makes Istra liveable, and I'm living on Istra. Plain?"

There was long silence. Tallen took a drink and stared at her, long and directly. "Do you represent someone?"

"I'm Meth-maren. Some used to call us hive-masters; it's a term we've always disliked, but it's descriptive. That's what I represent, though some dispute it."

"You control the majat?"

She shook her head. "No one—*controls* the majat.

Anyone who tells you he does . . . lies. I'm an intermediary. An interpreter."

" 'Though some dispute it,' you said."

"There are factions in the Family, seri, as aforesaid. You might hear others disputing everything I say. You'll have to make up your own mind, weighing your own risks. I've called you here, for one thing, simply to lay all things out in open question, so that you don't have to ask ITAK questions that are much easier to ask of me directly. You had to wonder how much secrecy you needed use with certain items of trade; you could have wasted a great deal of energy attempting to conceal a fact which is of no importance to me. I consider it courtesy to tell you."

"Your manners are very direct, Kont' Raen. And yet you don't say a word of why you've come."

"No, ser. I don't intend to." She lowered her eyes and took a drink, diminishing the harshness of that refusal, glanced up again. "I confess to a lively curiosity about you—about the Outside. How many worlds are there?"

"Above fifty around the human stars."

"Fifty . . . and non-human? Have you found other such?"

Tallen's eyes broke contact, and disappointed her, even, it seemed, with regret to do so. " A restricted matter, Kont' Raen."

She inclined her head, turned the glass in her hand, let the melting ice continue spinning, frowned—thinking on Outside, and on the ship at station, Outbound.

"We are concerned," Tallen said, "that the Reach remain stable."

"I do not doubt." She regarded him and his companions, male and female. "I doubt that I can answer your questions either."

"Do you invite them?" And when she shrugged: "Who governs? Who decides policies? Do majat or humans dominate here?"

"Moth governs; the Council decides; majat and humans are separate by nature."

"Yet you interpret."

"I interpret."

"And remain separate?"

"That, ser," she answered, having lost her self-possession for the second time, "remains a question." She frowned. "But there remains one more matter, seri, for which I asked you here. And I shall ask it and hope for the plain truth: among the bargains that you have made with concerns inside the Reach—is there any breach of quarantine? You're not—providing exit for any citizens of the Reach? You've not agreed to do so in future?"

They were disturbed by this, as they might be.

"No," Tallen said.

"Again, my personal position is one of complete disregard. No. Not complete. I would," she said with a shrug and a smile, "be personally interested. I would be very interested to see what's over the Edge. But this is not the case. There is no exit."

"None. It would not be tolerated, Kont' Raen, much as it is regrettable."

"I am satisfied, then. That was the one item which troubled me. You've answered me. I think that I believe you. All our business for my part is done. Perhaps a social meeting when there's leisure for it."

"It would be a pleasure, Kont' Raen."

She inclined her head, set her glass aside, giving them the excuse to do the same.

There were formalities, shaking of hands, parting courtesies: she went personally to the door and made sure that Warrior did not approach them as they entered their car and closed the doors.

"Max," she said, "see to the gate out there. Make sure our security is intact."

He was over-zealous; he went without more than his sunvisor, and she frowned over it, for Istra's sun was no kinder than Cerdin's. New azi. Anxious and over-anxious to please. It was worse in its way than dealing with housecomp.

The car reached the gate and exited; Max saw to the closing and walked back, Warrior gliding along at a little distance, keeping a critical majat eye on all that passed.

Max entered, sought more instruction. "Just protect yourself when you go out, after this," she said peevishly, and dismissed him. She was depressed by the encounter, had hoped otherwise, and logically could not say why.

She closed and sealed the door, blinking somewhat from the change of light, from the portico to the inner hall—looked up, for Jim was on the stairs, watching her.

He looked yet a little abstracted; deepstudy did that to one. And he had been upstairs longer than the tape had run . . . asleep, perhaps. It was a common reaction.

"You didn't repeat it, did you?" she asked, thinking of Max's excessive zeal, concerned for that.

"I listened aloud for several times."

"You were supposed to enjoy it."

"I thought I was supposed to learn it." He shrugged from the stare she gave him for that, glanced down briefly, a flinching. "Is there something I can do now?"

She shook her head, and went back to her work.

The supplies arrived: Jim went out with Max and Merry to fend off Warrior while they were unloaded; it evidently was managed without incident, for she heard nothing of it. Six of the neighbors called, advising that they were indeed seeking shelter elsewhere; three were silent, and calls to them raised no human answer, only housecomp. There were several more calls from various sources, including ITAK and ISPAK.

For the most part there was no sound in the house at all, not a stirring from Jim, wherever he was and whatever he did to pass the time. He appeared at last, prepared supper, shared it with her in silence and vanished again. She would have spoken with him at dinner, but she was preoccupied with the recollection of her work with the comp net, and with the hazard of dipping as she did into intercomp; it was nothing to touch lightly, a taut-strung web which could radiate alarms if jostled too severely. She did not need abstract discussion with an azi to unhinge her thought.

He was there after midnight, when she came to bed, and even then she was not in a mood for conversation; he sensed this, evidently, and did not attempt it. But the work was almost done, and she could, for a time, let it go.

She did so; he obliged, cheerfully, and seemed content.

iv

She went down alone in the morning, letting Jim sleep while he would; and the fear that some urgent message, some calamity, some profound change in circumstances might be waiting in the housecomp's memory, sent her stumbling down to check on it before her eyes were fully open.

Only the same sort of message that had been coming in during the last day and night. She scanned the message-function a second time, refusing to believe in her continued safety, and finally accepted that this was so—pushed her hair out of her eyes and wandered off to the kitchen to make a cup of coffee: Outsider-luxuries, cheaper here than in innerworlds, for all the threat of famine. Istra was not backward where it regarded what was obtained from Outsider trade.

She drank her breakfast standing up, staring glaze-eyed at the garden through the kitchen's long slit window, thinking even then that the house had far too many windows, too many accesses, and that the walls were a good deal too low to serve even against human intruders: they masked what went on outside and close to them, and were no defense, only a delay.

The rising of beta Hydri gave a wan light at this hour—wan by reason of the shaded glass. The light rimmed the walls, the edge of the azi-quarters which showed a gleam of interior light, and over the wall, far distant, showed a vague impression of the domes of another arm of the City, with brush and grassland intervening: another hazard. Within the walls was deep shadow. The light frosted edges of rocks, of hastate-leaved plants, of the garden's few trees, which were gnarled and twisted and looked dead until one realized that the limp strings which hung along the limbs were leaves. A vine which ran among the rocks like a brown snarl of old cable by day had miraculously spread leaves for the dawn. Other things likewise had leafed out or bloomed, for the one brief period of moderate light and coolness. By day the garden reverted to reality. It was much like Cerdin. The Eln-Kests had had an eye for gardens, for Istran beauty, declining to import showy exotics from Kalind, which would have died, neglected: these thrived. It was a quality of subtle taste unsuspected in folk whose front-room decor was as it was. Raen thought of the green-and-white bedroom, and the subtlety of that, and reckoned that the same mind must have planned both, a character unlike what she knew of betas.

A large shadow appeared in the window, stopping her heart; it was Warrior—at least majat, wanting in. She opened the door, hand on the gun she had in her pocket, but it was in truth only Warrior, who sat down on the floor and preened itself of dew.

A little sugar-water more than satisfied it; it sang for her while it drank, and she stroked the auditory palps very softly in thanks for this.

"Others come," it said then.

"Other blues? How do you know so, Warrior?"

It boomed a note of majat language. "Mind," it translated, probably approximating.

"Is blue-hive not far, then?"

It shifted, never ceasing to drink, into a new orientation. "There."

It faced down-arm from residence circle 4.

"Come that way," it informed her, then reoriented half about. "Blue-hive there, our-hill."

They would come an eighth of the way round the asterisk-city and up the wild interstice to the garden wall. And majat runners could cover that ground very quickly.

"When?"

It stopped drinking and measured with its body the future angle of the sun, a profound bow toward the far evening. Late, then. Twilight.

"This-hive hopes you remain with us, Warrior."

It began drinking again. "This-unit likes sweet. Good, Kethiuy-queen."

She laughed soundlessly. "Good, Warrior." She touched it, eliciting a hum of pleasure, and went about her business. Warrior would of course do what the hive determined, immune to bribery, but Warrior would at least give its little unit of resistance to being removed, as valid a unit of the Mind as any other.

And the hive was reacting. She went of her work, schooling herself to concentration, but burning with an inner fire all the same: the hive . . . had heard her, regarded her. The approach through Kalind Warrior had had its imprint.

It was there again, the contact which she had lost. Nearly twenty years, and many attempts, and this one had taken: she had allies, the power of the hives.

All possibilities shifted hereafter. Being here, at the Edge, was no longer a protracted act of suicide, a high refuge, a place where enemies could not so easily follow: the circular character of events struck her suddenly and amazed her with her own predictability. She had run, a second time, for the hive.

It was time to attack.

V

House records had indicated a vehicle in the garage: systems in it seemed up and operable. Max and Merry both, by their papers, had some skill in that regard. "Go out," she said, "and check it out by eye; I'm not inclined to trust housecomp's word on it."

They went. Citybank provided an atlas in printout. A sorrowfully thin atlas it proved to be, only a few pages thick, for an entire inhabited world. Newhope and Newport were *the* two cities, Newport seeming a very small place indeed; and the town of Upcoast was the other major concentration of population, only an administrative and warehousing area for the northern estates. The

rest of the population was dotted all over the map, in
the rain-belts, on farms and pumping stations and farms
which served as depots on the lacery of unpaved roads.
Over most of the land surface of Istra was nothing but
blankness, designated Uninhabited. There was the spec-
tacular upsurge of the High Range on East; and an extremely wide expanse of marsh southward on West,
marked Hazard, which given the habit of Istran nomen-
clature, might be the name of the place as well as its
character. Small numbers were written beside the dots
that were farms . . . 2, 6, 7, and those in black; and by
depots and by the cities, likewise, but ranging up to
15,896 at Newhope.

Population, she realized. A world so sparse that they
must give population in the outback by twos and threes.

In the several pages of the atlas, three were city-maps,
and they were all of the pattern of Newhope. The city
was simplicity itself: an eight-armed star with business
and residential circles dotted along its arms and with
wedges between wistfully titled Park . . . Park doubtless
being the ambition. Reality was outside, over the garden
wall, a sun-baked tangle of weeds and native trees which
could not have known human attention in centuries.
Newhope must have had ambitions once, in the days of
its birth . . . ambition, but no Kontrin presence to aid it:
no relief from taxes, no Kontrin funds feeding back into
its economy, for beautification, luxury, art.

Most of the building-circles were warehouses: the two
arms of the city nearest the Port were entirely that. There
were local factories, mostly locally consumed equipment for
agriculture, light arms, clothing, food processing. There
were services and their administrations; worker-apartments
for the ordinary run of betas; midclass apartments and
some residential circles for the midclass well-to-do; and
one arm was all elite residence-circles, like circle 4, which
this house occupied. The highest ITAK officials lodged
in circle 1, the lowest in 10. And the guest house was
second circle of the eighth arm: the Outsider-mission's
residency, while ITAK officers were dead center, zero-
circle.

Useful to know.

There was a closing of doors upstairs. She heard foot-falls, soft, wandering here and there. She punched time: the morning was well along.

The reflection in the dead screen showed her Jim standing in the doorway, and she pushed with her foot, turned the chair nearly full about.

"You certainly had your sleep this morning," she said cheerfully.

"No, sera."

She let go her breath, let pass the *sera*. "What, then? You weren't meddling with the tapes, were you?"

"I didn't remember them well. I tried them again."

"For enjoyment. I thought you would enjoy them. Maybe learn something."

"I'm trying to learn them, sera."

She shook her head. "Don't try beyond convenience. I only meant to give you something to fill your time."

"What will you want for lunch, sera?"

"Raen. I don't care. Make something. I've a little more to do here. I'll be through in half an hour. We should have staff here. You shouldn't have to serve as cook."

"I helped in galley sometimes," he said.

She did not answer that. Jim strayed out again. War-rior met him: she saw the encounter reflected when she had turned about again, and almost turned back to inter-vene. But to her gratification she saw Jim touch Warrior of his own accord and suffer no distress of it. Warrior sang softly, hive-song, that was strange in the human rooms; it trailed after Jim as he went kitchenward.

"Sugar-water," she heard from the kitchen, a deep har-mony of majat tones, and afterward a contented hum-ming.

The car functioned, with no problems. Raen watched the short street flow past the tinted windows and settled back with a deep breath. Merry drove, seeming happy with the opportunity. Max and Warrior, minutely in-structed regarding each other as well as intruders, were guarding the house and grounds; but Jim she would not

leave behind, to the mercy of chance and Max's skill at
defense. Jim sat in the back seat of the Eln-Kests' fine
vehicle, watching the scenery, she saw when she looked
back, with a look of complete absorption.

Doing very well with this much strangeness about him,
she reckoned of him. *Doing very well, considering.* She
smiled at him slightly, then gave her attention forward,
for the car dipped suddenly for the downramp to the
subway and Merry needed an address.

"D-branch circle 5," she said, the while Merry took
them smoothly onto the track for Center.

The program went in. The car gathered speed, entering
the central track.

Something wrong whipped past the window on Max's
side. Raen twisted in the seat, saw an impression of stilt-
limbed walkers along the transparent-walled footpath
that ran beside the tracks.

Tunnels. Natural to majat, easy as the wildland interstices. But there were beta walkers too, and no sign of
panic.

"Merry. So majat have free access here? Do they just
come and go as they please?"

"Yes," he said.

She thought of calling the house and warning Max; but
Max and Warrior had already been stringently warned.
There was no good adding a piece of information that
Max would already know. The danger was always there,
had been. She settled forward again, arms folded, scanning the broad tube, the lights of which flicked past them
faster and faster.

"Majat make free of all Newhope, then, and betas just
bear with it, do they?"

"Yes, sera."

"They work directly for betas?" She found amazement, even resentment, that majat would do so.

"Some places they do. Factories, mostly."

"So no one at the Port found a Warrior's presence
unusual. Everyone's gotten used to it. How long, Merry,
how long has this been going on?"

The azi kept his eyes on the tracks ahead, his squarish

face taut, as if the subject was an intensely uncomfortable one. "Half a year. . . . There was panic at first. No more. Hives don't bother people. Humans walk one side, majat the other, down the walkways. There are heat-signs."

Redsss, redsss, Warrior had tried to tell her. *Go here, go there. Redss pushhh.*

"What hive, Merry? One more than others?"

"I don't know, sera. I never understood there was a difference to be seen, until you showed me. I'll watch." His brow was creased with worry. Not so slow-witted, this azi. "Humans don't like them in the city, but they come anyway."

Raen bit at her lip, braced as the car went through a maneuver, scanned other majat on the walkway. They whipped into the great hub of Central and changed tracks at a leisurely pace. There were human walkers here, swathed in cloaks and anonymous in the sunsuits which Istra's bright outdoors made advisable; and by twos, there were armored police . . . ITAK security: everything here was ITAK.

They whipped out again on another tangent. D, the signs read.

More majat walkers.

Majat, casually coming and going in a daily contact with betas . . . with minds-who-died. Once majat had fled such contact, unable to bear it, even for the contacts which gave them azi, insisting to work only through Kontrin. Death had once worried majat—azi-deaths, no, as majat deaths were nothing—but betas they had always perceived as individual intelligences, and they had fled beta presence in horror, unable to manage the concepts which disrupted all majat understanding.

Now they walked familiarly with minds-who-died, unaffrighted.

And that sent a shiver over her skin, a suspicion of understanding.

D-track carried them along at increasing velocity; they took the through-track until the lights blurred past in a stream.

And suddenly they whisked over to slow-track, braking, gliding for the D circle 5 ramp. Merry took over manual as they disengaged, delivered them up into a shaded circle free of traffic and pedestrians, a vast area ringed by a pillared overhang of many stories—which must outwardly seem one of those enormous domes. The summit was a tinted shield which admitted light enough to glare down into the center of the well of pillars.

They drove deep beneath the overhand, and to the main entry, where transparent doors and white walls lent a cold austerity to the offices. LABOR REGISTRY, the neat letters proclaimed, 50-D, ITAK.

It was the beginning of understandings, at least. Raen contemplated it with apprehensions, reckoned whether she wanted to leave the azi both in the car or not, and decided against.

"Merry, I don't think we'll be bothered here. It's going to be hot; I'm sorry, but stay in the car and keep the doors locked and the windows sealed. Don't create trouble, but if it happens, shoot if you have to: I want this car here when I come out. You call Max every ten minutes and make sure things are all right at the house, but no conversation, understand?"

"Yes."

She climbed out and beckoned to Jim, who joined her on the walk and lagged a decorous half-pace behind as she started for the doors. She dropped a step and he caught up, walked with her into the foyer.

The offices were unnaturally still, desks vacant, halls empty. The air-conditioning was excessive, and the air held a strange taint, a combination of office-smells and antiseptic.

"Is this place going to bother you?" she asked of Jim, worried for that, but she reckoned hazards even of leaving him here at the door.

He shook his head very faintly. She looked about, saw a light on in an office down the corridor from the reception area. She walked that way, slowly, her footsteps and Jim's loud in the deserted building.

A man occupied the office—had heard their coming evidently and risen. It was modern, but untidy; the desk was stacked high with work. DIRECTOR, the sign by the door declared.

"Ser," Raen said. He surveyed them both, blinked, all at once seemed to take the full situation into account, for his face went from ruddy to pale; a Kontrin in Color, a man in impeccable innerworlds dress and with an azimark on his cheek.

"Sera."

"I understand," Raen said, "that there are numerous personnel to be contracted."

"We have available contracts, yes, sera."

"Numerous contracts. I'd like a full tour, ser—"

"Itavvy," he breathed.

"Itavvy. A tour of the whole facility, ser."

The smallish beta, graying, balding . . . looked utterly distressed. "The office—I've responsibility—"

"It really doesn't look as if you're overwhelmed with visitors. The whole facility, ser, floor by floor, the whole process, so long as it amuses me."

Itavvy nodded, reached for the communications switch on the desk. Raen stepped across the interval and put out her chitined hand, shook her head slowly. "No. You can guide us, I'm sure. Softly. Quietly. With minimum disturbance to the ordinary routine of the building. Do you object, ser?"

vi

The Labor Registry was a maze of curving corridors, all white, all the same. Lifts designated sub-basements down to the fifth level; Raen recalled as many as twenty stories above ground, although the lifts in this area only went to the seventh: she recalled the overhang. They passed row on row of halls, a great deal of seemingly pointless walking with ser Itavvy in the lead. There were doors, neat letters: LIBRARY: COMP I: LEVEL I: RED CARDS ONLY.

She made no sense of it, had no idea in fact what she was seeking, save that in this building was what should have been a thriving industry, and in the front of it were empty desks and silent halls.

Itavvy paused at last at a lift and showed them in, took them to third level, into other identical halls, places at least populated. Gray-suited techs stared at the intrusion of such visitors and stopped dead in their tracks, staring. White-suited azi, distinguishable by their tattoos, stepped from their path and then resumed their cleaning and their pushing of carts.

Itavvy led them farther.

"I'm tired of walking aimlessly," Raen said. "What do you propose to show us on this level? More doors?"

"The available contracts, sera."

Raen walked along in silence, scanning doors and labels, searching for something of information. Periodically corridors branched off from theirs, always on the right. Inevitably those corridors ended at the same interval, closed off by heavy security doors. RED CARD ONLY, the signs said.

She stopped, gestured toward the latest of them. "What's there, ser Itavvy?"

"General retention," Itavvy said, looking uncomfortable. "If sera will, please, there are more comfortable areas—"

"Unlock this one. I'd like to see."

Itavvy unhappily preceded them down the short corridor, produced his card and unlocked the door.

A second door lay beyond, similarly locked: they three stood within the narrow intervening space as the outer door boomed and sealed with a resounding noise of locks. Then Itavvy used his card on the second, and a wave of tainted air met them, a vastness of glaring lights and gray concrete, a web of catwalks.

The scent was again that of antiseptic, compounded this time with something else. Itavvy would too obviously have been glad to close the door with that brief look, but Raen walked stubbornly ahead, moving Itavvy out before her—no beta would have the chance to slam a door at her back—and looked about her.

Concrete, damp with antiseptic, and the stench of humanity and sewage.

Pits. Brightly lit doorless pits, a bit of matting and one human in each, like larvae bestowed in chambered comb. Five paces by five, if that; no doors, no halls between the cells . . . only the grid of catwalks above, with machinery to move them, with an extended process of ladders which could, only if lowered, afford the occupants exit, and that only a few at a time.

The whole stretched out of view around the curve of the building and far, far, across before them. Their steps echoed fearsomely on the steel grids. Faces looked up at them, only mildly curious.

Raen looked the full sweep of it, sickened, deliberately inhaled the stench.

"Are contracts on these available?"

"For onworld use, sera."

"No export license."

"No, sera."

"I understand that a great number of azi have been confiscated from estates. But the contracts on those azi would be entangled. Where are they housed? Among these?"

"There are facilities in the country."

"As elaborate as these?"

Itavvy said nothing. Raen calculated for herself what manner of facilities could be constructed in the sparsely populated countryside, in haste, by a pressured corporation-government. These facilities must be luxurious by comparison.

"Yet all of these," she said, "are warehoused. Is that the right word?"

"Essentially," Itavvy whispered.

"Are you still producing azi at the same rate?"

"Sera, if only you would inquire with ITAK Central— I'm sure I don't know the reasons of things."

"You're quite satisfactory, ser Itavvy. Answer the question. I assure you of your safety to do so."

"I don't know of any authorization for change. I'm not

over Embryonics. That's another administration, round
the other side, 51. Labor doesn't get them until the sixth
year. We haven't had any less of that age coming in. I
don't think . . . I don't think there can be any change.
The order was to produce."

"Origin of that order?"

"Kontrin licensing, sera." The answer was a hoarse
whisper. "Originally—we appealed for a moderate increase. The order came back quadrupled."

"In spite of the fact that there existed no Kontrin license to dispose of them when they reached eighteen.
The export quota wasn't changed."

"We . . . trusted, sera, that the license would be
granted when the time came. We've applied, sera. We've
even applied for permission to terminate. We can't do
that either. The estates—were all crowded above their
limits. They're supposed to turn them back after a year,
for training. But now—now they're running their operations primarily to feed their own workers . . . and they're
panicked, refusing to give them up, the permanent workers and the temporaries." Itavvy wiped at his face. "They
divert food—to maintain the work force and it doesn't
get to the depots. Our food. The station's food. ISPAK
has threatened a power cutoff if the estates go on holding
out, but ITAK has—reasoned with ISPAK. It wouldn't
stop the estate-holders. They have their own collectors,
their own power. And they won't give up the azi."

"Are the holders organized?"

The beta shook his head. "They're just outbackers.
Blind, hardheaded outbackers. They hold the azi because
they're manpower; and they're a means to hold out by
human labor if ISPAK follows through with its threat.
Always . . . always the farms were a part of the process;
azi went out there in the finishing of their training and
shifted back again, those that would be contracted for
specialized work—good for the azi, good for the farms.
But now, sera, the estates have been threatening to break
out of the corporation."

"Hardly sounds as if these holders are blind, ser
Itavvy . . . if it comes to a fight, they've the manpower."

"Azi."

"You don't think they'd fight."

Beta deference robbed her of an honest answer. Itavvy swallowed whatever he would have said; but he looked as if he would have disputed it.

"It hardly sounds as if they're without communication on the issue," Raen said, "since they're all doing alike. Aren't they?"

"I wouldn't know, sera."

"Only on East, or is West also afflicted?"

Itavvy moistened his lips. "I think it's general."

"Without organization. Without a plan to keep themselves from starving."

"There's already been work toward new irrigation. The river . . . that supplies Newhope . . . is threatened. They expand—"

"Unlicensed."

"Unlicensed, sera. ITAK protests, but again—we can do nothing. They feud among themselves. They fight for land and water. There are—" He mopped at the back of his neck. "Maybe two and three holders get together. And azi . . . muddle up out there. They're trading, these holders."

"Trading?"

"With each other. Goods. Azi. Moving them from place to place."

"You know so?"

"Police say so. Azi—are more on some farms than we put there."

Raen looked over all the cells, as far as the eye could see. "Weapons?"

"Holders—have always had them."

She walked forward, slowly, the little boxes shifting past. The ceiling weighed upon the senses. There was only gray and black and the white glare of light, no color but the shades of humanity, all gray-clothed.

"Why," she asked suddenly, "are they walled off one from the other? Security?"

"Each is specifically trained. Contact at random would make it more difficult to assure specificity."

"And you get them at six years? Is it different from this, the young ones?"

The beta did not answer. At last he gave a vague shrug.

"Show me," Raen said.

Itavvy started walking, around the curve. New vistas of cells presented themselves. The complex seemed endless. No walls were discernible, no limits, save a core where many catwalks converged, a vast concrete darkness against the floodlights.

"Do they ever leave this place?" Raen asked as they walked above the cells, provoking occasional curious stares from those below. "Don't they want for exercise?"

"There are facilities," the beta said, "by shifts."

"And factories. They work in the city factories?"

"Those trained for it." Perhaps Itavvy detected an edge to her voice. His grew defensive. "Six hours in the factories, two at exercise, two at deepstudy, then rest. We do the best we can under crowded circumstances, sera."

"And the infants?"

"Azi care for them."

"By shifts. Six hours on, two of exercise?"

"Yes, sera."

Their steps measured the metal catwalk another length. "But you're not sending these out to the estates anymore. You're more and more crowded week by week, and you're not able to move them."

"We do what we can, sera."

They reached the core, and the lift Itavvy used his card to open the door, and they stepped in. SEVEN, Itavvy pushed and the lift shot up with heart-dragging rapidity, set them out on that level with a crashing of locks and doors, echoes in vastness.

It was otherwise silent.

All these levels, she began to understand, all these levels were the same, endless cubicles, floor after floor, the same. Seven above ground. Five below. And there was silence. All that space, all those cells, all that humanity, and there was nowhere a voice, nowhere an outcry.

Itavvy led the way out onto the catwalk. Raen looked

down. These were all small children, six, seven years. The faces upturned held mild curiosity, no more. There were no games, no occupations. They sat or lay on their mats. Same gray coveralls, same shaven heads, same grave faces. At this age, one could not even tell their sex.

None cried, none laughed.

"God," she breathed, gripping the rail. Itavvy had stopped. She suddenly wanted out. She looked back. Jim stood at the rail, looking down. She wanted him out of this place, now, quickly.

"Is there a door out on this level?" she asked, perfectly controlled. Itavvy indicated the way ahead with a gesture. Raen walked at his unhurried pace, hearing Jim following.

"What's the average contract price?" she asked.

"Two thousand."

"You can't produce them for anything near that cost."

"No," said Itavvy. "We can't."

It was a long walk. There was nothing to fill the silence. She would not hurry, would not betray her reaction, disturbing betas whose interests were involved in this operation, stirring apprehensions. Nor would she turn and look at Jim. She did not want to.

They reached a door like the one on third—passed that and its mate into sterile halls and light and clean air. She breathed, breathed deeply. "I've seen what I came to see," she said. "Thank you, ser Itavvy. Suppose now we go back to your office."

He hesitated, as if he thought of asking a question; and did not. They rode the lift to main, and walked the long distance back to the front offices, all in silence. Itavvy had the air of a worried man. Raen let him fret.

And when they three stood once again in the beta's office, with the door closed: "I have an estate," Raen said, "ridiculously understaffed. And a security problem, which affords me no amusement at all. How many contracts are available here?"

Itavvy's face underwent a series of changes. "Surely enough to fill all your needs, Kontrin."

"The corporation does reward its people according to

the profits their divisions show, doesn't it? All these empty desks . . . this isn't a local holiday, is it?"

"No, sera."

Raen settled into a chair and Itavvy seated himself at his desk. Raen gestured to Jim, and he took the one beside her.

"So," she said. "And the number of contracts available for guard personnel, azi only?"

The beta consulted the computer. "Sufficient, sera."

"The exact number, please."

"Two thousand forty-eight, sera, nineteen hundred nine hundred eighty-two males, rest females; nineteen hundred four under thirty years, rest above."

"Counting confiscated azi, or are these on the premises?"

"On the premises."

"A very large number."

"Not proportionately, sera."

"Who usually absorbed them?"

"Corporation offices. Estate-holders . . . it's wild land out there."

"So a great number of those tangled contracts in custody in the country . . . would be guard-trained, wouldn't they?"

"A certain number, yes, sera."

Itavvy's eyes were feverish; his lips trembled. He murmured his words. Raen reckoned the man, at last nodded.

"I'll buy," she said, "all two thousand forty-eight. I also want sunsuits and sidearms. I trust an establishment which sends out guards sends them out equipped to work."

He moistened his lips. "Yes, sera, although some buyers have their own uniforms or equipment."

"You'll manage." She rose, walked about the office, to Itavvy's extreme nervousness, the while she looked at the manuals on the counter by the comp unit. She looked up a number, memorized it, turned and smiled faintly. "I'll take the others as fast as you can train them. Those tangled contracts . . . if you'll check tomorrow, you'll find the matter cleared and the contracts salable. I trust you can quietly transfer azi from there to here as spaces become available."

"Sera—"

"The children, ser Itavvy. However do you substitute for—human contact? Do tapes supply it all?"

Itavvy wiped at his lips. "At every minute stage of development . . . deepstudy tapes, yes, sera. The number of individuals, the economics . . . it would be virtually impossible for a private individual to have the time, the access to thousands of programs developed over centuries to accomplish this—"

"Eighteen years to maturity. No way to speed that process, is there?"

"For some purposes—they leave before eighteen."

"Majat azi."

"Yes."

"And moving them out without programming—as they are—"

"Chaos. Severe personality derangements."

She said nothing to that, only looked at him, at Jim, back again. "And more than the two thousand forty-eight . . . how long does it take for training? On what scale can it be done?"

"Minimally . . . a few days." Itavvy shuffled the papers spread across his desk, an action which gave him excuse to look elsewhere. "All channels could be turned to the same tapestudy—easier than doing it otherwise. But the legalities—the questions that would be raised on this world—they'd have to be moved, shipped, and ISPAK—"

"You know, ser Itavvy, that your loyalty is to ITAK. But ITAK is a Kontrin creation. You are aware then of a—higher morality. If I were to give you a certain—favor, if I were to ask your silence in return for that, and certain further cooperations, you would realize that this was not disloyalty to ITAK, but loyalty to the source of ITAK's very license to function."

The beta wiped at his face and nodded, the papers forgotten, his eyes fever-bright. He looked at her now. There was no possibility of divided attention.

"I'm creating an establishment," she said very softly,

"a permanent Kontrin presence, do you see? And such an establishment needs personnel. When this process is complete, when the training is accomplished as I wish, then I shall still need reliable personnel at other levels."

"Yes, sera," he breathed.

"The great estates, you see, these powers with their massed forces of azi—this thing which you so earnestly insist has no organization—could be handled without bloodshed, by superior force. Peace would come to Istra. You see what a cause you serve. A solution, a solution, ser, which would well serve ITAK. You realize that I have power to license, being in fact the total Kontrin presence: I can authorize export on the levels you need. I'm prepared to do so, to rescue this whole operation, if I receive the necessary cooperation from certain key individuals."

The man was trembling, visibly. He could not control his hands. "I am not, then, to contact my superiors."

She shook her head slowly. "Not if you plan to enjoy your life, ser. I am extremely cautious about security."

"You have my utmost cooperation."

She smiled bleakly, having found again the measure of betas. "Indeed, ser, thank you. Now, there's an old farm on B-branch, just outside the city, registered to a new owner, one ser Isan Tel. You'll manage to find some azi of managerial function, the best: its housecomp has instructions for them. Can you find such azi?"

Itavvy nodded.

"Excellent. All you can spare of them, and all of the guard-azi but two hundred males that I want transferred to my own estate . . . go to the establishment of Isan Tel. Provisioned and equipped. Can you do it?"

"We—can, yes."

She shook her head. "No plural. You. *You* will tend every detail personally. The rumor, if it escapes, will tell me precisely who let it escape; and if there is fault in the training—I need not say how I would react to that, ser. You would be quite, quite dead. On the other hand, you can become a very wealthy man . . . wealthy and secure. In addition to the other contracts, I want half a dozen domestics to my address; and ser Tel's estate will need a good thirty to care for the guard-azi. Possible?"

Itavvy nodded.

"Ser Itavvy, after today, an identity will be established, one ser Merek Sed. He will be a very wealthy man, with properties on several worlds, with trade license, and an account in intercomp, a number I shall give you. You will be that individual. He will be a creator of art. I shall purchase art for the decoration of my house . . . and so will ser Isan Tel. Be discreet at first, ser Itavvy. Too ostentatious a display of your new wealth would raise fatal questions. But if you are clever—Merek Sed can retire in great comfort. You have family, ser Itavvy?"

He nodded again, breathing with difficulty. "Wife. A daughter."

"They also can be built into Merek Sed's identity. Untraceable. Only you and I know how he was born. Once off Istra, utterly safe. I will put your wife and daughter into those records too, and give you their new citizen numbers . . . at a price."

"What—price?"

"Loyalty. To me. Discretion. Absolute." She tore off a sheet from a notepad and picked up a pen, wrote three numbers. "The first is a number by which you can contact me. Do so tomorrow. The second is the citizen number of ser Merek Sed. The third is an account number which will provide you an earnest of things to come. Use only cash-machines, no credit purchases . . . don't patronize the same store repeatedly. Create no patterns and don't let others know how much your fortunes have improved. Recall that if you're suspected, the consequences to me are mere annoyance; to you . . . rather more serious. For your family also. I can defend myself from my annoyances. But I fear that they would devour others, ser Itavvy." She held up the paper.

He took it.

"The delivery," she said, "of the guards for my house . . . today?"

"Yes."

"And all equipage with them?"

"Yes. That can be arranged. We have warehouse access."

"And the transfer of the azi to the Tel estate?"

"Will begin today, sera. I could suggest an abbreviated training, if only the use of arms is required, and not specialized security—"

"Hastening the program?"

"Hastening it by half, Kontrin."

"Acceptable."

"If the authorizations to clear the papers on the others could be given—"

"Not from this terminal, ser, but if you'll check after your delivery to my house, number 47A, if you'll kindly make a note of that, you may find that certain problems have vanished. And the Tel estate access is South Road 3. You have all that?"

"Yes, sera."

She smiled. "Thank you, ser Itavvy. Payment will clear at delivery. And a further matter: should you ever notice on your housecomp a call from ser Tel in person . . . check the Sed account at once. There'll be passage for Sed and family, to ISPAK and elsewhere. It would be wise at that point to use it. I do take care of my agents, ser, if it's ever necessary."

"Sera," he breathed.

"We're agreed, then." She rose, offered her chintin-sheathed hand with deliberation, knowing how betas hated contact with it. Itavvy took it with gingerly pleasure, rising.

"Jim," she said softly then, drew him with her, out of the office.

And in the foyer she looked back. Itavvy had not come out of his office . . . would not perhaps, for a small space. She took Jim's arm. "All right?" she asked.

Jim nodded. Upset, she thought, how not? But he showed no signs of worse disturbance. She pressed his arm, let it go, led the way to the door.

The car still waited. She looked right and left, walked out into the heat. The filtered light coming down the huge well to the pavement was not screened enough: the ventilation was insufficient. When they reached the car, Merry opened the door with a look of vast relief and started the air-conditioning at once. He was drenched with sweat, his blond hair plastered about his face.

"Everything all right?" she asked, letting Jim in.

"At the house . . . quiet. No trouble."

Raen closed the door, looked back yet again at Jim. He looked none the worse for the experience, even here, where he might have given way in private. He seemed quite composed, quite—she thought with disturbance— as composed as the faces which had looked up at them from the cells, silent, incapable of tears.

"Center," she directed Merry, settling forward in her seat again and folding her arms about her. "We're going to pay another call. ITAK's due one."

vii

It was very like the Labor Registry, the circle which was the heart of ITAK: it was only wider, taller, and perhaps deeper underground.

The Center drew a great deal of traffic, cars prowling the circle-drive . . . probably every car in East, every car on the continent resorted here regularly, in a city where everyone but the higher ITAK officials must rely on public transport. A space was available in front of the main doors, probably vacant because it was restricted; Raen directed and Merry eased into it, parked, let them out and locked the doors.

She and Jim were actually well into the building before the reaction set in among the betas. It began with shocked stares. Word apparently flashed then throughout the building, for by the time she reached the main hall, with its central glass sculpture, there was a delegation to meet her, minor executives anxious to escort her upstairs where, she was assured, the Board was hastily assembling to meet her.

She cast a glance at the sculpture, which ascended in a complex shaft to a light-well all its own, and took advantage of beta Hydri's glare to illumine colors and forms all the way down. "Lovely," she murmured, and looked at the betas. "Local, seri?"

Heads nodded. Anxious gestures tried to urge her elsewhere, hallward. She shrugged and went with them, Jim treading softly in her wake, playing at invisibility. No one spoke to him, no one acknowledged his presence: the tattoo let them know what he was despite his dress. Bodyguard, they would think him, not knowing his harmlessness, and therefore he served the function well. Betas crowded about them, one babbling on about the glass-artist, an Upcoast factor's son.

They entered the lift, rode it to the uppermost floors, entered directly from it a suite of offices the splendor of which equalled many an establishment on Andra, and a second crowd waited to greet the visitor: division heads, secretaries, minor officials, a chattering succession of introductions.

Raen smiled perfunctorily, reckoning those who might be worth recalling, met the Dain-Prossertys again, and ser Dain himself, the president, and two more Dains high on the staff. The inner office was opened, revealing chairs arranged about a vast hollow table, and the ITAK emblem blazoned on the wall like the Kontrin symbol in Council.

Illusions, illusions. She smiled to herself, and brought Jim in with her, offered him a seat at the table beside her, offending them all. Azi women appeared, to take requests for drinks. She ordered for herself and Jim, the same that he had ordered on-ship, and leaned back, waiting, while betas took their seats and made their orders and hissing whispers tried to solve the problem of a disturbed seating arrangement. A chair was brought in. The first drinks arrived: Raen's, Jim's, president Dain's and the Dain-Prossertys'.

Raen sipped at hers and studied them all, who had to wait on theirs. The serving-azi hastened breathlessly . . . decorative, Raen thought, eyeing the young women with a critic's cold eyes, reckoning whether they were home-bred or foreign, and whether they were equally to the taste of the beta women on the board.

Foreign, she decided. Mixed as populations were in the Reach, seven hundred years had brought some definition among azi, whose generations were short and subject to brief fads. These had the look of Meron's carnival decadence, elegant, sloe-eyed.

The last drinks appeared; the azi took themselves hence very quickly. Raen still mused the question of beta psych-sets, looked at Dain, who was murmuring some courtesy to her, and nudged herself out of her analysis to look on him as a man, plump, nearly bald, eyes full of anxiety. She kept seeing labs, and the Registry's gray honeycomb of cells.

"Ser Enis Dain," she said. "I recall your message." She smiled and regarded the others. "It's very kind of you to disarrange your schedules. I'll take very little of your time."

"Kont' Raen Meth-maren, we're very honored by your visit."

She nodded. "Thank you. Your people have been very cooperative. I've appreciated that. I know that my presence is a disturbance. And you're doubtless wanting to ask me questions; let me save you time and effort. You'd like to know if my coming is going to disturb your operations here, and most of all whether the seri Eln-Kest, personally lamented, had anything to do with bringing me here."

There was disturbance in their faces. They were not apparently accustomed to such directness. She sipped at her drink and three others did so by reflex.

"I know your difficulties here," she said. "And I know other details, and I shall not confide in any until I am sure what other agency arranged that reception of my party at the port, thank you."

"Sera," said Dain senior, "Kontrin—the hives—the hives are beyond our influence, beyond our power to restrain. We apologize profoundly for the incidence, but it was a hive matter."

She frowned darkly. This casting back of the Kontrin's eternal answer for majat intrusions had, on the lips of a beta, suspicion of irony. For a moment she readjusted her estimate of ser Dain's craft, and then, staring at his chin, which wobbled with anxiety, dismissed her suspicions of subtlety. "A hive matter. If so, ser, majat have come into possession of communications equipment—modified for their handling. Or how else would they have informed themselves? Tell me that, seri. How did they know we were coming?"

Dain made a helpless gesture. "The information was widespread."

"Public broadcast?" The notion appalled her.

"ITAK general channels," Dain answered faintly.

She waved her hand in disgust, dismissing the matter. "Trust that I shall find my own way and provide my own security. If you have any policy of allowing majat to walk freely in and out of ITAK agencies . . . revise it."

"We have protested—"

"If majat object to being evicted, mention my name and invoke the Pact. If you can't move them . . . Well, but you've let matters go too far, haven't you? They're all over the city."

"They've done no harm. They—"

"If you will believe me, seri, hive matters and Kontrin affairs are better avoided. And while I remind myself of it . . . since you're unaccustomed to the protocols of Kontrin presence . . . a bit of advice in self-protection. Houses have their differences. We all do. And if another Kontrin arrives here, your safest action is to inform me at once and stay neutral. Such a visitor would correctly assume that I have agents among you and that I have personal interests in protecting the world of Istra. A friend would of course treat you well—an enemy . . . *if* I were removed . . . could be very disruptive in his search for my agents, who would disrupt in their turn. . . . You do see your hazard, seri. I don't think Istra could easily bear that sort of thing.

"As for the benefits of my presence, you'll see them

very soon. You want licenses; I understand that some Kontrin somewhere has blocked all your appeals. I shall expect, in fact, that any opposition who turns up here will probably be that agency, do you see, seri? I can grant those licenses. I've already begun to purchase . . . extravagantly . . . items which will permit me to live in comfort and safety, of course to the aid of your tax balance and the security and prosperity of the company. Council on Cerdin hasn't received your appeals; you've been cut off deliberately; and if it goes on, your economy will collapse. I shall take immediate steps to improve matters. And I do imagine that that action will turn up enemies—mutual enemies—very quickly."

"Kontrin," said ser Dain, hard-breathing. "In no wise was the attack on your person of our doing. There is no one in ITAK who would desire—"

"You can only speak of your hopes, ser Dain, not certainties. I'll look to myself. Simply afford me your cooperation."

"Our utmost cooperation."

She gave them her almost-best smile. "Then I thank you, seri. I've found possibilities in Istra, a change from the ordinary. I'd like to travel a bit. An aircraft—"

"Your safety—"

"Trust me. An aircraft would be very useful. Armed, if you feel it necessary."

"We'll provide it," Dain said; the man at his left confirmed his uncertain look with a nod.

"I'll furnish my own security about my property; I'd appreciate ITAK security temporarily about the aircraft allotted to my use. All these things of course are not gifts: they'll be credited against ITAK's taxes. Kontrin presence is never financially disadvantageous, seri."

"We are enormously concerned—" This was sera Ren Milin, head of Agriculture, "enormously concerned for your personal safety. Dissidents and saboteurs are presently confined to attacks on depots, but one more deranged than the rest . . ."

"I do appreciate your concern. You have heavy

arms . . . for onworld security . . . surely. I'd appreciate it if a goodly number were delivered to my estate, say, sufficient for a thousand men."

Faces went uniformly stark with shock.

"Precaution, you see, against dissidents, saboteurs, and deranged persons. If it's generally known that we're armed, ITAK being so inclined to general broadcast channels, there will be less temptation. I certainly hope not to use them. But you wouldn't like the consequences of a Kontrin killed here . . . by your own locals. No. You'd be surprised how even Houses at odds with mine would look on that: the Family . . . would be forced to make a very strong answer to that. The facts of policy. Kindly see that the arms arrive. They're quite safe in my hands. My security, after all, is yours. And enough, enough unpleasantness. I'm quite delighted by your courtesy. I'll extend you my own hospitality as soon as I'm decently settled and housed. If there's entertainment to be had, I'd appreciate knowing. I suffer from boredom. I do hope there's some society here."

The pallor did not entirely depart. They murmured courtesies, professed themselves honored and delighted by the prospect of her company socially. She laughed softly.

"And Outsiders!" she exclaimed ingenuously. "Seri, I saw an Outsider ship at station . . . an ordinary sight for you, surely, but profoundly exciting for one from innerworlds. I've met these folk, had some chance to talk with them. Do you include them in your society?"

That brought silence, a moment of awkwardness.

"It could be arranged," sera Dain said.

"Excellent." Raen finished her drink and set it aside.

"We'll be pleased to provide what we can in all respects," ser Dain managed to say. "Would you care for another drink, Kont' Raen?"

"No, thank you." She gathered herself up and waited for Jim, deliberately slipped her hand within his arm. "I'm quite content with your courtesy. Very pleased. Thank you so much. And don't worry about what I shall uncover. I know that you've been driven to unusual methods, unusual sources. I give you warning that I know . . . and I shall refrain from seeing what perhaps shades your license. The maintenance of order here under trying circumstances is a tribute to your ingenuity. I don't find fault, seri. And do forgive me. My next call will be entirely social, I assure you."

Men moved to reach the door, to open it for her. She smiled at them one and all and walked out, with Jim beside her, in a crowd of security agents who made turmoil in the outer offices.

The agents, armored police, and Dain senior himself insisted on staying with them, in the lift and out into the foyer. She lingered there an instant, with the crowd milling about, looking up to the glass sculpture.

"Find me the artist's address," she said to Dain. "Send it to me this evening. Would you do that?"

"Honored," he said. "Honored to do so."

She walked on. The crowds broke and closed.

"You would find interest, perhaps," ser Dain rambled on, while the police in advance of them pushed folk from before the doors to clear passage, "in an example I have in my own house, if you would do me the honor to—"

Shadows moved beyond the tinted-glass doors, out beneath the pillars, about the car . . . too-tall shadows, fantastical.

"Sera," Jim protested.

Under her cloak she drew her gun, but ser Dain put out his hand, not touching—offering caution. "The police will move them. Please, sera!"

Raen paid him no heed, stayed with the rush of the agents and the police as they burst outside.

Greens. Warriors. They swarmed about the entrance, about the car. "Away!" a policeman shouted at them. "Move away!"

Auditory palps flicked out, back, refusal to listen. The majat did move back somewhat, averaging a line, a group.

"Green-hive!" Raen shouted at them, seeing the beginning formation. She brought her hand out into the open, gun and all. Auditory palps came forward, half. At her right was the car; Merry surely still had the doors locked. "Jim," she said. "Jim, get in the car. Get in."

"Blue," green leader intoned. "Blue-hive Kontrin."

"I'm Raen Meth-maren. What are greens doing in a beta City?"

"Hive-massster." There was more than one voice to that, and an ominous clicking from the others. They began to shift position, edging to the sides.

"Watch out!" Raen yelled, and fired as the greens skittered this way and that. Green leader went down squalling. Some leapt. She whirled and fired, careless of bystanders, took others. Police and security began firing, with Dain screaming orders, his voice drowned in bystanders' panic.

Then the greens broke and ran, with blinding rapidity, across the pavings, down into the subway ramp, down into tunnels, elsewhere.

Dying majat scraped frenetically on the concrete, limbs twitching. Humans babbled and sobbed. Raen looked back and saw Jim by the car, on his feet and all right; Dain, surrounded by security personnel, looked ill.

"Better find out if the rest of the building is secure," Raen said to one of the police. Another, armor-protected, was being dragged from the body of a dead majat; safe, he lay convulsing in shock. Someone was leaning over against the side of a column, vomiting. Two victims were decapitated. Raen looked away, fixed Dain with a stare. "This comes of trifling with the hives, ser. You see the consequences."

"Not our choosing. They come. They come, and we can't put them out. They—"

"They feed this world. They buy the grain. Don't they?"

"We can't put them out of the city." Dain's face poured sweat; his hands fluttered as he sought a handkerchief, and mopped at his pallid skin. For an instant Raen thought the aging beta might die on the spot, and so, evidently, did the guards, who moved to support him.

"I believe you, ser Dain," Raen assured him, moved to pity. "Leave them to me. Lock them out of your buildings; use locks, everywhere, ser Dain. Install security doors. Bars on windows. I can't stress strongly enough your danger. I know them. Believe me in this."

Dain answered nothing. His plump face was stark with terror.

Merry had the car doors open. She waved an angry gesture at Jim, who scrambled in and flung himself into the back seat. She settled into the front, clipped her gun to her belt, slammed the door. "Home," she told Merry. And then with a sharp look at the azi: "Can you?"

Merry was white with shock. She imagined what it must have been for him, with majat swarming all about the car, only glass between him and majat jaws. He managed to get the car down the ramp and engaged to the track, keyed in the corn-unit. "Max," he said hoarsely, "Max, it's all right. We're clear of them now."

She heard Max answer, reporting all secure elsewhere.

She looked back then. Jim was sitting in the back seat with his hands clasped before his mouth, eyes distracted. "I had my gun," he said. "I had it in my pocket. I had it in my pocket."

"Practice on still targets first," she said. "Not majat."

He drew a more stable bream, composed himself, azi-calm. The car lurched slightly, having found the home-track, gathered speed.

Out the back window she saw a group of majat along the walkway . . . the same or others; there was no knowing.

She faced forward again, wiped at her lips. She found herself sweating, shaken. The car whipped along too fast now for hazard: no passers-by could define them at their speed. The lights became a flickering blur.

No majat troubled the A4 ramp. And at the house there was no evidence of difficulty. Raen relaxed in her seat, glad, for once, of the sight of the beta police on guard at the gate. There was a track at a neighbor's: the furnishings were being removed. She regarded that bleakly, turned her head again as their own gate opened for them.

Merry took the car slowly up the drive, stopped under the portico and let them out, drove on to put the car in the garage, round the drive and under.

Warrior arrived around the corner of the house, through the narrow front-back access, Raen squinted in the light, anxious about any majat at the moment.

And Max opened the front door, let them both into the shade and coolness of the inner hall. "You're all right, sera?"

"All right," she confirmed. "Don't worry about it. Merry will tell you how it was."

Warrior stalked in, palps twitching.

"Do you scent greens?" Raen asked. "Greens attacked us. We killed some. They killed humans."

"Greensss." Warrior touched her nervously, calmed as she put her hand to its scent-patches, informing it. "Greenss make shift. Reds-golds-greens now. Weakest, greens. Easy to kill. Listen to red-Mind."

"Who listens, Warrior?"

"Always there. Warrior-Mind, redsss. I am apart. I am Warrior blue. Good you killed greens. Run away greens? Report?"

"Yes."

"Good?"

"They know I'm here now. Let them tell that to their hive."

"Good," Warrior concluded. "Good they taste this, Kethiuy-queen. Yess."

And it touched and stalked back outside.

Jim was standing over against the wall, his face strained. Raen touched his arm. "Go rest," she said.

And when he had wandered off to his own devices, she drew a deep breath, heard Merry coming in the side door—looked at Max. "No trouble at all while I was gone?"

He shook his head.

"A cold drink, would you?" She walked into the other room, on into the back of the house, toward the comp center.

Messages. The bank was full of them. The screen was flashing, as it would with an urgency.

She keyed in. The screen flipped half a dozen into her vision in rapid sequence. URGENT, most said. CALL DAIN.

One was different. I AM HERE, it said simply. P.R.H. *Pol.*

She sat down, stricken.

BOOK SEVEN

i

More reports. Chaos multiplied, even on Cerdin.

Moth regarded the stacks of printouts with a shiver, and then smiled, a faint and febrile smile.

She looked up at Tand.

"Have you made any progress toward the Istran statistics?"

"They're there, Eldest. Third stack."

She reached for them, suffered a fluttering of her hand which scattered them across the table: too little sleep, too little rest lately. She drew a few slow breaths, reached again to bring the papers closer. Tand gathered them and stacked them, laid them directly before her. It embarrassed and angered her.

"Doubtless," she said, "there are observations in some quarters that the old woman is failing."

From Tand there was silence.

She brushed through the papers, picked up the cup on the table deliberately to demonstrate the steadiness of her right hand . . . managed not to spill it, took a drink, set it down again firmly, her heart beating hard. "Get out," she said to Tand, having achieved the tiny triumph.

Tand started to go. She heard him hesitate. "Eldest," he said, and came back.

Near her.

"Eldest—"

"I'm not in want of anything."

"I hear rumors, Eldest." Tand sank on his knee at the arm of her chair; her heart lurched, so near he was. He

looked up into her face, with an earnestness surprising
in this man . . . excellent miming. "Listen to me, Eldest.
Perhaps . . . perhaps there comes a time that one ought
to quit, that one could let go, let things pass quietly.
Always there was Lian or Lian's kin; and now there's
you; and is it necessary that things pass this time by
your death?"

Bewilderment fell on her at this bizarre maneuver of
Tand Hald; and within her robes, her left hand held a
gun a span's remove from his chest. Perhaps he knew;
but his expression was innocent and desperately earnest.
"And always," she whispered in her age-broken voice,
"always I have survived the purges, Tand. Is it now? Do
you bring me warning?"

The last question was irony. Her finger almost pulled
the trigger, but he showed no apprehension of it. "Resign
from Council," he urged her. "Eldest, resign. Now. Pass
it on. You're feeling your years; you're tired; I see it . . .
so tired. But you could step aside and enjoy years yet,
in quiet, in peace. Haven't you earned that?"

She breathed a laugh, for this was indeed a strange
turn from a Hald. "But we're immortal," she whispered.
"Tand, perhaps I shall cheat them and not die . . . ever."

"Only if you resign."

The urgency in his voice was plain warning. Perhaps,
perhaps, she thought, the young Hald had actually conceived some softheartedness toward her. Perhaps all
these years together had meant something.

Resign Council; and let the records fall under more
critical eyes. Resign Council; and let one of their choice
have his hand to things.

No.

She gave a thin sigh, staring into Tand's dark and earnest eyes. "It's a long time since Council functioned without someone's direction. Who would take Eldest's place?
The Lind? He's not the man for this age. It would all
come undone. He'd not last the month. Who'd follow
him? The Brin? She'd be no better."

"You can't hold on forever."

She bit at her dry lips, and even yet the gun was on its target. "Perhaps," she said, allowing a tremor to her voice, "perhaps I should take some thought in that direction. I was so long, so many, many years at Lian's side before he passed; I think that I've managed rather well, have I not, Tand?"

"Yes, Eldest . . . *very* well."

"And power passed smoothly at Lian's death because I had been so long at his side. My hands were at the controls of things as often as his; and even his assassination couldn't wrench things out of order . . . because I was there. Because I knew all his systems and where all the necessary matters were stored. Resign . . . no. No. That would create chaos. And there are things I know—" Her voice sank to the faintest of whispers, "things I know that are life and death to the Family. My death by violence—or by accident—would be calamity. But perhaps it's time I began to let things go. Maybe you're right. I should take a partner, a co-regent."

Tand's eyes flickered with startlement.

"As I was with Lian . . . toward the last. I shall take a co-regent whoever presents the strongest face and the most solid backing. I shall let Council choose."

She watched the confusion mount, and kept a smile from her face.

"Young Tand," she whispered, "that is what I shall do." She waved her right hand, dismissing him; he seemed never to have realized where her left one was, or if he did, he had good nerves. He rose, gray and grim as iron now, all his polish gone. "I shall send out a message," she said, "convoking Council for tomorrow. You must carry it. You'll be my courier."

"Shall I tell the elders why?"

"No," she said, knowing that she would be disobeyed. "I'll present them the idea myself. Then they can have their time to choose. The transition of power," she said, boring with sudden concentration into Tand's dark eyes, "is always a problem in empires. Those which learn how to make the transfer smoothly . . . live. In general chaos who knows *who* might die?"

Tand stood still a moment. Moth gave him time to consider the matter. Then she waved her hand a second time, dismissing him. His departure was as deliberate and graceful as usual, although she reckoned what disturbance she had created in him.

And, alone, Moth bowed her head against her hands, trembling. The trembling became a laugh, and she leaned back in her chair in a sprawl, hands clasped across her middle.

Not many rulers had been privileged to be entertained by the wars of their own successions, she reckoned; and the humor of seeing the Hald and their minions blinking in the light with their cover ripped away, publicly *invited* to contend for power, while she still lived . . . That was worth laughter.

Her assassination had been prepared, imminent. Tand's action was puzzling . . . some strange affliction of sentiment perhaps, or even an offer relayed from the others; and with straight-faced humor she had returned the offer doubled. Of course they would kill her as soon as their choice was well-entrenched in power . . . but time . . . *time* was the important thing.

She grinned to herself, and the grin faded as she gathered up the falsified Istran reports, stacked them with the others.

The Meth-maren would have need of time.

To leave this place, Cerdin and Council and all of them, and have such a place as the old Houses had been, old friends, dead friends—that was the only retirement for which Moth yearned, to find again what had died long ago, those who had built—instead of those who used.

But one of the folders was the Meth-maren's, and Moth opened the record, stared morosely at the woman the child had become.

The data was random and the cross-connections inexplicable, and her old age grew toward mysticism, the only sanity . . . too much knowledge, too wide a pattern.

Lian also must have seen. He had complained of visions, toward the last, weakness which had encouraged assassins, and hastened his death.

He had died riveted in one of those visions, trembling and frothing, a horror that left no laughter at all in Moth.

She had had to do it.

"Eggs," Lian had cried in his dying, "eggs . . . eggs . . . eggs . . . eggs," as if recalling the beta children, the poor orphaned creatures, the parentless generation—the thousands growing up too soon, cared for en masse, assembly-lined into adulthood, men and women at ten, to care for others, and others . . . to bear natural children at permission, as they did all things at permission, forever. *Give them luxury,* Lian had said once. *Corrupt them, and we shall always control them. Teach them about work and rewards, and reward them with idleness and ambition. So we will always manage them.*

So betas, seeking idleness, created azi.

Eggs . . . eggs . . . eggs . . . eggs.

Eggs of eggs.

Moth shuddered, reliving the fissioning generations who had spawned all reality in the Reach.

Seven hundred years. From one world to many worlds, a rate of growth no longer controlled.

Eggs.

Potential.

I am the last, Moth thought, *who was once human. The last with humanity as it once was. Even the Meth-maren is not that.*

Least of all . . . that.

Eggs making eggs.

Family, she thought, and thought of an old saying about absolute power, and absolute corruption. *Only the azi,* she thought, *lack power. The azi are the only innocents.*

ii

Pol Hald sat down, propped his slim legs on a table, folded his hands and looked about him with a shrug of amusement.

Raen took the drink that Jim served her and leaned back, stared balefully as Pol accepted his and looked Jim up and down, drawing the obvious conclusions. Jim glanced down, an azi-reaction to such attention.

"Thank you, Jim," Raen said softly. For a very little she would have asked Jim to sit down and stay, but Pol was another matter than the ITAK board . . . cruel when he wished to be; and he often wished to be.

Jim vanished silently into the next room. Warrior did not. The majat sat in the corner next to the curio table, rigidly motionless as a piece of furniture.

"Beta-ish," Pol observed of the decor, of the whole house in general, a flourish of his hand. "You've a bizarre taste, Meth-maren. But the azi shows some discrimination."

"What are you doing here?"

Pol laughed, a deep and appealing chuckle. "It's been eighteen years since we shared a supper, Meth-maren. I had a mad impulse for another invitation."

"A far trip for little reward. Does Ros Hald's table not suffice?"

He had pricked at her. She nicked it back doubled, won a slight annoyance of him. That gaunt face had not changed with the years; he had reached that long stage where he would not. She added up numbers and reckoned at least over seventy. Experience. The gap was narrowed, but not by much.

"I've followed you for years," he said. "You're the only Meth-maren who ever amused me."

"You've done so very quietly, then. Did the Hald send you?"

"I came." He grinned. "You have a marvelous sense of humor. But your style of travel gave me ample time to catch up with you." He drank deeply and looked up again, set the glass down. "You know you've set things astir."

She shrugged.

"They'll kill you," Pol said.

"They?"

"Not I, Meth-maren."

"So why are you here?" she asked, mouth twisted in sarcasm. "To stand in the way?"

He made a loose gesture, looked at her from half-lidded eyes. "Meth-maren, I am jealous. You outdid me." He laughed outright. "I've studied to annoy Council for years, but I'll swear you've surpassed me, and so young, too. You know what you're doing here?"

She said nothing.

"I think you do," he said. "But it's time to call it off."

"Take yourself back to Cerdin, Pol Hald."

"I didn't come from Cerdin. I heard. I was willing to come out here. You're my personal superstition, you see. I don't want to see you go under. Get out of here. Now. To the other side of the Reach. They'll understand the gesture."

She rose. "Warrior," she said.

Warrior came to life, mandibles clashing, and reared up to its full height. Pol froze, looking at it.

"Warrior, tell me, of what hive is this Kontrin?"

"Green-hive," Warrior said, and boomed a note of majat language. "Green-hive Kontrin."

Pol moved his chitined right hand, a flippant gesture that was a satire of himself. "Am I to blame for the choice of hive? It's Meth-maren labs that set the patterns, that reserved blue for chosen friends . . . of which we were not."

"Indeed you were not."

Pol rose, walked to the window, walked back again, within reach of Warrior, deliberate bravado. "You're far beyond the limits. Do you know . . . do you understand what deep water you're into?"

"That my House died for others' ambitions? That something was set up two decades ago and no one has stopped it? How are they keeping it from Moth? Or are they?"

Pol's dark eyes flicked aside to Warrior, back to her. "I grow nervous when you become specific. I hope you'll consider carefully before you make any irrevocable moves."

"I learned, Hald. You taught me a lesson once. I've always held a remote affection for you on that account. No rancor. We said once we amused each other. Will you answer me now?"

He made a shrug of both hands. "I'm not in good favor among Halds. How could I know the answers you want?"

"But what you know you won't tell me."

"Moth has not long to live. That I know. For the rest of what I know: the Halds are your enemies . . . nothing personal, understand. The Halds want what Thel reached for."

"And no one has undone what Eron Thel did."

Pol made a gesture of helplessness. "I don't know; I don't know. I protest: I am not in their confidence."

It was possibly true. Raen kept watching the hands and the eyes, lest a weapon materialize. "I appreciate your concern, Pol."

"If you'd take my advice, get out of here . . . clear over to the far side, they would understand, Raen a Sul. They'd read that as a clear signal. Capitulation. Who cares? You'll outlive them if you guard your life. Running now is your only protection. My ship is onworld. I'd take you there. The Family wouldn't harm you. The Halds may not take me into their intimate confidence, but neither will they come at me."

She started to laugh, and saw Pol's face different from how she had ever know it, drawn and tense . . . no laughter, for one of a few times in his irreverent life.

"Go away," she said very softly. "Get yourself to that safety, Pol Hald. You'll survive."

He said nothing for a moment, looked doubtful. "What is it you have in mind?"

She did laugh. "I wonder, Pol Hald, if you don't surpass me after all. Maybe they did send you."

"I think you'll hear from the Family soon enough."

"Will I? Where's Morn, Pol?"

He shrugged. "I don't know. Cerdin, maybe. Or near these regions. It could be Morn. Or Tand. Or one of the Ren-barants. Or maybe none of them. When Moth falls, they'll pull your privileges, and then you'll be deaf, dumb and blind, grounded on Istra."

"Moth's on my side, is she?"

"She has been. I don't know who it will be. Truth. I

started from innerworlds when I was sure where you'd gone . . . when I knew for certain it wasn't a cover. Morn headed the other way. Tand moved inworlds, even earlier than that. He's likely with Moth. I'm handing you things that would break the Reach wide open *if* you called Moth."

"You're challenging me to do that?"

Again a shrug, a hint of mockery. "I'm betting the old woman knows a good part of it already."

"Or that it's already too late? It would take eight days for the shockwave to reach us."

"Possible," he said. "But not my reason."

"Then you believe I don't want the break right now. You could be mistaken."

Pol said nothing.

"You don't plan," Raen said in a hard voice, "to be setting up on Istra."

"I've a problem," Pol said. "If I go back, I'll be called in; and if I run alone . . . they'll know I heard something here that made it advisable. I've put myself in difficulty on your account, Meth-maren."

"If I believed any of it."

Pol made another of his elaborate gestures of offense. "I protest. I shall go back to my ship and wait until you think things over in a clearer mind. Someone else will come, mark me."

"Ah, I don't doubt that much. And help would be convenient. But likewise I remember the front porch at Kethiuy. You knew. You knew when you were talking to me. Didn't you?"

A profound sobriety came on Pol's face. He lowered his eyes, raised them steadily. "I knew, yes. And I left, with the rest of the Halds, before the attack. Revenge, Meth-maren, involving another generation. It had nothing to do with you."

"Now it does."

He had no answer for that. Neither did he flinch.

"This one's mine," she said. "I always had profound respect for your intelligence, Pol Hald. You were in Hald councils before I was born. You were alive when the

Meth-marens split, Sul from Ruil. You have contacts I don't. You've access to Cerdin. You've been staying alive and embarrassing Council twice my whole lifespan. You knew, back in Kethiuy. You're telling me now that you don't figure precisely what's in others' minds?''

Pol drew a long breath, nodded slowly, looking down. ''The plan was, you understand, to break out of the Reach. That was Thel's idea. To build. To breed. And it's all here on Istra, isn't it? You've put it together for yourself.''

''Enough to take it apart.''

''They'll kill you for sure. They'll drag Moth down and kill you before they let you expose their operation.''

''Their.''

''Their. I'm not in favor. I go my own way. As you do. I'll run when the time comes. I'll stay, while the mood takes me. Only you won't have that luxury. Is it worth this much, your vendetta?''

''It's beyond argument.''

He looked at Warrior, stared into the faceted eyes, glanced back with a faint touch of revulsion. ''Hive-masters. It's that, isn't it? Ruil Meth-maren tried to use the hives. And Thel wanted to use them. Look where that took us.''

''No one,'' she said, ''*uses* the hives. Hive-master was a Ruil word. Sul never used it. And Thon's still playing that dangerous game. Are red-hivers out again on Cerdin?''

''They make gifts to all the old contacts.''

Warrior's palps nicked nervously. ''Tact,'' it said.

Pol glanced that way in apprehension.

''Do you not understand the danger?'' Raen asked him. ''The hives don't have anything to gain . . . nothing Hald could want out of the exchange.''

''Azi,'' Pol said. ''They ask for more azi. For more land. More grain.''

''Hives grow,'' said Warrior. ''Hives here—grow.''

Raen looked on Warrior. Truth. It was clear truth. It fit with all the knowledge elsewhere gathered.

''Don't you understand?'' she appealed to Pol. Doesn't

Council? Who talked first of this expansion? Thel, Ruil . . . or red-hive?"

"Thel claimed unique partnership, claimed that even Drones could be brought into partnership with humans."

Her heart beat very fast. She laid her hand on one of Warrior's auditory palps, stroked it gently, gently. "O Pol. Don't they realize? Drones are the Memory. Humans can't touch that."

Pol shrugged, and yet his dark eyes were quick with worry. "The Meth-marens are dead. The hive-masters are dead, all but you. And Council doesn't have access to you, does it? Moth's kept saying that you were important."

"I'm flattered," she said hoarsely. "Hive-masters. Ruil deluded themselves. They were never hive-masters. They listened to the hives. Get out of here. Take your ship. Tell them they're all mad. I'll give you reasons enough to tell them."

He shook his head. "I wouldn't live to get there. And they wouldn't listen. Can't. It's gone too far. Moth will be dead by the time I could get there. Eight days, message-time or ship-time, at quickest. I couldn't—couldn't get there in time."

"And someone's on his way here."

"There's no way not."

Pol was talking clear sense. She continued to soothe Warrior, aware it was recording, aware of the nervous tremor of the palp against her hand. She felt it calm at last. "There are extensions of ITAK on the other continent. Are there blues with the other city, Warrior?"

"Yess. All hives, red, gold, green, blue. New-port."

"Same-Mind, Warrior?"

"Same-Mind."

"No queen."

"Warriorss. Workerss. From this-Hill."

She looked at Pol. "Suppose that I trusted you. Suppose that I asked you to do me a small favor. Have you your own staff?"

"Twelve azi. The ship is mine. My entire estate. I'm mobile. In these times it seems wise."

"I haven't an establishment on the other continent."

"You plan to take me out of the way."

"You can take West and be sure of the situation there in the matter of a day or two."

"You may not have that much time. They'll stop you. I mean that."

"Then it's wise that I cultivate *you,* isn't it? If they pull my authorizations you'll still have yours, won't you, Pol Hald?"

"You have a dazzling mutability. You'd rely on me?"

"One does what one must."

"You'd have my neck in the jaws with no compunction, wouldn't you?"

"I'm figuring you started from innerworlds first and farthest out. So there's a little time yet. You can do me that small service and still have time to run. And I'd run far, Pol. I would, in your place."

All posing fell aside. He stared at her. "I've told you something. I wish I understood the extent of it."

"The Halds should have asked my help. Or Moth should have. If they'd asked, I might have come." She gave Warrior's auditory palp a light brush, and Warrior turned its head, reacted in slight pleasure. "It's good to see you, Pol. I'd not say that of any of the rest of the Family, I assure you. My old acquaintances no longer interest me. The Family . . . no longer interests me. I've found here what you've been searching for all your life."

"And what do you take that to be, Raen a Sul?"

"The Edge. That which limits us."

"You don't have Ros Hald's ambitions."

She laughed, which was no laughter. "Mine are yours. To push until it gives. Here's the stopping-place. Beware red-hive. You understand me?"

"You have disquieted me."

"You never liked peace."

"What shall I look for in West?"

"Guard-azi. Buy up those you can. Ship them to East, to the Labor Registry. Arms as well."

"You're planning civil war."

She smiled again. "Tell the estate-holders in West . . . and ITAK there . . . to prepare for storm."

"How can I, when I don't know what you have in mind?"

"It's your choice. Go or stay."

"I know my choices, youngster."

"You'd better get yourself clear of this house, in any case. There'll be blue-hive thick about here in a little while, and that hand of yours is no guarantee of friendship. Get out of Newhope, in either direction you choose."

He put on a long face. "I'd thought of dinner, alas; and more things after."

"Later, Pol Hald. I confess you tempt me."

A twinkle danced in his eye, a favorite pose. "Then I'm not without hope. Alas, you've your azi for consolation, and I'm not without my own. Sad, is it not?"

"The time will come."

He bowed his head.

"You know my call number. It never changes."

"You know mine."

"Betas on Istra," she said, "have played the same dangerous game as Hald and Thon. Red-hive gives them gifts. I'll warrant red-hive walks where it will in West."

"I've no skill with majat."

"Keep it that way. Refuse to be approached. Shoot on the least excuse."

"Hazard," Warrior broke in, coming to life again. "Green-hive Drone, take care: danger. Red-hive kills humans, many, many, many. You are not green-hive Mind. No synthesis. None."

"What's it saying?" Pol asked. "I can never make sense of them."

"Perfect sense. It knows you're naïve of majat, and it warns you that without hive-friendship, green-hive chitin is no protection to you, even from greens. Red-hive and even greens have learned to kill intelligences. Red-hive has learned to make agreements with minds-that-die, and no longer has trouble with death. What's more . . . they've learned to *lie*. Consider the hive-Mind, Pol; consider that those who lie to majat have to be unMinded. But they can lie to humans without it . . . a profound discovery. Red-hive has gone as far from morality as majat can go. Hald and Thel and Thon helped . . . or otherwise. Get out of here. You've not much time. Be careful at the port. Are you armed?"

He moved his hands delicately. "Of course."

She offered her hand, warily; he took it, with a wry smile.

"I'll give you West," he said, letting go her hand. "Is that all you want?"

She grinned. "I'll be content with that." And soberly: "Keep within reach of your ship, Pol. It's life."

He took his leave, let himself out. In a moment she heard a car start and ease down the drive. She went to housecomp to open the gate, did so, picked him up briefly on remote. He cleared the gate and she closed it.

Warrior came, hovered at her shoulder. "This-unit heard things of other hives. Redsss. Trouble."

"This-unit is concerned, Warrior. This-unit begins to think that the hives know more than you've told me."

It drew back, jaws clicking. "Red-hive. Red-hive is—" It gave a booming and shrill of majat language. "No human word, Kontrin-queen. Long, long this red-hive, gold-hive—" Again the combination of sound, discord. "Red-hive is full of human-words: push-push-eggs-more-more."

"Expansion. They want expansion. Growth."

Warrior tried to assimilate that. It surely knew the words; they did not satisfy it.

"Synthesis," it said finally. "Red-hive messengers come. Many, many. Red-hive—easy, easy that messengers come. Kontrin permit. Goldss, yes. Greens, sometimes. Many, many, no blues."

"I know. But Kalind blue reached you. What did it tell you?"

"Kethiuy-queen . . . many, many, many messengers, reds, golds, greens. No blues. Blues have rested, not part

of push-push-push. No synthesis. Now blue messenger.
We taste Cerdin-Mind."

"Warrior. What was the message?"

"Revenge," Warrior said, which was the essence of
Kalind blue. And suddenly auditory palps flicked left.
"Hear. Others."

She shook her head. "I can't hear, Warrior. Human
range is small."

It was listening. "Blues, they say. Blues. They are coming. Many-many. Goodbye, Kethiuy-queen."

And it fled.

iii

The sun was almost below the horizon; it was no
longer necessary to wear cloaks or sunsuits or to fear for
the eyes. And the garden was alive with majat.

Raen kept Jim by her, constantly, and Max and Merry
as well, not trusting the nervous Warriors. She walked
the garden, making sure that Warriors saw their presence
clearly, to realize that they justly belonged there.

And suddenly others were there, rag-muffled figures,
swarming over the back garden wall among the Warriors;
and other majat accompanied them, smaller, with smaller
jaws: Workers, a horde of them.

Ragged human figures came to her and sought touch
with febrile hands and eyes visored even at dusk, and
their movements were strange, nervous. One and several
others unmasked, sought mouth-touch with Jim and Max
and Merry and danced away from their vicinity when
Raen bade them go.

"What are they?" Jim asked, horror in his voice.

"Don't worry for them," Raen said. "They belong to
the majat. They have majat habits." And seeing how all
three azi reacted to their majat counterparts: "Blue-hive
azi, go in, go inside the building, seek low-level and settle there."

"Yes," they said together, song-toned, and with that
mad-blind fix of hive-azi stares. They scampered off, to

seek the basement of the house, the dark places where they would be most at home.

Workers set to work without asking, began to pry up stones with their jaws, began to dig, through the pavings, into the moist earth.

And suddenly there was a buzz from the front gate.

Raen swore, waded off through the crowd of Warriors, beckoning Jim and Max and Merry to come with her. "Warrior," she shouted at the nearest. "Keep all majat out of sight behind the house. No enemies. No danger. Just stay here." And to Max and Merry: "Get down by the gate. I imagine that's the new azi coming in. You're in charge of them. See they don't wander loose. Get them in strict order and check them off against the invoice, by numbers, visually."

They hurried off at a run. She went inside with Jim as her shadow, unsealed the gate from the comp center when she saw the trucks by remote: they bore the Labor Registry designation. She kept watching, while the trucks disgorged azi and supplies, while Merry and Max called off numbers and ranged the men in groups of ten. The men stood; the boxes formed a square in the front garden. As each truck emptied, it pulled out, and when the last vehicle cleared the gate, Raen closed it and set the alarm again.

"They'll not like the majat at all," Raen said. "Jim, go find one of the quieter Warriors and ask it to come to the front of the house with you—alone. Better they see one before they see all of them."

He nodded and went. Raen put the outside lights on and went out the front door, walked out into the midst of the orderly groups, two hundred six men, by tens.

Max and Merry were checking numbers as she had said, a process the brighter lights made easier. Each was read, not by the stencil on the coveralls, but by the tattoo on the shoulder; and each man passed was directed into military order over by the portico. Neat, precise, the team of Max and Merry; and the two hundred were minds precisely like theirs . . . all too precisely, having come from the same tapes.

Every figure stiffened, looked houseward. Raen glanced and saw Jim with his unlikely shadow slow-stepping along in close company. "There are many such here," Raen said before panic could take hold. "*I* hold your contracts. I tell you that you're very safe with these particular majat. They'll help you in your duties, which are to protect this house. Understood?"

Each head inclined, the fix of their eyes now on her. Two hundred men. In the group were many who were duplicates, twin, triplet, quadruplet sets, alike even to age. There were two more Maxes and another Merry. They could accept. They would accept her and the majat as they would accept anything which held their contracts. It was their psych-set. Like Max and Merry, they fought only when they were directed, only when their contract-holder identified an enemy. But for their own lives, they would scarcely put up resistance. Did not. Until things were clear to them, they were docile. Warrior exercised curiosity about them, stalked down near them. They bore this: their contract-holder was present to instruct them if instructions were to be given.

Guard-function.

Specificity, Itavvy had called it.

"Warrior," she said, "come." And when it had joined her, with Jim shadowing, she soothed it with a touch and kept it by her, an act of mercy.

The process continued. But by one man both Max and Merry delayed, looked closely at the mark, disputed. "Sera," Max called.

The man bolted. Warrior moved. "No!" Raen yelled, but Warrior was deaf to that, auditory palps laid back, a blur of motion. Azi scattered.

But it was Max and Merry who had the fugitive; Raen raced through the chaotic midst, calmed the anxious Warrior. Jim stayed with her. Other azi stayed about, sober-faced, stunned, perhaps, that one of their number had done violence.

The azi in Max's grip stopped fighting, gazed past Raen's shoulder and surely understood what he had narrowly escaped. He was a man like the others, shaveheaded, gray-clad, a number stenciled on his coverall; but Merry pulled back the cloth from his shoulder and showed the tattoo as if there were something amiss.

"It's too dark, sera," Merry said. "Papers say twenty-nine, but the mark's bright."

The man's eyes shifted back to Raen, a face rigid with terror.

Such things had been done . . . a beta highly bribed, promised protection. "I'd believe a fluke of the dye," Raen said softly. "But not an azi who'd break and run. Who sent you?"

He gave no answer, but wrenched to free himself.

"Not an assassin," Raen said, though the hate in that face gave her pause to think so. "Betas don't go for that. Or—" she added, for the expression was nigh to madness, "maybe not beta at all. Are you?"

"He's little," Merry said, "for guard-type."

That was so too.

A smile took her, sudden surety. "Outsider. One of Tallen's folk."

It hit to the mark. The pale eyes shifted from hers.

"O man," she said softly. "To go to that extent . . . or did you know what you were getting into when you set that mark on yourself?"

There was no more resistance, none. In that moment she felt a touch of pity, seeing the young Outsider's desperation. Twenty-nine. He did not look that.

"What's your name?" she asked him.

"Tom Mundy."

"You *are* Tallen's. Easier with him, Max. I doubt he's here to do murder. I rather well think he realizes he's made a mistake. And I wonder if we haven't swept up something utterly by chance. Haven't we, Tom Mundy?"

"Let me go."

"Let him go, Max. But," she added at once as the young Outsider braced himself for escape, "you'll not make it across the City like that, Tom Mundy."

He looked as if he were on the brink of madness. Some shred of sense held him to listen.

"I'll *send* you to Tallen," she said, "without asking you

a thing. But if you'd like a drink and a place to sit down, while my people finish checking things out, it would be more convenient for us."

"Outsider-human," Warrior murmured in mingled tones.

The Outsider began to weep, tears running down his face; and would have sat down where he was, but that Jim and Merry took him in hand and led him up to the porch, to the door.

iv

There was at least for the time, quiet in the house—stirrings in the back, noises in the basement, but nothing visible in the main room.

And the azi who had been Tom Mundy sat on the couch clutching a drink in his hands and staring at the floor.

"I would like," Raen said softly, "one simple question answered, if you would." Jim was by her, and she indicated a place by her; Jim sat down, settled back with a disapproving look.

Mundy slowly lifted his head, apprehension on his face.

"How," Raen asked, "did you find yourself in such circumstances? Did you come to spy on me? Or did someone put you there?"

He said nothing.

"All right," she said. "I won't insist. But I'm guessing it looked like a means for information. And you made a mistake. A real azi number, real papers, guard-status: a spy could pick up a great deal of information that way, and no one would shut an azi away from communications equipment. I'd guess you make regular reports to Tallen, because no one would suspect you'd do such a thing. But it went wrong, I'm guessing."

He swallowed heavily. "You said that I could go."

"The car's being brought. Max and one of the others will deliver you to Tallen's doorstep—a surprise to him, perhaps. How long were you in those pits?"

"I don't know," he said hoarsely. "I don't know."

"You didn't plan coming here, then." She read the man's apprehensions and leaned back, shrugged off the question. "You'll get to Tallen alive, don't fear that. You'll come to no harm. How long have you been working on this world?"

Again an avoidance of her eyes.

"There are more of you," she said. "Aren't there?"

She obtained a distraught stare.

"Probably," she said, "I've bought more than one of you and haven't detected it. I own every guard-azi contract available on this continent. I'd sort you out if I could. You've been standing guard in ITAK establishments, gathering information, passing it along to Tallen. Of no possible concern to me. Actually I favor the enterprise. That's why I'm making a present of you to him. I'd advise you, though, *if* you know of others in that group, you tell me. There are others, aren't there?"

He took a drink, said nothing.

"Did you know what you were getting into?"

He wiped at his face and leaned his head on his hand, answer enough.

"Tell Tallen," she said, "I'll pull his men out if he'll give me the necessary numbers. I doubt you know them."

"I don't," he said.

"How did you end up in the Registry?"

"Took—took the place of an azi the majat killed. Tattoo . . . papers . . . a transport guard. Then the depots shut down. Company stopped operating. Been there—been there—"

"A long time."

He nodded.

A born-man, subjected to tapes and isolation. She regarded him pityingly. "And of course Tallen couldn't buy you out. An Outsider couldn't. Even knowing the numbers, he couldn't retrieve you. Did anyone think of that, before you let that number be tattooed on?"

"It was thought of."

"Do you fear us that much?" she asked softly. He avoided her eyes. "You do well to," she said, answering her own question. "And you know us. You've seen.

You've been there. Bear your report, Tom Mundy. You'll do well never to appear again in the Reach. If not for the strict quotas of export, you might have been—"

Her heart skipped a beat. She laughed aloud, and Tom Mundy looked at her in terror.

"Azi," she laughed. "Istra's primary export. Shipped everywhere." And then with apprehension, she looked on Jim.

"I am azi," Jim said, his own calm slightly ruffled. "Sera, I *am* azi."

She laid a hand on his arm. "There's no doubt. There's no doubt, Jim." There was the sound of a motor at the door. "That will be the car. Come along, ser Mundy."

Tom Mundy put the drink aside, preceded her to the door in evident anxiety. She followed out under the portico, where Max had the car waiting, Max standing by it.

"Max, seize him," Raen said.

Mundy sprang to escape; Max was as quick as the order, and fetched him up against the car, rolled with him to the pavement. Majat were at hand, Warriors. Jim himself made to interfere, but Raen put out a hand, restraining him.

Mundy struggled and cursed. Max shouted for human help, and several more azi arrived on the run.

It needed a struggle. "Don't harm him," Raen called out, when it began to look as if that would be the case; Mundy fought like a man demented, and it took a number of azi to put him down. Cords were searched up, all with a great deal of confusion. A shooting, Raen decided, watching the process, would have been far simpler; as it was the police at the gate wanted to intrude: she saw their lights down the drive, but the gate would keep them out, and she reckoned they would fret, but they would not dare climb a wall to investigate.

Mundy was held, finally, hands bound. He cursed and screamed until he was breathless, and lay heaving on the pavement. Max and another gathered him to his feet, and Raen stepped back as he spat at her.

"I'll keep my word," she said, "eventually. Don't try

me, Tom Mundy. The worst thing I could do is send you back. Isn't it?"

He stopped fighting then.

"How long have you been infiltrating?" she asked. "How many years?"

"I don't know. Would it make sense I'd know? I don't."

"Keep him under guard, Max. Don't take your eyes off him. One of the basement storerooms ought to be adequate. He won't *want* loose down there. Constant watch. See to it."

They drew him into the house, and through it. Raen lingered, looked at the disturbed Warriors, whose mandibles clicked with, nervousness. "Wrong-hive," she explained in terms they would understand. "Not enemy, not friend, wrong-hive. We will isolate that-unit. Pass this information. Warrior must guard that-unit."

They spent a moment analyzing those concepts, which were alien to the hive. A stranger should be ejected, not detained.

"That-unit will report if it escapes. We will let it go when it's good that it report."

"Yesss," they said together, comprehending, and themselves filed into the house, nightmare shapes in the Eln-Kests' hallway.

She started to go in, realized Jim was not with her, and turned back, saw him standing by the car, saw the blank horror on his face. She came back, took his hand. From inside the house came a scream of hysteria. She slipped her hand up to Jim's elbow; decided to walk round the long way, beneath the portico, past the corner, within the walkway to the back, where there was quiet.

"I *am* azi," Jim said.

She pressed his arm the more tightly. "I know so. I know so, Jim. Don't distress yourself. It's been a long, hard day."

She felt the tremor, wordless upset.

"The fall of the dice," she said, "was a fortunate thing for me. But what a place you've come to."

"I am azi."

"You do very well at it."

She walked with him out the arch into the back garden, into chaos, where guard-azi tried to set their supplies in order, where nervous Warriors stalked among humans and touched one and the other. It was pitiful that the azi did not object, that they simply stopped and endured, as no betas would have done, although they were surely afraid. Raen moved among them, sorted Warriors away from humans, nodded to Merry, who began hastily to motion his men into the shelter of the azi quarters. There was no hesitation among them.

The doors closed. Thereafter majat ruled in the garden, and majat azi scampered out the back door, naked, having shed their sun-protections, with their mad eyes and their cheerful grins, their ready acceptance of the touches of Workers and Warriors. They had come to help, and plunged quite happily into the excavations underway in the garden.

"They'll want feeding," Raen said. "They're our responsibility. Jim, go locate the domestics. Have them cook up enough for the whole lot. The majat azi will prefer boiled grain. There look to be about fifty of them."

Jim murmured agreement, and went, tired and shaken as he was. She watched him at the azi quarters gather up the six in question, watched him shepherd them across to the house, fending away the persistent majat azi. He managed. He managed well. She was able, for a moment, to relax . . . lingered, gazing on the shadow-forms of majat, the blue lights of the azi winking eerily in the shadowed places of the garden, where the tunnel was deepening.

"Worker," she said when one passed near her, "how far will the tunnel go?"

"Blue-hive," it said, which was answer, not inanity. A chill went over her skin. She surmised suddenly that there were tunnels begun elsewhere, an arm of the hive reached out into the city.

Mother accepted; Mother had ordered. The hive reached out to embrace them and protect. She wrapped her arms about her, found the lights shimmering in her vision.

There was a freshness in the air, of moisture and evening. A little drop fell on her arm and she looked up, at a sky mostly clouded. There was another rain coming. It would hardly trouble the majat, or their azi.

She wandered inside finally, as domestic azi came out, bearing foodstuffs, hastening for fear of the majat, to the kitchens in the azi quarters.

One remained in the house kitchen, under Jim's direction, preparing a different meal. "Thank you," Raen said to them both; she could have eaten azi porridge without compunction, so tired she was; but she was glad when a good dinner was set before her and Jim took his place at the end of the table.

The hive was about her. The song began. She could hear it in the house, illusory and soft as the rainfall, as old dreams.

Then she thought of the basement, and the cup hesitated at her lips; she drank, and began reckoning of other things.

Of Itavvy, and promises; of Pol Hald; of Tallen.

Of the Family.

There were messages upon messages. Comp spat them out in inane profusion; and she sat and searched them, the while thunder rumbled overhead.

One was ser Dain. MY HUMBLEST APOLOGIES. THE ARTIST IS SER TOL ERRIN, 1028D UPCOAST. There was more, mostly babble. She rubbed her eyes, took a sip of coffee, and entered worldcomp to pull a citizen number, to link it with another program.

One was Pol Hald. NEWPORT IS DISMAL. MY SUFFERING IS EXTREME. REJOICE.

She drank more coffee, sulking into the rhythms of the majat song which ran through the house, nerved herself for intercomp. The dataflow never stopped, world to station, station to station, station to world, jumping information like ships from point to point. Data launched could not be recalled.

She called up the prepared program regarding contracts, and export quotas, the oft-denied permits.

GRANTED, she entered, to all of them.

In an hour the board would be jammed with queries, chaos, the deadlock broken. Cerdin would not know it for eight days.

She called up the city guest house, and drew a sleepy Outsider out of bed. "Call Tallen," she said, using her own image and direct voice, which she had not used on Istra.

Tallen appeared quickly, his person disordered, his face flushed. "Kont' Raen," he said.

"I've an azi," she said, "who knows you. His name is Tom Mundy."

Tallen started to speak, changed his mind. Whatever of sleep there was about him vanished.

"He's not harmed," she said. "Won't be. But I want to know how long this has been going on, ser Tallen. I want an answer. How much and how many and how far?"

"I'll meet with you."

She shook her head. "Just a plain answer, ser. Monitored or not. How far has the net spread itself?"

"I have no desire to discuss this long-distance."

"Shall I ask Mundy?"

Tallen's face went stark. "You'll do as you please, I imagine. The trade mission—"

"Is under Reach law. Kontrin law. I do as I please, yes. He's safe for the moment. I'll give him back to you, so you needn't do anything rash. I merely advise you that you've done a very unwise thing, ser. Give me those numbers and I'll do what I can to sort things out for you; you understand me. I can act where you can't. I'm willing to do so . . . a matter of humanity. Give me the numbers."

Tallen broke contact.

She had feared so. She shook her head, swallowed down a stricture in her throat with a mouthful of cooling coffee, finally turned housecomp over to automatic.

She drank the rest of the coffee, grimacing at the taste,

followed it with half a measure of liquor, and sat listening to the thunder.

"Sera," Jim said, startling her. She glanced at the doorway.

"Go to bed," she told him. "What about the azi downstairs? Settled?"

He nodded.

"Go on," she said. "Go rest. You've done what you can."

He was not willing to leave; he did so, and she listened as his footsteps went upstairs. She sat still a moment, listening to the hive-song, then rose and went downstairs, into the dark territory of the basement.

Majat-azi gathered about her. She bade them away, suffered with more patience the touch of Workers and Warriors. There was a door guarded by Warriors. She opened it, and two guard-azi rose to their feet, from the chairs inside. The third huddled in the corner, on a mat of blankets.

"I've spoken with Tallen," she said. "He's very upset. Is there anything I can get for your comfort?"

A jerk of the head, refusal. He would not look at her face. They had taken the cords off him. There was the double guard to restrain him.

"You were a transport guard. Were you sensible enough to understand that what you're seeing on this world is not the usual, that things have gone vastly amiss?"

Still he would say nothing, which in his place, was the wiser course.

She sank down, rested her arms across her knees, stared at him. I'll hazard a guess, ser 113-489-6798, that all you've done has been a failure: that Tallen would have known *me* had it succeeded. You've scattered azi off this world, if at all, only to have the embargo stall them, if not here, on Pedra, on Jin. And do you know where they'll be? In cases similar to your own. You entered that faculty when the depots were closed . . . about half a year ago. What do you think will become of those stalled there for years, as some are—two years already, for some? What do you think will come out of that? You think they'll be sane? I doubt it. And how many azi have access to transmission of messages via intercomp? None, ser. You've thrown men away. Like yourself."

Eyes fixed on hers, hollow, in a shaven skull. Thin hands clasped knees against his chest. He would never, she thought, be the man he would have been. Youth, cast away in such a venture. More than one of them. He might break. Most would, if majat asked the questions. But she much doubted that he knew anything beyond himself.

"Majat," she said, "killed the azi you replaced. Was that a hazard, running the depots?"

"They're all over," he said hoarsely. "Farms—armed camps for fear of them."

Cold settled on her at that. She nodded. "Ever see them in the open?"

"Once. Far across the fields. We drove out of it, fast as we could."

"What do you suppose they would do?"

"There'd been trucks lost. They'd find the tracks. Nothing else."

She nodded slowly. "It fits, ser Mundy. It does fit. Thank you. Rest now. Get some sleep. You'll not be bothered. And I'll get you back to Tallen in one piece if you'll stay in this room. Please don't try my guards. A scratch from a majat is deadly as a bite. But they won't come into this room."

She rose, left, walked out among the Warriors. The door closed behind her. She singled out one of the larger ones, touched it, soothed it. "Warrior, many azi, many, in blue-hive? Weapons?"

"Yes."

"The hives have taken azi, taken food?"

There was a working of mandibles, a little disturbance at this question. "Take, yesss. Red-hive takes, goldss take, greens take, blue-hive, yessss. Store much, much. Mother says *take, keep, prevent other-hives.*"

"Warrior, has blue-hive killed humans?"

"No. Take azi. Keep."

"Many azi?"

"Many," Warrior agreed.

V

Jim sat on the bed, massaged his temples, tried to still the pounding in his skull. *Never panic; never panic. Stop. Think. Thinking is good service. It is good to serve well.*

He seldom recalled the tapes verbatim. The thoughts were simply there, inwoven. This night he remembered, and struggled to remember. He was unbearably tired. Strange sights, everything strange—he trembled with the burden of it.

The other Kontrin had gone, that at least, away around the world; but the majat would not go, nor this flood of azi. He remained unique: he sensed this, clung to it.

He had *here,* and the others did not. He had this room, this place he shared with her, and the others did not.

He rose finally, and went through all the appropriate actions, born-man motions, for although the *Jewel* had rigid rules about cleanliness, there had been no facilities such as these, even in upper decks. He showered, coated himself liberally with soap, once, twice, three times . . . in sheer enjoyment of the fragrance, so unlike the bitter detergent that had come automatically through the azi-deck system, stinging eyes and noses. He worked very hard at his personal appearance: he understood it for duty to *her,* to match all these fine things she had, the use of which she gave him; and *she* was the measure of all the wide world through which she drew him. He had seen rich men, powerful men, in absolute terror of her; and majat who feared her and majat who obeyed her; and another Kontrin who treated her carefully; and he himself was closest to her, an importance as heady as wine. On the ship he had been terrified by the reaction of others to her; he had not known how it would be to live on the other side of it, shielded within it.

He was *in* the house, and others were not. He had seen new things, the details of which were still a muddle to him, most even without words to call them or recall them, without comparisons to which to join them, only some that her tapes had given him. He had been with her in places far more important than even those powerful rich men had been, that society which drifted through the salon of the *Jewel,* offering snippets of their lives to his confused inspection, a stream dark before and dark after. He had gone out, into that unimaginable width in which born-men lived, and *she* was there, so that he was never lost.

He had stood back over the pens, which he had half-forgotten, as all that time before the *Jewel* was confused in his memory, hard to touch from the present, for it had been so empty, so void of detail. Today he had looked down, as he had looked down in earlier times, and known that he was not on his way back from exercise, to return again to the pens and the half-world of the tapes breathing through his mind. This time he had come to look, and to walk away again, at *her* back, until the stink purged itself into clean air and light. There was no fear of that place again, forever.

She prevented.

She was there, in the night, in the dark, when his dreams were of being alone, within the walls, and only the white glare of spotlights above the tangled webs of metal, the catwalks . . . when one huddled in the corner, because the walls were at least some touch, somewhere to put one's back and feel comforted. On the azi-deck everyone slept close, trying to gain this feeling, and the worst thing was being Out, and no one willing to touch. Being Out had been the most terrible part of the long voyage here, when he had borne the Kontrin like a mark on him, and no one had dared come near him. But she did . . . and more than that, more even than the few passengers who had engaged him for a night or even a short voyage, several with impulses to generosity and one that he tried never to remember . . . she stayed. The rich folk had let him touch, had shown him impressions of experiences and luxury and other things forever beyond an azi's reach; each time he would believe for a while in the existence of such things, in comfort beyond the blind nestlings-together on the azi-deck. *Love,* they would say; but then the rich folk would go their way, and his contract rested with the ship forever, where the only lasting warmth was that of all azi, whatever one could gain by doing one's work and going to the mats at night. In with everyone, nestled close.

Then there was Raen. There was Raen, who was all these things, and who had his contract, and who was therefore forever.

Warm from the shower he lay down between the cool sheets, and thought of her, and stared at the clouds which flickered lightnings over the dome, at rain, that spotted the dome and fractured the lightnings in runnels.

He had no liking for thunder. He had never had, from the first that he had worked his year in Andra's fields, before the *Jewel.* He liked it no better now. Nonsense ran through his head, fragments of deepstudy. He recited them silently, shuddering at the lightnings.

> *To some eyes, colors are invisible;*
> *To others, the invisible has many colors.*
> *And both are true. And both are not.*
> *And one is false. And neither is.*

He squeezed shut his eyes, and saw majat; and the horrid naked azi, the bearers of blue lights; and an azi who was no azi, but a born-man who had gone mad in the pens, listening to azi-tapes. The lights above the pens had never flickered; sounds were rare, and all meaningful.

The lightning flung everything stark white; the thunder followed, deafening. He jumped, and lay still again, his heart pounding. Again it happened. He was ready this time, and did not flinch overmuch. He would not have her to know that he was afraid.

She delayed coming. That disturbed him more than the thunder.

He slept finally, of sheer exhaustion.

He wakened at a noise in the room, that was above the faint humming of the majat Raen was there; and she did not go to the bath as she had on the nights before, but moved about fully dressed, gathering things quietly together.

"I'm awake," he said, so that she would not think she had to be quiet.

She came to the bed and sat down, reached for his hand as he sat up, held it. The jewels on the back of hers glittered cold and colorless in the almost-dark. Rain still spattered the dome, gently now, and the lightnings only rarely flickered.

"I'm leaving the house," she said softly. "A short trip, and back again. You're safest here on this one."

"No," he protested at once, and his heart beat painfully, for *no* was not a permitted word. He would have made haste to disengage himself from the sheets, to gather his own belongings as she was gathering hers.

She held his arm firmly and shook her head. "I need you here. You've skills necessary to run this house. What would Max do without you to tell him what to do? What would the others do who depend on his orders? You're not afraid of the majat. You can manage them, better than some Kontrin."

He was enormously flattered by this, however much he was shaking at the thought. He knew that it was truth, for she said it.

"Where are you going?" he asked.

"A question? You amaze me, Jim."

"Sera?"

"And you must spoil it in the same breath." She smoothed his hair from his face, which was a touch infinitely kind, taking away the sting of her disappointment in him. "I daren't answer your question, understand? But call the Tel estate if you must contact me. Ask comp for Isan Tel. Can you do that?"

He nodded.

"But you do that only in extreme emergency," she said. "You understand that?"

He nodded. "I'll help you pack," he offered.

She did not forbid him that. He gathered himself out of bed, reached for a robe against the chill of the air-conditioning. She turned the lights on, and he wrapped the robe about himself, pushed the hair out of his eyes and sought the single brown case she asked for.

In truth she did not pack much; and that encouraged him, that most of her belongings would remain here, and she would come back for them, for him. He was shivering violently, neatly rearranging the things she threw in haphazardly.

"There's no reason to be upset," she said sharply. "There's no cause. You can manage the house. You can trust Max to keep order outside, and you can manage the inside."

"Who's going with you?" he asked, thinking of that suddenly, chilled to think of her alone with new azi, strange azi. "Merry and a good number of the new guards. They'll serve. We're taking Mundy, too. You won't have to worry about him. We'll be back before anything can develop."

He did not like it. He could not say so. He watched her take another, heavier cloak from the closet. She left her blue one. "These azi," he said, "these—*strange* azi—"

"Majat azi."

"How can I talk to them?" he exclaimed, choked with revulsion at the thought of them.

"They speak. They understand words. They'll stay with the majat. They *are* majat, after a fashion. They'll fight well if they must. Let the majat deal with their own azi; tell Warrior what you want them to do."

"I can't recognize which is which."

"No matter with majat. Any Warrior is Warrior. Give it taste and talk to it; it'll respond. You're not going to freeze on me, are you? You won't do that."

He shook his head emphatically.

She clicked her case shut. "The car's ready downstairs. Go back to bed. I'm sorry. I know you want to go. But it's as I said: you're more useful here."

She stared away.

"Raen." He forced the word. His face flushed with the effort.

She looked back. He was ashamed of himself. His face

was hot and he had no control of his lips and he was sick at his stomach for reasons he could not clearly analyze, only that one felt so when one went against Right.

"A wonder," she murmured, and came back and kissed him on the mouth. He hardly felt it, the sickness was so great. Then she left, hurrying down the stairs, carrying her own luggage because he had not thought in time to offer. He went after her, down the stairs barefoot . . . stood useless in the downstairs hall as she hastened out into the rainy dark with a scattering of other azi.

Majat were there, hovering near the car with a great deal of booming and humming to each other. Max was there; Merry was driving. There were vehicles that did not belong to the house, trucks which the other azi boarded, carrying their rifles. Merry turned the car for the gate and the trucks followed.

Max looked at him. He thrust his hands into the pockets of his bathrobe and looked nervously about. "Everything goes on as usual," he told Max. "Guard the house." And he went inside then, closed the door after him, . . . saw huge shapes deep in the shadows, the far reaches of the hall, heard sounds below.

He was alone with them. He crossed the hall toward the stairs and one stirred, that could have been a piece of furniture. It clicked at him.

"Be still," he told it, shuddering. "Keep away!"

It withdrew from him, and he fled up the stairs, darted into the safety of the bedroom.

One had gotten in. He saw the moving shadow, froze as it skittered near him, touched him. "Out!" he cried at it. "Go out!"

It left, clicking nervously. He felt after the light switch, trembling, fearing the dark, the emptiness. The room leapt into stark white and green. He closed the door on the dark of the hall, locked it. There were noises downstairs, scrapings of furniture, and deeper still, at the foundations. He did not want to know what happened there, in that dark, in that place where the strange azi were lodged.

He was human, and they were not.

And yet the same labs had produced them. The tapes . . . were the difference. He had heard the man Itavvy say so: that in only a matter of days an azi could be diverted from one function to another. A born man put in the pens had come out shattered by the experience.

I am not real, he thought suddenly, as he had never thought in his life. *I am only those tapes.*

And then he wiped at his eyes, for tears blinded him, and he went into the bath and was sick, protractedly, weeping and vomiting in alternation until he had thrown up all his supper and was too weak to gather himself off the floor.

When he could, when he regained control of his limbs, he bathed repeatedly in disgust, and finally, wrapped in towels, tucked up in a knot in the empty bed, shivering his way through what remained of the night.

vi

The freight-shuttle bulked large on the apron, a dismal half-ovoid on spider legs, glistening with the rain, that puddled and pocked the ill-repaired field and reflected back the floodlights.

There were guards, a station just inside the fence. Raen ordered the car to the very barrier and received the expected challenge. "Open," she radioed back, curt and sharp. "Kontrin authorization. And hurry about it."

She had her apprehensions. There could be delays; there could be complications; ITAK could prove recalcitrant at this point. The azi with her were untried, all but Merry. As for Mundy, in the truck behind . . . she reckoned well what he would do if he could.

The gates swung open. "Go," she told Merry.

Her own aircraft, guarded by ITAK, was at the other end of the port. She ignored it, as she had always intended to ignore it, simply giving ITAK a convenient target for sabotage if they wished one.

It was the shuttle she wanted. Beta police and a handful of guard-azi were not sufficient to stop her, if her own azi kept their wits about them.

Shuttle-struts loomed up in the windshield. Merry braked and half-turned, and the truck did so too, hard beside them. Raen contacted the station again. "Have the shuttle drop the lift," she ordered. There were guards pelting across the apron toward them, but her own azi were out of the track, forming a hedge of rifles, and that advance slowed abruptly.

Evidently the call went through. The shuttle's freight lift lowered with a groaning of hydraulics that drowned other sound, a vast column with an open side, lighted within.

"Crew is not aboard," she heard over the radio. "Only ground watch. We can't take off. We're not licensed—"

"Merry," she said, ignoring the rest of it. "Get a squad aboard and take controls. Have them call crew and ground service to get this thing off, and take no argument about it. Shoot as last resort . . . move! My azi," she said into the microphone, "will board. No resistance and there'll be no damage."

Merry had bailed out of the car and gathered the nearest squad. She opened the door, the gun in one hand, microphone in the other. Other figures exited the track, dragging one who resisted: Mundy; stilt-limbed ones followed. The police line disordered itself, steadied.

"Kontrin," a voice said over the radio, "please. We are willing to cooperate."

Rain blew in the open door of the car, drenched her, slanted down across the floodlights, hazing the stalemated lines, Mundy fought and cursed, disturbing the momentary silence: nuisance, nothing more. Police would not move for so slight a cause, not against a Kontrin; policy would work on higher levels.

There was a sound of machinery inside the open cargo lift: the lights were extinguished . . . Merry's orders. They would make no targets.

Shadows passed the car: the three Warriors skittered

over the wet pavement and into the lift, following their own sight, that cared nothing for darkness.

No one moved. An inestimable time later she heard Merry's voice over the radio advising her they had the ship.

She left the car. "By squads," she shouted. "Board!"

She went with the first, that drew Mundy along with them—reached the dark security of the lift. Mundy screamed at the police, a voice swiftly muffled again. The next ten started their retreat.

"Be still," she said, annoyed by continued struggles from the Outsider. "They'll do nothing for you. Don't try my patience."

The last squad was coming in, rifles still directed at the police. Her attention was fixed on that. And suddenly there was another truck coming. She expelled a long breath of tension, held it again as the truck scattered bewildered police, as it came straight for the cargo lift and jolted up within, rain-wet and loud, the azi with her dodging it. More of her men poured from it, dragging prisoners.

Tallen. They had got him, and all his folk. She found her heart able to beat stably again, and shouted orders as the track backed out again. It almost clipped the hatch, missed. The azi driver bailed out while it was still moving and raced for the hatch, pelted aboard.

She hit the close-switch, and the lift jolted up, taking them up, while the ITAK police gazed at the diminishing view of them. Just at total dark, she hit the lights, and looked over the azi and the Warriors and the shaken prisoners.

"Ser Tallen," she said, and nodded toward Tom Mundy, who had no joy to see his own people. Pity took her, for Mundy turned his face away as far as he could, and when she bade Tallen released to see to him, Mundy wanted only to turn away, a shaven ghost in gray.

"You're going home." she said to Tallen. She had no time for other things. She gave brief orders to an older azi, setting him in charge, and set herself in the personnel lift, rode it up to more immediate problems.

A nervous pointing of weapons welcomed her above; she waved them aside and looked past Merry to the watch crew, who huddled under the threat of guns, way from controls, in the small passenger compartment.

"Kontrin," the officer-in-charge said, and rose: the azi let him. He was, she noted, ISPAK, not ITAK. "We've done everything requested."

"Thank you. Come forward, ser, and run me some instrument checks; I suppose that you can do that, until the crew shows."

The ISPAK beta wiped at his face and came with her, well-guarded, showed her the functioning of the board; it was exceedingly simple, lacking a number of convenient automations. Outside, there was the ministration of ground-service. That, she reflected, simply had to be trusted: one simply minimized the chances.

She settled into the nearest of the cushions, folded her arms and closed her eyes as the first touch of dawn began to show, for she was robbed of sleep this night, and she reckoned that this frightened beta would hardly risk anything with so many armed azi at her back.

Then crew arrived, with a flurry of distressed calls to the bridge; they were no more relaxed by the time they had negotiated the personnel lift, past the azi below and the Warriors with them, and into the upper level to the welcome of Merry's armed squad.

"Just do your job," Raen advised them. They settled in, speaking only in fragments and that when they must. "We're not scheduled," was the captain's only protest. "We may not have a berth up there."

"We'll get one," Raen said. She reached for the com switch herself, requested lift clearance, obtained it, priority. If traffic was in the way, it would be diverted or aborted. The shuttle's engines were in function; it settled earthward as its stilts drew in, and engaged its moving-gear, trundled ponderously out toward the lifting area.

"Merry," she asked of the passenger area. "All right back there?"

"Yes, sera."

"Have Tallen up after lift. Strict security on the rest."

They were entering position, wings extruding, gathering speed. Then wings locked, and they made their run. "Use the handholds," she remembered to snap at the azi still standing, and they left the ground, under heart-dragging acceleration.

Pol, she thought in that vulnerable moment, Pol was onworld, ship-based—could down a shuttle if he would, if she had guessed wrong; and there was ISPAK to contend with. She doubted then, whether she should not have gone back to ISPAK at once, taken it first, instead of delaying onworld.

But there was also blue-hive. Principally, there was blue-hive.

They passed the worst of lift, launched on an angled ascent that would carry them at last to intercept with station. The deck would slant for the duration. "Rest," she bade the standing azi, lest they tire, "half at a time. Sit down." They settled, by their own way of choosing, but all kept weapons ready, and held to the safety grips, for the sensation of flight was new to them.

The lift had activated: she saw the indication on the board, and left her cushion, negotiated her way back to it.

Tallen. An armed azi escorted the man, and waited while he caught the handhold and exited the lift . . . no pleasant sensation, the personnel lift during flight, and the man was old—not as Kontrin aged, Raen thought sorrowfully, but as betas did. It was sad to understand.

"Apologies, ser," she welcomed him. "Are your folk all right?"

"Our rooms raided, ourselves handled as we were—"

"Apologies," she said in a cold voice. "But no regrets. You're off Istra. You're alive. Be grateful, ser."

"What's going on?"

"There are very private affairs of the Reach involved here, ser Outsider." She gestured him into the corner by the passenger compartment, where they could stand more comfortably, and waited until he had braced himself. "Listen to me: you were not well-advised to have cut off my warning. You've Mundy back; you've information, for what it's worth. But you've killed the others. You understand that. It's too late for them. Listen to me now, and save something. Your spies have not been effective, have they?"

"I don't know what you're talking about."

"You do, ser. You do. And the only protection you have is myself, ser. The betas surely can't offer you any, whatever their assurances to the contrary."

"Betas."

"Betas. Beta generation. The children of the labs, ser. The plastic civilization."

"The eggs." Comprehension came to his eyes. "The children of the eggs."

"They're set up to obey. We've conditioned them to that. Do you understand the pattern you see now? Your spies haven't helped you. You've dropped them into the vast dark, ser, and they're gone, swallowed up in the Reach."

"These—" he looked about him at the guards. "These creatures—"

"Don't," she said, offended. "Don't misname them. The azi are quite as human as the betas, ser. And unlike the betas, they're quite aware they're programmed. They've no illusions, but they deserve respect."

"And you go on creating them. You've pushed a world to the breaking point. Why?"

"I think you suspect, ser Tallen; and yet you go on feeding them. No more. No more."

"Be clear, Kont' Raen."

"You've understood. You've been gathering all the majat goods we and the betas can sell you, swallowing them up, shipping them out. Warehousing them—against a time of shortage, if you've been wise, taking what you could get while you could get it. But to do that, you've been doing the worst thing you could have done. You've been feeding the force that means to expand out of the Reach. And worse, ser, much worse—you've been feeding the hives. This generation for industrialization, the next for the real move. And you've fed it."

He turned a shade yet paler than he had been. "What do you propose, Kont' Raen?"

"Shut down. Shut down trade for a few years. Now. The Reach can't support these numbers. The movement will collapse under its own weight."

"What's your profit in telling us?"

"Call it internal politics."

"It's mad. How do we know what authority you have to do this?"

She lifted a hand toward the azi. "You see it. I could have handled this otherwise. I could have pulled licenses. But that wouldn't have told you why. I am telling you now. I mean what I say, ser: that your continued trade is supplying a force that will try to break out of the Reach. That a few years of deprivation will destroy that hope and make a point to them. We're not without our vulnerabilities. Yours is the need for what we alone supply. But you've been oversupplied in these last few years. You can survive a time of shut-down. I assure you you can't come in and *take* these things: trying to take them would destroy the source of them . . . or worse things . . ." She looked directly into his eyes. "You would stand where we do, and be what we are."

"How can I carry a report to my authorites based on one person's word? There's another of your people in Istra. We've heard. This could be an attempt to prevent our contacting—"

"Ah, he'd tell you differently, perhaps. Or perhaps he'd shrug and say do as pleased you. *His* reasons you'd not understand at all."

"You play games with us. Or maybe you have other motives."

"Invade us. Come in with your ships. Fire on betas and innocent azi, break through, to Cerdin and take all that we have. Then where will you be? The hives won't deal with minds-that-die; no, they'll lead you in directions you don't anticipate. I give you a hive-master's advice, ser, that I've withheld from others. Is it not so, that your desperation is because you need us? Your technology relies on what we produce? And do we not serve well? You're safe, because we know well what we do. Now a hive-master says: stop, wait, danger, and you take it for deception."

"Get my agents out."

She shook her head. "It's too late. I've given you warning. A decade or two, ser. An azi generation. A time of silence. Believe me now. We'll get you to your ships. A chance to run, to get out of here with what lives I can give you."

He stared at her. The ship was already coming into release from Istra's gravity, and there was a feeling of instability. She beckoned him toward the lift.

"Believe me," she said. "It's the only gift I can give. And whatever you do, you'd best get down to your people, ser Tallen. They'll wonder. They'll need your advice. See it's the right advice. My men will let you free, and you'll do what you please on that dock."

Tallen gave her a hard and long look, and sought the lift; the guard went with him.

Raen hand-over-handed her way back to the cushion, scanned instruments, looked at the crew. "Put us next the Outsider ships. If we need to clear a berth, we'll do that."

The captain nodded, and she settled, arms folded, with station communications beginning to hurl frantic questions at them.

vii

"It's settled," the Ren-barant said.

The Hald looked about him in the swirl of brightly clad heads of septs and Houses, and at the Thel, the Delt, the Ilit and others of the inner circle. Here were the key votes, the heads of various factions. They went armed into Council, remembering Moth, remembering another day. Ros Hald felt more than a touch of fear.

"I don't trust the old woman," the Ilit said. "I won't feel easy until this is past." His eyes darted left and right, his voice lowered. "This could as easily be a way to identify us, eliminate the opposition. We could go the way the others did, even yet."

"No," Ros Hald said fiercely. "No. Easiest of all if she gives over the keys we need. She'll do that. She's buying living time and she knows it."

"Then she knows other things too," said the Delt.

Hald thought of that, as he had thought of it a hundred times, and saw no other course. The others were filing into the Council chamber. He nodded to his companions and went.

The seats were filled, one by one, with nervous men and women, heirs of the last purge.

Doubtless there were many weapons concealed now, within robes of Color of House and sept.

But when Moth entered, and all those present rose in respect—even the Hald and his faction rose, because respect cost nothing—she had Tand for her support and seemed incredibly frail. Before now, she had doddered somewhat; now she had difficulty even lifting her head to speak before Council.

"I don't trust this," the Ren-barant whispered, fell silent at the press of the Hald's hand.

"I have come to a difficult decision," Moth began, and rambled on about the weight of empire and the changes in the Council, which had cast more and more weight on First Seat, which had made of her the dictator she avowed she would not be, that none of them had meant to be.

Her voice faltered and faded often. The Council listened with rare patience, though none of this was at all surprising, for Tand and rumor had spread her intent throughout the Family, even into factions which would not have been powerful enough to have their own spies. There could not be a representative present that did not know the meaning of this meeting.

She spoke of the hives, ramblings of which they were even yet patient.

And suddenly she began to laugh, so that more than one hand in the hall felt after a weapon and her life hung on a thread; but her own two hands were in sight, and one had to wonder who her agents were and where they might be positioned.

"The hives, my friends, my cousins—the hives have come asking and offering now, have they? And the hive-masters divided on the question, and now they're gone. I'm tired. I am tired, cousins. I see what you don't see, what no one else is old enough to see, and no one cares to see." She looked about, blinking in the glare of lights, and Ros Hald tensed, wondering about weapons. "Vote," she said. "You've come here ready, have you not, already prepared, not waiting on me? Not waiting for long debate? You've been ready for years. So vote. I'm going to my chambers. Tell me which of you will share responsibility for the Family. I'll accept your choice."

There was a murmur, and silence; she looked about at them, perhaps surprised by that silence, that was a touch of awe. And in that silence, Moth turned off the microphone, and walked up the steps among them, slowly, on Tand's arm, in profound stillness.

Ros Hald rose. So did Ren-barant, and Ilit, and Serat and Dessen and all the many, many others. For a moment, at the top of the stairs, Moth stopped, seeming to realize the gesture, and yet did not turn to see. She walked out, and the door closed. The standing heads of House and sept sank down again into seats. The silence continued a moment.

Next-eldest rose and declared the matter at hand, the nomination of one to stand by Moth, successor to Moth's knowledge and position. The dictatorship which had become fact without acknowledgment under Lian's last years, became acknowledged fact now, with Moth's request for a legal heir.

Ren-barant rose to put forward the name of Ros Hald.

There was no name put in opposition. A few frowned, huddled together. Ros Hald marked them with his eyes, the next group that would try for power in the Family, the next that needed watching. Four Colors were not represented today; four Houses were in mourning. The opposition had no leaders.

"The vote," next-eldest asked.

The signs flashed to the board. No opposition, seven abstentions, four absent.

It was fact.

A cheer went up from Council, raucous and harsh after the long silence.

viii

The shuttle docked, jolted into lock next to one of the Outsider vessels. The azi caught at support, and one fell—shame-faced, recovered his footing. "All right, all right," Raen comforted him, touching his shoulder, never taking her eyes from the crew. "Squad two, stay with this ship and keep your guns aimed at the crew. They may try to trick you; you're quite innocent of some maneuvers, fresh as you are from Registry. Don't reason. Just shoot if they touch anything on that control panel."

"Yes, sera," said the squad leader, who had seen service before. The crew stayed frozen. She gathered up Merry and squad one and rode the overcrowded lift down to the lock, where the other squads and the Warriors stood guard over the Outsiders.

They were free of restraint, Tallen and his folk, huddled in a corner with the guns of eighty-odd azi to advise them against rashness. Raen beckoned them to her and they came, cautiously, across the dark cavern of the hold. One of their own men had Mundy in hand, had him calmed, had restored him to a fragile human dignity, and Mundy glared at her with hate: no matter to her. He was neither help nor harm.

"We're going out," she said to Tallen. "Ser, there's one of your ships beside us and its hatch is open. We've warned them. When you're aboard, take my advice and pull all Outsider ships from station as quickly as you can undock. Run for it."

Tallen's seamed face betrayed disturbance, as it betrayed little. "That far, is it?"

"I've risked considerable to get you here. I've given you free what you spent men to learn. Believe *me,* ser, because from the agents the Reach has swallowed you'll *never* hear. If it's clear they're not azi, they'll perish as assassins, one by one. It's our natural assumption. I'll give you as much time as I can to get clear of station. But don't expect too much, ser."

Merry was by the switch. She signalled. He opened up to the ramp.

It was as she remembered the dock, vast and shadowy and cold, an ugly place. Security agents and armored ISPAK police ringed the area. She walked out, her own azi about her, rifles slung hip-level from the shoulder. She wore no Color, but plain beige, no sleeve-armor. It was likely that they knew with whom they had to deal, all the same, for all the terseness of the messages she had returned their anxious inquiries.

Next to them, the Outsider ship waited. "Go," she told Tallen, whose group followed. "Get over there, before something breaks loose here."

He delayed. She saw in surprise that he offered his hand, publicly. "Kent' Raen," he said, "can *we* help *you?*"

"No," she said, shaken by the realization of finality. Her eyes went to the Outsider's ramp, the lighted interior.

To go with them, to see, to know—

Their duty forbade. And so did something she vaguely conceived as her own. She found tears starting from her eyes, that were utterly unaccustomed.

"Just get out of here," she said, breaking the grip. "And believe me."

He apparently did, for he walked away quickly then, and his people with him, as quickly as could not be called a run. They reached the ramp, rode it up. The hatch sealed after.

Raen folded her arms within her cloak, the one hand still holding her gun, and stared at the ISPAK security force, which her on azi faced with lowered weapons. Breath frosted in the icy air.

"Sera," one called to her. "ISPAK board has asked to see you. Please. We will escort you."

"I will see them here," she said, "on the dock."

There was consternation among them. Several in civilian dress consulted with each other and one made a call on his belt unit. Raen stood still, shivering with the chill and the lack of sleep, while they proposed debate.

She was too tired. She could not bear the standing any longer. Her legs were shaking under her. "Stand your ground," she bade the azi. "Fire only if fired upon. Tell them I'll come down when the board arrives. Watch them carefully."

And quietly she withdrew, leaving Merry in charge on the dock, trusting his sense and experience. In the new azi she had little confidence; they would not break, perhaps, if it came to a fire fight, but they would die in their tracks quite as uselessly.

She touched the Warriors who hovered in the hatchway, calming them. "We wait," she said, and went on to the lift, to the bridge, to the security of the unit which guarded the crew and the comfort of a place to sit.

Likely, she thought, *they'll arrive at the dock now, now that I've come all this way up.*

They did not. She reached past the frozen crew and punched in station operations, listened to the chatter, that at the moment was frantic. Outsider ships were disengaging from dock one after the other, necessitating adjustments, three, four of them, five, six. She grinned, and listened further, watched them on the screens as they came within view, every Outsider in the Reach kiting outward in a developing formation.

Going home.

A new note intruded, another accent in station chatter. She detected agitation in beta voices.

She pirated their long-scan, and froze, heart pounding as she saw the speed of the incoming dot, and its bearing.

She keyed outside broadcast "Merry! Withdraw. Withdraw everyone into the ship at once."

The dot advanced steadily, ominous by its speed near a station, cutting across approach lanes.

They would not have sent any common ship, not if it were in their power to liberate a warship for the purpose. Swift and deadly, one of the never-seen Family warships: Istra station was in panic.

And the Outsider ships were freighters, likely unarmed.

"Sera!" Merry's voice came over the intercom. "We're aboard!"

A light indicated hatch-operation.

"Back off," Raen said to the beta captain. "Undock us and get us out of here."

He stared into the aperture of her handgun and hastened about it, giving low-voiced orders to his men.

"Drop us into station-shadow," Raen said. "And get us down, fast."

The captain kept an eye to the incoming ship, that had not yet decreased speed. Station chatter came, one-sided—ISPAK informing the incoming pilot the cluster formation was Outsider, that no one understood why.

For the first time there was deviation in the invader's course, a veering toward the freighters.

The shuttle drifted free now, powering out of a sudden, in shadow.

"Put us in his view," Raen ordered. The captain turned them and did so, crossing lanes, but nothing around the station was moving, only themselves, the freighters, and the incomer.

Raen took deep breaths, wondering whether she should have gambled everything, a mad assault on station central, to seize ISPAK . . . trusting the warship would not fire.

It fired now. Outsiders must not have heeded orders to stop. She picked it up visually, swore under her breath; the Outsiders returned fire: one of that helpless flock had some kind of weapon. It was a mistake. The next shot was real.

She punched in numbers, snatched a microphone. "Kontrin ship! This is the Meth-maren. You're forbidden station."

The invader fired no more shots. He was, perhaps, aware of another mote on his screens; he changed course, leaving pursuit of Outsiders.

"It's coming for us!" a beta hissed.

Raen scanned positions, theirs, the warship's, the station's, the world. In her ear another channel babbled converse with the invader. *Shuttle . . .* she heard. *One onworld . . . one aloft . . . Plead with you . . .*

"Sera," the captain moaned.

"It can't land," she said. "Head us for Istra."

They applied thrust and tumbled, applied a stabilizing burst and started their run.

"Shadow!" Raen ordered, and they veered into it, shielded by station's body, at least for the instant.

"We can't do it," someone said. "Sera, please—"

"Do what it can't do," she said. "Dive for it." Her elbow was on the rest; she leaned her hand against her lips, found it cold and shaking. There was nothing to do but ride it through. The calculation had been marginal, an unfamiliar ship, a wallowing mote of a shuttle, diving nearly headlong for Istra's deep.

Metal sang; instruments jumped and lights on the board flicked red, then green again. "That was fire," Raen commented, swallowing heavily. A voice in her ear was pleading with the invader. The shuttle's approach-curve graph was flashing panic.

They hit atmosphere. Warning telltales began flashing; a siren began a scream and someone killed it.

"We're not going to make it," the captain said between his teeth. He was working desperately, trying to engage a failed system. "Wings won't extend." The co-pilot took over the effort with admirable coolness, trying again to reset the fouled system.

"Pull in and try again," Raen said. The beta hit retract, waited, lips moving, hit the sequence again. Of a sudden the lights greened, the recalcitrant wings began to spread, and the betas cried aloud with joy.

"Get us down, blast you!" Raen shouted at them, and the ship angled, heart-dragging stress, every board flashing panic.

They hit a roughness of air, rumbling as if they were rolling over stone, but the lights started winking again to green.

"Shall we die?" an azi asked of his squad leader.

"It seems not yet," squad-leader answered.

Raen fought laughter, that was hysteria, and she knew it. She clung to the armrest and listened to the static that filled her ear, stared with mad fixation on the hands of the terrified betas and on the screens.

Pol, she kept thinking, *Pol, Pol, Pol, blast you, another lesson.*

Or it was for him also, too late.

ix

"So it's you," Moth said, leaned back in her chair, wrapped in her robes. She stared up at Ros Hald, with Tand; and the Ren-barant, the Ilit. "It's Halds, is it?"

"Council's choice," Ros Hald said.

Moth gave a twisted smile. She had seen the four vacant seats, action taken before she had even announced her intent. "Of course you are," she said, and did not let much of the sarcasm through. "You're welcome, very welcome beside me, Ros Hald. Tand, go find some of the staff. We should offer hospitality to my partner-in-rule."

Tand went. Ros Hald kept watching her nervously. That amused her. "What," she asked, "do you imagine I've let you be chosen . . . to arrange your assassination, to behead the opposition?"

Of course it occurred to him, to all of them. They would all be armed.

"But I was sincere," she said. "I shall be turning more and more affairs into your hands."

"Access," he said, "to all records."

You've managed that all along, she thought, smiling. *Bastard!*

"And," he said, "to all levels of command, all the codes."

She swept a hand at the room, the control panels, the

records. The hand shook. She was perpetually amazed by her own body. She had been young—so very long; but flesh in this last age turned traitor, caused hands to shake, voice to tremble, joints to stiffen. She could not make a firm gesture, even now. "There," she said.

And fired.

The Hald fell, the Ilit; the Ren-barant fired and burned her arm, and she burned him, to the heart. Tand appeared in the doorway, hung there, mouth open.

And died.

"Stupid," she muttered, beginning then to feel the pain. The stench was terrible. She felt of her own arm, feeling damage; but the right one had not been the strong one, not for a long time.

Azi servants crept in finally, "clear this out," she said. Her jaw trembled. She closed the door when they had gone, and locked it. There was food secreted about, an old woman's senile habit; there was wine, bottles of it; there was the comp center.

She sat, rocking with the pain of her wound, smiling to herself without mirth.

X

The ground was coming up fast and the air was full of burning. They broke through haze and came in over bleak land, desert. It was not what the display showed on the screen; the ship's computer was fouled. The sweating betas labored over the board, retaining control over the ship, jolting them with bursts of the braking engines. There was no knowing where they were; cloud and panic had obscured that. They might yet land.

And all at once a mountain wall loomed up in front of them, vast beyond reason.

"Blast!" Raen shouted. "Altitude, will you?"

"That's the High Range," one of the betas said. "The winds—the winds—the shuttle's not built for it, Kontrin."

"We're on the way home, we're over East, blast you: take us up and get over it!"

The deck slanted. They were launching themselves for what altitude they could gain for that sky-reaching ridge. A beta cursed softly, and wept. The High Range loomed up, snow-crowned. Jagged peaks thrust up above the clouds which wreathed them. The mad thought came to Raen that if one must die, this was at least a thing worth seeing—that such a glorious thing existed, uncultivated by Kontrin, who hungered after new things: hers.

Istra, the High Range, the desert—all explored, all possessed, in this mad instant of ripping across the world.

The azi were silent, frozen in their places. The crew worked frantically, sighted their slot in that oncoming wall and aimed for it, the lowest way, between two peaks.

"No!" Raen cried, reckoning the winds that must howl down that funnel. She hit the captain's arm and pointed, a place where needle-spires thrust against the sky—cursed and insisted, having flown more worlds than earthbound betas knew. He veered, tried it, through turbulence that jolted them. Needles reared up in the screens. Someone screamed.

They went over, whipped over that needled ridge and sucked down a slope that wrung outcries from born-men and azi, downdrafted, hurtling down a vast rock face and outward. She saw spires in the slot they had not taken, reckoned with a wrench at the stomach what they had narrowly done.

"Controls aren't responding," the captain muttered. "Something's jammed up."

"Take what you can," Raen said.

The man asked help; the co-pilot lent a hand, muttered something about hydraulics. Raen set her lips and stayed still the while the frantic crew tried their strength and their wits. The rocks flew under them, turned to gold and gray-green, and ahead, the white-hot flare that was water under beta Hydri's light, serpentine, the River, and horizon-wide, the Sea.

Poor chance they had if they were carried out into *that* maelstrom of Istran storms, of endless water, and glare.

The captain made the right decision: retros jolted

them, and they began losing airspeed with such abruptness it felt as if they were halting midair. "Hold on," she shouted at the azi, trying not to think of belowdecks, nigh a hundred men without safety harness. The engines continued to slam at them in short bursts, until they were lumbering along at a wallowing pace and dropping by sickening lurches.

Beyond recall now, with the controls locked up.

"Merry," Raen called to below, "brace up hard down there; we're going to belly in if we're lucky."

Another lurch downward, with alternate trees and grassland before them, with sometime bursts of the engines to give them more glide, and wrestlings by manual at the attitude controls.

Hills sprang up in their path. *We'll not make it,* Raen thought, for the betas were at the end of their resources; and then the jolt of braking engines nigh took the breath out of them and they lumbered into a tilt, feathered with the attitude jets.

She braced then, for they were committed beyond recall, and the valley walls were right in front of them. The engines jolted, one and then the other, compensating for a damaged wing.

The nose kept up. Raen watched the land hurtle toward them, waiting for the contact; it hit, slewed—the straps cut in. Then the nose flew up, slammed down, and somebody hurtled past Raen on his way to the control panel. Another hit her in the back. A gun discharged.

And she remained conscious through impact, with azi bodies before her and about her, while sirens screamed and the shriek of metal testified what was happening below. She cursed through it, watching horrified as the azi in front of her bled his life out on the control panel and the betas screamed. The worse horror was that the azi did not.

And when the ship was still—when it was evident that the feared fire had not taken place, and the shriek of metal had died—there was still no outcry from the azi. Two of the betas were unconscious, a half dozen of the azi so. Raen gathered herself up on the sloping deck and looked about her. Azi faces surrounded her, calm, bewildered. The betas cursed and wept.

"We can manual this lock," Merry's voice came over the intercom. "Sera? Sera?"

She answered, looked at the betas, who had begun working at the emergency chute. Hot air and glare flooded the opened hatchway. Merry, down below, was attempting his own solution. Fire still remained a possibility.

"Get supplies," she said. "All the emergency kits." They were not going to be adequate for so many men. She opened a locker and found at least a reserve of sunsuits, lingered to put one on the while azi clambered out, and slid down—her own men, she thanked her foresight, with such clothing, and with weapons. Her own suit was in her luggage, and one of the azi had brought it, but at the moment she had no idea where it was . . . cared nothing.

Injured azi moved themselves; the betas she left to betas, and made the slide to safety, into the arms of her azi below, steadied herself and looked about: the hold chute was deployed, and men were exiting there. She staggered across the grass, angry that her knees so betrayed her, found Merry, whose battered face wept blood along a scraped cheek. "The hold—many dead?"

"Six. Some bad, sera."

So few hours, from the null of the pens, and to die, after eighteen years of preparing. She drew a deep breath and forced it out again. "Get them all out." She sat down on the grass where she was, head bowed against her knees, pulled up the sunsuit hood, adjusted her gloves, small, weary movements. They had to get clear of the ship. The ship was a target. They had to move. She shut her eyes a moment and oriented herself, slipped the visor to a more comfortable place on her nose, adjusted up the cloth about her lower face, as anonymous as the azi.

Warriors living-chained down from the hatch, hale and whole. She called to them and rose, bared a hand to identify herself. They came, humming and booming in distress at their experience, offered touch. "Life-fluids," they kept saying, alarmed by the deaths.

"Watch," she said, gesturing at all that empty horizon of fields, thinking of raided depots and murdered azi. "Let no majat come on us."

"Yess," they agreed, and hovered never far away.

An azi brought her luggage, her battered brown case, and she laughed with the touch of hysteria for that, extracted her kit of lotions and medicines and jammed those in her side pocket, cast the rest away.

The azi were all out, she reckoned. She walked among them, saw that Merry had taken her at her word, for the dead lay in a group, half a dozen not counting the one above, on the bridge; and a little apart from them were four with disabling injuries; and apart from them was a large group of wounded; and a group which bore virtually none. She looked back that course again, suddenly understanding how they were grouped, that the wounded, huddled together, simply waited, knotted up as she had seen Jim do when he was disturbed.

Waiting termination.

She cast about in distress, reckoned what would be the lot of any left in beta care. "We carry those that can't walk," she told Merry, and cursed the luck, and her softness, and turned it to curses at the hale ones, ordering the emergency litters, ordering packs made, until men were hurrying about like a disturbed hive.

And the beta captain limped to her . . . she recognized the graying brows through the mask. "Stay with the ship," he urged her.

"Stay yourself." Her head throbbed and the sun beat through the cloth; she forced herself to gentle language. "Take your chances here, ser. Kontrin feud. Stay out of it."

And seeing her own folk ready, she shouted hoarse orders and bade them move.

North.

Toward Newhope, toward any place with a computer link.

xi

Morn Hald paced the office of the ISPAK station command, waited, settled again at the console.

Such resources as the Family had at its command he called into use; a code number summoned what vessels waited at Meron, and long as it would take for the message to run via intercomp, as long as it would take those ships to reach Istra—they were as good as on their way.

He relied on the Hald for that.

The Meth-maren had provided the overt provocation the Movement needed, the chaos she had wrought at station, that elevated the matter above a feud of Houses. Panicked Outsiders were running, refusing all appeals to return—had *fired* on a Kontrin vessel. Morn's thin hands were emphatic on the keys, violent with rage.

His witness, under *his* witness the Meth-maren had managed such a thing; and he was stung in his pride. Outsiders were involved. He had hesitated between destroying them and not; and the thought of embroiling himself with that while the Meth-maren found herself escape and weapons—for that he had pulled away, to his prime target, to the dangerous one. There was no knowing in what she had her hand, where her agents were placed by now.

Revenge: she had never sought it, in all the long years, had wended her insouciant way from dissipation to withdrawal, and retaliated for only present injuries. The Family had tolerated her occasional provocations, which were mild, and seldom; and her life, which crossed none; and her style, which was palest imitation of Pol's.

Morn read the comp records and cursed, realizing the extent of what she had wrought in so few days: the azi programs disrupted, export authorizations granted, winning the allegiance of ITAK, which was therefore no longer reliable—she knew, she *knew,* and Outsiders, perhaps not the first to do so, were scattering for safety in their own space. News of that belonged in the hands of the Movement before it reached Council: he sent it, via Meron, under Istran-code, which would be intercepted.

So she might have launched instructions to Meron, to Andra, to whatever places an agent might have become established over two decades. They had worked to prevent it, had found no agent of the Meth-maren in all the years of their observation; and that, considering what she had done on Istra, disturbed all his confidence.

Betas hovered distressedly in the background of the command center, as yet simply dazed by the passage of events—betas who had learned to avoid his anger. But any of them—any of them—could be hers. His own azi stood among them, armored and armed, discouraging rashness.

To disentangle a Kontrin from a world was no easy matter. It was one which he did not, in any fashion, relish. His own style was more subtle, and quieter.

He put in a second call to Pol, waited the reasonable time for it to have relayed wherever he was lodged, and for Pol to have responded. He kept at it, sat with his chitined hand pressed against his lips, staring balefully at the flickering screen.

SALUTATIONS, the answer came back.

He punched in vocal, his own face instead of the Kontrin serpent that masked his other communications; Pol's came through on his screen, mirror-wise, but Pol's was smiling.

"Don't be light with me, cousin," Morn said. "Where are you?"

"Newport."

"She's been here," Morn said. "Was here to meet me, as you were not."

Pol's face went sober. He quirked a brow, looked offended. "I confess myself surprised. A meeting, then, not productive."

"Where is she based?"

"Newhope. You've not been clear. What happened?"

"She cleared in a shuttle and station picks up nothing."

"Careless, Morn."

Morn gave a cold stare to the set's eye, suffered Pol's humor as he had suffered it patiently for years. "I'm holding station, cousin, and I'll explain in detail later why *you* should have taken that precaution. It may not please you to learn. Get after her. I'd trade posts with you, but I trust you haven't been idle in your hours here."

He had sobered Pol somewhat "Yes," Pol said. "I'll find her. Enough?"

"Enough," Morn said.

BOOK EIGHT

i

Jim went about the day's routines, trying to find in them reason for activity. He had washed, dressed immaculately, seen to a general cleaning for what rooms of the house were free of majat. But the sound of them filled the house, and what jobs could occupy the mind were soon done, and the day was empty. One frightened domestic azi held command of the kitchen, and together they prepared the day's meals on schedule, two useless creatures, for Jim found himself with no appetite and likely the other azi did not either, only that it was routine, and maintenance of their health was dutiful, so that they both ate.

There was supper, finally, with no cessation of the frenetic hurryings in the garden, the movements at the foundations. Night would come. He did not want to think on that.

"Meth-maren."

A Warrior invaded the doorway, and the domestic scrambled from the table over against the wall, throwing a dish to the floor in his panic. "Be still," Jim said harshly, rising. "Your contract is here and the majat won't hurt you."

And when it came farther, seeking taste and touch, he gave it "Meth-maren azi," it identified him. "Jimmm. This-unit seeks Meth-maren queen."

"She's not here," he told it, forcing himself to steadiness for the touch of the chelae, the second brush at his lips, between the great jaws. He shuddered in spite of himself, but the conviction that it would not, after all, harm him, made it bearable—more than that, for she was gone, and the majat at least were something connected with her. He touched Warrior as he had seen her do, and calmed it.

"Need Meth-maren," it insisted. "Need. Need. Urgent."

"I don't know where she is," he said. "She left. She said she would come back soon. I don't know."

It rushed away, through the door to the garden, damaging the doorframe in its haste. Jim followed it past the demoralized house-azi, looked out into the ravaged back garden where a deepening pit delved into the earth, where the neighbor's wall had been undermined. Guard-azi stood their posts faithfully, but as close to the azi quarters door as they might. He went out past the excavation, past the guards—sought Max, and having located him in the azi quarters, told him of Warrior's request, not knowing what he ought to have answered.

"We must stay here as we were told," Max concluded, his squarish face grimly set, and there was in his eyes a hint of disapproval for the azi who suggested a violation of those instructions. Jim caught it and bit off an answer, turned and hesitated in the door, irresolution gnawing at him with a persistence that made his belly hurt. The hive wanted: Raen would have been disturbed at an urgent message from the hive. She needed to know.

And he was charged simply to keep the house in order.

That was not, now, what she needed. The look that had been in her eyes when she left him had been one of worry, anxiousness, he thought wretchedly, because she must leave him in charge, *him* who could not understand the half of what he ought.

He looked back, shivering. "Max," he said.

The big guard-azi waited. "Orders?" Max asked, that being the way Raen had arranged things.

"I'm going upstairs. You're in charge down here."

"She said you were to work."

"She said I was to take care of things. I'm going upstairs. I have something to do for her. You're in charge down here. That's the order I'm giving you. I'm responsible. I'll admit to it."

Max inclined his head, accepting, and Jim strode back the way he had come, across the devastation of the garden, past the domestic azi in the kitchen, who was mopping up the broken dish—past the comp center, the screens of which flashed with messages which waited on Raen. The walls vibrated with song. Warriors hulked here and there in the dark places of the hall. A majat-azi scampered out of the farther doors, female, naked, bearing a blue light that glowed feebly in the shadow. She grinned and trailed fingers across his shoulder as she passed, and he shuddered at the madness in that laughing face. A male followed, younger than left the pens to any other service, and the same wildness was in his eyes. A whole stream of them began to pour up from the basement with a Worker behind them, fluting orders for haste.

He fled in horror, lest he be swept up with them by accident, herded with them into the dark pit outside. He ran the stairs, hurled himself into the bedroom, saw it safely vacant and locked the doors.

It was a moment before he could unknot his clenched hands and arms and straighten. One part of him did not want to go farther . . . would rather seek the corner of the room and tuck up there and cease.

Like the lower azi, when they reached the limit of their functions.

Raen needed more than that. This tall, gaunt Kontrin had come, and talked with her, and she had been distressed: the strange born-man azi had distressed her further. He understood that there were connections he could not comprehend, that perhaps she was somewhere with *him,* who was of her kind—and that in hazardous things an azi of his training was useless.

Keep the house in order.

It was far from what she needed, but it was the limit of his function. He had seen betas, who could make up what to do: Kontrin, whose function he could not conceive, but who simply *knew*. He had seen the pens and knew himself.

Dimly he realized that if Raen were lost, he would be terminated: someone had told him that they did not pass on their azi; but he failed to take alarm at that. He thought should that happen, he would simply sit down and wait for termination, out of interest in other things, without further use. There was an unfamiliar tightness in his throat that had bided there most of the day, a tenseness that would not go away.

Be calm, old tapes echoed in his mind. *Calm is always good. When you cannot be calm, you are useless. A useless azi is nothing. Turn off all disturbance. Instruction will come. You are blameless if you are calm and waiting for instruction.*

Next came the punishment, if he let the emotion well up, the inbuilt nausea. He was shaking, torn between the tightness in his throat and the sickness which heaved at his stomach, and knew that if he let the one go, the other would follow. He had no time for this. He fought down the hysteria with a simple exercise of self-distraction, refusing to think in the direction of his feelings. *Calm, calm, calm is good. Good is happy. Happy is useful. Good azi are always useful.*

He busied himself at once, taking the deepstudy unit out of the closet, opening the case with the tapes. *Calm, calm, calm,* he insisted to himself, for his hand shook as he deliberately chose the tapes with the black cases, the forbidden ones. The disobedience increased the pain in his stomach. *For her,* he kept telling himself; and, *Good azi are always useful,* playing one tape against the other. If he had what was in her tapes he would know what she knew; if he knew what she knew, he would understand what to do.

He propped up a divider from the case, contrived a way to brace the stack which he made in the play-slot, for they were far more than the machine was designed to hold. Focus the mind, concentrate only on the physical action: that was the means to keep calm in crisis. Never mind where the action was tending; it was only necessary to do, until all was done.

He prepared the machine. He prepared the chair, throwing over it a blanket for padding; last of all he prepared himself, stripped completely, smoothed the blanket so that there would be not the least wrinkle to crease his skin during the long collapse, and found the pill bottle where he had left it last, in the bath. He sat down then, with the pill clenched in his teeth, attached the leads. Last of all he drew the edges of the blanket over himself and swallowed the pill, waiting for the numbness to begin.

I shall change, he thought, and panic rose in him, for he had always liked the individual he was, and this was self-murder.

He felt the haziness begin, bade himself goodbye, and threw the switch—composed his arms loosely to his sides and leaned back, waiting.

The machine cycled in.

He was not unconscious; he was hyperconscious, but not of things around him—gripped and shaken by the alienness that poured in.

Attitudes. Information. Contradictions. The minds of immortals, the creators of the Reach. He absorbed until body began to scream out distantly to mind that there was hazard, and went on absorbing.

He could not want to stop, save in the small pauses where instruction ceased. Then he would try to scream for help. But he was not truly conscious, and body would not respond at all. The stream began again, and volition ceased.

ii

"Meth-maren," Mother intoned, distraught. "Find, find this queen." Workers soothed Her; Drones sang their dismay. There was/had been impression of separation, the hive-consciousness that had been established for a time stretched thin, soaring as in flight.

Then disaster.

Workers labored, frantically. The hive reached out and sought Meth-maren hive, one with it. Workers died in the stress, jaws worn away, bodies exhausted, and the husks were caught up and carried away as the work boiled forward. Azi fell beneath their burdens and drank and rested and staggered back to their work, to die there.

There was in the hive the frightened taste of a green scout, who had fallen to Warriors. Disorientation was in its hive also, the memory of Meth-marens of ages past, before the sun had risen at such an angle and the world had changed colors.

And it in turn had tasted the minds of golds, who tasted of reds, whose fierceness now had a taint of hesitancy, less push and more of fear.

"Kill," the Warrior portion of blue-Mind urged. "Restore health. Kill the unhealthy."

Drones sang of memory, and the balance of the hive shifted toward Warrior-thoughts and shifted back again to Mother, as She wrenched it to Herself, fierceness greater than theirs, for it embraced eggs, survival.

BUILD, the command went out, and the Workers hastened in frenzy.

iii

They huddled, an exhausted group, in the shade of a hedge. Raen slipped fingers under her visor and wiped sweat from her eyes, withdrew them, adjusted the rim to a new place and grimaced it back to the old. The hood of her sunsuit was back, the gloves off, the sleeves unfastened to the elbow; toward evening as it was, still the heat lingered as the residue of a furnace. The suits that saved from burn, ventilated as they were by majat-silk insets, left the skin sticky with perspiration, clung with every movement. A dead azi's rifle was on her knees, weight on sore muscles; she had food and a canteen from the emergency stores and would not drink, tormenting herself with the thought of it—supplies meant for ten, and a cluster of thirsty men about her: neither did others drink, being azi, and waiting. The wounded bore their wounds, and the insects, without a sound: it was only surprise could get an outcry from them, and there was none of that. They knew what the situation was. They were the lighter by two they had started with, the worst-wounded; the bearers had been glad, and she did not delude herself otherwise. In that day she had reconsidered her mercy, and gazed at two others as bad, and at the grasslands endless about them, and she had almost turned the gun on them. Instead she had given them a sip of water, that compounded the idiocy, and the same to the bearers: for herself and the others there was only the chance to moisten mouths and spit it back, and no one defied instructions.

She was, however long ago, of Cerdin, and Cerdin's sun was no kinder; she was, for the rest, accustomed to exercise, and most of these were not. She had Merry by her, poor Merry, his lips as cracked as hers felt, his face bruised as well as scraped; she trusted him more than the others, these babes new from the pens. Merry helped, used his wits; the others obeyed.

There was a stirring, a shrilling; they snatched rifles up nervously, but it was one Warrior, their own, that bore a white rag tied on a forelimb so that the azi could tell it. It ran low, scuttled up waving its palps and seeking scent.

"Here," Raen said, turning her hand to it. It came, offered taste, the sweet fluids of its own body, and it was welcome. She touched the scent-patches, soothed it, for it had been moving hard, and air pulsed from the chambers so it had difficulty with human speech.

"Mennn. Humannsss. Human-hive."

She gave a great breath of relief. Every face was turned toward it, faces suddenly touched with hope. She caressed the quivering palps. "Warrior, good, very good. Where are other Warriors?"

"Watching men."

"Far?"

It quivered slowly. Not far, then. "We leave the wounded and five to help them," she said. "We'll come back for you injured when we've gotten transport. I say so. Understood?"

Heads inclined, all together.

"Come on," she told Merry. "Choose those to stay and let's move."

Warrior moved ahead of their concealment, a black shape in the starlight. Likely Warrior was screaming orders; human ears could not pick it up. In a moment all three came back to the hedgerow, clicking with excitement.

"Guardss," Warrior said, with two neat bows in the appropriate directions: majat vision in the cool of night could hardly miss a human.

"No majat?" Raen asked.

"Humanss. Human-hive."

Fifty men were, in the last twos, grouping behind her. Lights showed ahead, floodlights about the fields, the farmyard. An azi barracks showed light from the windows; the farmhouse had the same, windows barred, proof against majat.

"Door's nothing," she said to Merry. "A burn will take it. Azi won't fight if we can get the betas first."

"Take the guards out," Merry said. "Three men each, no mistakes. I'll take one."

She shook her head. "Stay by me at the door. I'll get it, ten men with me take the house, twenty round the side door. You get down by that porch and take any charge starts out the door of the barracks."

"Understood," Merry said, and orders passed, quick and terse, by units.

"No firing unless fired on," Raen said, and took the nearest Warrior by the forelimb. "Warrior: you three stay here. Guard this-place until I call."

"Warrior-function: come," it lamented.

"I order, Meth-maren, hive-friend. Necessary."

"Yess," it sighed.

"I go first," she said, to the distress of Merry and the

others, but they said no word of objection. She stood up, gripped her rifle by its body, and started out into the road, dejected, limping. Her eyes, her head still downcast, flicked nervously from one to the other of the guardposts she knew were there, in the hedges.

"Stop!" someone shouted at her.

She did so, looked fecklessly in that direction, with no move of her rifle. "Accident," she said. "Aircraft went down—" and pointed back. The azi came from their concealment, both of them, naïve that they were. "I need help," she said. "I need to call help."

One of them determined to walk with her. The other stayed. She limped on toward the house, toward the door, studying the lay of the place, the situation of windows; the barracks was at her back, the porch before.

And the azi with her went up the steps ahead of her, rang at the door, pressed the housecom button. "Ser?"

Someone passed a window to the door.

"Ser, there's a woman here—"

"Istra shuttle went down," she cried past him. "Survivors. I need to call for help."

The door unlocked, opened. A graying beta stood in it. She slipped inside, leaned against the wall, whipped the rifle up.

"Don't touch the switch, ser. Don't move."

The beta froze, mouth open. The guard-azi did likewise, and in that instant a rush of men pelted across the yard. The guard whirled, found targets, fired in confusion, and the rush that hit the door threw him over, swept the beta against the wall, ringing him with weapons. Her azi kept going, and elsewhere in the house were shots and outcries. "No killing!" she shouted. "Secure the house! Go, I've got him." She held her rifle on the man, and the azi swept after their comrades.

It was a matter of moments then, the frightened family herded together into their own living room, the azi servants, one injured, along with them.

Merry held the front porch. The first shot into the azi barracks had convinced the others. Her men regrouped, meditating that problem.

"Ser," Raen said to the householder, "protect your azi. Call them out unarmed. No one will be hurt."

He did so, standing on the porch with enough rifles about to assure he made no errors. In the house, the family waited, holding to one another, the wife and a young couple that was likely related in some way, with an infant. The baby cried, and they tried to hush it.

And fearfully the farm's azi came out as they were told; she bade Merry and some of the men search the barracks and the azi themselves for weapons.

But most of all was water, food. She gave them permission as quickly as she could, and they drank their fill—brought her a cup, which she received gratefully, and a grimy fistful of dried fruit. She chewed at it and kept the rifle slung hip-level, pocketed some, drank at the water. The householder was allowed to rejoin his family on the chairs in the livingroom. "Ser," Raen said, "apologies. I told the truth: we've injured among us. I need food, water, transport, and your silence. You're in the midst of a Kontrin matter.—Kont' Raen, seri, with profound apologies. We'll not damage anything if we can help it."

A cluster of beta faces stared back at her, gray with terror, whether for their attack or for what she told them, she was not sure.

"Take what you want," the man said.

The baby started crying. Raen gave the child a glance and the woman gathered it to her; the injured azi touched it and tried to soothe it. Raen took a deep breath for patience and looked at the lot of them. "You've a truck here, some sort of transport?"

Heads nodded.

She went off to the center of the house, hunting comp, located it, a sorry little machine pasted with grocery notices and unexplained call-numbers. She keyed in, called the house in Newhope, the number she had arranged for emergency.

"Jim?" she called. And again: "Jim!"

There was no response.

Her hand began to shake on the board. She clenched it and leaned her mouth against it, considering in her desperation how far she could trust Itavvy or Dain or anyone else in ITAK. "Jim," she said, pleading, and swore.

There was still no response. JIM, she keyed through, to leave a written message, STAND BY. EMERGENCY.

She put the next one through to Isan Tel's estate, where a few managerial azi kept the fiction of a working estate, unsupervised azi and a horde of guards. STAND BY. EMERGENCY. EMERGENCY.

And a third one to the Labor Registry. EMERGENCY, TEL CONTRACT. PLEASE STAND BY.

None used her name. She dared not. She rose and took two of the men with her, walked out past Merry's unit to the road, and up it to the place where they had left the Warriors. They were there, fretting and anxious. "All safe," she told them. To each she gave two pieces of the dried fruit, which they greatly relished. "I need one-unit to stay with me, two for a message," she said.

"Yess," they agreed, speaking together.

"Just tell Mother what's happened. Tell her I'm coming to Newhope, but I'm slow. I need help, blue-hive azi, weapons. Fast."

There was an exchange of tones. "Good," one said. "Go now?"

"Go," she said; and two darted off with eye-blurring speed, lost at once in the night and the hedges. The other remained, shadowed her with slow-motion steps as she and her guards returned to the house.

"Merry," she said, when she had come to his group, where they huddled on the porch, tired men with rifles braced on knees toward the azi barracks. Merry gathered himself up, haggard, the light from the door showing darkly on his wounded cheek, his blond hair plastered with sweat and dust. "One of the two of us," she said hoarsely, "has to get the truck back after those men. You've land-sense. Can you do it? Are you able to? I need you back; I rely on you too much."

Pride shone in the azi's eyes. "I'll get back," he said; she had never imagined such a look of intensity from stolid Merry. It approached passion. Such expression, she saw suddenly, rested not alone in his face, but in those of others. She did not understand it. It had something to do with the tapes, she thought, and yet it was no less real, and disturbed her.

"Truck ought to be in the equipment shed. Watch yourselves, walking around out here. We think we've accounted for everyone. I haven't had time to check comp thoroughly."

"I need three men."

She nodded; Merry singled out his men and left for the side of the house. She stationed Warrior by the side of the porch by the other azi and left them so, limped up the steps and into the house, giving only a glance to the captive betas. Her legs shook under her, adrenalin drained away. She sank down and wiped her face with her hand.

"Get a water-container," she told one of the azi. And to the beta, "ser, is there a key for that vehicle?"

"By the door."

She looked and saw it hanging. "Take that to Merry," she told the azi. "Take a bit of that dried fruit too. There'll be at least some can appreciate it."

The azi gathered up the items and left, came back again; distantly there was a moaning of an engine, that turned off where the road would be: Merry was on his way.

"True that the shuttle crashed?" the beta woman asked.

Raen nodded. "Broken limbs in plenty, sera. And dead. We had a hundred men aboard that ship."

The betas' faces reflected compassion for that.

"I'm sorry," Raen said, "for breaking in. It's necessary. Your names, seri? I'd rate you compensation if it were safe. It's not, at the moment."

"Ny," the man said, nodded at his wife. "Berden. My son and his wife. Grandchild. Kontrin, you can have anything, only so you leave us all right."

"There's majat," the young man said. "We've got to have our defenses whole. Have to, Kontrin."

"I've heard how that is. I've heard how the farms won't give up their azi."

"All the protection we have," Ny said.

Raen looked at them, at the house, recalling the situation of buildings and the fields. "But you could rather well survive in such a place, could you not—producing your own food and power? And ITAK and ISPAK both know it. You don't have to yield up your grain; and they know that too."

"Need it," Ny said. "We need the azi; azi've no desire at all to go back to the pens either. They've lived loose here, lived well, here. We don't turn them back, no, Kontrin. We don't."

It was a bold speech for a beta. It did not offend her. "Indeed," she said, "you've a secure and enviable land here. I'd a notion to destroy your comp at least; but you're not ITAK folk nor ISPAK, are you? You have a map of the area?"

"Comp room," Berden said. "Drawer under the machine."

"I thank you," she said quietly, rose on aching limbs and limped off to the cluttered little room.

The map was there. She sat down before the unit and studied it, found their location conveniently marked, a rough two hundred kilometers south of a major tributary of the River, nearly a thousand from Newhope.

She hesitated a moment, then coded in one of her several male personas, keyed in a purchase of passage; the program under that name was already set. One sped to the persona of Merek Sed and family, a matter of honor. One sped to the real person of one ser Tol Errin 1028D Upcoast, a worker in glass, with his family, with offer of an immediate commission on Meron, freighter-passage.

A mad gesture. A whim. Some things were worth saving.

It took an instant of time. She nerved herself again and keyed Newhope, again on emergency. "Jim!" she snapped, and gave instructions in case any other azi was in hearing, to answer her.

There was nothing. She broke connection quickly.

She sat then with her hand pressed against her mouth, staring at the board distressedly and trying to reckon now what to do.

She looked about her. There had gathered a quiet ring of surplus azi, exhausted, slitting on the floor and all about, young faces looking toward her with anxious eyes.

They all had Merry's look.

iv

There were dreams, horrid dreams, and one of them was a shadow, tall and gaunt, leaning across the light.

It seized and shook, and Jim tore his arm free and cried out, clawing at the leads which were no longer there, trying to free himself of the nightmare. He had no strength. The grip closed on him and held him still, and for a time there was only his pulse for reality, a throbbing in his ears and a dull wash of rose across his eyes.

"Wait outside," a voice said above him.

"Dying." The tones were song, deep and sorrowful.

"Wait outside." Harsher now. "Go."

"Stranger," the song mourned. "Stranger, stranger, green-hive."

But it retreated, as far as the door. He could hear it clicking.

Hands caught his face between. "Azi," the male voice said. "Azi, come back, come back, wake up. Quietly now. Was it suicide? Did she order you to this?"

The words made sense and then did not. Senses grayed out again, his whole body numb and heavy. Then there was sharp pain, and he came back, feeling it, but unable to reckon where the pain was centered.

"He's coming out of it," the voice said. "Stay back. Let him be."

"Green-hive," the other fretted, retreated again, muttering deep notes of distress. He turned his head, opened his mouth to cry to it for help.

"No." A hand covered his mouth, hard. He struggled at that, vision clearing. He knew the face that leaned above him: not simply recognized, but *knew*—

Knew the Halds, and the man Pol, who was dangerous, whose House and sept had clear reason to hate the Methmarens. He fought the muffling hand, and had no strength in his limbs or his hands, scarcely even the power to lift them.

"Be very still." Pol leaned close, his breath fanning his cheek. "I've talked my way in here, you see. The majat is watching . . . such moves as they have eyes to see. Do you hear me, azi?"

He tried to nod against the hand. He could scarcely breathe; words passed out of sense again.

"I told you to stay downstairs."

"Let him go." Max's voice. Jim struggled back toward the sound, toward understanding. "I shouldn't have let you in."

"But you have. Get the Warrior out of here. Guard the door if you like. Leave me with him."

Max, Jim wanted to say. He murmured something. Max did not answer.

"Get downstairs," Pol Hald said. "Hear me?"

The crack of authority was in his voice. Jim winced at it. Max went. The door closed. Pol Hald rose and locked it, and Jim rolled onto his side, holding the chair arm, fighting to move at all. Pol returned, caught his arms, jerked at him. His head snapped back with a crack: muscle control was gone. He could not even lift it.

"Shuttle's down," Pol said, "but not in either port. Where is she? Come out of it and answer me."

He could not. He tried to shake his head to protest the fact. Pol flung him down, let him alone; steps retreated, came back—he was roughly lifted and a cup held to his lips.

"Drink it, hear? If there's a mind left in you. Was it her order you did this?"

He drank. The water eased his throat. Pol let him back

then, and touched wet fingers to his temples. He shut his eyes and drifted, came back again to a faint rattling of plastic.

"Kontrin tapes," Pol muttered. "History. Law. Comp theory—blast! where did she get that one?" He thought that it was safe to rest while the voice railed elsewhere, but suddenly the hands fastened into his toneless limbs again and pressed to the bone. "Why, azi?"

He lay still, looking at Pol, and Pol at him.

"You know me," Pol said. "*Don't you?* You know me."

He blinked, no more than that. It was truth. Pol understood it.

And slowly Pol sank down beside the chair, gripped his arm quite gently. "You're sane. Don't think you can pretend it undid you. I've seen suicides by deepstudy. You're not gone. You're lying there with your teeth shut on everything, but I understand, you hear? You've studied what you ought not. I'm not dealing with an azi, am I? You're something else. How long have you been delving into those particular tapes?"

He answered nothing, and there was knowledge in his mind, memory of the Family, what he could expect of Halds.

"She ordered this? She set you to suicide?"

"Not suicide." The accusation that touched her, stung him. "No. *I.* My choice. To learn."

"And what have you learned, azi?"

"My name is *Jim.*"

"You *have,* haven't you?"

He thought that Pol would kill him. He expected so, but there was nothing he could do about it; he tried to move, and Pol helped instead of hindering, hauled him forward to sit on the edge, put a glass into his hands. He expected water and got juice, gagged on it. "Drink it," Pol snapped at him, and when he had done so, dragged him bodily into the bath and into the shower, turned the water on him. He sank down, too weak to stand, and leaned against the glass.

It was Max who pulled him from it. Max's strong hands lifted him, half-carried him to the bed.

"Pol," he objected. "Where is he?"

"Downstairs." The guard-azi looked at him in anguish. "He came to the gate outside—said *she's* in trouble. What do we do? What orders?"

Max was asking him. He stared at the azi. Nothing made sense. There was only the single word. *She.*

He snatched at his abandoned clothing, looked up suddenly at a move in the open doorway. Pol stood there, a shape among shadows.

"The mind's working now, isn't it? More than these that could be argued into letting the likes of me into the house."

It was. Jim looked reproach at Max, and suddenly realized a gulf between. He did not know what he should and knew more than gave him comfort. His knees went out from under him and he had to lean, caught wildly at the chair.

"You've thrown yourself into shock," Pol said. "The body won't stand that kind of insult; throws metabolism into erratic patterns. Help him, azi."

Max did so, caught him and set him down, grasped his arms. "What do we do?" Max asked of him. "He's not armed. We saw to that." Max tugged and pulled the clothes onto him, shook at his arms. "Warriors are all about. He *can't* do any damage. Can he, Jim? He talks about her, about some trouble. What are we supposed to do? You're to give the orders. What?"

He fought nausea, looked up at the Hald. "The first thing is not to trust him. He's older and wiser than we."

Pol grinned. "You've studied Raen's tapes. Her mind-set. You reckon that, azi? That you *are* her mind-set?"

"The second thing," Jim said, resisting the soft voice that unraveled him, "is to make doubly sure that he isn't armed."

Pol solemnly spread open his hands. "I swear."

"And never believe him." He was shaking, violently. He sat still, conserving the energy he had in him, tried to think past the pains in his joints and the contractions of his stomach. *Blood pressure,* a forgotten tidbit of information surfaced, explaining the intense feeling that his head was bursting. "You think you can take this house. You won't."

The Family would kill him, he thought. If Raen were lost, he would die. If Raen survived, it was possible that she would kill him for what he had done. Neither was important at the moment. The necessity was not to let the Hald get control of the staff.

"Search him again, Max," he said.

Pol bristled. Max approached him with deference—evidence of how little thorough that first search had been; but Pol submitted, and it was done, with great care.

"I'm not alone now," Pol said, the while Max proceeded. "There's another of the Family here. I have to contact the Meth-maren. You understand me. The time has come. He'll be here. He'll not be subtle; he'll not need to be. The whole house is vulnerable."

"Who?" Jim asked.

"Morn. Morn a Ren hant Hald."

That name too he knew. First cousin to Pol. Traveling companion. Experienced in assassination.

"You often appear together," Jim said. "You make jokes. He kills."

Pol's face reacted, to Max's searching or to an azi's presumption. He frowned and nodded slowly. "Morn is nothing to trifle with. You understand that at least. I'll get her out of here. You listen to me, azi."

"Jim."

"I can get her off this world. Elsewhere. Out of the Family's hands. I have a ship waiting at the port. I have to reach her in time."

Jim shook his head slowly.

"You know," Pol said, as Max finished; he brushed distastefully at his clothing. "You know where she is."

"No, ser. You know well she wouldn't tell me."

"She would have established other contacts. Other points. Numbers, records. Names."

"She wouldn't have confided them to me."

"There had to be records."

"Max!" Jim said. "Have Warrior keep a guard about the comp center. Now. Do it! Warrior!"

Max moved, drew his gun: Pol's instant move was stopped cold. The Hald stepped back, then.

And there was a shadow in the door, that filled it, moiré eyes that swept them. "This-unit guardsss," it said.

"This stranger," Jim said, "must not go near the comp."

"Understandss. Comp center: many-machine. Sssafe."

Pol's eyes hooded. "You've killed us all. Morn won't hesitate at wiping out this whole house. Do you understand that?"

"I understand it very well. *We're* only azi."

Perhaps Pol caught that sarcasm. He gave him a long and penetrating look. "It's Raen's mind-set," he said. "Male, she's no different."

Jim swallowed at the sickness in his throat. *Calm, calm,* an old tape kept insisting somewhere. And: *Distraction is argument that needs no logic,* another advised him, Kontrin. Pol was skilled in the tactic. Jim painted a smile on his face and tucked a corner of the blanket about him against a tendency to chill, reckoning that what happened would at least be quick, unless Pol or Morn directly laid hands on him. "The staff," he said, "will make you comfortable, ser. But you'll stay away from the computer."

"You realize a direct strike could wipe this house out. That with the stakes I fear she's playing—the Family may not care that betas or a Kontrin die in the process." Pol's mouth twisted as though the words choked him. "I don't care for a few betas or a houseful of azi and majat. But *she's* another matter with me. You hear me. I'll not be taken down by a houseful of azi."

"There are majat."

The Kontrin went stone-faced.

"The staff," Jim repeated, "will make you comfortable in this room. But you'll not leave it."

Pol folded his arms.

"She'll come back," Jim said.

Pol shook his head. "I doubt that she can, azi. The

shuttle was never meant for landing elsewhere. She'll die, if she's not dead already."

It undermined his confidence of things. He could not keep that from his face.

"You know," Pol said reasonably, "that she admitted me here herself. She'd never have let an enemy that close to her. You have her mind. You know that better than anyone would. She wouldn't have let me in the door to see the lay of things, if she didn't know that I wasn't the enemy."

"I don't try to think as she does." Jim hugged the blanket about him, stared bleakly at the Hald. "I don't know enough. I only know what she told me, which was to stay and hold this house. You can say what you wish, ser. It may entertain you. It won't make any difference."

Pol cursed him, and Warrior stirred in the doorway.

"Green-hive," Warrior moaned.

"That is another reason," Jim said. "We simply wait for her. Maybe she'll tell me then that I was wrong."

"She's never going to have the chance."

Jim shrugged, tucked his feet up, crosslegged on the bed. "How shall we pass the time, ser? I am passably skilled at Sej."

v

The queasiness of docking upset the child. Wes Itavvy hugged her against him, looked at his wife, mute, full of things he should have said. They held Meris between them, clasping her hands, saying nothing. The shuttle made this run nearly empty: they three, a family of five from Upcoast, whose faces were no less worried. The port had been a-bristle with police. IDs were checked, and Itavvy had endured that in terror, expecting at any moment there would be someone who knew his face, who could detect the false numbers, the lies behind the precious tickets.

They had gone through. They had taken almost nothing in baggage, in their haste. There was disaster at their backs. It was palpable, throughout the city, through the subways, where armored police patrolled, with rifles levelled, in shops closed, in newslines censored, broadcasts cancelled.

They had made it through. Station let them dock. The procedure completed itself and the crew unsealed the hatches.

"Come on," he said, feeling his pocket for the authorizations. There was a freighter . . . the tickets advised so . . . it was the best place to go now, no lingering on station. They carried their own baggage off, jostling the Upcoast family in their haste.

Police.

And not police. Armored men with a serpent for an emblem, levelling rifles at them.

"Papers," one said.

Itavvy produced them. For a brief, agonizing moment he thought that they would then be waved on; but the man kept them, checked those likewise of the Upcoast group.

"Both for the *Phoenix*," he said into his com-unit.

"Faces check?" a voice came back.

"No likeness."

Itavvy reached, to have the papers. The faceless man held them, and the others, motioned at them with the rifle. "Waiting room," he said.

"We'll miss our boarding," a youth from Upcoast protested.

"Nothing's leaving," the armored man said.

Azi, Itavvy realized in indignation. No Kontrin, but an azi force was holding them. He opened his mouth to protest: the rifles gestured, and he closed it. Meris started to cry; his wife gathered her up, and he took the burden from her, went after the Upcoasters into the designated waiting area.

DOCK 6, BERTH 9, he could see on the signs outside the clear doors as they were ushered through. Berth 11 was their ship, safety.

From here, past azi guns, there was no reaching it. He looked at the Upcoasters, at his wife, hugged Meris to

him. A guard deposited their baggage inside the door
and unmasked to search through it, disarranging one and
proceeding to the next, putting nothing back.

vi

"Nothing," the azi reported, and Morn scowled, folded
his arms.

"No more flights," he said, looking at the ISPAK president. "Nothing moves out, no more come up."

"Kont' Morn," the beta breathed, appalled.

He cared little for that. He had no trust at all for
ITAK, and believed in ISPAK's loyalty only while guns
were on them and in the command center.

And from Pol there was yet no word. Pol was down
in Newhope; that much was certain; his ship pulsed out
a steady flow of status information, but there were only
azi aboard.

The Meth-maren had weapons enough at her disposal
if she had linked into ITAK. She had still the resources
of the Family with which to buy beta loyalties. And to
take those privileges needed Council.

Except by one procedure.

"She's dead," Morn said suddenly, bewildering the
beta. "I'll enter in the banks that the Meth-maren's dead.
And ISPAK will witness it. Then it'll be true, by the
law—do you agree, ser?"

"Yes, Kont' Morn," the man said; as it had been yes,
Kont' Pol, and Kont' Raen before that.

"All Kontrin and a world's corporations are sufficient
witness." He glared at the beta to see the reaction to
this, and the beta simply looked frightened. He motioned
to the console. "Get ITAK in link. Use your persuasion."

The man sat down and keyed a message through, the
while Morn leaned above him, one hand on his chair,
one on the panel's rim; and often the man's hands trembled over a letter, but he made no errors. ITAK protested; NO CHOICE, the ISPAK beta returned. It was
untidy; it fed into intercomp, to be examined and made

permanent record. Morn scowled and let it. The records were only as dangerous as Council chose to regard them, and Council—was as Council went. Risks had to be taken.

ITAK complied, under threat, registering protest. *Brave little betas,* Morn thought, with respect for the Meth-maren's hold on them. It amused him. He watched the ISPAK beta trembling with psych-set guilt and that amused him the more. "Move over," he said, thrust the man out of the way, glared until the man moved far away, by the door. Then he set his own fingers to the keys, with both ITAK and ISPAK signatories, coded in his own number . . . and Pol's: for that he had gained long ago, comitted it to memory: he had taken that precaution, as he tolerated nothing near him he could not control—save Pol. All a world's Kontrin and the corporations: the latter, K-codes could forge; but only on Istra did it come down to so small a body of the Family.

Worldcomp accepted it; it leaped to intercomp. Morn smiled, which he did rarely.

Officially dead, so far as Istra was concerned; universally dead in the eight to sixteen days it would take for the message to reach homeworld and fan out again in intercomp. She could not use her codes or her credit: they were wiped.

He pushed back from the console, rose, turned to the azi who waited. "Get the shuttle ready," he said. "My own."

One left. He turned to the ISPAK beta.

And suddenly the comp screens began to flash with alarm.

He was at the panel in an instant, keyed through a query.

No answer returned to him. He sat down and plied the keys, obtained only idiocy. Panic flashed into him. With all the speed he could manage he K-coded intercomp out-of-link, separating it from the deadness that was Istra.

The cold reached his stomach. Worldbank was wiped. All records, all finance, *null.*

The Meth-maren's death-notice.

It was keyed to that, and he had done it.

"Kill the power!" he shouted, rounding on the ISPAK beta. "Kill all the power on Istra. Dead, you understand me?"

There was silence. Nothing of the sort had ever been done before, the threat never carried out, the withdrawal of station power from a world.

"Yes, Kontrin," the beta stammered hoarsely. "But how long, how long are we talking about?"

"Until you hear from me to restore it. Shut it down." He turned to the board, keyed a message to his ship, ordering more azi to the command center. "I'm going down," he said to the azi present, to Leo, who was chief of them. The azi looked troubled at that, no more. "There's no more time to spend with this. You know procedures."

Leo nodded. Twenty years Leo had been in his service, the last five as senior. Efficiency and intelligence. There was no beta would get past him, no one who would get near controls. Azi lined the room, thirty of them, armed and armored, impersonal as the majat, and that resemblance was no chance. Beta psych-set was terrified by it. There was no one of them about to make a move under those guns.

He looked about him, saw the screens which monitored the collectors, saw the incredible sight of vanes turning, all at the same time, averting into shadow.

"*We* must have power," the ISPAK beta objected.

"Without dispute," he said. The beta looked abjectly grateful.

Morn ignored him and, gathering two of the azi to accompany him, left the center.

There was a Kontrin ship onworld, Pol's; and Pol remained silent, leaving only azi to report.

It was the first law, in the Family, to trust no one.

vii

Figures rippled across the comp screen. Raen saw the sudden dissolution of information and sprang back from it with a curse.

Dead. They had gotten to that, then, to pull her privileges.

And all Kontrin onworld had to agree to it.

Pol, she thought. *You bastard!*

She swore volubly and kept working, fed in the Newhope call number. "Jim," she said. "Jim. Any staff, punch five and answer."

There was no answer.

JIM, she sent, BEWARE POL HALD.

She suddenly found chaos in the machine, nonsense, and finally only house-functions.

"Power's down in the main banks," she said, turning to look at one of the older azi, who attended her shadow-wise, armed, wherever she went in the house. She cut the unit off and walked back into the doorway of the living room, where the Ny-Berdens and their family remained with the house-azi. "Worldcomp's undone," she said, and at their blankly incredulous stares: "Power's going to go soon, I'd imagine. Very soon. You've some collectors here. Is that enough to keep your house running?"

They only stared.

"I hope for your sakes that such is the case," she said, looking about her at the smallish rooms, the hand-done touches, the rough and unstylish furnishings. She turned again and raised her voice to them. "You understand, don't you? Istra's been cut off. Power will be cut. Worldcomp's been dissolved—wiped. No records, no communications, nothing exists any longer."

The ser and sera gathered their son and daughter-in-law and grandchild close about them and continued to stare at her. *Your doing,* their eyes said. She did not argue with them. It was so. Her azi sat still, waiting. The azi belonging to the estate sat outside, ranged in orderly rows in the shade of the azi-quarters, under the guns of her own. There had been need to feed them, to give them at least a little relief from the confinement. Silence prevailed everywhere about the house and grounds.

"Is your local power," Raen asked yet again, "enough for you?"

"If nothing's damaged," ser Ny answered at last, and faintly.

"Confound it, I'm not proposing to harm you. I'd not do that. We'll leave you your cells and your farm machinery. I'm worried about your survival. You understand that?"

They seemed perhaps a little reassured. The child whimpered. The young mother hugged and soothed her.

"Thank you," ser Ny said tautly.

An azi came up beside her, offered a cup of juice, bowed. *Blast, what triggered that impulse?* she wondered, concerned for the azi's stability, for she had not ordered it. She sipped it gratefully all the same. The air-conditioning might not last, not unless the farm collectors could carry it. More than likely it would have to be sacrificed for the farm's more essential machinery, the pumps to irrigate, refrigeration for stored goods.

Distantly there was the sound of an engine.

"Sera!" an azi shouted from the porch. "The truck's back!"

Everyone started to his feet, save the Ny-Berdens and their family: the azi guarding them did not let the guns turn aside. The truck groaned and rumbled its way to the porch. Raen put on her sun visor and took her rifle in hand, walked out to meet it.

It was a wretched sight, the covered vehicle laden with injured, with men bleeding through their bandages or, deep in shock, trying to protect unset bones. Warrior danced about anxiously, scenting life-fluids: "Go, out of the way," Raen bade it. Merry climbed down, and the three he had taken to help him climbed out of the back, exhausted and staggering themselves from the heat. Raen ordered cold water for them, ordered the others to work while Merry and his companions slumped in the shade of the truck.

Willing hands off-loaded the injured into the air-conditioned house, to the bedrooms, the carpeted floors, everywhere there was room. They gave them water, and what medicines they could find in the house. Some were likely dying. All were in great pain, quiet as azi were always quiet, so long as they retained any consciousness of what they were doing. Some moaned, beyond that awareness.

Raen walked back into the living room, where her sun-suit lay over the back of a chair. She looked at the kitchen door, where Merry stood, shadow-eyed and bruised and bloody. "There's no taking them farther," she said hoarsely. "It's too cruel. Some, maybe. Some." She looked at Ny and Berden. "You tell me, seri. What would happen to those men here, in your care? I can terminate the worst or I can leave them—but not for you to do it. You tell me."

"We can manage for them," Ny said. "Want to." He pressed Berden's hand. "Never killed anybody. Don't want anybody killed in this house."

She believed that, by means having nothing to do with logic.

"Are you," Berden asked, "leaving us our own azi?"

She had intended otherwise until that moment. She looked at the beta woman and nodded. "Keep them. Likely you'll need their help yourselves, and probably they're no use in a fight."

The youth stood up, provoking a nervous reaction of his wife and of the armed azi. "I'm coming with," he said. "You're going to the City; you're going to fight. I'm coming with. There's others too. From other farms."

She was bewildered by that, saw his parents and wife almost protest, and not; saw ser Ny nod his head in slow agreement.

"I have the place to hold," Ny said sorrowfully. "But Nes'd go if he wants. Take some of the guard-azi with him, ours. We can spare. Settle with those citymen, and 'bove-worlders."

"You don't understand," Raen protested. "You can't help. It's not ISPAK; it's not ITAK either."

"What, then?" asked the younger Ny, his brow wrinkling. "What are you going to fight, Kontrin?"

It was a good question, better than he might know. Raen looked about her at their refuge, the farm, that might survive the chaos to come . . . looked back at him and shrugged. "Hive-matter. Things that have wanted settling for a long time."

"There's men would go," the young beta insisted. "Farms like ours and big estates too, belly-full with the way ITAK's run us. There's men all over would go to settle this once for all, would go with you, Kontrin."

"No."

"Sera," Merry objected. "This is sense he offers."

"This is the tapes," she said, looked about at all their faces, azi and beta. "*Tapes* . . . you understand that? You owe me nothing. We taped it into your ancestors seven hundred years ago. All your loyalty, all your fear of us, your desire to obey. It's all psych-set. Your azi know where their ideas come from. I'm telling you about yours. You're following a program. Stop, before it ruins you."

There was silence, stark silence, and the young man stood stricken and the young woman held her child close.

"Be free," Raen said. You've your farm. Let the cities go. I doubt there'll be more azi. These are the last. They'll go at their forty-year. Have children. Never mind the quotas. Have children, and be done with azi and with us."

"It's treason," the older Ny said.

"We created you; is that a reason to die with us? Outsiders have left the Reach, for a time long in *your* terms. The old woman who rules on Cerdin will fall soon, if not already: that they've come for me openly says something of that; and there'll be chaos after. Save what you can. Depend on no one."

"You stay, then," said Berden. "You stay with us, sera." She looked at the beta in affront, and the gentleness in that woman's face and voice minded her of old Lia; it hurt. "Tapes," she said. "Come on, Merry. Load the truck." She glanced again at the Ny-Berdens. "I'm sorry about taking from you; all I can give you in return is advice. You've the lifetime of these azi to prepare yourselves for years without them, for a time when there'll only be your children to farm the land. And never—*never* meddle with the hives."

The azi gathered themselves, packed up food and water, headed for the waiting truck. Raen turned her back on the betas, pulled on the sunsuit, took up her rifle again, went out down the steps. Warrior hovered there, clicking with anxiety. Merry was tying on containers of extra fuel, a can and a half. "All we have?" she asked; Merry shrugged. "All, sera. I drained it."

Already the azi were boarding, all who could come and many who should not, insisting they were guard-azi and not farmers.

For them she felt most grief, for men who could imagine nothing more than to come with her. Even some of the farm azi rose and started forward, as if they thought that they were supposed to come, but she ordered them back, and they did not.

Then Merry climbed aboard, waiting on her. She saw two more waiting . . . long-faced, and the back of the truck was jammed; she motioned them into the cab, two more that they could manage, for in the back, men sat three deep, rifles leaned where they could; or stood, leaning on the frame. Heat went up from the ground and the truck in waves.

She squeezed herself in with Merry and the two others, pulled the door shut: no air-conditioning . . . they needed the fuel. There was a last scurrying and scrabbling atop the truck. Warrior was minded to ride for a space, boarded even as Merry put the vehicle in motion and it labored out, swaying and groaning, toward the dirt road.

"Left," Raen said when they reached the branching, directing them toward the River, and abandoned depots and the City.

She had the map, on her knee, and the hope that the vehicle would hold together long enough. She looked at

Merry, past the two azi who shared the cab with them. Merry's face was solid and stolid as ever, no sign of dread for what they faced.

How could there be, she wondered, for the likes of them, who knew their own limits, that they were designed and bred for what they did, and did it well?

They had not even the luxury of doubt.

We are outmoded, they and I, she thought, closing her hands about the smooth stock of the rifle. *Appropriate, that we go together.*

BOOK NINE

i

There was a presence at the door, beyond the sealed steel. Moth did not let it hasten her, carefully poured wine into the crystal with a steady left hand. The right hung useless. It throbbed, and the fingers were too swollen to bend. She did not look at it. The bandages sufficed; the robes covered it; and she deliberately forced herself to move about, ignoring it.

Something hissed at the door. She caught a flicker from the consoles about the room, a sudden shriek of alarm after. She set the wine down quickly and keyed broadcast to the hall outside.

"Stop it," she snapped. "If you want these systems intact, don't try it."

"She's alive," she heard in the background. "Eldest," an old voice overrode it, a familiar voice. She tried through the haze of pain to place it. Thon. That was Nel Thon. "Eldest, only your friends are here. Open the doors. Please open the doors." She said nothing to that.

"Crazy," someone said farther away. "Her mind has gone." Someone hissed that voice to silence.

"No," she answered it. "Quite sane. That you, Nel?"

"Eldest!" the voice overflowed with relief. "Please, open the doors. It's settled, over with. The forces loyal to you have won. Use the intercomp channels and confirm it for yourself."

"Loyal to *me?*" Pain made her voice harsh and she fought to make it even again. "Go back to the hives, Thon. Tell *them* your loyalty."

"Everything is stable, Eldest. Unlock the doors."

"Go your way, Nel Thon. Lord it in Council without me. Try your own terminals to intercomp. They'll work . . . so far." She drew a deep breath and cared little now how her voice sounded. "That door opens from the inside, cousins. Force it and you'll trigger a wipe."

There was a burst of voices from outside. She could not distinguish words.

"Please," said Nel Thon. "Is there some condition you want? Is there any assurance you want?"

"The same goes," she continued, "for trying to gain access to the banks, dear cousins. My key is fed in with a destruct order. When I go, it goes. Figure your way around *that*, cousins."

There was profound silence outside.

In time a whispering of anguished voices retreated from the area. She left the set on broadcast and settled back again, picked up the goblet and drank, sipped at it slowly, for the wine had to last.

ii

The ship was there, on the field, a sleek, familiar shape too graceful for the ground. Morn took time for a glance, attended to the necessary business of landing: the shuttle was not made for fine maneuvers.

Touchdown. He ignored the field patterns; tower was dead, and there were no lights to relieve the evening haze. He used the moving gear to take the shuttle up to the rear of the starship, out of the track of its armament.

"They answer," the azi at com told him quietly. "They're Hald azi and they're upset."

"Time they responded," Morn said. He began shutdown, closed off systems. "Standard procedures." He looked back through the ship, to the dozen who were with him, armored and armed. Chatter crackled in his left ear: no port control, but the Istra shuttle coming in with thirty more of his men, hard behind him. "Ask where Pol is."

"They say," the com-azi reported back slowly, "that he's gone into the City some time ago, hunting the Methmaren face to face. They weren't told how he's proceeding, or where."

"Is Sam with him?" Morn asked, for that one of Pol's azi was his most reliable.

"No. It's Sam I'm talking to."

"Tell him to open that ship." Morn rose, ducking the overhead, felt for his gun and gathered up his sun-kit and his rifle. One-unit readied itself to accompany him.

"Sam says," the com-azi called after him, "that he doesn't want to open. He says he's not sure he should."

Morn looked at the com-azi, his breath shortened by temper. "Tell Sam he has no choice," he said, and opened the hatch.

There was a thunder of engines outside, the Istra shuttle coming in. "Have them form up beside this ship," he directed two-unit leader, and rode the extending ladder down: one-unit was quickly at his heels.

He had a prickling at his nape, being in the open, near the terminal building. Betas might occupy that point, that flat roof, ITAK betas, who were likely *hers* to a man, and dangerous. He darted glances to all likely points for snipers, and half-ran the space to Pol's sleek *Moriah,* careless of dignity. Sam was capitulating, lowering the ramp, having come to his senses.

He climbed it with half his escort, stood inside, breathing the cold air of the hatchway. Pol's whole staff gathered there, Sam prominent among them, a sandy-haired azi with a scar at his brow.

"Out of my way," Morn said, and elbowed Sam aside; the others moved, pushed aside by his armored escort. He walked into controls with Sam anxiously struggling his way through after—sat down and read through what there was to read.

There was nothing. He turned around, a frown gathered on his face. "Sam. What kind of operation has he out there? What force is with him?"

The azi ducked his head in distress. "Alone, ser. He went alone."

Morn drew in his breath, eyes flicking over the staff of *Moriah,* finding them far too many: it was likely truth. Guard-azi. Dark-haired Hana, a female azi who was Pol's eccentricity, not even particularly beautiful. Tim, like Sam, Pol's accustomed shadow.

"Where," Morn asked, "is the Meth-maren based? City? ITAK Central?"

"We don't know."

It was truth. Sam was distressed; the whole staff was distraught.

"Stay and hold this ship," Morn directed his own men. "If Pol shows up, tell him to stay here."

A stifling feeling of things wrong assailed him. He thrust his way past them, out, down the ramp again where the other half of one-unit waited. The second shuttle had disgorged its occupants. Thirty more men waited orders.

A long partnership, his with Pol: forty years. They had shared much, had hunted together—and not only in sport. He tolerated Pol's humor and Pol supported his grimmer amusements.

Pol's humor. He looked about him, at dead buildings, at a sky void of traffic, the only sound that of the wind tugging at cloth and the popping of cooling metal. It was not a time or place for an exercise of whim, not even Pol's.

He had sent Pol, in advance of the order which sent him: Pol's humor, to ask this of him.

Pol . . . who avoided Cerdin of late; who avoided many old connections, and the hold at Ehlvillon—and, avowing her tedious, . . . Moth.

He paused, hard-breathing, looking back at *Moriah,* Pol avowed he had no sense of humor. Pol contrived, finally, to disturb his self-possession.

He shouted an order to the azi, stalked off toward the buildings of the terminal. Azi hastened to cluster themselves about him, shielding him with their armor and their bodies; he took this for granted, it being their function, and himself conspicuous for the Color that he wore.

Sun's glare still reflected off windows, but there was more than one window missing, betokening more than a quiet power shutdown here. That drew him, promising some insight into what had happened in the City.

And in the terminal, scattered over the polished floors, there were dead, male and female, young and old.

With live majat.

"Don't fire!" Morn snapped. One stepped lightly toward them, in the doorway. He saw the badges on it: it was a red, that had never been trouble for Hald.

"Kontrin," it moaned, when he held up his fist. "Green-hive."

"Hald. Morn a Ren hant Hald."

Palps swept forward. "Hhhald. Friend. Giffftss."

The tone of that chilled the flesh. But one took allies where one could, when family failed. "I'll settle with the Meth-maren for you. I need to locate her base. Her-hive. Understand?"

"Yes. Understand." It shifted forward, and the azi flinched, torn between terror and duty. It extended a forelimb, touched at his chest, and he suffered it, concealing his loathing, reckoning he might have to accept worse than this. "Red-hive knows Meth-maren hive, yes. Blues guard. This-unit will call othersss, many, many, many Warriors, reds, golds, greens, all move. Come kill, yess."

"Yes," he confirmed—did not touch it; that risk was one he did not choose to run, and the Warrior did not offer.

Others moved, to a shrilling command only partially in human hearing. They gathered, out of all the recesses of the terminal, a living sea of chitinous bodies.

"Tunnels," the Warrior said. "Tunnels for beta-machines. Ssubwayss."

iii

The house stirred and hummed with activity. One could hear it, even in the upper floors, the stir of many feet, the singing of majat voices. Jim sat still in the semi-dark beneath the dome, on the bed, hands loose over his crossed legs, watching the Kontrin who slumped angrily in the chair opposite. They were at a silence, and Jim found that profound relief, for Pol Hald reasoned well, and wounded accurately when he wanted to.

The power was gone, had been for hours; he believed now that it would not return.

There's no more comp, Pol had advised him. *Nothing. If you'd listened earlier, something might have been done. Something still might. Listen to me.*

Jim gave no answers. He could not argue with such a fluency: he could only steadfastly refuse. Max, downstairs, gave him the means to refuse. Warrior, standing faithfully outside, was a guard against which even Pol Hald's reasoning could not prevail.

Newhope's dead, Pol had said. *There's nothing here for her. Only trouble. He's here. Morn's here. He'll be coming, and she'll know that.*

He could not listen to such logic. It made sense.

Below, the majat swarmed and stirred and tugged at foundations.

And in the dome above, the stars began to show in a darkening sky, the majat song to swell louder.

"Does it never stop?" Pol demanded.

Jim shook his head. "Rarely."

Pol hurled himself suddenly to his feet. Jim rose, alarmed. "Relax," Pol said. "I'm tired of sitting."

"Sit down," Jim said, received of Pol a cold and sarcastic look. There was a certain incongruity in the situation.

And abruptly the song fragmented to a shrilling note.

Outside, Warrior dived for the stairs, scuttled away. "Come back!" Jim shouted at it, and jerked from his pocket the gun which he had for his protection, an azi against a Kontrin. Pol saw it, raised both hands and turned his face aside, miming peace.

Jim held the gun in both hands to steady it. "Max!" he shouted, panic hammering in him.

"Please," Pol said fervently. "I'd not be shot by mistake."

Steps tramped up the stairs, not human ones, but spurred feet which caught on the carpet fiber, with the hollow gasp of majat breathing. Warrior loomed up in the doorway again.

"Many, many," it announced. "Trouble."

Jim did not take his eyes off Pol—motioned nervously with the gun, indicated the chair. Pol subsided, his gaunt face anxious.

"Where's Max?" Jim asked of Warrior.

"Down. All down in outside. Warrior-azi, yess. Much danger. Reds, golds, greens are grouping. Blues are here, Jim-unit. Kill this green, take taste to Mother, yesss."

Pol looked for once sober, his hands held in plain sight. "Argue with it, azi."

"Stay still!" Jim tried to control his breathing, tried to reason. "I hold this place," he said. "No, Warrior. This is Raen's. She'll understand it when she comes."

"Queen." Warrior seemed to accept that logic. "Where? Where is Meth-maren queen, Jim?"

"I don't know."

Warrior clicked to itself, edged forward. "Mother wants. Mother sends Warriors out, seek, seek, find. I guard. This-chamber is no good, too high. Come, this-unit guides, down, down, where safety is, good places, deep."

"No," Pol advised softly, alarm in his voice.

"I trust Warrior more. Up, ser. Up. We're going downstairs."

Pol made a gesture of exasperation and rose, and this sudden lack of seriousness in him, Jim watched with the greatest apprehension. Pol sauntered out, past him, and Warrior led them downstairs, Jim last and with the gun at Pol's back.

The center of the house, windowless, was plunged in darkness, blue lights bobbing and flaring on the walls and making strange shadows of their bearers. Majat-azi skipped about them, touching them, Pol as well. The Kontrin cursed them from him, and they laughed and scampered off, taking the light with them.

Other azi remained, in the blackness. "Jim," Max's

voice said. "They urged us to come in. Was it right to do? I thought maybe we shouldn't, but they pushed us and kept pushing."

"You did right," Jim said, although in his mind was the horrible possibility of being swept up with the majat-azi, herded deep below. "The Hald is with us. Watch him."

"Tape-fed obstinance," Pol's voice came, outraged, for they laid hands on him. "If you would listen—"

"I won't."

"At least check comp."

Jim hesitated. It ceased to be an attempt to unsettle him, began to seem plain advice. He felt his way aside, into the comp center, shuddered as a majat-azi brushed his shoulder. He caught a slim female arm. "Stay, come," he asked of her, for the light's sake, and took her with him, into the face of the dead machinery, the dark screens.

But paper had fed out, printout, in the machine's dying.

He was stricken, suddenly, with the realization Pol had been urging him to what he should have done. He drew the majat-azi to the machine, tore off the print and laid it on the counter. "Light," he said, "light," and she lent it, leaning on his shoulder with her arm about him. He ignored her and ran through the messages as rapidly as he could read the dim print in azi-light. Most were of no meaning to him; he had known so. Pol might understand, and he knew that Pol would urge him to show them to him: but he dared not, would not. It was useless; the key to these was not in the tapes he had stolen.

JIM, one said plainly. STAND BY. EMERGENCY.

It was not signed. But only one who knew his name could have used a comp board.

Sent before her trouble, perhaps; the possibility hit his stomach like a blow, that she had needed him, and he had been upstairs, unhearing.

"Stay!" he begged of the azi, who had tired of what she did not understand. He caught at her wrist and held her light still upon the paper, ran his eye over the other messages.

JIM, the last said, BEWARE POL HALD.

He thought to check the time of transmission; it was not on this one, but on the one before . . . an ITAK message . . . One in the night and one in the morning.

He looked up, at a commotion in the doorway, where dancing azi-lights cast Pol Hald and Max and others into a flickering blue visibility.

Alive, his heart beat in him. *Alive, alive, alive.*

And they had let Pol in.

"Is it from her?" Pol asked. *"Is it from her?"*

"Max, get him down to the basement."

Pol resisted; there were azi enough to hold him, though they had trouble moving him. "Please," Jim said sharply, rolling up the precious message, and the struggle ceased. He felt the insistent hands of the majat-azi touching him, wanting something of him. He ignored her, for she was mad. "Please go," he asked of the Kontrin. "Her orders, yes. This house is still hers."

Pol went then, led by the guard-azi. Jim stood still in the dark, conscious of others who remained, majat shapes. All through the house bodies moved, and round about it, a never-ceasing stream.

"Warrior," Jim asked, "Warrior? Raen's alive. She sent a message through the comp before it died. Do you understand?"

"Yess." A shadow scuttled forward. "Kethiuy-queen. Where?"

"I don't know. I don't know that. But she'll come." He looked about him at the shapes in the dark, that flowed steadily toward the front doors. "Where are they going?"

"Tunnels," Warrior answered. "Human-hive tunnels. Reds are moving to attack; golds, greens, all move, seek here, seek Kethiuy-queen. We fight in tunnels."

"They're coming up the subway," Jim breathed.

"Yes. From port. Kontrin leads, green-hive: we taste this presence in reds. This-hive and blue-hive now touch;

tunnel is finished. All come. Fight." It sucked air, reached for him, touched nervously and uncertainly he sought to calm it, but Warrior would have none of it. It clicked its jaws and moved on, joining the dark stream of others that flowed toward the doors.

Azi went, majat-azi, bearing blue lights in one hand and weapons in the other, naked and wild. Warriors hastened them on. Jim tried to pass them, almost gathered up in their number, but that he ducked and went the other way, down the hall and down the stairs.

Blue azi-lights were there, hanging from majat fiber, and a draft breathed out of an earth-rimmed pit, the floor much-trampled with muddy feet. Max and the other azi were there in a recess by the stairs, and Pol Hald among them.

Pol rose to his feet, looking up at him on the stairs. Azi surrounded him with weapons. "There's nothing," Pol said, "so dangerous as one who thinks he knows what he's doing. If you had checked comp while it was still alive—when I told you to—you could have contacted her and been of some use."

That was true, and it struck home. "Yes," he admitted freely.

"Still," Pol said, "I could help her."

He shook his head. "No, ser. I won't listen." He sank down where he stood, on the steps. At the bottom a majat-azi huddled, a wretched thing, female, whose hands were torn and bleeding and whose tangled hair and naked body were equally muddied. It was uncommon: never had he seen one so undone. The azi's sides heaved. She seemed ill. Perhaps her termination was on her, for she was not young.

"See to her," he told one of the guard-azi. The man tried; others did, and the woman would take a little water, but sank down again.

And suddenly it occurred to him that it was much quieter than it had been, the house silent; that of all the Workers which had labored hereabouts—not one remained.

The tunnel breathed at them, a breath neither warm

nor cold, but damp. And from deep within it, came a humming that was very far and strange.

"Max," Jim said hoarsely. "They've gone for the subways of the city. A red force is coming this way."

Pol sank down with a shake of his head and a deep-voiced curse.

Jim tucked his arms about his knees and wished to go to that null place that had always been there, that he saw some of the guard-azi attain, waiting orders. He could not find it now. Tape-thoughts ran and cycled endlessly, questions open and without neat answers.

He stared at Max and at the Kontrin, at the Kontrin most of all, for in those dark and angry eyes was a mutual understanding. It became quieter finally, that glance, as if some recognition passed between them.

"If you've her mind-set," Pol said, "use it. We're sitting in the most dangerous place in the city."

He looked into the dark and answered out of that mindset, consciously. "The hive," he said, "is safety." Pol's retort was short and bitter.

iv

Itavvy rose and walked to the door, walked back again and looked at his wife Velin as the infant squirmed and fretted in her arms, taxing her strength. One of the Upcoast women offered a diversion, an attempt to distract the child from her tears. Meris screamed in exhausted misery . . . hunger. The azi outside the glass, with their guns, their faceless sameness, maintained their watch.

"I'll ask again," Itavvy said.

"Don't," Velin pleaded.

"They don't have anger. It isn't in them. There are ways to reason past them. I've dealt—" He stopped, remembered his identity as Merek Sed, who knew little of azi, swallowed convulsively.

"Let me." The gangling young Upcoaster who had spent his time in the corner, sketch-pad on his knee, left his work lying and went to the door, rapped on it.

The azi ignored it. The young artist pushed the door open; rifles immediately lowered at him. "The child's sick," the youth said. "She needs milk. Food. Something."

The azi stood with their guns aimed at him . . . confused, Itavvy thought, in an access of tension. Presented with crisis. Well-done.

"If you'd call the kitchens," the artist said, "someone would bring food up."

Meris kept crying. The azi hesitated, unnerved, swung the rifle in that direction. Itavvy's heart jumped.

Azi can't understand, he realized. *No children. No tears.*

He edged between, facing the rifle. "Please," he said to the masked face. "She'll be quiet if she's fed."

The azi moved, lifted the rifle, closed the door forcefully. Itavvy shut his eyes, swallowed hard at nausea. The young artist turned, set a hand on his shoulder.

"Sit down," the youth said. "Sit down, ser. Try to quiet her."

He did so. Meris exhausted herself, fell whimpering into sleep. Velin lifted bruised eyes and held her fast.

Then, finally, an azi in ISPAK uniform brought a tray to the door, handed it in, under guard.

Drink, sandwiches, dried fruit. Meris fretted and ceased, given the comfort of a full belly. Itavvy sat and ate because it was something to do.

The identity of Merek Sed would collapse. They were being detained because someone was running checks. Perhaps it had already been proven false. They would die.

Meris too. The azi had no feeling of difference.

He dropped his head into his hands and wept.

v

The truck labored, ground up the slope from the riverbed, picking up dry road in the headlights. Raen threw it to idle at the crest, let what men had gotten off climb on again, the truck sinking on its suspension as it accepted its burden. She read the fuel gauge and the odometer, cast a look at Merry, who opened the door to look out on his side. "They're all aboard," he said.

"Then go back to sleep." She said it for him and the two azi crowded in between them, and eased the truck forward, walking it over ruts that jolted it insanely and wrenched at her sore arms. A thousand kilometers. That was one thing on the map, and quite another as Istrans built roads. The track was only as wide as the truck. The headlights showed ruts and stones, man-high grass on either side of the road, obscuring all view.

A nightmare shape danced into the lights before them, left again: Warrior stayed with them, but the jolting on this stretch was such that it chose to go on its own feet.

By the map, this was the only road. They were on the last of their fuel, that which they had brought in containers, having used the stored power and both main and reserve tanks. They might nurse a kilometer back out of batteries after the fuel ran out. Cab light went on. Merry was checking the map again, counting with his fingers and making obvious conclusions.

"It's six hundred to go," Raen said, "and it pulls too much. We're loaded way beyond limits and we're not going to do it."

"Map shows good road past the depot."

"Easier walking, then." Raen looked to the side as a black body hit the door, scraped and scrambled its way to the roof of the truck. Warrior had decided to ride again. Six hundred kilometers more: easy on a good road with an unburdened track. As exhausted men would walk it . . . days.

"Could be fuel there," Merry offered.

"One hopes. If we get that far."

"I'll drive again, sera."

"We'll change over at the depot. Rest."

Merry turned the light out. He did not seem to sleep, but he said nothing, and in him, in the two with them—

likely in all those men in the rear—there was evident that familiar blankness. They lost themselves in that, and perhaps found refuge.

She had no such. There was a stitch in her back which had been growing worse over the hours, and fighting the steering aggravated it; the right shoulder ached, until finally she chose to let the right hand rest in her lap, however much that tired the left. The jolt of the crash, she reckoned. Pain was something she had long since learned to ignore. A stoppered bottle sat beside her; she moved the right hand to it, flipped the cap with her thumb, took a drink of water, capped it again. It helped keep her awake. She worked a bit of dried fruit from her pocket, bit off a little and sucked at that: the sugar helped too.

The road worsened again, after a little smoothness; she applied both hands for the while, relaxed again when it passed. Imagination constructed a picture of the men in the back, jammed in so that some must constantly stand, or lie on others, whose muscles must cramp and joints stiffen, all jolted cruelly with every hole she could not avoid and every lean and lurch of the turns.

Figures flicked past on the odometer, a red pulse far too slow. The fuel registered lower and lower, most gone now out of the last filling.

Then the road smoothed out on a flat high enough to see no flooding. She kicked them up to a better pace, and Merry came out of his trance and shifted position, causing the other two men to do the same.

"Should be coming up on the depot," she said.

Merry leaned to take a look at the fuel and said nothing.

There was a scraping overhead. A spiny limb extended itself over the windshield. Warrior slid partially down, and Raen swore at that, for they had no margin for delays. It scraped at the glass, insisting on her attention, and at the realization it was urgent her heart began to beat the faster.

She let off the accelerator, coasted, rolled down the window lefthanded. Warrior scrambled off when they slowed enough, paced them, the while the headlights picked out only dusty ruts and high weeds.

"Others," Warrior breathed. "Hear? Hear?"

She could not. She braked, threw the engine to idle, quieter.

"Many," Warrior said. "All around us."

"The depot," Merry said hoarsely. "They've got it." Raen nodded, a sinking feeling in her stomach.

"Get the men out," she said. "They'd better limber up, be ready for it, be ready to dive back in on an instant. Third thorax ring, center; or top collar-ring, if they don't know. Make sure they understand where it counts."

Merry bailed out, staggering, felt his way around to the back. Warrior was dancing in impatience beside the truck. The two men in the cab edged out and followed Merry.

"How far?" Raen asked. Warrior quivered very rapidly. Near, then. She felt the truck lighten of its load, eased off the brake and set it in gear, not to waste precious fuel. Merry's door was open. She left it so; he might need it in a hurry. "Warrior—hear me: you must not fight. You're a messenger. Understand?"

"Yess." It accepted this. It was majat strategy. No heroism, she thought suddenly, not among majat: only function and common sense, expediency to the limit. Warrior was very dangerous at the moment, excited. It paced the slow-moving truck as the men did. "Give message."

"Not yet. I don't want you to go yet."

The road curved, took a small decline, rose again. Then blockish shapes hove up in the starlight, among the distinctive structures of collectors.

The depot. The road went through it, that cluster of buildings that likely spelled ambush. Raen kept the truck rolling, watched the fuel that was registering just slightly: enough to carry them through—maybe.

Then the shrilling of Warriors erupted from the left of the road. She began to feel the jolting of the truck, men climbing aboard in haste. She kept it slow.

"Warrior," she said, "don't answer them."

"Yes," it agreed. "I am very quiet, Kethiuy-queen."

"Can you—" The wheels jerked into a rut and she wrenched it over again. "Can you tell their hive?"

"Goldsss."

That made sense. Golds even on Cerdin had chosen the open places, the fields, avoiding men. Once reds had done so too.

The headlights picked out girders, the frame of a collector, the wall of a weathered building, with barred and broken windows. The light flashed back off jagged glass.

Objects lay in the road, where it widened to include the buildings. Corpses, she realized, avoiding one. Human forms, desiccated by heat and sun, scattered in a pattern of flight from the central building. Another shape hove up, brown metal—the rear of a truck, with open doors.

Merry darted past, running to it, a group of men with him. Her eyes picked out something better: pumps, a fuel delivery in the shadow of the truck, a spidery tantalus with lines intact.

She pulled in, braked, bailed out and ran round to the side; Merry was before her, the nozzle in.

"It needs a pump," he said, anguished; and then nicked a glance up, at the collectors. She had the same thought. "Go," she said to the man nearest. "Should be a switch in the building. It ought to work."

The azi ran. All about them now, the shrilling was ominously louder.

"Golds," Warrior boomed. "Here, here, watch out!" It moved, swiftly, dancing in its anxiety. Fire spat in the building.

"Watch it!" Raen cried, ran for the door of it; Merry was in the same stride with her.

A Warrior sprang out at them; she fired from the hip and crippled it, as Warrior pounced. Two others were on them: azi-fire raked past and took them. Raen clutched the rifle and kicked the door wider, on a dark room and an azi convulsing on the floor, majat-bitten. There were no others; Warrior shouldered past her, and she was sure by that. Merry found the comp, called out, and she punched POWER-ON. Lights came on, inside and out, blinding. . . . local reserve, from the collectors.

"Works!" she heard an azi call from outside. "Works!"
And the shrilling was moving in on them.

"We could use that other truck," Merry said.

"Don't be greedy."

"Less load, better time."

"Try it," Raen said. "Hurrry."

He left, running. She walked out after. They were no
clearer to majat eyes in the lights than in the dark; but
the heat of the lights themselves was an advertisement.
The golds knew beyond doubt now, perhaps delayed in
the process of Grouping.

Warrior had darted out again; it rose from the corpse
of a gold, mandibles clicking. "Other blues," it translated
for her.

"Both dead. Gold-hive killed blue messengers. Lost
Message in gold-hive now. Bad, Kethiuy-queen, bad thing.
This-unit goes now."

"Wait," she said. It would not get through, not with
golds ringing them. She bit her lips and kept scanning
beyond the lights, reckoning how blind they were to the
land outside the circle of them.

And the majat were cut off by the cluster of buildings;
that was why there was no rush as yet. Majat sought
them visually, and the buildings were between. The
group-mind had to be informed, to make nexus.

Quickly now she passed among the azi still outside,
touched shoulders, ordered them into the truck with the
tank most full. Warrior danced about in her wake, quivering with anxiety, wanting instruction. "You too," she told
it. "Get inside, inside the front of the truck, this side, understand? Merry, we may have to give up on the second."

"First is full." Merry snatched the nozzle from the first
truck and passed it to another man, who swung the tantalus over to the second. He put the cap on. "We can make
it, sera. And if one should break down on the road—"

"I'm putting most of the men in my truck. We'll sort
things out if we both get out of here."

"Good, sera. Leave me two men, that's all."

"Get up there and be sure this thing starts," she yelled
at him, over a rising in the majat-sound. She hastened

then, saw that Warrior had contrived to work its unyielding body into the cab. She slammed the door on it, raced round the back, giving last orders to the men jammed inside, vulnerable with the rear of the truck open to the air. "Get the tanks when we're clear," she shouted at them. "Pick your time and do it."

"Sera!" several cried suddenly.

She looked over her shoulder. A glittering tide swept under the lights and the girders, with speed almost too great for the eye to comprehend.

"Merry!" she screamed, and ran, flung herself into her seat, slammed the door, rolled the window tip as she started the motor. It took. She slung the truck back and around, screening Merry for the instant, saw him and his partners dive for the cab and get the doors closed. The truck rocked, and all at once majat were all over them, tearing at the metal and battering at the glass. Some had weapons, and sought targets for their vision.

Merry's truck started moving, lurched forward at full; she hit the accelerator hard behind him. The tantalus ripped loose and raked the majat clinging to the front; Warrior, tucked beside her, squirmed and shrilled in its own language, deafening, itself blind by reason of the glass about it. "Sit still," Raen shouted at it, trying to rake majat against the corner of a building.

Suddenly everything flared with light.

The tanks. One of the men had gotten them. Majat dropped from the truck; rear-mirrors showed an inferno and majat scattering across the face of it, blinded in that maelstrom of heat. Red fire laced in their wake, and open road and grass showed before them, the whole area alight with that burning. Buildings caught, and blazed red.

She sucked in a breath, fought the wheel to keep in Merry's wake, down the road, her own vehicle overladen, but free. A sound pierced her ears, Warrior's shrill voice, passing down into human range. "Kill," Warrior said, seeming satisfied.

The road smoothed out. They began to make time, blind as they were in Merry's dust cloud.

And when the light was out of sight over several hills she punched in the com and raised Merry. "Good work. Are you all right up there?"

"All right," he confirmed.

"Pull off and leave the motor running."

He did so, easing to a comfortable stop. She pulled in behind and ran round the front to open the door for Warrior before it panicked. It disentangled itself, climbed down, grooming itself in distaste, muttering of gold-scent.

"Life-fluids," it said. "Kill many."

"Go now," she bade it. "Tell all you know to Mother. And tell Mother these azi and I are coming to blue-hive's Hill, to the new human-hive nearest it. Let Warriors meet us there."

"Know this place," Warrior confirmed. "Strange azi."

"Tell Mother these things. Go as quickly as you can."

"Yess," it agreed, bowed for taste, that for its kind was the essence of message. She gave it, that gesture very like a kiss, and the majat drew back. "Kethiuy-queen," it said. And strangely: "Sugar-water."

It fled then, quickly.

"Sera." Merry came running up behind her; she turned, saw him, saw his partners sorting men from truck to truck.

"We have casualties?"

"Eight dead, no injured."

She grimaced and shook her head. "Leave them," she said, and walked back to supervise, put several men on watch, one to each point, for the headlights showed only grass about, and that not far. The glow was still bright over the hills.

The dead were laid out by the road, neatly: their only ceremony. Units organized themselves, all with dispatch.

"Sera!" a lookout hissed, pointed.

There were lights, blue, floating off across the grass.

"Hive-azi," she exclaimed. "We're near something. Hurry, Merry!"

Everyone ran; men flung themselves into one truck or the other, and Raen dived behind the wheel of her own, slammed the door, passed Merry in moving out: she had the map. The truck, relieved of half its weight, moved with a new freedom.

And suddenly there was the promised paving, where the depot road joined the Great South. Raen slammed on the brakes for the jolt, climbed onto it, spun the wheel over and took to it with a surge of hope.

Behind them, reflected in the mirrors, the fire reached the fields.

vi

The sound of hammering resounded through the halls of ITAK upstairs. Metal sheeting was going into place, barriers to the outside. The hammer-blows echoed even into the nether floors, the levels below. In the absence of air-conditioning and lights, the lower levels assumed a strange character, the luxury of upstairs furnishings crowded into what had been lower offices, fine liquor poured by the lighting of handtorches.

Enis Dain lifted his glass, example to the others, his board members, their families, and the officials, whoever had been entitled to shelter here. There were still, from above, through the doors still open, the sound of hammering.

Some had fled for the port. Unwise. There was a Kontrin reported there, the Enemy that the Meth-maren had warned them would come. Likely they had met with him, to their sorrow. Dain drank; all drank, the board members, his daughter, who sat by Prosserty—a useless man, Prosserty, Dain had never liked him.

"It's close in here," Prosserty complained. Dain only stared at him, and, remembering the batteries, cut off the handtorch, leaving them only the one set atop the table. He began calculating how long a night it would be.

"About sixteen days of it," he said. "About time for Council to get a message from the Meth-maren. We can last that long. They'll do something. Until then, we last it out. We've comfort enough to do that."

The hammering stopped upstairs.

"They're through up there," Hela Dain said. "They'll be sealing us in now."

Then glass splintered, far above.

And someone screamed.

The lights were out. 117-789-5457 sat tucked in the corner on her mat, mental null. The lights had been out what subjectively seemed long, and the temperature was up. Sounds reached her, but none were ordinary. She knew a little unease at this, wondering if food would come soon, and water, for water no longer came from the tap, and it always had, whatever cubicle she had occupied.

Always the lights had been above, and the air had been tolerable.

But now there was nothing.

Sounds. Sounds without meaning. The quick patter of soft feet. 117-789-5457 untucked and looked up. There was a strange glow in the blackness, blue lights, that wove and bobbed above, not on the catwalks, but on the very rims of the cells. Faces, blue-lighted; naked bodies; wild unkempt hair; these folk squatted on the rim of her own cell, stared down, grinning.

Hands beckoned. Eyes danced in the lights. "Come," they said, voices overlapping. "Come. We help. Come, azi."

She rose, for they reached hands to her, and one leaned down very far, helped by the others, caught her hands and drew her, by all their efforts, up.

117-789-5457 looked about her, balancing on the wall, held by strong, thin hands. Lights wove and bobbed everywhere. Laughter echoed in the silent places. Out of all the cells, azi were drawn.

"Take all azi, young, old, yess," one laughed, and danced away. "Come, come, come, come."

117-789-5457 followed, along the walls, for she had never refused an order. She smiled, for that seemed the way to please these who ordered her.

*   *   *

"There's fire in the city," the voice from downworld continued thinly, azi-calm, and Leo K14-756-4806 listened without looking, taking deeply to heart his instructions, which placed him in charge of station command. Morn depended on him. He listened, and did not waver, although he was distressed for what he heard.

Regarding his own men he could not tell: they kept their masks, that being Morn's general instruction; and he could not read their reactions to the voice from the shuttle, that brought them ill news. But there was wavering certainly in the ranks of the captive betas, and of the guard-azi who belonged to the station, who stood under levelled rifles, along with the betas.

"We must restore power," the head beta appealed to him. "The city must have it."

"The fires are in every quarter," the impartial voice continued. "We've had no contact with Morn since he entered the terminal. What shall we do, Leo?"

"Wait for orders," Leo answered, looked about the center, at betas and station azi. No one moved. The betas did not dare and the station azi would not, lacking instruction.

"This is *Moriah*," another azi voice broke in. "We're getting nothing from city communications any longer. Everything's in complete chaos."

"Just stand by your posts," Leo said. There was nothing else to say. He paced back across the command center, arms folded, looked constantly at the betas, challenging them to advance any more ideas of their own.

They did not.

Warriors were back, great bodies shifting through all the rooms of the house, shrilling and booming signals that hurt the ears. Jim ventured the stairs to the turning, met some coming down and flung himself aside, for the Warriors were in haste, and had no inclination to speak. Pol's oath erupted out of the blue-lit depths.

"They're running," the Kontrin said.

"Max," Jim pleaded, at the edge of panic. "Max—"

Max came; all the azi followed, bringing Pol, scrambling up the stairs against the spiny flood of majat down them. Furniture crashed throughout the house, the press of too many bodies. The house boiled with them; the dark rooms hummed with distress and anger.

And the glow of fires shone through the back windows, distant ruddy smoke billowing up.

"They're blind in fire," Pol said. "Some betas have figured one way to fight them."

"Windows," Max said. "Stations."

Azi moved, each rifleman to a window.

"Your blues are beaten," Pol said above the hum of majat-voices. "I'd suggest we get out of here." Jim shook his head fiercely, strode up the hall to look out the open door, where dark shapes scurried about the front garden. "They're not running, not all of them. They're still going to hold this place."

Max cast a look too, and at him. "I'd suggest we get out there, work ourselves into cover in the rocks. Harder to dislodge us that way."

"I can't say." Jim swallowed heavily. "Do it. I don't think walls can stop them."

"Want advice?"

Jim looked about, back to the wall, at Pol Hald. The gaunt Kontrin stood between his guards, without threat.

"I've some interest in the management of this," Pol said. "The man's right; but occupy those windows with vantage, front and back for screening fire if you need it. And get your own Warriors behind you; your men can't tell blues from reds in the dark."

"It's sense," Max said.

A sound began . . . started with the feeling of pressure in the ears, so that many pressed their hands to them; and then became pain, a shrilling that grated in the bones.

It was all around them. The Warriors in the house retreated into a knot, grouping, booming to each other in panic.

"Warrior!" Jim cried. "Stay!"

They clicked and shrilled in reply, nicking palps this way and that, and majat-azi who had come with them scampered from their vicinity, faces stark with fright. Jim started forward.

"No," Pol exclaimed, reached out to grip his arm. "No, blast it, you're not Meth-maren. Stay back from them."

That too was good advice. He retreated outside with Max, settled in the rocks with a Kontrin of Hald beside them, and shook his head to clear his ears, pressure that would not go away.

We're going to die, he thought, and panicked entirely, for it was a born-man thought, a born-man fear: the tapes had done it to him, prepared him only for this, this sick dread. Max's face was calm. The Kontrin gave him a twisted smile, as if he had read his mind, and mocked him in the fear they shared.

Sound rose about them, madness.

vii

The truck jolted, badly. Raen caught at the door, rubbed her blurred eyes, looked askance at the azi who, however indifferent a driver, kept the pace, tailing Merry.

"How's the fuel holding?" she asked, leaning to see. It was reserve tank, half full. They were still all right.

And the odometer: ten kilometers from their goal. The lights of the city should have been visible, but she expected none. She folded her arms and sat regarding the sweep of the horizon, finding yet no sight of their goal, nothing in the faint glimmering of dawn, which began to fade the stars.

But there were no stars northward.

She sat up, her heart beating hard against her ribs. She had slept. There was no drowsiness in her now.

"Merry," she said into the com. "Merry. Are you awake up there?"

"Sera?"

"Smoke. Smoke over the city."

"Yes. I see it, sera."

"We're going to pass. Turn's coming up. Stand by. Go round him, Will. We've a little space yet."

Five kilometers. The truck accelerated; Merry dropped back. Four. She started watching on the right closely, wondering in agony about the accuracy of the maps.

The kilometers ticked off. "Slow down," she said. The driver eased down. There was a stake with an illegible number, a spur, a mere eroded place off the paved road, but trucks had passed it: crushed weeds showed in the dawning.

"Take it," she said. The driver did so, eased them onto it, carefully, while the truck swayed and lurched and weeds whispered against the doors.

They were blind in this place. She would have given much then for Warrior's sight and hearing. Turn after turn took them out of sight of the road, and the only comfort was Merry's vehicle showing in the mirror by her window.

A turning, a descent of the road, a brief climb around the curve of a hill: a weathered cluster of buildings showed before them, a desolate place . . . but someone had been cutting weeds.

Itavvy, she thought, *prosperity on your house.*

Doors opened; men came out, sunsuited, rifles levelled, to meet the trucks. Beside her, Will reached for his own rifle. She gathered up hers, opened the door.

"Isan Tel," she said. "Come code 579-4645-687."

One man nodded to the others, his rifle lifted out of the line of fire; other weapons were turned away. Sun-masks and visors came off. There were several among them female; several of more clerical look than guard-type, some unarmed.

"I'm your contract," she said. "I can't clear it on comp; you know that. Ask your azi-in-charge: did you not find orders in comp to keep to these buildings and fight only majat that attacked you?"

"That's truth," a man said, quiet voice, quiet manner, minding her of Jim. Faces all about took on a look of great relief, as if their entire world had suddenly settled into order: it had asked much of them until now, that azi alone hold the place. She saw their eyes fixed on her, with that deep calm that did not belong in the situation: contract-loyalty.

"The hives are moving," she said. "Have you had trouble here?"

The manager-azi lifted an arm toward the south, the open fields. "Majat came in. We took a few. They went back again."

She indicated the northeast. "Nothing from that direction."

"No, sera."

She nodded. "You're on blue-hive's doorstep; but they're not human-killers. The others were golds, more than likely. You've already done your proper service, sitting here, guarding blue-hive. I have your contract. We go further now, but only azi that won't freeze or panic."

Their calm was disturbed by talk of blue-hive. She saw the ripple of dismay, turned and waved at Merry. "Out! We're going afoot from here. Any who'll come, any who are able."

Her own azi climbed out, none hesitating, with rifles and what gear they had; weary as they were, she looked on them with some hope. "We're going to fight *for* a hive," she said. "For blue-hive, our own, back in the city. We have to go among them; into it, if we can. Stay, if that's too much for you."

She started walking . . . knew Merry, at least, would join her. He was there, at once, and hardly slower, the others, filthy, sorry-looking men; she looked back, and not one had stayed. The Tel estate azi were on their heels, plain by their clean clothing and their energy. In the rear, the managers and the domestics trailed along, perhaps reckoning now they were safer not to be left in the deserted buildings.

They climbed, pushing aside the high weeds, finding trails overgrown and forgotten in the hills. "Majat trails," she said to Merry. "Abandoned ones."

"Blue-hive?"

"Better be."

Something urged at her hearing. She kept her eyes to the high rocks, the folds of the land.

A majat warning boomed out. She spun left; rifles jerked about, hovered unfired on the person of a Warrior, testament to azi discipline. She turned her fist to it, that stood against the sky.

"Meth-maren," it intoned.

"Warrior, you're too far for my eyes. Come closer."

It shifted forward, a blue beyond doubt. Others appeared out of the rocks, jaws clicking with excitement.

"Here are azi of my-hive," she said. "They've held the valley til now; now they'll fight where needed."

It lowered itself, offered touch and taste, and she took and gave it, moving carefully lest some new azi take alarm. "Good, good," it pronounced then. "Mother sends. Come, come quick, Kethiuy-queen. Bring, bring, bring."

She looked back; none who followed had fled; none offered to go back now. Warrior danced with impatience and she touched Merry's arm and started after it, following the devious ways it led, over stone and through brush.

Suddenly the hive gaped before them, a dark pit, seeming void of defense; but Warriors materialized out of the weeds, the stones of the hills, boiled out from the darkness. She hesitated not at all, hearing their guide boom a response to them; and one Warrior touched her—by that move, one who knew her personally.

"Warrior?" she asked it.

"This-unit guides. Come. Come, bring azi."

Blue lights bobbed in the pit. She went without question toward them, Merry beside her, others close at her heels. The darkness enveloped them, and majat-azi scampered just ahead, wretched creatures who no longer laughed, but stumbled and faltered with exhaustion. Blue light ran chaotically over the walls, showing them the way. Warrior-song shrilled in the dark.

And the majat-azi touched her, urged her on, breathlessly, faster and faster. "Mother," they cried, "Mother, Mother, Mother."

Raen gasped for air and kept moving, stumbling on the uneven floor, catching herself against the rough walls.

All at once the blue lights were not sufficient. Vast darkness breathed about them, and they streamed along the midst of it. A great pale form loomed ahead, that dragged itself painfully before them, huge, filling all the tunnel.

It was Mother, who moved.

Who heaved Herself along the tunnel prepared for Her vast bulk. The walls echoed with Her breathing. About Her were small majat who glittered with jewels; and before Her moved a dark heaving flood of bodies, dotted with azi-lights.

Majat-language boomed and shrilled in the tunnel, deafening. And, terrible in its volume, came Her voice, which vibrated in the earth.

Raen gathered herself and passed beside that great body, moving faster than ever Mother could. There was room, barely, that she and the men with her could avoid the sweep of Mother's limbs, that struggled with even thrusts to drive Her vast body along, at every rumbling intake of Her breath.

"I am here!" Raen cried.

"Kethiuy-queen," She answered. The great head did not turn, could not; Mother remained fixed upon Her goal.

"Am I welcome, Mother? Where are you going?"

"I go," Mother said simply, and the earth quivered with the moving of Her. Air sucked in again. "I go. Haste. Haste, young queen."

Anxiety overwhelmed her. She increased her pace, moving now among the Drones, whose chittering voices hurt her ears.

Then the Workers, all that vast horde, azi scattered among them; and the strange-jawed egg-tenders, leaving their work, precious eggs abandoned.

She looked back. Mother had almost vanished in the shadows. She saw Merry's bruised face in the faint blue glow, felt the touch of his hand.

"We're going north," she said, comprehension suddenly coming on her, the Workers who had plied the basement, the preparation of a way.

"To fight for them?" Merry asked hoarsely, and glanced back himself, for there were men who still followed. Perhaps they all did; strung out through the tunnel, it was no longer possible to see. Perhaps some collapsed in withdrawal, gone mad from fear; or perhaps training held, and they had no sensible dread.

"I belong," she said, "where this merges."

"Where, sera?"

"Home," she said.

viii

A horde of steps approached the steel doors, a surge of panicked voices. Moth stirred, lifted her head, although to do so took more strength than she had left to spend on them, who troubled her sleeping and merged with dreams.

"Moth!" A voice came out of the turmoil. She knew this one too, old Moran, and fear trembled in that sound. "Moth! Thon is gone—*gone*. The hive-masters couldn't hold them. They're in the City. Everywhere—"

She touched her microphone, braced before her on the console, beside the wine bottle and her gun. "Then lock your own doors, Moran. Follow my example."

"We need the codes. Moth, do something."

She grinned, her head bobbing slightly with weakness. "But haven't you figured it out yet, Moran? I am."

"The city's in wreckage," the voice from *Moriah* said. "Leo, Leo, we've still had no contact with him. There were majat here. Even they've left, moved elsewhere. He should have been in contact by now."

"Hold the ships," Leo repeated, and looked up at the other azi, his own and the station's. They were exhausted. There had been no food, no off-shift. He thought that he ought to send for something to eat. He was not sure that he had appetite for it.

The betas sat in a knot over to the side of the door. One of them had become ill, holding his heart. He was an older beta. They fed him medicines and he seemed to have recovered somewhat; this was of no concern, for he was not a necessary beta. None were, individually.

"Call the galley," Leo said to one of the others. "Have food brought up here."

The beta rose, came, moved very carefully while he was at the com board. He spoke precisely the request and retreated again among his fellows. Leo stood watching them.

Moriah and the shuttle called again, on the quarter hour; and again.

Then a light flashed at the door, and a cart arrived from the galleys, redolent with food and drink. Azi brought it, unloaded it, bent to unload the lower tray.

Suddenly a gun was in one azi hand and a bolt flew for comp, raked it. Leo fired, and the azi spun back against the doorway, slid down. Others froze in dismay, died so.

Lights flickered. Sirens started sounding, lights all over the board flaring red.

"He's a plant," one said, bending over the azi who had fired. He wiped with his thumb at the too-bright tattoo. "A ringer."

The sirens multiplied. The betas rushed to the boards and worked at them frantically, and Leo hesitated from one threat to the other, null-mind pressing at him. "Get away!" he shouted at the betas. One of his men fired, and a beta died at the main board, slumped over it.

A sign began flashing in the overhead. DISENGAGE ALL SHIPS, it ordered.

The ship. Sanity returned with that responsibility. Leo fired, taking out the betas who would not obey his shouted orders, and leaned over com, punched it wide-broadcast. "*Eros* crew." His voice fed from the corridors outside and throughout the station. "This is Leo. Return to the ship at once. Return to the ship at once."

It was necessary to hold that, above all else. Morn would expect it. "Go," he shouted at the others with him.

And then because it occurred to him that he dared not leave betas near controls, he killed them, every one.

"They're running," the young Upcoaster said, leaning against the glass and pressed to it, staring up the outside concourse.

"Don't!" another cried, when he pushed the door open.

There were no shots, only a breath of cold air off the docks.

"Come on!" Itavvy cried at his wife, snatched Meris from her arms; and the Upcoasters sprang for the doors too, all of them starting to run, baggage left, everything left.

The floodlights on the vast docks were flickering, red lights flashing warnings, sirens braying. Itavvy sucked a lungful of the thin cold air and pelted after the artist, cast a look over his shoulder to see that Velin followed. Tears blurred the lights when he looked round again, a flickering that spelled out *Phoenix*. The ramp was ahead of them, through a tangle of lines. Someone fell behind him, scrambled up again. The artist took the ramp; Itavvy did, Meris wailing in his ear, and for that, for *her* he did not fall, although he felt pain in his side and his chest. They ran the frozen ramp, over the plates that should have moved to help them.

And the hatch was shut.

"*Let us in!*" he screamed at it. Others caught up with him, hammered at the metal with their fists. Itavvy wept, tears streaming his face, and Velin flung her arms about them both, him and Meris.

It was the oldest Upcoaster who found the intercom recessed in the ramp housing. He shouted into it. "Shut up!" he yelled back at them when they added their voices; and from the intercom: "*Stand by.*"

The hatch hummed, parted. Azi crewmen, their faces sober and unamazed, stood waiting to help them aboard.

They stood inside, with trembling hands proffered tickets, evidence of passage.

The hatch sealed behind them.

"Brace where you are," a voice grated from the intercom overhead. "We're disengaging and getting out of here."

ix

The shrilling was louder, front walls, back walls, on all sides of them, and what had begun in the dark of night refused to go away by day, when light streamed over the garden. It should dispel the nightmare. It instead made it real, picking out the shapes of poised Warriors, the husks and bodies of the dead piled in the corner of the garden, and the cracks in the outer wall where assault had already been made and repulsed.

Jim wiped at his face, crouching by Max's side among the rocks. Pol was by him: they spared one young azi to keep a gun in Pol's ribs constantly, for whatever the Kontrin was, he was a born-man and old in such maneuverings, able to forewarn them what the hives might do . . . most of all what the human mind among them might do.

He's there, Pol had said, when the last assault had nearly carried to them, when cracks had appeared in the wall and fire from the gate had distracted them. *That's Morn behind that. The next thing is to watch our backs.*

And that proved true.

"He's delayed over-long," Pol said after a time. "I'm surprised. He should have tried by now. That means he and his allies are up to something that takes a little time."

Jim looked at him. The Kontrin's accustomed manner was mockery; Pol used little of that in recent hours. His gaunt face was yet more hollowed, his eyes shadowed with the exhaustion which sat on them all. The high heat would come by mid-morning; they wore sunsuits, but neither masks nor visors in place, and the sleeves were all unfastened for comfort. Azi rested in their places, slumped against rocks or walls, seeking what sleep could be gotten, for they had had little in the night. Pol leaned his head back against the rock that sheltered them, eyes shut.

"What would take time?" Max wondered aloud.

"Tunnels," Jim said, the thought leaping unwanted into his mind. He swallowed heavily and tried to reason around it. "But Warriors don't dig and Workers don't fight."

Pol lifted his head. "Azi do both," he said, and shifted around to face forward. "Look at the cracks in that wall. They're wider."

It was so. Jim bit at his lips, rose and went aside, where one of the Warriors crouched . . . touched its offered scent-patches.

"Jim. Yess."

"Warrior, the wall's cracking over there. Pol Hald thinks there could be digging."

The great head rotated, body shifted, directed toward the wall. "Human eyes . . . certain, Jim?"

"I can see it, Warrior. A crack in the shape of a tree, spreading and branching. It gets wider."

Chelae brushed him; palps flicked over his cheek. "Good, good," Warrior approved, and scuttled off. It sought and locked jaws with the next, and that one moved off into the house, while Warrior continued, touching jaws with each of the Warriors nearest, who spread in turn to pass the message further.

Jim slid back into position next Max and Pol. "It's disturbed about it," he panted. He shivered despite the warmth, suddenly realizing that he was terrified. They had fought in the night; he had never fired his gun. Now at the prospect of their shelter breached by daylight he sat trembling.

"Easy," Pol said, put out a thin hand and closed it on his leg until it hurt. The pain focused things. He looked at the Kontrin, suddenly aware of a vast silence, that the shrilling which had surrounded them had fallen away.

"You're always with Morn," Jim said hoarsely, for it did not make sense, the tapes with the behavior of Pol Hald. "You're out of his house. You wouldn't go against him."

"A long partnership." The hand did not move, though it was gentler. "In the Family, such are rare."

Treachery, what he had learned warned him. He stared at the Kontrin, paralyzed by the touch he should never have allowed.

"Strange," Pol said, "that at times you have even her look about you."

The shrilling erupted again; and a portion of the garden sank away, gaping darkness aboil with earth and majat bodies. Blues sprang, engaged; shots streaked from azi weapons.

The wall went down, collapsed in a cloud of dust: through it came a horde of majat, azi among them.

Jim braced the gun and sighted, tried to pull the trigger. Beside him a body collapsed, limp.

It was Max. A shot had gone through his brain. Jim stared down at him, numb with horror.

The azi on the other side cried warning, sprawled back unconscious. Pol had Max's rifle and whipped it from a backward blow at his guard to aim it up, putting shots into the majat horde, dropping azi and majat with no distinction.

Jim sighted amid them and pulled the trigger, firing into the oncoming mass, unsure what damage he did, his eyes blurred so that it was impossible to see anything clearly.

The sound swelled in his ears, a horrid chirring that ascended out of range. Majat poured from the house behind them, more Warriors than he had known were there. Majat swarmed from the pit before them and through the breached wall, and came on them like a living wave. Pol fired indiscriminately; he did; more came to replace the fallen, as a wider portion of the wall collapsed, exposing their flank.

"Move back!" Pol shouted at him. "Get your men back!" The Kontrin sprang up low and took a new position.

Jim shouted a half-coherent order and scrambled after, slid in at Pol's side and started firing again.

Then eerie figures appeared among the majat, like

majat in the mold of men, bearing each an insignia on the shoulder.

And one was among them that was clearly a man, in Hald Color.

"Morn," Pol said, and stopped firing.

Jim sighted for that target, missed; and fire came back, grazed his arm. Pol seized him, pulled him over as a lacery of fire cut overhead.

Majat voices boomed, and stone cracked. One of the portico pillars came down in the sudden rush of majat from the house, a sea of bodies; and among them ran naked majat-azi and azi in sunsuits brown with mud and blood.

Fire cut both ways. Majat and azi fell dying and were trampled by those behind. And one there was slighter than most, with black hair flying and a gun in a chitined fist. The azi by her died, rolled sprawling.

Jim fought to loose himself, flung himself over and saw Morn in the center of the yard. Raen was blind to him. "Look out!" he screamed.

"*Morn!*" Pol yelled, hurled himself to his feet and fired.

Morn crumpled, the look of startlement still on his face. And startlement was on Raen's face too, horror as she averted the gun. Pol sank to one knee, swore, and Jim seized at him, but Pol stood without his help, braced, fired a flurry of shots into the armored invaders, who stood as if paralyzed.

Raen did the same, and majat swept past the lines of her men, who hurled accurate fire into the opposing tide, majat meeting body to body, waves that collided and broke upon each other, with shrilling and booming. Heads rolled. Bodies thrashed in convulsions. More of the wall collapsed, and again they were flanked. Jim turned fire in that direction, and saw to his horror the majat sweeping down on them.

Pol's accurate fire cut into them, shots pelting one after the other, precisely timed.

A body slid in from their rear: Merry, putting shots where they counted; and Raen next, whose fire was, like

Pol's, accurate. The shrilling died away; majat rushed
from their rear, narrowly missing them in their blinding
rush, and they dropped, tucked for protection.

But Pol did not go on firing. He laid his head against
the rock, staring blankly before him. Raen touched him,
bent, pressed a gentle touch of her lips to his brow.

"That's once," Pol said faintly, and the face lost its
life; a shudder went through his limbs, and ceased.

Raen averted her face, looked instead at the wave of
majat that was breaking, flooding back toward the walls.

And with a curse she sprang up and ran; Merry followed, and other azi. Jim slipped his hand from Pol's
shoulder and snatched at his rifle to follow, past the
cover of the rocks.

A dark body hurtled into him, spurs ripping. He
sprawled, went under, body upon body rushing over him,
until pain stopped.

X

Agony . . . Mother existed in it, in each powerful drive
of Her legs that drove Her vast weight another half-
length. Drones moved, themselves unaccustomed to such
exertions, their breathing harsh pipings. Workers danced
back and forth, offering nourishment from their jaws,
the depleted fluids of their own bodies, feeding Her and
the Drones.

Their colors grew strange, the blue mottled light and
dark, with here and there a blackness. The sight disturbed Her, and She moaned as She thrust Her way
along, following the new tunnel, the making of the
Workers.

Mother, the Workers sang, *Mother, Mother.*

And She led them.

I have made the way, the Warrior-mind reported, one
of its units touching at Her. *Enemies are retreating. Need
of Workers now to move the stones.*

Well done, She said, tasting of life-fluids and of victory.

Warrior scurried away, staggering in its exhaustion and

its haste. *Follow this-unit,* Warrior gave taste to Workers. *Follow, follow me.*

xi

"Sera?"

Raen caught herself, caught her breath between the wall and Merry's solid body. An azi-light swung from her wrist. She blinked clear the subway, the vacant tracks coursed by majat. One of the men offered her a flask. She drank a mouthful; it went the round among them, forlorn humans huddled at the side of the arching tunnel. They panted for breath, lost in the strange sounds, the rush of chitined bodies, of spurred feet. One of them, hurt, slumped in a knot against the wall. Raen reached and touched him, obtained a lifting of the head, an attempt to focus. Another gave him a drink.

They were twelve, only twelve, out of all of them. She swallowed heavily and rested her hand on Merry's shoulder, breathing in slower and slower gasps.

"City central's up there," she said. "Blues have A branch. The reds are probably in E, that goes to the port. Greens . . . I don't know. Golds . . . likely C, due south. They'll mass in central, under ITAK headquarters."

"Three hives against them," Merry said faintly. "Sera, the blues can't do it."

She slid her hand down, pressed his arm. "I don't think so either, but there's no stopping them. We've kept them alive this long. Merry, take the men, go back. Go back from here. I'll not throw the rest of you away."

"Sera—send them back, not me."

Other voices protested, faces anxious in the blue glow.

"Any of you who wants to stay back, stay," she said, and rose up and started to walk again, slung the burden of the riflestrap to her shoulder.

They came. Perhaps it was fear of the majat without her. She thought that it might be. She suspected something else, that she was too rational to believe. She wiped at her face, struck the tears away with no realization of hurt or grief, only that she was very tired and her eyes watered. The tunnel smelled of majat, like musty paper; and they passed strange sights as they walked, found vehicles frozen on the tracks, wherever they had been when power failed; and terrible sights, the sweet-sour reek of death, where betas had died, some sprawled on the tracks, some in vehicles the glass of which had shattered, dead of majat bite or terror—brushed constantly now by the steady rush of Warriors.

But now there appeared other types amid the press . . . blue-hive azi, staggering with exhaustion and mindless with haste; and after them, Workers, fluting shrill, plaintive cries.

"They're all going," Merry breathed beside her. "Even the queen will follow. Sera, is it wise to be here at all?"

"No," she said plainly, "it's not."

But she did not stop walking, or hesitate. The Worker-cries became song, that filled her ears, ran through her nerves, and banished thought.

Daylight shafted down ahead, where bodies milled, that vast terminal that was central, zero, with day falling down from skylights. Song came up from that heaving mass, and Warriors within it surged this way and that. Workers added themselves, climbing over the bodies of others.

More, Raen thought, far more than blue-hive alone: all, all hives, met there.

And majat died there, of weakness and wounds, crushed down. The song numbed. Merry held his ears and cried out soundlessly in the chaos; and Raen pressed hands to her own, all of them seeking the retreat of the walls, any place aside from that flood of bodies which kept coming.

The ground shook, the walls quivered.

A faint far glimmering in jewels and azi-lights, Mother came, struggling forward.

Mother drew breath, heaved forward, breathed again, dazed with pain. Her own limbs, reaching out and shifting again out of view, were mottled now, bright blue and dark. About Her moved insanity, Warriors whose colors had gone mad, whose bodies glowed blue and extremities red, whose midlimbs gold, all mottled with green.

Queens were at hand: She heard Them, others, other-hives. Desperation possessed Her, the instinct certain now of direction. There was nothing else.

She saw Them, in a seething mass of colors, among Warriors and Workers and Drones who had gone mad. One of the queens was red, with darker mottlings: She, fiercest; one gold, tinged with red; one green, with shadings of blue, incipient chaos.

Red queen shifted forward, ominous, and went for green, for the tainted and nearest one, breathing out hate.

Red was the killer, the Warrior-fragment, as green was the Worker-mind.

Mother hesitated, trembling, and saw green die, life-fluids drunk.

Blue, red queen breathed, and the Warriors quivered aside, pressing themselves out of the way in terror.

A second queen was dead. Raen shuddered, the hard grip of her azi about her, putting their own bodies between her and the press, a small knot of humanity, blue-lit. Other azi sheltered with them, naked creatures male and female, trembling and holding their ears against the battering sound. Lighter majat clambered over them, Drones, glittering with living jewels, perhaps adding their own screams to the thunder of the queens.

Merry shivered against her. Raen caught his hand and held it, that crushed bone against bone in hers: likely he had no wit left to know; she had none to care.

The battle raged in ponderous slow-motion, hazy shafts of sunlight enveloping the queens atop the living hill, reflecting jewel-colors. Strength held against strength: then came a darting move.

The third queen died, head severed.

The hill of bodies came undone about the survivor, sweeping over and about Her. Drones streamed through, to gather with other Drones; and Workers with Workers;

and Warriors with Warriors, ringed about the living
queen. The dead were hauled away. The living circles
widened, spread throughout the terminal.

The queen moved, shifted position; so did all the others. She breathed out a note that made the walls shake,
and after that was quiet.

A human wept, audible, soft sobs.

Raen leaned against Merry a moment, then gathered
herself from him, from all the azi, and rose—walked
among the still shapes of majat, Warriors, Workers, with
the badges of blue-hive, red-hive, green and gold comin-
gled. The rifle was still slung from her shoulder. She
realized it, and dropped it echoing to the pavement, for
there was no way out but to kill a queen, the last Mother
of a world, and that she would not do.

She walked within reach of Her, without weapons in
hand, and gazed up into the great jewelled face, the
moiré eyes, heard the sough of Her breathing.

It was a gold. The pattern was on Her, for those who
could read it.

"Mother," she said, "I'm Raen a Sul, Meth-maren."

Air sucked in. "Meth-maren," She sighed, and the
huge head lowered, sought taste.

Raen kissed Her, touched the scent-patches, waited for
the vast jaws to close; and they did not.

"Meth-maren," Mother said. "Kethiuy-queen."

It was blue queen's memory.

xiii

The sun was unbearable. Jim felt the burn of it before
he felt anything more, and struggled to shade his face
from it. He was held, and had to think which way to
turn; and that meant consciousness.

His hands met spines and hair and chitin. He focused
at that, and shoved in horror at the stiffening limbs that
lay over him, the intertwined corpses of a majat and
an azi.

All about him were corpses, shimmering and running

in the tears the sun brought to his eyes. He struggled to pull the visor which hung about his neck up to his eyes, to see—and found nothing living anywhere.

The house was ruined, gaping rubble; and bodies lay thickly over the garden, save in one vast track which led to the broken walls . . . bodies majat and human, naked and clothed. Insects flitted about him as they settled on the dead; he batted at them, fought with fingers stiffening with sunburn to fasten the sunsuit.

Rock moved, a shifting outside the wall. He gathered up a rifle, staggered in that direction, his senses wavering in and out of focus.

He climbed over the rubble, blinked, saw a shadow on the ground and whirled, whipped the rifle up, but the majat's leap was faster. The gun went off, torn from his hands. Another was on him, pulling from the other side. Chelae gripped his arm, cutting flesh.

Red: he saw the badge and tried to pull from it; the badge of the second was green. It lowered its head, jaws wide, and the palps brushed his lips, his face.

And it drew back. "Jim," it intoned.

He lived. The fact numbed him. He ceased to struggle, understanding nothing any longer.

"Meth-maren sendss," red Warrior said.

"Let me go," he asked then, his heart lurching a beat. "Let me go, Warrior; I'll come with you."

It released him. He clutched his injured arm and followed it, trailed by the green, down into the circle of the street, into the dark entry of the subway, into the deep places of the city, where no lights shone at all. At times he stumbled, blind, and his hands met bodies, yielding ones of majat-azi or the spiny hardness of majat. Chelae urged at him, hastening him, lifting him each time he fell.

Blue lights drifted toward him. At first he shrank from meeting them, not wanting delay, not wanting to be left: but he saw *her* bearing one of those lights, and he thrust his way free of the Warriors and ran, stumbling, toward her.

She met him, held him off at arm's length to look at him. "You're all right," she said, a question in her impatient manner; but her voice trembled. There was Merry by her, and other faces that he knew.

She hugged him then, and he nearly wept for joy; but she did not know, he thought, the things that he must admit, the knowledge that he had stolen, the thing he had made of himself.

He tried to tell her. "I used all the tapes," he said, "even the black ones. I didn't know what else to do." She touched his face and told him to be quiet, with a shift of her eyes toward Merry and the others.

"It's rained back there," he said then. "Everything's ruined. Where will we go now?"

"In, for a time. Till the cycle completes itself." Her hand entwined with his: he felt the jewels rough and warm beneath his fingers. She gestured, walked with assurance the way from which she had come. Warriors walked about them; armed majat-azi followed. "It's going to be a while before I think of outside, a long while, perhaps. Majat-time."

"I've nineteen years," he said, anticipating all of them, and well-content.

Her fingers tightened on his.

Soft singing filled the air, the peaceful sound of Workers, with the stirrings and movings of many bodies in the tunnels.

"Hive-song," she said. "They've long lives. A turning of nature, a pulse of the cycle, to merge all colors, to divide again. *This-sun,* they say now. *Home-hive.* Against those cycles, my own life is nothing at all. Wait with me."

There was a ship, he thought, recalling Pol. There were betas who might live, who might serve her. He objected to these things one by one, and she shook her head, silent.

He asked no more.

xiii

Moth, the voices shouted, *Moth, Moth!*

Eggs, she thought back at them, and mocked them for what they were.

A different sound came through the speakers, the shrilling of majat voices, the crash of metal and wood.

From the vents came a curious paper-scent. Human voices had ceased long ago.

Moth poured the last of the wine, drank it.

And pushed the button.

BOOK TEN

i

The hatch opened, let in the flood of evening air, the gentle light of the setting sun.

"Stay put," Tallen heard. *"Sir, we're picking up movement out there."*

"Wouldn't do to run," he said into the com unit. "Whatever happens—no response, hear me?"

"Be careful."

Majat. He heard the ominous chirring, and walked forward, very slowly.

Newhope had stood here. Weeds had taken the ruins. At center rose a hill, monstrous, where no hill had been. He had seen the pictures smuggled out, heard the reports and memorized them, along with family tales.

And in the long passage of years, in the fading of the Wars, *this* waited, where no Outsider dared trespass, until now.

We were wrong, the one side argued, ever to have relied on them.

But governments rose and fell and rose again, and rumors persisted . . . that life stirred in the forbidden Reach, that the wealth which had made the Alliance what it had been was there to be had, if any power could contrive to obtain it.

And the hives refused contact.

There were human folk on Istra, farmers, who lived out across the wide plains, who told wild tales and traded occasional jewels and rolls of majat-silk.

Tallen had met with them, these sullen, furtive men,

suspicious of any ship that called; and there was warning here, for there were no few ships resting derelict in Istran fields.

Sixty years the contact had lapsed: collapse, chaos, war . . . worlds breaking from the Alliance in panic, warships forcing them in again, all for the scarcity of certain goods and the widespread rumors of majat breakout.

It was told in Tallen's family that men and majat had co-existed here, had walked together in city streets, had cooperated one with the other.

It was told somewhere in Alliance files that this was so.

He heard the sound nearer now, and walked warily, stopped at last as a glittering creature rose out of the rocks and brush.

A trembling came on him, a loss of will. *Natural,* he thought, recalling the tales his grandfather had told, who claimed to have stood close to them. *Humans react to them out of deep instinct. One has to overcome that.*

They see differently: that too, from old Tallen, and from reports deep in the archives. He spread his hands wide from his sides, making clear to it that he had no weapons.

It came closer. He shut his eyes, for he quite lost his courage to look at it near at hand. He heard its loud breathing, felt the bristly touch of its forelimbs. A shadow fell on his closed eyes; something touched his mouth—he shuddered convulsively at that, and the touch and the shadow drew back.

"Stranger," it said, a harmony of sounds that joined into a word.

"Friend," he said, and opened his eyes.

It was still near, the moiré eyes shifted through the spectrum at each minute turn of the head. "Beta human?" it asked him.

ii

A stirring ran through the hive. Raen lifted her head, read it in the voices, the shift of bodies, needing no vision in the dark.

Stranger-human, the message came to her, and that pricked at curiosity, for betas would never come this far: they did their grain-trading far out on the riverside, where they brought their sick, such as majat could heal.

And the azi had gone long ago.

She missed them sorely. The hives did, likewise, mourning them in Drone-songs.

Merry had gone, neither first nor last, a sudden seizure of the heart. And she had wept for that, though Merry would hardly have understood it. *I am azi,* he had said once, refusing to be otherwise. *I would not want to out-live my time.* And so, one by one, the others had chosen.

It was strange, now, that a beta would have ventured into majat land, under the great Hill.

"Jim," she said.

"I hear." He found her hand, needing sight no more than she, as he was in other ways skilled with her skills.

Of all of them, Jim remained, a costly gift of Worker lives, and of his own will, more than Merry had had, who had wanted things his own way, in old patterns, in terms he understood.

For a long time she had cared for nothing beyond that, to know that there was one human to share the dark with her.

Now Warrior came, immortal as she, as he, in one of its many persons. "Outsider," it said, troubled, perhaps, in the perception of changes. "Unit called *Tallen.*"

iii

Tallen blinked in the twilight, watching them come . . . two, woman and man, robed in gauzy majat-silk. They wore it as if it were nothing, priceless though it was, as if their own will were cloak enough.

They stopped near to him, and Tallen shivered in their regard, that strange coolness and lack of fear. There was a mark on the man, beneath the eye and on the shoulder: *azi.* The old Tallen had reported such, but not such as he, whose gaze he could not bear. The mark on the woman was of jewels; of her kind too there were remembrances.

"Ab Tallen," she said, strangely accented, "would be an old, old man."

"Dead," Tallen answered. "I'm his grandson. Your people remember him?"

Her eyes flickered, seemed possessive of secrets. She held out her right hand and he took it, hesitating at the strange warmth of the jewels that covered it.

"Raen Meth-maren," she said. "Yes, there's memory of him. Kind memory."

"Your name is hers, that he mentioned."

She smiled faintly, and questions of kinship went uninvited. She nodded to the man beside her. "Jim," she said, and that was all.

Tallen took the other offered hand, regarded them both anxiously, for majat hovered about, escort, guards, soldiery—there was no knowing what.

"You delayed longer than you should," she said.

"We had our years of trouble. I'm afraid there may have been landings here of a sort we'd not have allowed. Our apologies, for such intrusions."

She shrugged. "Most have learned, have they not?"

That was truth, and chilling in her manner. "We've come here twice—peacefully, hunting some contact."

"Now," she said, "we're pleased to answer you. Is it trade you want?"

He nodded, all his careful speeches destroyed, forgotten in that direct stare.

"I'm Meth-maren. Hive friend. Intermediary. I can arrange what you want." She looked about her, and at him. "I speak and translate."

"We need lab-goods, more than the jewels the farmers have been trading."

"Then give us computers. You'll get your lab products."

"And some sort of licensing for regular trade."

She nodded toward the plains, the beta-holds. "There are those who will deal with you as we arrange."

"There's no station any longer. It's gone."

"Crashed. We saw it, Jim and I. It fell into the sea, a long time ago. But stations can be rebuilt."

"Come aboard my ship," he invited her. "We'll talk specifics."

She shook her head, smiled faintly. "No, ser. Take your ship from the vicinity of the hive tonight, within the hour. Go to riverside. I'll find you there with no trouble. But don't linger near the hive."

And she walked away, leaving him standing. The majat remained, and the man, who looked at him with remotely curious eyes and then walked away.

"All things end," she said. "Does the Outside frighten you, Jim?"

"No," he said. She thought it truth. Their minds were much alike.

"There's *Moriah*." She nodded in the direction of the port, where the only whole buildings in Newhope remained.

"There's the Reach or Outside. We're human. There's a time to remember that."

He looked at her, saying nothing.

She linked her fingers in his, chitined hand in human one.

"It begins again," she said.

RULES FOR SEJ

Pieces: one pair six-sided dice; trio of four-sided wands: first wand face black, second blue with ship symbol; third white; fourth orange with star symbol.

Object: first player to accumulate 100 points wins. To start play: high roll of dice determines starting player. The Starting Player throws the wands, and play proceeds. To score: The players roll dice for possession of the points represented by the wands. The casting of wands proceeds in alternation, one player and the next. The wand-thrower has the option of the first cast of dice; the dice then proceed in alternation during the Hand (this particular casting of the wands). High roll takes the wand or wands in contention, and points are recorded as follows. Value of wands: stars are 12 points each; ships are 10; white and white with black are 5 points for the white pair combined, but the black is played separately and with its own value; white assumes the value of any wand-of-color, always the highest in the Hand . . . and assumes the value of black only if both other wands in the Hand are black; black cancels all points in the possession of whichever player "wins" the black wand, but cancellation of points is limited to the Game itself. Play always proceeds from ships to stars to black: that is, in a Hand, the dice must be rolled first for possession of the ships, then for the stars, and last of all for possession of the black. If a tie occurs in the roll of the dice, the dice are rolled again. If the wands come up doubled or tripled stars or ships or white, the winner of the first of the double or triple set automatically takes the others of that color; for this purpose also, white matches the highest wand of the Hand.

Should triple white show, the winner automatically takes Game. Should triple black show, the winner automatically loses Game.

Passing: In this matter rests the skill of the game, judging when to pass and when to risk play. A Hand containing a single black wand or any number of black wands may be declined by the thrower of wands, thus entirely voiding the Hand, the dice will not be rolled; the wands pass into the hand of the next player, who will cast again, with all privileges of the wand-thrower. Further, a player with the option to throw either wands or dice may voluntarily pass that option to the next player, who is not, however, obliged to accept: the player who has passed will receive the wands or dice again in alternation. The latter is a matter of courtesy and custom of the game: highest or decisive points are played last.

CJ Cherryh
Classic Series in New Omnibus Editions

THE DREAMING TREE
Contains the complete duology *The Dreamstone* and *The Tree of Swords and Jewels*.   0-88677-782-8

THE FADED SUN TRILOGY
Contains the complete novels *Kesrith*, *Shon'jir*, and *Kutath*.   0-88677-836-0

THE MORGAINE SAGA
Contains the complete novels *Gate of Ivrel*, *Well of Shiuan*, and *Fires of Azeroth*.   0-88677-877-8

THE CHANUR SAGA
Contains the complete novels *The Pride of Chanur*, *Chanur's Venture* and *The Kif Strike Back*.
0-88677-930-8

ALTERNATE REALITIES
Contains the complete novels *Port Eterntiy*, *Voyager in Night*, and *Wave Without a Shore*   0-88677-946-4

AT THE EDGE OF SPACE
Contains the complete novels *Brothers of Earth* and *Hunter of Worlds*.   0-7564-0160-7

To Order Call: 1-800-788-6262

CJ Cherryh
EXPLORER

"Serious space opera at its very best by one of the leading SF writers in the field today." —*Publishers Weekly*

The *Foreigner* novels introduced readers to the epic story of a lost human colony struggling to survive on the hostile world of the alien atevi. In this final installment to the second sequence of the series, diplomat Bren Cameron, trapped in a distant star system, faces a potentially bellicose alien ship, and must try to prevent interspecies war, when the secretive Pilot's Guild won't even cooperate with their own ship.

Be sure to read the first five books in this action-packed series:

FOREIGNER	0-88677-637-6
INVADER	0-88677-687-2
INHERITOR	0-88677-728-3
PRECURSOR	0-88677-910-3
DEFENDER	0-7564-0020-1

0-7564-0131-3

To Order Call: 1-800-788-6262

Julie E. Czerneda

THE TRADE PACT UNIVERSE

"Space adventure mixes with romance...a heck of a lot of fun." —*Locus*

Sira holds the answer to the survival of her species, the Clan, within the multi-species Trade Pact. But it will take a Human's courage to show her the way.

A THOUSAND WORDS FOR STRANGER
0- 88677-769-0
TIES OF POWER
0-88677-850-6
TO TRADE THE STARS
0-7564-0075-9

To Order Call: 1-800-788-6262

C.S. Friedman

The Best in Science Fiction

THIS ALIEN SHORE   0-88677-799-2
A *New York Times* Notable Book of the Year
"Breathlessly plotted, emotionally savvy. A potent
metaphor for the toleration of diversity"
—*The New York Times*

THE MADNESS SEASON   0-88677-444-6
"Exceptionally imaginative and compelling"
—*Publishers Weekly*

IN CONQUEST BORN   0-7564-0043-0
"Space opera in the best sense: high stakes adventure
with a strong focus on ideas, and characters an intelligent reader can care about."—*Newsday*

THE WILDING   0-7564-0164-X
The long-awaited follow-up to *In Conquest Born*.

To Order Call: 1-800-788-6262

DAW 17

C.S. Friedman

The Coldfire Trilogy

"A feast for those who like their fantasies dark, and as
emotionally heady as a rich red wine." —*Locus*

Centuries after being stranded on the planet
Erna, humans have achieved an uneasy stalemate with the fae, a terrifying natural force with
the power to prey upon people's minds. Damien
Vryce, the warrior priest, and Gerald Tarrant, the
undead sorcerer must join together in an uneasy
alliance confront a power that threatens the very
essence of the human spirit, in a battle which
could cost them not only their lives, but the soul
of all mankind.

BLACK SUN RISING   0-88677-527-2
WHEN TRUE NIGHT FALLS 0-88677-615-5
CROWN OF SHADOWS   0-88677-717-8

To Order Call: 1-800-788-6262